BALANCE

BALANCE

BOOK ONE

INGHILD ØKLAND

DRAGONSONG PUBLISHING

BALANCE

Copyright © 2022 by Inghild Økland

All rights reserved. No part of this book may be reproduced or used in any manner without written permission of the copyright owner except for the use of quotations in a book review.

This is a work of fiction. Names, characters, places, and incidents either are the product of the author's imagination or are used fictitiously. Any resemblance to actual persons, living or dead, events, or locales is entirely coincidental.

For more information, contact:
inghild@inghildokland.com

Dragonsong Publishing
First Printing, 2022
ISBN: 9798737476892

Cover Artwork © Merilliza Chan
Dragonheart Artwork by Lisa Le
Content Edit by Rachel Garber
Copy Edit by Lauren Nicholls
Proofreading by Rebecca Reid

To my fiancé,
For laughter and love.
Thank you for believing in me,
For supporting this dream.

A MARE OF THE NIGHT

If the nightmares are real, this will not be the end.

A shiver traced down my back despite the hot air. I shook my head, dispelling the voice from my mind. My voice. Instead of lingering on phantom echoes from a nasty dream, I should enjoy this moment. My freedom. Fiar's streets were bustling with life, with carts and crates and lively people. Which, of course, was fine, but . . .

"I know my braid is messy, but do they all have to stare?"

Sir Sigve, my guardian, sent me a bemused look. "I don't think the braid is to blame."

I crossed my arms. "Well, excuse my looks. I know I'm not at my best after three weeks at sea."

"Lady Vildi, that was not what I implied and you know it."

"Yes, yes." Sir Sigve was too well-behaved to insult me. Openly, at least. "And didn't I tell you to stop with the 'lady'?"

"Yes, you did, my lady. You look . . . presentable, for being here. I think your colors are to blame for the attention."

I let my eyes wander, meeting a few pairs of dark brown eyes that quickly looked away. Certainly, my wheat blonde hair drew a stark contrast to their raven locks. Then again, the fault might lie with Sir Sigve all along, with his russet beard against the clean-shaved young men sauntering through the streets. Or maybe the sword at his hip.

A man in his thirties gave me a winning smile in passing. Right. It was me, after all. I stepped a little closer to Sir Sigve, drawing from the dense air.

"Lady Vildi, are you still unwell? We should find a pleasant inn and rest for today. This heat seems to be detrimental to your health, so I'll arrange for a ship to take us home, fast as possible—"

"Perish that thought, and do it now. I'm not going home." Nothing but arranged marriages awaited there, and a mother who hounded my every move. No way. "Besides, I haven't forgiven you yet for barging in this morning."

"I had to. You were screaming, my lady."

Pain flared through my throat, and a spell of dizziness made me stumble. My fingers crept up, but my skin was whole, unmarred, unbroken. Nothing there. "Never mind, let's explore that street." I pointed down a wide road, where chalked buildings stood cramped upon each other, and shops vied for attention with wares varying from silks and pearls to intricate glass wares. "I bet we'll find some food."

Sir Sigve sighed. "Very well."

The street soon opened to a market square. In the center of the square, a statue rose from the ground, two stone dragons with sleek bodies winding toward the sky, their foreheads resting against each other.

I retrieved a coin from my pocket, flipping it in my palm. Dragon side down. Dragon side up. The dragons' eyes gleamed, and I lifted my gaze to the stone equivalents. With a trick of the sun, one seemed to stare me right in the eye. This was it. Strange lands, new cultures, stories that got the blood pumping. My fairy-tale adventure. And this was by far the strangest yet. Lakari, Land of the Sun. Considering the entirety of my first seventeen years had been spent far north, in cold and dark Rimdalir, how could I help myself?

"Only the softest silks for the lady. Have a look at the finest . . ."

"Spices, oi, spices, the best and greatest, spice up your meals, for every occasion, spices . . ."

"Delicate jewelry, the very best of metalwork, the sharpest knives—we have it here, we have it all . . ."

I smiled at the vendors, watching Sir Sigve from the corner of my eye. "Can you at least keep to our story this time, *dad?*"

"I don't see how it would make any difference, but very well, *daughter.*"

I snorted. Didn't he understand it would make all the difference in the world? No nobles, no formalities, and best of all, no suitors. No Lord Gaute of forty years and desperate gifts, and no Vinjar the Worm. Here, I could simply let myself be 'merchant's daughter Vildi.' "Why, *thank* you. With that settled, I'll get myself some food."

A wonderful whiff teased my nose, more tempting than a gift from the gods. By the corner of the square stood a stall overflowing with small, delicate cakes. My legs moved as if I'd walked the distance a hundred times over.

Sir Sigve didn't quite match my admiration. "My l—dear daughter, we should not eat sweets for breakfast." His words were like hearing Maya, my lady's maid at home. She had surely entrusted Sir Sigve with strict instructions, despite his hasty departure, chasing me. A girl couldn't even avoid rebuke on her runaway trip.

My stomach protested the statement with a groan. "You're right. I'll only have that pink little thing then. Oh, and that golden cake!" As a glutton at heart, was it not my duty to partake?

The girl selling cakes handed me the pastries with careful fingers and a seller's charm, her tan skin accentuating white teeth in a bright face. She was as happy with the coins as I with the sweets. Sir Sigve scowled as I put the pink, swirly delicacy into my mouth. It was sugary and crunchy, and it melted on my tongue. The greatest treasure, however, was the golden cake, with paper-thin layers of dough held together by thick, sticky honey. Truly, it was heaven in small bites.

"Have you heard the news?" A voice like a bird's song brought me out of my stupor.

"Sorry, we arrived today. Will you tell me?"

"You like that cake? You may want another, perhaps?" A sensible proposal, although judging by her wide and glinting eyes, the girl would spill her news regardless.

I bought one more—not one to waste such a perfect excuse for us both.

"So, you know about the prince, right?"

I swallowed my disappointment. "No."

The market girl sighed, her gaze reaching for heaven. "It's *so* romantic. Tragic. Our prince is finally getting married!"

"Oh. Why is that tragic?" With her starry eyes, I could scarcely believe the girl shared my thoughts on matrimony.

"Well, this is his second time." The girl clutched her chest. "And he is still so young, our poor prince. Even as an arranged marriage, it's said they loved each other very much. But he lost his wife in childbirth, and you see, neither of them survived."

Any possible amusement for her poor word choice, hinting that a man died in childbirth, got overshadowed by the grave subject. I was the sister of at least three siblings I never got to meet, perhaps more. Thank the gods for the two I never lost. Bowing my head for the dead, I listened to the girl's tale.

"And they used to be *such* a cute couple too. They came riding through this very town once. *Oh,* it was a beautiful sight! When the princess passed on to Rashim, we all felt his pain. Sorrow is never easy, but he lost himself to it for so long, our grieving, handsome prince." The confectioner took a deep breath, then cast away her gloom with a bright grin. "But he finally found a new bride!"

Meeting the girl's expectant eyes, I gave in. Surely I could endure this a little longer. "Who is she?"

"Well, I don't know. Some foreign princess, I think." The girl crossed her arms, eyebrows furrowing together. Perhaps this unsightly void in her otherwise full recount of the prince's affairs annoyed her.

"Let's hope it goes well," I said, my mood softened by sugar.

"Yes. He is such a wonderful person."

"I'm sure he is. The cakes were delicious. Thank you."

"Have a pleasant stay, miss." The girl's full smile made me feel at ease, as it was quite similar to Madalyn's. My sister would have enjoyed the cakes too. Another bite, and honey flooded my senses as we walked among the market stalls. Behind us, the girl was already working on her next customers, her voice drifting with the wind. "Would you want a cake? Oh, and have you *heard* about the prince . . . ?"

Sir Sigve cast me a sideways glance, lips pulling down in a grimace. "I wish you would stop. What will your parents say? And your marriage prospects, if you get bigger than in your paintings?"

I tried not to choke on the last bit of cake. Sir Sigve was dead serious, having the audacity to look concerned. Why, I couldn't fathom. I was still slim enough. "Yes indeed, what a great tragedy. But I fail to see how this concerns you."

He averted his eyes, thin lips pressed together.

I sped up, heading deeper into the market. "Let's have some breakfast."

"Do you even want breakfast anymore?" He stared at my last mouthfuls of cake as if they personally offended him.

"Of course. Let's go before I starve."

~

Later in the day, we explored the outskirts of town, reaching an establishment of wide, low buildings and a row of stalls. Strange, shaggy animals poked their heads out. They had bulbs on their backs, as I had only ever seen as drawings in books. They were cute, with enormous eyes encircled by envy-worthy lashes, and their noses looked soft like velvet. "Are those camels?"

Sir Sigve hummed. "I think they may be."

A huge caravan—several heavily loaded wagons, merchants, and even three traveling families—crossed our path, leaving town along the main road. The company drifted into the desert, soon hidden behind a rise and bend in the path. The immense sea of sand seemed to lead to the very end of the world. My gut twisted, my vision drenched with blood, making mud of sand like a crimson flash flood. I blinked, and it was gone. "Sir Sigve, I think I would like to rest after all."

"Very well."

My body didn't seem to agree well with this climate and I fought off nausea for a while, hiding my condition. Sir Sigve was too quick to worry.

"Around this corner is a place to dine," I guessed, as a sandy gust peppered my cheek. We turned to see taverns lining the street, merry light spilling out their windows. "Hah, I was right. Is this the third time?"

"You're just getting lucky," Sir Sigve pointed out. "We should settle on a place to stay."

Cold crept down my arms.

"Do you see over there? It's even near your beloved camels. If the inside matches the outside, I think we've found our place." His eyes gleamed with the anticipation of strong drinks. "Let's put our bags down for the evening."

Crammed between a smithy and a closed grocer's shop, a small inn was visible beyond his pointed finger. Torches illuminated a facade of dragons on each side of the entrance, welcoming travelers through a door made from old wood.

"Fine. Take a skaal with me?" A toast with Sir Sigve wasn't the worst thing to do after a long boat ride.

Our entrance barely disturbed a hum of laughter and easy banter. Behind a gleaming counter, an innkeeper methodically wiped glass mugs as his wife flitted about, distributing drinks and food. A few men had gathered around the tables, all of them of leathery skin and gray in their beards, looking as if they were more comfortable with each other than their homes. It was a place for playing games and sharing news. A common, ordinary, in-all-ways-typical tavern.

My breath heaved. The air was surely all too stagnant. "No." My voice cracked. "Let's go. I don't feel like staying here."

In truth, it seemed like a respectable establishment, where a good drink and an even better story should be possible to come by. And yet, as I turned for the door, my condition instantly improved—until my stomach took a plunge. From the dim light of the doorway, two men emerged, cloaked by darkness.

I tried acting normal—I really did. Greeting with a smile, relaxed posture, and arms at ease by my sides. I failed. My lungs heaved, gasping for air which was suddenly too sparse.

And they all gawked. Every person in the room turned for a glimpse of the hysterical girl by the entrance. Of course they did.

The man closest to me leaned forward, hitting my nose with a pungent odor. "It is her," he declared, his voice dull.

"Are you sure?" This one was younger, though no less gruff. He had to bend around his companion to get a better view, his mouth slightly ajar. When he moved again, the light caught something glinting from the shadow of his cape.

"Do you see other girls with golden hair around?" The older man adjusted his stance, a tinge of rust coming from him in waves.

"And her eyes. Yes, that must be her," the young one said, stepping forward. The candles shining down on him revealed clothes stained over and over until the color had turned a patchy, strange brown. "I think I liked the portrait better." His voice was *just* loud enough for me to hear, and he had the indecency to smirk. As if I wasn't already aware of my travel-worn self.

Sir Sigve glared down at the men.

"I don't care about your likes," the first said, sparing his partner a taste of fish and stale ale before again facing me. "You, come here."

"You have the wrong person. I'm not who you think." I backed up a step, clammy palms pressed against the fabric of my dress.

They shared a look.

"No. You're exactly who we think. Now come along, *Princess* Alvildi." The man held a hand at his belt. Between his fingers, I caught a glint of steel. A chill ran down my back. Kidnapping?

"On whose authority?" Thank the gods for Sir Sigve. He stepped forward, obscuring my view of the men.

I glanced behind us. Throughout the room, people were busy pretending a confrontation was not happening by the entrance.

The man reached inside his cloak to reveal an official-looking scroll. "We have our orders. The princess has been su—"

"It's fake." As the words tumbled out, I knew them to be true.

The man narrowed his eyes, his hand sinking like a stone in water.

I took another step back, throat constricting. "I'm not coming, whatever you say or show." Only the fingers digging into Sir Sigve's arm kept me from crumbling to the floor.

The rude one sneered, facing my companion. "Your princess will come with us."

"I'm afraid I cannot allow that." Sir Sigve stood his ground, right hand finding the hilt at his hip.

"Do you still wish to do this the discreet way?" the man asked.

"No," the other said. His eyes were pinned on me. "Better here than not at all." Curved daggers spun into two pairs of hands. They moved as one.

"Vildi—" Drawing his sword, my companion held off the advancing men. He met their daggers with a twist of his blade. Metal screeched as blade ground against blade and Sir Sigve sidestepped, his sword flowing like an extension of his arm. The rude man threw knives, the other reached for more blades at his belt. Ducking and intercepting their path, Sir Sigve's labored breath already hit as bolts of lightning. "Go, Princess. *Run.*"

They came at him with renewed vigor and twin grins, promising pain, the sharp edges ready to deliver death.

Kicking and upending a stool, Sir Sigve created some distance, desperate eyes piercing me for a fleeting moment as he whirled around.

There had to be another exit. Sir Sigve would be fine. He was such an accomplished fighter, striving, heaving, protecting me. A table toppled over, halting the strangers for a second. A blade cleaved the air; Sir Sigve dodged, losing balance and falling hard against the bar. The men advanced. As if Sir Sigve was a pesky inconvenience, their eyes followed me. Perhaps if I fled, they would leave him be. A back door. Surely, if I only reached the other side of the room, I would find a way.

The scent of copper reached me from behind, a grunt and the poor person coughing. But Sir Sigve was fine, so skilled—a thud, the dull impact of flesh against hard stone and another immediately after—and then came the steps, following fast, and it was *not* Sir Sigve because his were heavier and these, so light.

Blood hung in the air. I pushed past a table, a stool crashing down in my wake. A glance behind—glassy, gray eyes—and I stumbled forward, nausea again flooding my senses. I grasped for something to hold, clutching the bar counter and meeting the stare of a pale innkeeper. Behind me was a blotched cloak, a figure dashing toward me. My heartbeat was in my ears, and every other sound came to me as if through water.

A hand grabbed for me—grasping only at air—and I stumbled forward. The wall towered before me and there was no door, nowhere to go. He would never expect a princess to fight back, but surely, I could punch even though I had never hit anyone in my life. My only option. His breath was at my neck, and so I turned—

Wide, pleasantly surprised eyes stared into mine as his dagger plunged into my stomach.

THE JOY OF A SOLID SOLUTION

A shrill sound pierced the silence, and sleep was lost to me. The shriek caught in my throat, and I realized it was mine. Chipped nails clawed at my chest. The air in the room grew thick as mud, and I struggled to breathe. I grasped my stomach and found unmarred skin underneath fine linen, but every muscle inside cramped around a nightmare wound.

Within the echoes of my dream, I felt like throwing up all over again. No spark of life, not even a glint of misplaced humor. That husk on the floor which once housed Sir Sigve, staring at me with empty eyes. A shudder traced down my back.

"I heard—Lady Vildi! What's wrong?" He barged in, my companion. Somehow, I knew he would.

He shouldn't be here. *I* shouldn't be here. Though this was my room, my possessions. From the window and shining around us was the brilliant morning light, and the glimmering blue sea reaching for the sun. Sweat made my nightgown sticky. I drew a palm across my forehead, sweeping sweaty hair from my skin. Sir Sigve's gaze lingered as he finally let go of the hilt at his belt. *What's wrong?* The question echoed in my mind like a voice cast back and forth against the hills of a vacant valley. "Nothing at all," I said at last.

"Forgive me, but . . . you do *not* sound fine at all."

Well, there was nothing to be done for my dull tone.

"And . . . you don't look so good."

"Why, thank you." *Fine,* I didn't have Mother's pretty oval face or high cheekbones, but—

"You look sick. And you're staring, my lady."

"I think . . ." What could I say? Even the images were fading from my grasp, too faint to retain. "Just a bad dream. That's all."

"I see." Sir Sigve glanced out the window. "The *Disandri* reached Fiar an hour ago. I'll wait for you on deck." He was already halfway out the door when he added, "Unless . . . we could return to Rimdalir right away."

"You can go, I didn't ask you to come along." I stuck my nose up, hating my own snobby attitude a little. But it often proved effective.

"I promised I'd protect you."

"I can barely remember." Of course, I knew about it. Sir Sigve had never been allowed to forget, but I had trouble recalling the incident. I had only been nine. Vivid in my memory was the image of Hogne, stringing his bow for one last, successful shot in the royal tournament. Sir Sigve kneeling, in a jest promising to protect me? Not so much.

"But your father does—regrettably," Sir Sigve said, his words uttered through clenched teeth. It was a pitiable sight, though he had made this bed quite on his own.

I met my companion's eyes. "And he allowed me to travel."

"Only if I stayed with you," Sir Sigve reminded me, arms crossed in front of him.

"And I implore you, be more careful."

Sir Sigve's tense face eased up. "My lady, I'm barely old enough to *be* your father. This makes me feel old. And if I was," he said, "though thank the gods I'm not—we would definitely not be here."

"But you're not my father, and thank the gods."

He nodded, turning toward the door. "Right."

"Sir Sigve? Being your daughter wouldn't have been too bad, I think."

He cast me a bewildered look.

"Fewer suitors," I explained.

I caught his small smile. We were related if one searched far enough down the family lineage, but he was more an uncle to me than my real uncles. He had been present my entire childhood, trying—and failing—to teach me the use of weapons, watching over me and my sister Madalyn. Sir Sigve was family.

He left me, knowing no monsters had gobbled me up yet. I dressed and packed with sluggish movements, taking a moment to tuck my carved wooden pony close to my chest, then followed my guardian up on deck. The ocean spread out until it merged with the sky, and if I turned, the port. Workers labored in the hot, dense air, while travelers disappeared into the city proper. A few leafy palm trees rustled in the wind.

My stomach twisted. My body heaved, trying to expel some lingering emptiness. Cold moisture spread from my neck to my forehead; a weakness began in the thighs and ran down my legs. I had to grip the railing for support.

A deep breath, another one, and it settled. Still, I failed to summon my earlier excitement for Fiar. Maybe Sir Sigve was right, and I was sick. We could stay on the ship, let it whisk us away to a new place waiting to be explored.

One of the *Disandri*'s sailors walked by.

"Excuse me? When will this ship leave again?"

"Not in another fortnight, miss." He could as well have hit me across my face.

Mind blank, my mouth opened. "So long."

"Is something bothering you, miss?" The sailor's not-so-subtle, lingering glances toward the ship, his shuffling feet, told me he only stayed to avoid insulting me.

I forced a smile to the surface. It was easily done, with enough practice. Still, it was stiff and wrong somehow. "No, never mind."

This was my adventure—of course I should explore Fiar, and no nightmare would stop me. I felt better anyway, and Sir Sigve should be spared from needless worries. With a deep breath, I skipped to his side, my shoulders relaxing as Sir Sigve's troubled expression lifted.

I toyed with a single coin between my fingers, flipping it up to reflect light with its blank surface. The dragons gleamed at me. From the moment the coin had come into my hand, I wanted to see the country it belonged to. And finally, we were here. Lakari, Land of the Sun.

Sir Sigve possessed a considerably heavier coin purse. I would have to lure—no—*guide* him to invest our money properly. For example, he had no understanding of the true value of food.

On my first steps into Fiar, everything somehow seemed *right*. The kind where nothing is amiss, every house, ship, and barrel is where it should be—a sense of *knowing*, which would disappear if something was removed or changed. Like the cart filled with carpets. Or the men with midnight skin buzzing back and forth on a neighboring ship. One of them waved and grinned at me.

With land beneath me again after weeks at sea, the ground seemed to be leisurely bobbing up and down like a small boat on waves. The bumps in the road seemed set on tripping me, but my feet weaved around them with ease. Ahead was the overflowing main street leading to the local market. Nothing was *new* to me.

Eyes stared at us. Granted, we appeared as foreign to this land as we were and probably rich too, but they made me queasy. People performed their everyday routines, and I could see nothing unexpected for a busy, bubbly city. Bright colors with deep shadows.

We arrived at the market square. Voices called from stands and corners. People surrounded us, reaching out with their wares, staring, shouting, pointing . . .

"Have a taste of our famous cakes, sweets—oh, miss! You look terribly ill. Poor you, come here." A girl some years younger than me waved us over, putting a hand at my back.

"Over here, sit down, I'll fetch some water so please, just relax." There was something strange about receiving such caring gestures, seeing the motherly air of someone so young.

"I'm fine. Not used to the heat."

She ignored my mumbling. "Take a cake, miss. Which one do you want?" Before me was an assortment of delicious little baked things. A golden-brown pastry caught my eyes and was quickly deposited in one hand, a glass of water in the other.

"Say, miss, I'll tell you the latest news." Eyes gleaming, excitement sprang to life in the girl's tan face. Such impressive determination to lift my spirit.

I almost expelled the long sip of my drink, pearls of sweat breaking out on my forehead as a fresh wave washed over me. After a few breaths, it passed. I never knew my body hated heat to this extent.

The girl fussed, moving objects around in her stall restlessly, probably waiting for me to calm down. She would soon burst from elation.

"Your prince is getting married," I said. In front of me, the stone dragons gleamed in the sun.

"Yes!" The market girl spun on the spot. "To a foreign princess, I heard, and she's supposed to be *very* beautiful. Miss, you already knew!"

"I . . . did." I swallowed through a thickness in my throat. I must have heard it somewhere. There was a strange, tight sensation in my chest.

The girl droned on, lost in herself. "Oh, this wedding is the most exciting thing happening in *years*. They might even hold the Ceremony of Bonding. My mom says they probably won't, but perhaps they will after all."

"How nice." I failed to bring life to my voice. The lack of enthusiasm about *marriage* could be attributed to my faint condition, right? A *royal* marriage. Political, no doubt. Probably forced, that poor girl.

"Yes! It is a joyous occasion." The girl flashed her white teeth, eyes too far off to notice the lack of a response in her listeners. As surely as we were victims to her thoughts, here was another victim of romance and naïvety. "He can't take the throne without a new wife." Ah, and there came the real reason.

"Why is that?" Sir Sigve pulled at his beard, showing a spark of interest. In Rimdalir, the firstborn took the throne. Heirs were of course needed, but Madalyn could rule just fine without a husband if she had to. Lakari seemed to be different. Personally, I found little fun in politics.

The girl eyed him. "Why? It's law. The king and queen rule together. They keep the throne together. And since our queen died—may she rest with Rashim—Lakari needs a new ruling pair."

"So romantic." Nothing veiled the sarcasm drying up my voice.

The girl blinked, perhaps sensing perilous ground under her feet. "Well, no, but . . ."

I drained the water. Due to our walk under Lakari's harsh sun, it disappeared faster even than Torvald's raspberry juice. I hoped, by the gods, I conveyed some gratitude despite my mood. "What's your name?"

"Sarina." Her white smile returned, apparently never gone for long. For some reason, I thought of my sister. It was with slight regret I missed Madalyn's new budding love, her growing feelings for the only non-family noble I could tolerate. Although my sister, if anyone, understood the sudden need to get away from Eldaborg.

"Nice to meet you, Sarina. Thank you for helping me."

"It was no problem, miss. Here, take this, I insist." Sarina pushed an orange little pastry into my hand.

As I met Sarina's eyes, I knew we were of twin minds, and we turned upon Sir Sigve as one. Parting with his coins, he delivered a sigh that sounded like it came from the depth of his soul.

Sarina's radiance was only matched by mine. A fellowship meant to be.

"I'll pay you back, you know." My promise did little to appease Sir Sigve's grumbling face.

"I'll take that as it comes," he said. "We should be able to get proper food over there." My companion pointed to a small establishment, a tavern or inn of sorts.

We wandered through the streets after a *splendid*—and very late—breakfast, which might or might not have included a piece of honey-filled cake. And if they sold it practically everywhere, who could blame me for indulging?

The walk was slow. On the pretext of leisure, I hid how the heat sent my head spinning and weakened my legs. We mostly kept to the meager shadows of houses, staving off the worst burn. At the outskirts of town, dust swirled across the ground and the green met an end. The very last building was a worn but vast stable.

The camels seemed peaceful enough until one of them aimed a glob of spit directly at Sir Sigve. He sidestepped quickly.

"Don't disappoint the poor animals now," I said, struggling not to laugh.

My companion threw me a wary glance. "Indeed. What a tragedy that would be." By the gods' skaal, that man lacked humor. "I'm relieved to see you still have your wit, if nothing else, Lady Vildi."

A caravan came into sight, trudging out of town with dust clouds settling in its wake—but I should be a part of that group. My limbs were so *heavy*. I grasped for thoughts but found only fog. Fatigue—like my body and mind had been wrung and torn too many times. I struggled through the humidity for another intake of air. This place, despite the golden cakes, was set on suffocating me—and the group leaving Fiar felt like a lifeline waving goodbye.

It must have shown.

"That's Golden Road, miss. Leads to the big city, it does, you interested?" A man in his fifties—if his wrinkles were to be trusted—came up behind us, armed with charming, yellow teeth and a heavy accent to his fragmented Alltongue. "It leaves every two days, it does, big caravan. This be the most important trading route for the royals, you see."

"How nice." I eyed the cloud of dust being kicked up in the distance.

"Yes, and it be a glorious trip too, you see oasis, beautiful island of life, yes?" In this place where the air was thick with water and heat beat on us through a haze, such a thing seemed irresistible. Encouraged by my expression, the man continued. "And it be ruins on the way, magnificent monuments from olden times."

"Really?" None of the port-towns so far had offered excursions to ancient, abandoned ruins, and the thought sent a thrill through me.

"Yes! I fix trip for you, mister, miss, to the royal city Aransis. There be another caravan, great for travelers like yourselves. And there be other people too, having a fabulous journey thanks to our services." The man bowed, giving us his best jovial grin with all his remaining teeth.

"Fabulous?"

Perhaps we had different opinions on the concept. His caravan, or what was visible from this distance, seemed an interesting mix of dust and rudimental solutions, with three well-used wagons and few provisions. But the sights were sure to be worth the inconvenience.

"Ah, it be a pleasant journey, miss, because *I*, Rahid, guarantee it." Rahid flung his arms out in a grand gesture, showing off his worn clothes.

"Good. Let's leave today." I turned to Sir Sigve, delivering my delight in response to his raised, bushy brows.

Rahid's wrinkles arranged themselves in overly sad folds. "Sorry, miss, so so sorry, I am. No caravan leaving today. That one was last, it was." He waved in the general direction of the dust cloud.

I twirled the end of my admittedly dreary tangle of hair. "Could you rent us two—maybe three—animals? We don't *have* to travel with a caravan, right?"

"No is no, miss! If you arrive before, perhaps, but now is too late. You have to wait. Come back day after tomorrow, and I give you place in next caravan, I do. And fair price too." Rahid plastered a jolly smile on his face, whisking away the frown as if it had never marred his face.

I wanted to insist, ignoring Sir Sigve as he looked like madness had befallen me. But this was important and I had no idea why, yet the man before me would not budge. My shoulders slumped as a queasy stone settled in my stomach. "Fine. We'll leave with the next caravan."

"Certainly, miss!" Rahid's beaming face was brighter than sunshine, yellowing teeth included.

As we left in silence, I glanced at my companion. "Please don't ask. I just don't like it here."

Sir Sigve shrugged, hoisting our cumbersome luggage to a more secure hold. I felt bad for him, just a little. "All right. But it *is* unlike you."

I pulled my clothes closer around me, huddling despite the warm weather.

"Don't you miss the horses, Vildi?" Sir Sigve watched me, a certain calculating, familiar glint in his eyes. "If you want to ride, you don't need camels—Tyra waits at home. I'm sure she misses you too."

"Good attempt, *Papa*. I'm not swayed."

Sir Sigve smirked. "A man has to try, daughter of mine."

Snorting, I hid a smile with my hand. "Right." A black cat strolled across the street. Did such a thing bring bad luck? My stomach flopped, and I glanced behind me. No one there.

The sun reached its zenith, suffocating the evening dew. I was always hungry, but the warmth seemed to drain away my appetite. And I usually had a strong constitution too. Still, dinner would restore me because I was Vildi, and if I lacked a will to eat, there was something gravely wrong with me.

We found a tavern with a few outside tables and a splendid view of the sea, where they served a thick and wonderful soup—it slid down, no effort required. Still, judging by Sir Sigve's stew, this was a country of cake.

I had to admit, seeing the sun sink into the ocean in orange-yellow flames caught my breath. A heavy fragrance of deep purple flowers filled the air, from thick and uneven petals on green stems. With the warmth of the pavement beneath my feet, I found myself slipping off a shoe. The setting would have been romantic too, alas the one sitting across from me was Sir Sigve. But not even a lad straight from the fairy tales would have made a difference. I was better off without such foolish thoughts.

"Perhaps I can like this place," I said, breaking a prolonged silence.

Sir Sigve looked over, finally forgiving me for my tenth cake. "Lots of people here," he said. "Good for trading."

"I guess. Let's go to the market tomorrow since we didn't get to see much of it today."

"Fiar has people visiting from several nations." Sir Sigve spoke in the same tone he would use with his recruits, generous with the wisdom of his observations. "The market it is. I might find some new weapons, and we both need fresh clothes."

"Makes it easier to blend in," I mused.

Sir Sigve shook his head. "You still stand out. No sane person would eat as you do."

"Or drink like you," I bit back.

"Skaal!" With a wry grin, he emptied his glass. "For the gods."

I gave in, emptying my own. "I suppose. The gods it is."

"The sun setting in the water reminds one of summer at home, doesn't it?" Sir Sigve said. "The view from the western windows upstairs."

"I guess." I looked down at my empty cup. "It is a little similar."

"Don't you miss Eldaborg?"

"No. Well, Madalyn. And Brage when he doesn't play with my books."

"We can go back, you know. If we left now, we could return to the ripening of strawberries by the roadside."

"No."

Sir Sigve lifted the luggage miserably. "In that case my l—Vildi, we should find lodging soon. You have watched that sunset for a while now, and it's getting dark."

It was true. Only a sliver of gold was left on the horizon. I stood up, hand lingering on the table. This was a comfortable spot, just sitting in the same place was fine by me.

Sir Sigve coughed.

"Fine, fine."

"One is enough, Vildi." He sighed. Raising me to be a prim and proper part of society was not his usual pastime.

Quiet and darkness hung over Fiar like a wool blanket as we trudged through the streets. Still, there was life around us. From happy Lakarians, their language like a song in the night. It was in lights streaming out the windows, promising a festive atmosphere if we stepped inside.

"That place seems suitable, don't you think?" Sir Sigve gestured toward a door, lit up by merry torches. Laughter reached out as if beckoning us to join them. Like a siren's song, it was tempting.

My knees wobbled, ready to betray me. My companion moved forward—he would die. My hand shot out, grasping his shirt.

"Lady Vildi?" Sir Sigve looked concerned, but his voice sounded far away. "You're pale. You've been sick the whole day, haven't you? Let's get inside . . ."

"Lady . . . Vildi? As in Princess Alvildi?"

I whirled around and saw two men. My legs turned to lead, stiff then melting. I recognized those patchy, dark brown clothes.

"Golden hair, green eyes, that's her." The oldest man spoke with chopped and stunted words, eyes sharp on me.

"I think I preferred the painting," the other one smirked. Well, *I* would have preferred the minimal decency of his lowered voice. Where did they get my portrait anyway, with Lakari such a long distance from Rimdalir?

A stench of fish and stale ale hit me. "Please excuse his rude behavior, Princess. Now, if you will come with us, you've been summoned to—"

"NO!" Every nerve in my body screamed against these men. "I don't know you." *Strangers.* And somehow, despite his words, my mind warned me of danger. I would not survive this encounter.

My legs shook, too frail to keep me standing.

"Quit bothering my daughter." Bless Sir Sigve for stepping in—and even keeping to our story. His hand clenched the hilt of his sword.

"Daughter?" The leader laughed, a guffaw soon joined by his partner. "I think not. This is Princess Alvildi of Rimdalir, and she *will* come with us."

"What do you want with her? Unless you have some solid proof of authority, I won't allow this."

"Step down. The princess has been summoned to the court of—"

"No." Bile rose to my throat. Only the fingers clenching Sir Sigve's shirt kept me above ground, but if we followed these men his blood would sieve through sand, draining away among the dunes. "Fake. Please, Sigve, don't let them—"

"She will be handed over." The man stood his ground, eyes level and unwavering. He talked as if everything had been decided.

To stress the statement, the rude underling flicked his wrist to let the firelight reflect on what could only be weapons, knives resting in his hand as naturally as food in mine.

"Over my dead body." Sir Sigve's blade rang into the night. The fluidity of the battle bore a grotesque resemblance to a dance. Stab, duck, counterattack, dodge, turn, reaction to accompany each action. Sir Sigve's breath was heavy, ragged. "*Run,* Princess!"

My legs wouldn't move.

"Lady Vildi!" He took a cut to the flank. Sir Sigve's once perfect movements became chopped as a hiss of pain left his lips. Even as his sword bit flesh in return, the strangers were too much. My companion was losing.

I sank down upon the cobbled street.

A blade flashed in the firelight, sent flying toward Sir Sigve, but of course: years had tuned his body to react. He dodged, parrying at the same time an attack from the side—and the knife sailed past him, right at me.

All movement stopped, and three pairs of wide eyes blurred in my vision. I saw the worn handle before I felt a cold pain in my chest. Pulling at the blade, I looked up as it fell to the ground in front of me. Heard the *clank* as it hit stone. Or maybe it was Sir Sigve's sword, fallen from his slack grip. Guilt-ridden gray eyes faded into black.

"Well, that is one solution," a cheery voice said.

WILDERNESS SHELTER

The images slammed into me—dying with a knife through my stomach, a blade to the chest—and I woke up drenched in sweat. The crisp sheets mocked me with their pure whiteness as if saying: *no blood here.*

The nightmare stayed with me even as I sat up, imprinted on my mind as if it had violated my sleep many, many times. But around me was the glorified room—golden carvings framing a window to the glittering sea, a glaring contrast to my visions.

The door burst open. "Are you well, Lady Vildi, I heard—"

I turned. "Are you?"

"What?" Sir Sigve blinked, forgetting to close his mouth.

"Are you well?"

"I'm fine." His hand crept back to the sword.

I pushed away the hair that hung in front of my eyes. "You are not hurt? No wounds?"

"Of course not. My la—"

"Sorry, just checking—" *To see, if my sanity was damaged beyond repair.* "I had a nightmare," I said. The words came with ease as if rehearsed.

"I see." Sir Sigve held out his arms, face softening. "I'm perfectly fine, as you can see. We'll get some breakfast, and you'll feel better, I promise."

"Thank you." Shaking hands stilled in my lap at last.

Bolting off the ship with Sir Sigve in tow, I rushed across the harbor, through a few dense streets. Stretching further. Faster. I couldn't help it. Everywhere I laid my eyes, the view was exactly as expected. The barrels, the bumps in the pavement, the shops lining the main street. Everything was just perfect. I swallowed, reminding myself to breathe, struggling not to succumb to the bile rising to my throat. It was a nightmare, *only* a nightmare, a stupid dream—because what else could it be? Thunder in my heart hit my ears like drums, and it still felt like I would never reach.

"I wonder how my recruits are doing," Sir Sigve said, the clumsy attempt at conversation revealing his unease. He clenched and unclenched his hand around the hilt at his belt.

A girl waved at us, smiling as if the world was *such* a happy place. I had eaten an unreasonable amount of her golden honey cakes. That smell . . . one small bite would bring me to heaven for sure. Sarina's voice drifted toward me, words of "the prince" carrying on the wind. I shuddered, my stomach lurching. I had to keep moving.

The market girl looked sad as we strode past her, but I had to reach the other side of town. Even though I had no idea what waited—or perhaps did not wait—over there.

Sir Sigve kept glancing my way, a frown consolidating into his features. I pretended not to notice. Of course, that only worked for so long. "You have such vigor in your steps today, Lady Vildi, truly, you walk fast."

"Mhm." We passed the dragon statue, from which merchant eyes followed us.

"*Very* fast. You might, well, there is no need—"

"I'm just exercising." Up ahead was the end of the market square, where we would re-enter the narrow street and get away from stares and calls. My hair, hanging loose, covered my face, falling in my eyes even as I pushed it away. I should have braided it after all.

"Yes, I should be glad—you might resemble your portraits yet—but it's not like you." Sir Sigve's steps were brisk beside me.

"You're just getting slow, *Papa*." I spared him a glance. Did his crow's feet grow today?

Sir Sigve promptly scoffed and picked up his pace, looking everywhere but at me. He was so sensitive, my companion. He kicked aside a pebble in his path. "We've been rushing through the city."

"Of course. You must feel weary in your old bones, dear, poor *Papa*."

"I'm only thirty-six!"

A stand displaying brilliantly shining metalwork caught my eye from the reflected sun. The table contained all sorts of trinkets, jewelry, necklaces, leather belts with metal ornaments—and knives.

"I'm going to have a closer look. Please wait here?"

"Why? What are you plotting now?"

"Nothing! Well, I'm buying a gift for Madalyn, and I don't want her to know . . ."

Sir Sigve got a softer hue in his eyes, lasting less than a second. "Your sister is not here at the moment. How would she know?"

"Yes, but I don't want *anyone* to see it before I present it to her. Please." If this didn't work, I would have to give up. Still, a pleading voice usually did the trick. Plus, it was for my sister. He would not deny her.

Sir Sigve brightened. "I assume you intend to get home in time for Madalyn's birthday." He didn't even bother to disguise it as a question anymore.

I exhaled, forcing restless fingers to be still at my sides. Did he forget we spent over five months traveling to Fiar? "Maybe we could, if we left yesterday," I said, bypassing a few children running through the square, disappearing in an alley to our right. After fifteen years as a disappointment and two years on display, five months of freedom was simply not enough. But the plague of a dizzying, scourging city called Fiar was finished for me.

Sir Sigve sighed, kneading his fingers into an abused forehead. Perhaps he had a headache. "Very well. Go buy her the not-birthday present."

I skipped across the cobblestones to the small stall with all its shiny trinkets.

The merchant was an elderly man of leathery complexion and a graying beard, wearing one of the white hats that resembled a tangled bandage. It looked like excellent protection against the heat. Should I try it too? The seller's eyes lit up as I approached. "What can I do for you, young lady?"

"I need a knife."

"Fair lady, that's not something those delicate hands should touch. What about a beautiful necklace, how about it, miss?" He gestured to his fine assortment.

"I need a knife."

"A necklace," he said, "will look just marvelous on you. What about this? It is said to soothe the soul as well as a drop from the Desert Diamond." He held up a gem glittering as the ocean. "No? I have this one here, you see. This stone is jade, it is, a rare gem. But for you, I give a good price. Because it was made for your beautiful green eyes, eh?" He bestowed on me a blinding smile, effortlessly ignoring my request.

"Please, I only want a knife. If you cannot provide one, I'll find somewhere else."

With a piercing stare below upturned eyebrows, the man's skepticism seemed to only grow. "Now, miss, I—"

"*Please.*" I lowered my voice, struggling to not let my feelings seep out. I tipped my head toward Sir Sigve, standing with his back to us as promised. "See, it's for my father, his birthday."

The merchant sighed, looking the full extent of his age. To have such pitying brown eyes set upon me was almost unbearable. "All right. I'll sell you a small one. Be careful, though, miss. And if you change your mind, the necklace will be here for you."

"Thank you!" My breath rushed out as I exchanged coin for knife.

The blade gleamed in the sun, with a handle of ebony and quality in every curve. Although forged as decoration or perhaps for ceremonial instances, it was excellent craftsmanship, and above all: sharp. I tucked it behind the belt of my dress, grateful for the layers of clothes hiding it from view. Sir Sigve would never let me keep it if he found out.

Lucky for me, he was true to his word, steadfastly looking elsewhere. We would finally get out of Fiar because the city was worn and crowded, and if I stayed, I would fall ill for sure.

"Finished?"

"Yes." I glanced up from wringing hands. "The merchant had a very nice necklace; it suits anyone with green eyes splendidly."

"Lady Madalyn has blue eyes."

"I'm sure she will be happy," I said.

His eyes narrowed. "I thought I wasn't supposed to know what it was?"

Right. My poor, forgotten excuse. "Uh, yeah, well, you haven't seen what it looks like yet! Just . . . don't tell her, please?"

"I can't, she's not here." Sir Sigve tapped his foot, his frown deepening in a worrying tempo.

"Good," I chirped.

He shook his head, perhaps too exasperated to doubt the smile I had refined through all my seventeen years of suffering Maya's lessons. "I assume you'll deliver this gift to Lady Madalyn on her birthday?"

"You misunderstand." On purpose too. "I'm not ready to go home."

"Of course not. This is your grand adventure." Sir Sigve rolled his eyes. "You need not travel this far to experience something new. Lady Madalyn only went to Silverberg. Remember how much she grew?"

"Yes, and stupid suitors would leave me alone in Silverberg, or Nordsletta—"

Sir Sigve grimaced.

"—or any and all of Rimdalir. I could have *such* a pleasant journey." I snorted. "You don't believe that. I don't believe that." I would *not* stand on display for them like some hunter's trophy.

"You assume a court of suitors is lurking at every turn," Sir Sigve said. "You are running. Going from place to place, not staying long enough to enjoy anything."

"I left home because I discovered my words were not enough. You know I despise them."

"No, you're fleeing," Sir Sigve insisted, "and it will do you no good. You need to face your—"

"I told you, words were not enough! My title helps even less. I'm a girl, and not a strong one. I can't fight with just a needle and thread. Can't win a physical fight."

"Did any of them—"

I shook my head. "It's fine. Well, it's not, but nothing really happened." I felt ill from the memory.

"My lady, tell me."

"It was only . . . an unpleasant conversation. Nothing more." Except his wandering hands, fingers grasping as he whispered against my ear. "I would have left someday, anyway."

Sir Sigve's brows drew tight over a glare. "You could have told us. Your father would not—"

"It's fine." I swept hair from my eyes, rubbed away the stinging sensation pushing to the surface. "*When* I eventually go home, I'll tell you everything. Is that acceptable?"

Sir Sigve nodded. "I can already guess who. Tell me when you're ready."

I exhaled, spotting a black cat crossing our path. Didn't such a thing bring bad luck? Maya said something on the subject once or twice, mumbling her prayers as she threw salt everywhere.

Sir Sigve looked calm, a hand coming up to quench an incoming yawn. He was not of the superstitious kind. Naturally, neither was I.

"Do you miss Maya?" I asked, glancing up at him.

"I miss all of them equally," he said. To my satisfaction, his face flamed, betraying him. He sped up the pace, brisk steps pulling in front of me.

I wish Maya had seen that.

We reached the outskirts of town to the sight of native men walking and working, a turmoil of wagons and wares. A caravan, soon ready to depart. And I just knew it: that assembly was my life, my goal, my everything.

A man stood at the center of the chaos, with lists rustling from a clenched fist as he vigorously pointed around him.

"Excuse me? Do you have room for two more?" A stone took residence in my stomach, as if I had eaten a big rock, and forth from it a myriad of butterflies took flight.

"Ah, miss, welcome. I am Rahid. This here is caravan to the royal city Aransis. You want to go?"

"Yes!" The butterflies disappeared all at once.

"It be a little late. You should wait for next, it leave in two days. Better, yes? No stress." Rahid bobbed his head as if to agree with his own statement.

"No! It *has* to be today." The people near us turned to look, and the man before me raised a black, bushy eyebrow. I forced my lips to lift and softened my voice, with my head tilted just so. "Please, surely you can fit us in?"

"Ah, miss, how can I say no to such beautiful face, eh?" He beamed, and I knew it would be okay, despite his nonsense words.

"Do I have a say in this?" Sir Sigve looked ready to rebel, arms crossed tightly like the furrows between his eyes.

"Please?" I turned my begging looks on him. "This is just another port town, after all. I want to see the capital!"

Bless Sir Sigve, accepting my eccentricity with relative ease. "All right, as you wish. As always." Did he sound a little bitter?

"Hey, lad!" Rahid's voice boomed across the yard.

A boy younger than me, deeply embedded in loads of leather reins and other gear, raised his gaze with a start and dashed over.

"You bring them camels. And rations for two." Rahid looked us over once more. "And equipment. Quick, quick."

The poor soul nodded, hurrying away.

Rahid turned, a solid grin in place. "You see? It be okay."

"Fine." Sir Sigve watched his pouch with sorrow. "It's decided."

With an outstretched hand, the man received his payment. His smile was surely meant to charm us. "Pleased to have you with my caravan." In the next moment, Rahid was gone, and we were left waiting.

Soon, two animals came trotting behind the poor child from before. "This is Rai." He relinquished the reins to Sir Sigve. "And this is Balt." The boy didn't quite look at me, and the skin draped across his cheekbones darkened as he handed me the reins. "He's young, but he will take good care of you, lady."

"Thank you."

"Lad! No time to loiter. You work!" Rahid's voice boomed from behind his important papers. The youngling cast us another glance before he fled—off to labor in the heat.

My camel was smaller than the rest. He had beautiful, flaxen fur, smoother to the touch than it looked. Balt seemed to possess a calm intellect—but perhaps he just was a creature of leisure and laziness.

His movements were strange to me, differing from a horse with big, quirky, and not quite balanced swaying, but I wasn't a bad rider, so I got used to it during the first hour. Sir Sigve seemed less inclined to enjoy the ride, his whole face scrunched in a scowl. Perhaps he preferred horses, or more likely, lamented moving further away from returning to Rimdalir. Still, the road was pretty straight and easily traveled, old and trampled down by a thousand feet. Chances were, you had to be a terrible rider to fall off.

Hogne would have hated it. I could envision him atop Odin, the kindest, oldest little pony in the stable, with too long legs clamped around the belly as they trudged after the other horses. Poor Hogne, how many times we had forced

BALANCE

him to come with us. At least he was spared this particular ride.

The caravan consisted of two wealthy families, wearing finer clothes than Sir Sigve and I. Five merchants—real, unlike us—rode on camels alongside the wagons, three of them balancing impressive piles of headwear atop once-black hair. A guide led the party.

The dunes of sand, many times higher than us, branched out far off into an unending pale horizon. One of our local guides told us how wind moved the sand, shaping it into formations like long parallel bands or even stars. Yet in some places the ground was barren, with shiny pebbles and a cover of bigger stones as if man-made. But no, the guide told us, this was from the wind too.

The road seemed simple enough to follow, and I told our guide so. Yes, he answered, but even without wildlife and heat, there was danger in the very wind. If unlucky, sand would obscure the path until everywhere looked the same. He said that was why traveling with an experienced group was so important.

If the city had been hot, with salt and humidity hanging in the air, it was nothing to the direct, beating sun. Even the white shawl borrowed from the caravan helped little.

One merchant, darker by far than the rest of us, was generous with his blinding white smile. In good spirit he was unmatched—although it was an easy feat in the company of grave men and delicate ladies. His songs weaved into the silence from the very start, in a language I couldn't comprehend. The sounds he made followed a rhythm which never got boring, filling me with sorrow in one moment, yet spurred forth happiness and laughter in the next. Unlike anything I had ever heard, it exceeded any folk music or great skald—northern poet—of Rimdalir.

The merchant let one last tune fade into nothing as we reached our first resting site, a tiny spot of sudden blue and green. My first oasis.

The water was alluring, glittering like a sapphire encased by the desert. As we sprawled on the ground, the refreshing sights stressed hours in sweltering heat and whipped sand. I wanted that water so badly. To fall in, feel it against my skin, and swim in it—let it soak me and finally evaporate from my body in the sun. I looked at Sir Sigve, and he seemed all but ready to jump in himself—until he glanced my way. "Don't even think about it."

"Fine." I buried my face in my arms, exhaling. The caravan guide placed my share of rations in my hands, and other needs occupied me. But there was one thing I couldn't resist. Kicking off my shoes and stockings, I sat down by the edge with water swirling around my legs. The revered gentlemen and ladies in our company widened their eyes, and while the men turned away in embarrassment, the women whispered with scandalized, condescending delight, looking down their noses at me. The kind of people to be almost but not quite nobility, rich but not powerful, always judging others to put themselves apart.

It seemed bare feet were scowled upon in Lakari. But if I could be of help and serve as easy entertainment, it was fine with me. I had the pleasure of a cool sensation sweeping against skin, and dried meat and fruits to fill my wailing stomach.

With lunch over and the sun lowering from its highest peak, I once again mounted Balt. When we left the oasis, none of us were hungry or thirsty anymore, but only I was refreshed. Those eyes of condemnation turned to envy.

Most of us were not used to traveling in the desert and felt the heat, the trip taking its toll. Except for brief conversations which I—the crazy waterhole girl—was not privy to, people were silent. Sand-watching had been exciting for the first three hours. Maybe even the fourth. Not the tenth, and one thing was for certain: Sir Sigve was no help. I nudged Balt forward, catching up with our guide.

"I'm impressed by Lakari so far. You thrive in such tough conditions."

"Thanks, miss. We do our best, we do. These can be harsh lands, aye, but they are our lands. And we have an excellent king," the guide said with his rolling Alltongue, looking through his black curls up at me.

Quenching a sigh, I plastered on a smile. I had hoped he would tell me about their customs, not politics. "I saw much trade back in Fiar. Such peace and prosperity would not be possible without a good leader."

"Aye," the guide said. We walked on in silence, one comfortable, one decidedly disappointed. Well, this trip was of my own choice, and I would just have to resign myself to boredom. The guide started talking again. "In truth, we have kind neighbors."

Ah. More politics. "Yes," I agreed, thinking Mother and Maya would have been proud of my excellent politeness.

"But it be some disturbance of late," the guide continued, looking like he was conversing with the sandy road rather than me. "Unrest in Tolona . . . only a rumor though." The man glanced over at me. "Ah, nothing to worry miss, nothing to worry at all. You be fine." So, he *did* remember I was there.

Sadly, he lost all interest in speaking after that. I had nothing to do but trot along atop Balt, and all too soon I was too hot, anyway. The huge dunes didn't really help. Rather than sheltering us, I could imagine disaster hiding behind them, ready to devour me any second. Swallowing, I glanced around before drying off my clammy hands on the dress. As I steered Balt to walk beside Sir Sigve again, the feeling receded. My fantasy always had this tendency to run a little wild, but I reined it in right along with Balt. With a sour soldier on my left and such a down-to-earth creature under me, I grounded myself.

The journey continued through the day, with nothing more exciting than the occasional protruding rock or the screech of a scrawny bird flying above us. No incidents. When the sky took on a dark, violet-blue hue, we saw lights in the distance. It was a small assembly surrounding a bigger oasis—our destination for the night. Crafty plants: spiky cacti, bushes, grass—even some trees—made up the lush island around three springs. These people had created a home here, a tiny spot of life in the middle of a sea of sand. Though, if need be, they only had a day's trip to reach Fiar.

These surroundings gave an illusion of a sheltered wilderness. My shoulders eased up. Apparently, the owner liked her guests clean and the floor sand-free, so we did a quick wash up in a hut. A sign that read: *The Thirsty Traveler* greeted us, and as I stepped inside the inn, I finally relaxed, untangling even the teeny knot resting in my stomach. There was nothing here to give me sickness-inducing nightmares.

THE FAIRY-TALE LIE

For being such a hot place, the air chilled rapidly as the sun disappeared beyond towering dunes. It was a relief when the last of our party closed the door, shutting the night out behind us. Of the few sandy white-chalked buildings by the oasis, *The Thirsty Traveler* was by far the warmest and most welcoming. The hostess was a lively woman, instilling respect by both stature and smile. Her long braid thumped on her back in steady beats with her steps, reminding me of boots tramping the rhythms of song at a good feast. Dinner was ready when we arrived, and she served it with pleasant efficiency. Her name was Kaira, and she invaded our table at the first opportunity.

"Your skin is lovely, my dear."

Did she greet all guests like that? This might be normal for desert people. Or perhaps nice skin was rare here, with the ever-present sun? "Thank you . . ."

"You must have traveled very far," Kaira said, hands flat on the table as she leaned in, her slanted lips rivaling the sparkle in her eyes.

"Quite far," I agreed, dipping my spoon into the soup, then blowing off some steam. There was an angry tummy to appease. The food tasted like sweet heaven with a sizzle of spices, possibly because of the long day and my travel-worn condition. The small piece of bread was fresh out of the oven, sugary with a hint of something more. As I looked up, I stared right into Kaira's dark eyes. "Do you run this place by yourself?" I asked, feeling rather polite.

She shifted her weight, popping a hip to put her hand on. "Oh no, I have help. Three pairs of excellent hands, my sister one of them. But after my late husband died . . ." she drew a deep breath. "Well, I am the sole owner now."

Kaira was not, by appearance, an old woman. She was in her late twenties or early thirties, if I had to guess. It would seem the desert claimed people at a young age too, as the frost did at home. Or maybe her husband had been old to begin with.

"I'm sorry," I said. Behind Kaira, another woman appeared, rushing about to please the remaining guests as the proprietress herself indulged her curiosity at our table.

"Thank you." Her smile was a sad one, bearing the heavy melancholy and silent strength only death could instill. "He left me this place—a good life." Kaira gazed down at the ring still resting on her finger. When she looked up again,

BALANCE

her lips tilted, small dimples in her cheek. "Where do you come from?"

My spoon took another trip to the stew. Wouldn't do to let it go cold. With a mouth full of food, it would be impolite to talk.

Kaira yet again demonstrated our very different senses of personal space, her fingers finding one of my escaped locks trailing the table. "Your hair is like the sun. Such a fair color is a rare sight."

I swallowed. "Thank you."

Kaira let go. "And you—your beard could be the flames of Rashim." She leaned in further until Sir Sigve had to look away, his cheeks tinted red like his praised facial hairs. The local fashion was not what one would call modest, and he was her current target of interest. "You must come from far, far away." On second thought, she was perhaps a little *too* curious.

"Well," he coughed. "We come from—"

"A land up north. Probably haven't heard of it, being so far off, and small, and unremarkable." I smiled for good measure.

"North." Her eyes absolutely sparkled, and I realized my mistake. "Oh, is it true you have four *seasons*?"

I laughed. "Indeed. Would you not tell her about it, Papa?"

Sir Sigve's eyes trailed down where they had no business being. "W—well, there is winter of course, you know, with snow and cold."

Kaira nodded eagerly. It was a boring description, though.

"And fall . . . is when the leaves fall off," Sir Sigve continued, clearly getting the hang of things and looking more comfortable.

Kaira leaned back in her chair, clearly losing interest.

"Spring is—"

"—when everything comes to life. From nothing, with a few mild days, the hills go green, and all kinds of flowers and animals appear in the forest. The birds return, and they wake you with song each morning. And what else . . . we have a spring feast, to celebrate fresh food and warmth. It is my favorite season," I said. Someone had to defend my poor kingdom.

"I would like to see that." Kaira sighed, eyes glazed. "We don't have seasons." I almost pitied her, having the same sight outside her home every day, the whole year.

"There are trolls too," I said with a whisper, which earned a smile. "In the mountains. And the Hulder people live in the forest, though they try to sneak into human society. And if you encounter them in the woods, they'll seduce you. They have *tails*."

"*Vildi.*" Sir Sigve eyed me with *that* kind of frown, etching into his features.

"Yes, yes." I rolled my eyes. Sir Sigve was no fan of fairy tales, apparently. Maybe he would like them if Maya was the storyteller.

Our hostess blinked.

"It is part of our folklore," I explained to a rather bewildered looking Kaira. "But I always loved the fairy tales of beautiful princesses and brave lads the most."

"Say, what is your kingdom called?"

"Rimdalir." Sir Sigve sat up straighter, squaring his shoulders. I suppressed a sigh. It was such a short way from Vildi to Rimdalir and finally Alvildi. What about the listening ears possibly lurking around? Stupid Sir Sigve.

And stupid me. Perhaps keeping 'Vildi' had been too bold. I glanced at my companion. No. Even if I came up with a new name, Sir Sigve would have persisted with his 'lady' nonsense anyway, with no regard for the ramifications.

"I think I've heard that name before," Kaira said, lowering her gaze to the table. "Now how was it?" She leaned back, eyes far off and unfocused as she dug through her memories. "Rimdalir . . ."

"What about Lakari?" I asked, hoping I could nudge the conversation in a good direction. "Do you have any folklore? You must hear a lot of stories from those passing by?"

A knowing grin came to her face. Kaira leaned over the table again, her firm hands spread out flat against the surface. "Indeed, I do. Say, let's have a drink together. Finish your meal, let me take care of some chores, and I'll be back. I'll tell you some grand stories, my dear."

"I look forward to it." I returned the full extent of my concentration toward my soup-stew and now cold bread.

We ate the rest in silence. Perhaps we both felt the long day settle in. Especially Sir Sigve, with his old bones. He neared forty, poor man.

None too soon, two big mugs of brew were placed in front of us. While Sir Sigve grabbed his for a big swig, I sniffed mine. The drink emitted a fragrance of herbs, but it was dark like roasted nuts. I had a sip, and then one more. It was sweet, yet almost too spicy. If my poor taste buds hadn't already faced several burned experiences along our way, it would have been a problem. Sir Sigve was growing in redness—and not from the alcohol, although we would feel those effects in due time. Nothing like the mead back home, though.

Kaira sipped at her own drink, comfortably resting in our company. It was funny, with an assortment of fine guests, how she chose us. Then again, with our skin we stood out like the Northern star in the night sky.

"So," Kaira said. "Where should I begin . . . anything piquing your interest?"

My attention snapped back to the innkeeper. "I'm curious about . . . the ruins along Golden Road," I finally said.

"Ah, those." Kaira took a sip of her brew, nodding. "There are several, but one place in particular stands out. It's not exactly along the road, but this one is the most entrancing, in my opinion. Its story cuts to the very heart of Lakari, though I'm afraid I don't know all the details. This happened long before my time."

"That's okay. I can do without the boring facts. Old things and mysteries fascinate me."

"In that case, this should be the story for you." Kaira gazed at us both, folding her hands on the table. "From what I know, these ruins are ancient, from the origin of Lakari. You see, once upon a time this land was fragmented and fragile. War raged, and people were poor." Kaira's voice was low, but each word was precise and strong. "This region has always been stricken by desert. Only the coast, the occasional oasis, and Haya River grant a way to live. Naturally, people fought over water, livestock, and the few places suitable for farming. Small clans controlled these places, defending them from intruders, sometimes attacking themselves. Fiar is one such place. This is another." Kaira cast a fond, warm gaze across the room, her lovely inn. Shaking her head, she took a good swig of her drink, the smile gone when the mug hit the table.

"To lose your home was a death sentence. In a land where everything was scarce, getting a hold of additional food and water could save your children in the next drought. These dire times at last came to an end. A catastrophe hit the land. How much do you know about starvation?"

I peeked at Sir Sigve, noticing the small, telltale groove as his brows furrowed ever so slightly together, the rigid lines of his lips. I certainly looked the same.

"A prolonged drought can take a terrible toll on a person," Kaira said, with a tremble in her tone. "We have trade now and good neighbors. But imagine watching your crops shrivel up, drops of precious milk dry out until you're forced to slaughter your last animal . . . and no one can help you. As the body dehydrates, the mind wanders. You start seeing things. You lose control of your impulses, and even the faint promise of water drives you desperate. Because you can do nothing, even as your children cry with dry eyes." Kaira drew a deep breath. This no longer sounded like just a story. Our hostess raised her head, her gaze once again steady.

"The fights became vicious. And then, it is said, came sickness. It preyed upon weakened people, spread by desperation. Entire clans succumbed." Kaira's voice was scarce more than a whisper now, a soft wind carrying the scent of death.

I glanced at Sir Sigve. The lovely meal chunked up in my stomach. My companion looked with rapt focus at Kaira, but as if feeling my stare, he turned back to me. It was a comfort, seeing the gentle change in his eyes and knowing I was not alone with my thoughts, my memories like hollow echoes of empty plates and frozen ground, fires spreading a stench through Eldaborg.

Kaira hummed a sympathetic tune as she observed the reactions of her audience. "From this shattered land, a man and woman came forth. The heirs of the biggest remaining clans, once bitter enemies. The man and woman formed an alliance, recognizing the strength of a bond. They helped their families through the sickness, nourished the people with food and water, and shared the workload. By calling the people to them, they prevailed. Eventually, they led the nation to peace. Thus Lakari was born, and they reigned as the first king and queen. Although the kingdom has had its difficulties, Lakari has never again faced such dire times. Under the royal family, descendants of our founders, the desert prospers. The ruins are said to be the city they built together, centered around the Desert Diamond."

I let out a breath, noticing the need for air. "Incredible. I can't imagine how they were able to create something good from those conditions."

Kaira's lips lifted, taking on the telltale signs of a secret. "How indeed." She glanced at Sir Sigve, gazed upon me, then laughed a little—at me, waiting and wondering. "They received the gift of Hima from the gods."

I blinked. "Hima, is that Lakari's faith?"

"The protection. Hima is the bond between one of the royal family and their beloved."

"Romance." That was familiar ground. I took a new sip of my drink, feeling a spark of my old self, the child from before I came of age. The one who loved fairy tales and thought the world was like those adventures and one day, meeting a destined someone was as much an inevitability as the sun rising.

"Yes." Kaira's fingers worked on turning the mug, spinning, spinning in her hands. "Hima allowed the first king and queen to survive and win the trust of people coming to them for wisdom, protection, and strength. Or so the tale goes. It's too long ago to know for certain what transpired, and the scripts are few and badly preserved."

"This Hima, is it something magical?"

"Magic?" Kaira shook her head. Pointing at the purse at Sir Sigve's belt, she reached out, palm up. "Let me show you."

Like a man moving through mud, he handed over a bronze coin.

Giving him a heavy, generous smile, she put the coin on the table, tapping on the portrait of two small dragons. "It is a power from the gods, Liva and Avil. And even now, every few generations, it will manifest in the one of royal blood destined for the throne and their love."

"I like that," I said. "True, fairy-tale romance. A pity reality can't be so nice."

Kaira raised her eyebrow. "Reality, my dear? We have a saying in Lakari: *Hima never comes alone.* If Lakari ever stands on the brink of disaster, the gods intervene. With Hima comes great distress, although an age of prosperity always follows. None have received the gift in my lifetime. But Grandmother used to tell me about the last happening: the grandparents of the reigning king. Well, that's also a story, but maybe for another time."

"Indeed." Sir Sigve opened his eyes. They had slipped for a moment, just long enough to reveal his sleeping state. "It's getting late, L—Vildi."

"You are . . . not wrong." The mug was lukewarm in my hands. It still had a few sips left, if I drank in small portions, and besides, my drink deserved the proper treatment of being savored, not gobbled down. Tomorrow we would ride further along Golden Road, perhaps see some of these places where a myth was born. "How come there's only ruins left? If it was such a great city, the first of Lakari even."

Kaira shrugged, fingers lacing loosely together. "Well, I think the desert took hold, and they had to move."

"That's sad." One sip.

"A tragedy," Sir Sigve said, his voice flat and indifferent. Second sip.

"It's such a long time ago. Besides, we have Aransis now." Third sip. Kaira tilted her head. "I think you'll like our capital."

Sir Sigve stared at me through slipping lids. "I'm sure we will."

Final sip. "Thank you so much for the story and the drink. I enjoyed them both."

"Oh, deary, not a problem at all." Kaira swept up our empty mugs, expertly balancing them as she pushed her stool in place. "As thanks, tell me more about Rimdalir if you pass through again, will you?"

"Yes," I said, pulling a smile through my yawn. We could stop by here on our way back from Aransis.

Sir Sigve nodded, although with less enthusiasm. He paid his gratitude in coins.

With tired goodnights, we retreated to our separate sleeping arrangements. The room I got was small, struggling to fit both the bed and me, but I had it alone. A tiny window shed some moonlight into this tight space, reflected in light surfaces and spilling on my bedsheets.

The tangle resembling my hair would have to wait. After shaking out most of the sand, a nice combing in the morning could do the rest, I decided. There was no one to impress. I was worn and my body heavy, as if ten great ruins resided in me. I tucked myself in under the blankets and tried to stave off the cold creeping in. The pillow was coarse, but comfortable enough. My breaths grew deep, and my eyes slipped.

LUCK OF A GOOD HAND

My night was quiet and peaceful—no nightmares. It was actually my best sleep in a while. When I woke up, it was to the sight of chalked white walls and the murmur of voices from the people up and about downstairs. It was something *new*, waking up for the first time in this cramped yet comfortable room. Such a small thing, and still it was enough to bring the world into a radiant shine. My body was strong, my mind clear, and as had been usual for my journey, a fresh welcome of energy spurred me forth to receive the novelty a new place could provide.

Kaira chirped a "good morning" as I came down the stairs. She gestured me over to the same table we had occupied the night before, slightly sheltered in the innermost corner of the room. My steps were so light, I almost danced across the floor. Sir Sigve was already there, sipping something dark and hot.

"I'll come with your food, dear," Kaira said, disappearing behind the counter. A moment later I received a plate filled with thick slices of meat, an assortment of dried fruit, and soft, white bread.

"What about you?" I asked, looking at the suspiciously empty space in front of Sir Sigve.

"Already ate," he said. "I woke early. The cold room did nothing good for my sleep, and the blankets are too thin. I miss my pelts."

"The nights are surprisingly cold." A piece of meat migrated to my mouth. It left a strange aftertaste, but I flushed it down with water. Food was too precious to waste.

Sir Sigve stared at my meal. "Did you sleep?"

"Yes." The fruits were saccharine and juicy. "Very well, actually. I'm all rested and ready." The slight wave of nausea would disappear with a solid breakfast. "I didn't have a nightmare."

"You don't usually have those, do you?"

"I know, but since we came here, I feel like they haunt me. Nightmare upon nightm—no, now that I think about it, there was only one. But it felt so real." The bread warmed my fingers and melted on my tongue. "I used to have bad dreams, of course, when I was eleven."

"The cold winter?" Sir Sigve pulled his brows into a frown, gaze lingering on the piece of ham I was about to eat. "Didn't we all."

My stomach flipped around inside me. I let out a sigh. "I know. But I've been mostly nightmare-free since, until we got here. And this feels different."

"How so?"

"I don't know." My fists clenched into tight knots. With a lack of pebbles to kick, I tore into the meat anew.

Sir Sigve nodded, still not taking his eyes off my food. "Well, I'm glad you're better today. Good."

"You're still hungry." I laughed as he snapped to attention. "Have some meat. I won't be able to finish, anyway."

"I already ate," Sir Sigve said, but his hand was already on the slabs. His brow furrowed as he chewed. The rest of my breakfast disappeared, shared between us. If only the dizziness would go away.

I reached for more water to soothe the tingle in my throat. "Do you think we'll see the ruins today? Perhaps explore them too?"

The cup slipped between my fingers and broke against the floor. All eyes turned to me.

My hand was frozen in place, looking like I was reaching for empty air. I forced a smile but felt my lips tremble. "I'm sorry, I'm such a klutz."

"Don't worry about it, dear," Kaira said, glancing over at me.

"I'll be more careful." I bent down to retrieve the shards.

"Leave it," Kaira admonished. "I don't want my precious guest to hurt herself doing my job." She took the shards from me, sweeping in the same motion with a dishcloth. Most of the spilled drink and remaining fragments came with it, and she disappeared in a flurry of movements with the evidence of my clumsiness.

With a hand clutching for support, I rose to see the room spinning around me, the chair tipping and clattering to the floor. I swallowed, shook my head.

"Vildi?" I heard Sir Sigve's anxious voice.

The urge to throw up intensified. Kaira watched me from across the room, her foot tapping against the floor as she wrung the dishcloth around and around, the beginning of movements as if she was about to come to me, and yet she was rooted to her spot. I felt around me for something, anything to steady me, trying to find the table. My arms were leaden—I couldn't get a hold.

"Lady Vildi!" I felt Sir Sigve's hand grabbing my arm, hoisting me up. I was like a heavy sack against him, almost tripping us both. And then I sensed him fall, support vanishing as if cutting a string. Snap. On the floor, Sir Sigve expelled white froth, gasping as I reached for him, but I could not draw air at all and the room blurred in patchy browns. As my gaze moved over the guests staring at me, I noticed two dark shapes. Grinning.

∾

Why?

Tiny room, coarse bedsheets, and white, old walls. My eyes snapped open, taking in my surroundings. The inn. Dawn seeped in through a small window and warmth returned to the air. Nausea washed over me, rolling like a breath of fog in the mountains, leaving just as slow. A nightmare. Bile rose to my throat, breath heaving in hot, stifling air, and a tear pressed itself out, clouding the vision of my trembling fingers. Despite this, my heart beat strong in my chest.

How?

A mare of the night. It couldn't *be* more than a nightmare. *Impossible.* And I had to go down there, eat a poisoned breakfast, and then see Sir Sigve die with me because it had happened. Where was the air in this small, closed room where anyone could get in? The bed sheets were wet beneath my clenched fingers, like the liquid seeping down my cheeks.

On some level, I had known. I had bought the knife. I had blown through Fiar as if chased, choosing to forcefully push for a place in the caravan rather than stay and take in the sights of a city which should have been new to me.

How many times? No fairy tale described this. No one in Rimdalir had ever mentioned such magic. The gods embraced the dead—they never sent them back. A wisp of air reached my lungs. I gasped for more and found it. My shaking form stilled, cocooned in a blanket. "Please, Hogne, protect me."

Another tear fell, the last. Holding my hands in front of me, I clenched and unclenched them a few times. Traced the scars from when Father tried to teach me archery. My soft fingers made for a small fist, a grasp unsuited and unaccustomed to wielding a knife.

Reality or not, I didn't want to linger and find out, and if not poison then there were daggers and knives. Froth or blood. The thought of going back to Fiar sent cold shivers down my arms. Worse, Sir Sigve had died because of me. A fresh burst of bitter, growing bile traveled up my throat. How many times now?

I had to leave, without Sir Sigve. The thought, once formed, settled in my mind, turning my limbs to lead. He could not come with me, and he should not die for me.

I waited for the wave of sickness to pass, finally able to sweep up my few belongings. I scribbled a hasty note on an old envelope, hoping he would find it. He was safe with me gone, and I could manage without him. It would be just like camping in the woods, only without trees. And with sand everywhere. Alone.

Balt greeted me with bleary, blinking eyes from his bed of straw. It was still early enough that the stable was quiet. I took my camel, its equipment, grabbed some food, and left, easy as that. Well, the way of saddling a camel was a mystery to me, but I had excellent help from Balt. He knew how things worked, and when I reached forward with an assembly of leather straps meant for his head, he stuck his muzzle into it and suddenly it looked right. All I needed was that—for it to function, more or less. I learned how to ride the animal the day before and had no trouble getting him to come with me.

Safe. Although lights soon were lit in the buildings, the oasis was already a fair distance off. No bad meat would get to me. No twin grins.

I followed the paved road in the capital's direction for a while, and behind us Balt's tracks disappeared with a brush of breeze. When I could no longer see the lights from the buildings, we diverged from the main route and entered the desert. As the dunes grew around us, Balt made deeper tracks in the sand. The wind would whip them away, eventually.

I quickly discovered that traveling alone is boring.

The rising sun tinged the east with red, slowly tracing a path into the great sky. For hours I rode, chewing on the dried fruit and meat and getting thirsty between each sip of stale water. I followed a dune, its ridge leaning toward me. From its foot to the next a path formed, like a valley made from grains of sand, all in the same size and color. I rode through this tract as if it was a passage made especially for me. Perhaps I was the first to ever travel here. The narrow track between the dunes was sometimes straight, sometimes curving, but as I passed heaps and heaps of sand, it became hard to tell. The sun was high above us. Few shadows stretched in this endless brown sea. Did the dune lead in the right direction? My flaxen friend was calm and patient, never complaining as I steered him in—I hoped, surely—a big circle to the capital.

The branching dunes leaned over us, hulking like mountains. Gusts grasped the sand and sent it in ripples across the dunes. The sun burned through my insufficient, slight tan and heated me up, trapped me inside a dress meant for a colder climate. I wrapped the light linen of the borrowed shawl around my head.

I put the waterskin to my mouth. After half a sip, one last single drop dripped onto my tongue. Already? In my haste, I had forgotten to fill another before leaving, and I was still thirsty. But I would arrive soon; Balt had been walking for hours.

Did I still follow the right path? Well, *I* did not go in circles, only my mind did. Soon I would spot Fiar—no,

BALANCE

Aransis, the capital. Adventure. I fisted some of Balt's shaggy mane between my fingers, like Tyra's back home as she trotted leisurely through the woods, and before long I would sit around the dinner table with Father, Mother, Madalyn, and Brage.

My mouth—no, my entire being—craved something to drink.

But I would see the first buildings any time now, or at least an oasis. My face felt stiff with sand, and my dry tongue might as well be more sand. If only I had one sip of water, a can—no, a barrel of freshly brewed mead, the kind Torvald made in spring from plants plucked the same day and rich amounts of honey. My stomach was empty. Like my waterskin, with its leather slack and sunken inward, attempting to fold on itself. I turned the sack upside down over my mouth, waiting. Not one drop came out.

The air shimmered like pearls, and I noticed for the first time that in front of me, not far off at all, was something green and lush, and the glittering blue of water.

My skin protested against the beating sun. Perhaps I had looked too long at towering sand dunes, but for whatever reason their shapes blurred and melted together. My mouth was parched, but I was *so* close.

Shapes circled above me, big scrawny birds, their shrieks piercing the air.

The water was right in front of me. The sea? Soon I would bathe with Madalyn; Hogne and Eirik could come too. I swayed with the wind. The shadows above me drew near, wings flapping and sending gusts to my face. Light brown dots began forming at the edges of my vision but quickly spread, filling out my view.

Water should be right there, almost within reach. Oasis. A flare of life in unending dead, just a few steps away.

That leathery thing—skin, once upon a time—was sweltering, bubbly boiling across my cheekbones. My throat was parched. The reins felt slack and slippery between my fingers. The world tilted, or I did. Coarse grains flayed my hands.

Sharp, needle-like pain pricked at my arms, my legs, against my stomach, prodding, tearing. I lifted a hand but it fell back down. The brown let up, just enough to watch the lush green by the horizon vanishing as if it had never been there. Pale, beige-brown spots retook my vision, fading into darkness.

∼

I woke up to something sourly familiar. Instead of sand, what met my eyes was an old, white-chalked wall and a dust of light from the window. It was daybreak. The skin on my arms was hot and sore, yet unblemished and white. I had suffered in the desert for half a day with nothing to show for it. Excellent. Clearly, my efforts were worth little to the gods, to go so unrewarded. With a trembling exhale, I was ready to start over. Another repeat. A . . . Do-Again? No name could do the experience justice.

My throat was dusty. I reached out with blind eyes, flimsily throwing my hand out there until I sensed leather beneath my fingertips. Grasping it, I held on tight and gobbled down every drop. Water had never tasted so sweet. It was not enough.

Someone knocked rapidly on my door. "My lady, it would be no good to sleep in and let our company wait."

"Um . . ."

"And if you don't hurry, you'll miss breakfast."

My stomach flipped, twisting into a knot. "You can go without me."

"Absolutely not!"

"Don't be difficult. I'll be right there."

"Fine, fine." I could hear him sigh through the door.

"Don't you always tell me once is enough?" Maybe I had rubbed off on him? Would I even like to deal with a Sir Sigve behaving like me? The prospect seemed exhausting.

"Huh?"

"Never mind." I fell back down on the bed, allowing my eyes to close for a moment longer.

Sir Sigve's heavy footsteps plodded down the corridor. He would be fine down there, eating his breakfast, as long as I stayed away.

Of course, it wasn't that easy. I had to go through the salon to get out, past all the fine people, Kaira at the bar counter, and worse, Sir Sigve. "Vildi?"

"Just checking up on Balt. And I want to see the water—um, oasis before we go."

Sir Sigve rose before I finished speaking, his plate still half full.

"Please, sit. I can go alone, it's only the stables. I'll join you in good time before we leave."

"I find it unwise, my l . . ." Coughing, he seemed to remember the people surrounding us. He let out one of those deep sighs that had become so common for him. "As you wish. Be careful and don't be late." Just as he finally sounded like a true parent, Sir Sigve let me go.

Although the morning appeared to drain away, I worked fast and with sure fingers. This time, I gulped down water until I could stomach no more, then brought enough to satiate ten thirsty me. I took my share of the rations and a blanket for the night. For my second trip to the desert, I would survive.

Two men arrived at *The Thirsty Traveler* just as I waved it goodbye from behind a dune. An icy chill swept like winter winds down my back, but I released a pent-up breath. With them chasing me here, the capital or even Fiar should be safe. Sir Sigve would resent me for taking matters into my own hands, but I would send him a letter to explain. He wasn't safe, and this was the only solution. He had to understand.

It was certainly hot, but the day was bearable. I rode hard until the sun had left the horizon and the oasis was far behind. Although I stayed at a half-circle course along the road, I changed paths often enough that I should be difficult to track, keeping from the prominent ridges and never exposing my silhouette to the horizon, should they follow. And if the view offered only sand and brown in a surrounding sea, that was to be expected. Of course, this long way around would take time, and I could not hope to see anything before well into the next day, probably. I would re-enter the road and go straight to the capital. Have my adventure.

When the sun was at its peak, I led my camel to the very bottom of a deep dune. We could at least have a resemblance of shade, and Balt was kind enough to lend me his own shadow.

The evening was the best time to travel, but it rapidly turned so uninviting even I had to relent. The stars did not provide sufficient light to see where the next step would land, and the cold set in. It was strange. I had experienced frigid and unforgiving frost before, far more severe than this. It turned out, the body didn't like the quick change from sweltering hot to desert night. Ridiculous as it was, even with my blanket, the shivers rode me. Again, Balt was my savior, lending me warmth as I stole a spot beside him.

My sleep was peaceful, the night went by with little event, and waking up was how one would expect. All around was the sea of sand. I had survived another day, it would seem. Was it cause for celebration, perhaps? Where did a day even start, where did it end?

My only company was my flaxen friend. He looked clever enough. "What should I do?"

After careful consideration, Balt put his legs underneath himself and sank to the ground.

I broke off a piece of hard, flat bread, letting my breakfast disappear between his lips. Balt's hairs tickled my palm. "I have no idea anymore. I'm here, I'm alive—for now—but this is no help. Home is far away. And my family—they're all out of reach. Even if I get home, they'll eventually force me to marry one of those lords." And by the curse of his silver tongue, Mother still favored the worm. I'd rather marry Lord Gaute of forty, or the first Lakarian to cross my path. No! I would not lose my adventure. "But can I keep traveling by myself?" A sting needled my chest. "Sir

Sigve was convenient to have around; no one asks too many questions when they see a merchant and his daughter. Still, I had to leave him."

Balt cocked his head, looking skeptical.

"Really, I had to," I said, with a prayer to the Asir, the gods above that he was safe without me. This camel had no right to judge me. "Don't you know he almost died protecting me?" I blew a stray lock of hair out of my face. "I want to see Madalyn." I grimaced. "But I don't want my suitors. And I can't stay in this kingdom so set on killing me. But I still want to explore; I'm not ready to get trapped yet." I blinked against a pressure building behind my eyes. Crying never solved problems. Besides, it was a waste of water. "I miss my sister."

The creature looked at me, his gaze full of sympathy and compassion. He smacked his lips. A phlegm of spit came flying at me. Luckily, my reflexes were pretty decent.

"*Fine.* I won't ask you again. I can handle this just fine on my own."

Balt blinked, eyes big and innocent. The camel didn't seem to regret this loss of faith, as if my good favor was unimportant. Perhaps he forgot, but *I* kept the food in this relationship.

At least he brought me through the day without complaint, walking as if it didn't feel like we would travel endlessly in this landscape. By midday I scouted the horizon for change, any sign that the city or the coast drew near. I would gladly take either. In that vast, coarse brown, there were no traces of plants or water. I had thought winter back home—deep, cold, and unrelenting to the end—was the very embodiment of death. But this desert was another thing entirely. It was a world without life, in which me and my little camel dared to intrude.

Come night, I had yet to see any evidence of the desert ending.

"Do you think we are near?"

Balt eyed me silently before he continued to chew his share of the rations.

"Don't camels have a sixth sense of sorts? Like 'go find water!'"

He didn't seem much inclined to heed my request.

"Um, was that some other animal?"

Balt blew some grains out of his nose and shook his head. At least we shared that—the sand got in everywhere, yet the wind was too weak to soothe when the sun burned.

"I know, it's annoying. Just be patient a little longer. We'll get out of here."

He seemed satisfied with that, tucking his nose between folded legs. I relaxed against the rough hairs of his back, sharing warmth. We were breathing the same, dry air. Although Balt was a silent and sometimes cross companion, he didn't scrunch his nose at me once. And I was not alone.

I sighed, snuggling more closely with my head against Balt's flank. He was warm. Alive. "G'night, Balt." I let the night take me, sinking into what I thought would be a merciful sleep. However, I had never been lucky.

Something stung my hand, startling me awake. A disgruntled animal of sorts trudged away on its many legs, stark black with a single arched and pointy tail. It was alluring, a pale moon reflecting off the hard exterior. The beauty you find in danger.

Turns out there *was* life in the desert.

As the creature's arrow-like tail disappeared behind a dune, my skin burned. I shook, a wet cough disrupting my breath. I exhaled, expelled, gasped. Invisible flames spread throughout my body like wildfire, and soon that sensation was everything.

Then nothing.

∽

The black creature crept upon me, stinging me, and I felt the pain, the animal swimming in front of me as I clutched my hand. But this was a nightmare, a dream.

My own shrill scream awoke me as my hand stung. The creature scuttled away as flames erupted in my arm, my body heaving to the pale silver of a waning moon. A short darkness, a mercy of nothing before it started again, the nightmare torture seamlessly transcending into reality as I woke too late to move my hand.

Nothing.

Nightmare pain.

Sting.

The flames burned within my body and I shook, wet coughs and bile.

Starting again like needles, tendrils gripping my inside and wringing, and it was never over, an endless Do-Again. New and old and melting together, agony. Infinite night, infinite death.

If only I didn't have that hand.

If I could just *wake up*.

STRANGE LIKE A STORM

My wake-up call was abrupt, a saving grace. It was Hogne looking out for me, the gods protecting me. Someone seized my arm and jerked me backward. "Foolish girl, don't you know the wildlife here can kill you?" Rude, but I could live with that. Opening my eyes, I saw the scuttle of a midnight-black animal with its pointed tail curling up, steeling itself for an attack, as if ready to plunge an arrow into my flesh. The sight set ablaze the phantom pain of a dream, growing through me like tendrils, still alive in my memory.

Please, no more repeats.

The darkness pressed in on me as if the light from the moon could not reach and the stars were twinkling for someone else. The sand, though, was very much present. It prickled underneath me, and somehow it had snuck through layers of clothes. I was drenched in sweat, yet shivering. My breaths stilled, heart calming to let my eyes once again see the lights far away. The creature was gone.

"Can you hear me?"

I blinked against a startling shade of blue—like a stormy night sky—in a sharp but handsome face. The moon revealed hair as black as raven's feathers and wild like a tree crown in strong wind. With skin as golden as honey cake, he was definitely local despite his eyes. And too close. My muscles tensed, ready to tear my arm away when suddenly, I was free.

The stranger folded his hands, tucking them under his chin to make himself so very comfortable in the sand. "How do you feel?" he asked, with a stare fixed on me.

I wrapped my arms around my middle. There was *something*, a strange tugging on my mind, but no memory attached itself to the sensation. "Who are you?"

He looked worn, shoulders slumped around his frame and movements sluggish as he raked hair out of his face. "Does it matter?"

I narrowed my eyes.

He peered back through slipping lids and tired lines. "Why are you alone out here? That's like asking to die."

There was no one else intruding on my camp, only him and his camel. "You're alone." And he had no right to lecture me, he was no Maya or Sir Sigve. At most, he had just a few years over me, despite his drawn face.

"That's ... different." He stuck his nose up, as if arrogance sparked some leftover energy. "*I* know what I'm doing."

"Well, *I* had no choice." I would not die again. Better to brave the elements of nature. At least nature didn't kill me for being me.

"Really." His eyebrow shot up.

I tucked my legs beneath me, barely refraining from scratching at itching skin. The sand made for uncomfortable seating. "Yes, really," I said, trying to sound firm and convincing. Surely my choice of fleeing had been the right one? But leaving Sir Sigve . . . it was hard to say.

"Well, *I* had no choice either." My savior seemed to be a stubborn one, sitting down in the sand beside me for a better view, as if I was some strange animal.

I cast my eyes down to the sand at my feet. My body still burned from the memory of agony. Too many Do-Agains to count, and there was no mist to obscure my last nightmares. Only my arm was warm, as if the stranger left an imprint of himself on it. "I . . . I thank you for saving me."

Parting his lips, the stranger showed his white teeth. "I'm glad I reached you in time."

I swallowed, failing to rid myself of the thick sensation in my throat. "Why are you here?"

He was silent for a moment, then he shrugged. "Traveling through. Saw some tracks leading into nothing and decided to follow."

I looked him over once more, glancing through my veiled hair to be less obvious. Thick, black lashes rested against his skin rather than framing open eyes. The man wore typical travel clothes, a worn, white cloak draped across his shoulders and protecting him from sun, sand, and wind. Partly visible beneath was an inner layer of dark fabrics. The sight pulled on a memory, or perhaps a dream. No. Not a dream. Men in blotched, dark clothes finding me, knife, poison . . . but why? Who benefitted from the unimportant second princess of Rimdalir dying? Especially here, so far from home. The man in front of me offered no answers in his curious, blue eyes. Worse, could he be with them? He didn't *seem* like a killer . . . but how was an assassin even supposed to look? He had found me here, followed the tracks . . .

Though he *had* saved me. As long as he kept his distance, it was better than the arrow-tail of a scorpion. If he was with them, he would have let the creature sting me. A shiver ran down my back. But even if it did, I didn't truly die, I would just start over—

"Are you well? You look pale." The stranger reached into his pack, roaming about until he pulled out a waterskin. "Here, drink. You might feel better."

A cup slipping between my fingers, shattering upon impact with the floor. Froth. I shook my head.

The man held out the drink, shaking it as if sloshing the content made it any more tempting.

"I have my own," I said, fumbling with weak fingers until I pried my waterskin open. I drank deep as he examined me.

He let his hand fall, the drink he had offered retreating untouched. Still, he gazed at me, as if trying to discern something. Either that, or he was sleepy. His eyes slipped once, betraying him.

"Please go?" My voice was thin. "I can't have you here."

"It's the middle of the night. I need rest." He fell back in the sand, as if his spine could no longer carry him. "Besides, do you really want to be alone? You know the scorpion was moments away from poisoning you, right?"

A fresh shiver ran down my back. I could have been killed by the very creature that represented my sign of the zodiac. The thought of such a betrayal made it my worst Do-Again yet, trapped in a loop of pain. Still, a few days of loneliness could not kill. People could. That foreign person coughed, capturing my attention anew. My mouth dragged down at the corner. "And *you* will keep me safe?"

He drew a deep breath, releasing air in a hiss through his teeth. "I'll stay over there. See?" He stuck his thumb out toward the far edge of the dump which sadly was my camp. "And I swear, I'll protect you from wildlife and whatever else might come along, and as long as you keep near me, you'll be safe." The stranger set his eyes upon me, a glint of something more in their night-sky blue. Or it was simply the moon shining down on him. Regardless, he *looked* honest. An act?

"How chivalrous," I said at last.

"I certainly am." Stranger looked smug even through the throes of a yawn.

"Why would you promise that to someone you don't even know?"

"Why wouldn't I? Perhaps it's in my nature to help someone in need," he said with a slight smirk. When my face didn't change, he clutched his chest and continued: "All this dismissal, your skepticism . . . it hurts a little, you know?" It was a good act, I'd give him that.

I glanced around. The scorpion was gone, and I was grateful—truly, happy my savior had forced me awake. No need to keep him around anymore. He was a stranger. And he just happened to come along conveniently when I needed it? What if he was one of the attackers after all? Maybe the other hid behind the nearest dune, waiting for me to relax. But in his defense, I didn't feel sick when I looked at the man. "Will you not leave?"

He shook his head.

A tiredness clutched onto both body and mind. Although I had just slept, it felt more like going limp after hours of strain. My eyes were heavy, closing, I forced them open anyway and really, who needed sleep? My limbs ached from memories, but surely, this was my last Do-Again. The agony was over.

"Here, it'll keep you warm, at least." He threw me a blanket. Well, that's what I found when I dug my way out from underneath it. I hadn't even noticed my body shivering.

"I do appreciate your nice way of presenting this fine gift." I curled inside the soft wool, welcoming the return of warmth, with only my eyes and a stray lock of hair exposed.

The stranger stifled another yawn. "Good."

Not quite knowing how to respond, I settled for the obvious. The lines in his face, eyes yet again drooping while the smile slowly faded. "You look ready to drop. You don't know how to care for yourself, do you?"

"Wrong. But I've slept little these last days."

"Why?"

"Many reasons," he said. The man turned away, more interested in unloading equipment off his camel. A big sleeping bag was demonstratively rolled out.

I squinted through the moonlight, and he caught my stare.

"I'm redeeming my tired state. Besides, you should not be out here alone." He gave his animal food, whispering something low and soothing while stroking its neck. The creature leaned to the touch.

"Balt, do you think it's okay? Is he dangerous?"

My friend blinked.

"I can hear you just fine." We both ignored him.

Balt's gaze moved from me to the man. He smacked his lips, then made a strange, throaty sound, leaning toward the stranger as far as his neck allowed. It stung like betrayal. The man looked up, let his hand slide off his camel, and with slow steps, came over to us. He moved with languid care, methodically giving Balt the same treatment, and *my* companion seemed to accept him completely.

I had to trust either Balt's judgment of character or his love for food.

This person *had* saved me. Did he expect to profit from it later?

My lids slipped, obscuring my surroundings for a moment. I yanked them all back, forcing those eyes open.

Balt munched on his unexpected snack with eyes half closed, ears lazily perking forward.

Through darkness, the silhouette of my strange savior was barely visible.

The blanket was thick and smelled of citrus and sandalwood. The stars glinted from the stark black above us. My eyes slid again. The stranger shuffled around, settling in.

MAGNIFICENT

The rest of my night was uneventful. If I dreamt anything, it was lost the next morning save for a slight unease. I awoke to a stiffness in my body and sand beneath me. With the sight of the nameless stranger sleeping beside his camel just a short distance away, a restlessness carried over into the morning. I gathered my belongings, sacrificing slumber for speed. As I rolled up the blanket, he woke.

The stranger blinked the sleep from his eyes, gazing with a blank expression for a few seconds before he focused. He was actually younger than I expected and even more surprising, he was clean. His squint bounced from me, Balt, my few possessions, and lastly to the blanket he had lent me, folded—just as I had received it—in a messy pile beside him. "Good morning," he said, voice rough with sleep.

BALANCE

"Morning," I answered, holding his stare. I lifted my sack and fastened my belongings to Balt's saddle, arms heavy and fingers working the straps with some difficulty. I was almost ready.

He rose, stretching the sleep out of slender but strong limbs—a build reminding me of Father's young fighters. Without ceremony and ignoring my scrutiny, he shook sand out of his bedroll. "Did you sleep well?"

"Fairly well." My voice wavered without my consent. He didn't seem to notice.

"Have you had breakfast yet?" He pulled some packs from his saddlebag, unwinding a cloth and revealing what passed for good travel provisions in these parts. It was certainly better than my scraps. "I have enough for two, if you're hungry."

I shook my head. My stomach almost betrayed me, its rumbling too low for anyone else to hear, thank the gods. I had no hope of slipping away now. And he had done nothing to hurt me so far, so perhaps I could endure his company a little longer, at least long enough to satiate my hollow inside. "I have my own food." Grabbing my travel bag, I pulled out the sad resemblance of a meal.

We ate with the slow reluctance of someone pulling rotten teeth. I could not quite shake the feeling I was eating the desert itself.

"You know I have to ask," the stranger said, decimating our wonderful, prolonged silence. "How did you end up lost in the desert?"

His bluntness cut into my mind and left me staring at blue. *I'm on the run because my nightmares told me I'd get killed?* And explaining how those were not dreams at all but probably a lost reality would not exactly aid my plight. I let my gaze slide to the cloudless sky. "I'm traveling with my papa. Sigve Sturlason?" I gave the name as if he was a famous, renowned merchant.

Stranger shrugged, no recognition in his eyes.

I offered my best indulgent smile. "We got separated, and I have to find my way back alone. We were supposed to visit the capital." That was enough to do the job. A little truth to cover my lies.

The stranger appeared as convinced as Sir Sigve on a bad day. "Why didn't you follow the road? You must have been on it at *some* point. All traveling goes along set routes, to avoid situations exactly like yours."

By the gods' skaal! Why should I explain myself to him? Or speak at all? I pressed my lips together.

The man leaned forward, his chin resting on folded hands.

"I . . . lost the road. With all the sand and wind and sandstorms, I simply could not see it anymore." Through my clumsy explanation, I cursed that man for his curiosity. "It must happen occasionally, right?"

He nodded, thank the gods. "I guess it does. Without good guides, foreigners get lost easily."

"See? It was not my fault." I stuffed one last piece of fruit in my mouth. It was both sweet and sour, a strange combination which insisted on being tasty as if to spite reason.

His mood seemed to improve with a full belly. White teeth glinted in the sun. He stood up, shaking sand off his clothes, and then reached out a hand. "I'm going to Aransis too. Come on."

"Good for you. Thank you and have a nice life."

"What?" Forgetting to seal his lips, the stranger seemed like he truly didn't comprehend.

"I'm not coming with you. Go on, be on your way, and I'll go along mine."

I saw realization dawn on him. "I cannot leave you here. You'll die." He appeared absolutely, insultingly certain, crossing his arms. "This is plain silly. I must escort you. At least until we're out of this wasteland. Besides, you don't know where to go, do you?"

I looked along the path carved by sloping dunes.

"Yes, I'm sure you want to extend this exciting tour by going *deeper into the desert*." He shook his head, as if lingering on my stupidity was so important.

Well, that eliminated one direction. I glanced down the opposite side of the camp.

"Still wrong." His knuckles turned as white as his clenched teeth. "Just come with me. I'll lead you safely out."

"*You* are a stranger." And *I* was a fugitive.

He stared, hand carving through already disheveled hair. "You want to go by yourself? Do you want to die of thirst too? If you're lucky, maybe a sandstorm will take you—I can promise the grains will get in everywhere."

"They already do," I quipped, but my voice sounded faint and murky.

"*Fine.*" He took a step forward, glaring daggers at me. "All right. Perhaps some wolves would be a fine way to die? They have nice, sharp teeth. Or the vultures, once you're too weak to move. Being ripped apart always seemed like a good way to go. No?"

"And I'm sure the company of your excellent, morbid self will be just a ray of sunshine. Please, guide me. Give me more of your dark negativity." I didn't have to imagine my body drying up, vision fading before an unyielding sun. As if I needed his kind reminder. And I had no idea how fangs against skin, flesh, and bone felt, but it would be worse than a quick slice, for sure. I swallowed. The nausea was back, a sickening, sinking stone in my stomach, throat burning. My hands grasped at my clothes, whitening.

"See?" His voice mellowed, face softening as his fists opened. "I'm trying to help." As if it was settled, he seized my hand and pulled me up. Heat from his fingers shot through my arm, flaring in my cheeks. I stepped back.

He matched me with stride, never breaking the connection of our eyes. I felt the warmth from his chest radiate like the morning sun, awakening something within me.

"I have to stay with you." He crossed his arms. "If you choose not to come along, I have to follow you. My way is much more comfortable and a lot safer."

"Stupid sand." My eyes prickled. I released a shaky breath. "*Fine*, I'll go with you. If you tell me your name."

"Good." He smiled, eyes glinting. "I'm Sirion."

"Vildi."

Despite the drained appearance of the rider, Sirion's camel was sleek and muscular with a glossy coat. I even saw a symbol shaved into its flank: two shapes entwined. Such a contrast to Balt's shaggy mane.

Sirion took the lead, carving out a path in the sand with confident strides. Even though every twist of a dune revealed another, similar looking dune, he never faltered.

BALANCE

Balt's head bobbed down with each fall of his hooves, a rhythm lazy with leisure, my camel appearing happy to stare into the rear of his kin.

Traveling was slow and grueling work, not much more fun with this man than just going by myself. And though the sun shone stronger for each lift into the sky, I could see no actual change to the landscape. We rode, ate, and rode again.

"We need a little conversation at least," Sirion finally said.

I bit my lip, shielding my face with a veil of hair. It might have been different if I didn't know that somewhere out there were men who wished to kill me. If I didn't keep seeing myself die over and over again, I might actually be able to enjoy Sirion's ability to pull a conversation out of thin air.

"It could be anything," he continued, easing past my mute self. "I could compliment you on your riding skills, assuming from your fair skin that this is your first time in the desert, and thus on a camel."

Balt moved with steady, swaying steps. The reins were coarse and the saddle big, but nothing else was worth mentioning. Nothing out of the ordinary. Certainly nothing worth a compliment.

"Of course, you might ask about my excellent navigation skills." Apparently, Sirion had deemed our pleasant silence too long. "And I would tell you, they are hard earned. I have endured many nights under the stars, traveling through all parts of the desert. I know it well. We're currently not too far away from the capital, in fact. By the angle of the sun, we should reach Aransis at noon."

"Only half of what you said is of any use—or of interest—to me," I said. "And I don't want to talk." I sent him one of my best, hard stares, one of those expressions I had polished through long hours of forced mingling with desperate suitors. I knew how to throw a glare and deliver my replies to silence the most proud, arrogant, and grubby old men thrown at me. It should have been pretty effective.

"So hostile," Sirion said, amusement lilting in his tone. "You'll want to talk later."

His words did not deserve a response.

∼

We rode at first on uneven ground, crossing dunes and ridges as we went. After a few hours, we came out on a path of wind-polished stone and hard-trampled dirt.

"Isn't this supposed to be the main road through Lakari?" Except for us, Golden Road was empty in both directions. "This is no less wasteland than where we came from."

"You could sit here one day and not see another living being, but the next you could be swept up by a crowd. People travel in groups through this place." Sirion gave a half-shrug of his shoulder. "Also, the road isn't as straight as it looks, and you lose sight of it both up front and behind."

"People can hide behind the dunes." I cast a glance to both sides, but there were no tracks, nothing except the ones we had made ourselves, getting on the road.

Arching an eyebrow, Sirion studied the heaps of sand on his side. "It's possible, of course."

A shiver went down my back, and I swallowed. There was no use in thinking about it, but it was so, so difficult to ignore. Strangers, men grinning as Sir Sigve gasped his last breaths and a cup slipping between my fingers . . .

"Vildi? Do you feel well?" Sirion peered at me from atop his camel, and I had no way of knowing how long I had spaced out.

"Yes," I said, forcing my lips to lift. "I do. It's just the heat."

"It'll soon get warmer than this." Sirion's gaze lingered on my hair. "You should cover your head, it helps." He pulled at the white, worn cloak draped across his shoulders. "Do you have something like this?"

"No, not like that." Besides the white one I wore, my other dress was quite dark, and none of them had a hood like the one he hid beneath. "I have this." I stretched into my bag, producing the shawl I had . . . borrowed, with every intention of returning, from the caravan.

"It's better than nothing." Sirion examined the piece of dirty-white, camel-smelling linen hanging from my fingers. "But too thin."

"I have some blue fabric, but I was saving it for—"

"Dark or light?"

"Dark."

Slowing down, Sirion shrugged out of his cloak and gave it an inviting shake. "Take it. I'm used to this." His eyebrow arched in an elegant bend. "Don't want you to faint, one rescue is enough for me."

My hesitation lasted only a moment. Sirion had a normal build for a man, but I was small for my age and sex. Even if someone watched from the dunes, I would hardly be visible inside this piece of cloth piling up around me.

Sirion, on the other hand, lost his protection against the heat. His attire was linen, simple in a practical and thought through way. But it was dark. At his belt, poking up, I saw the hilt of at least one blade. There might very well be more of them, and I hadn't seen the side facing away from me. How many knives had he kept out of sight? How fast could he reach for the hilt, how quickly could I flee if Balt ran? Sirion's camel was better groomed, probably fast too. Balt was no match.

"It's for protection."

"What?"

"The dagger," Sirion said.

Blinking, I lifted my gaze to meet his. "What kind of protection?"

"It could be anything." Sirion's hand swept out, though the gesture did little but accentuate the abundance of nothing around us. "Cutting the stem of a cactus, partaking of wildlife, severing a rope or trimming a piece of cloth, fighting off bandits although I've never met any, or—more important—taking out curious scorpions."

"There's no end to its uses, is there?" It was a good reminder of the prominent weight of my own knife, secure at my hip. "Did you have to mention the scorpion too?"

Sirion put his finger in the air. "One can never learn about one's own folly too often," he said, with a grave and overly serious voice. His lips lifted at the corner. "At least that's what I'm told."

"I see." It sounded a bit like something Hogne could have said, on a good day. Perhaps that time long ago when he bested Eirik in archery. Glancing over, I was met with glittering eyes—and I was smiling back. With a slow exhale,

BALANCE

I set my eyes on the road and the never changing view of Balt's neck and ears dipping up and down.

Sirion was friendly enough, but he was a stranger. And even though he had yet to use them, he kept blades at his belt.

∽

The sun was almost at zenith when the uneven bumps and smudges on the horizon revealed themselves as buildings. They grew bigger, towering up from the desert. The constructions turned out to be only the first establishments of a larger city. As we came closer, small shrubs and cacti became common, replacing the bare sand. Our path changed from trampled sand to cobbled stone, widening to fit ten camels in breadth and turning noiseless steps into soft thuds. As if proving worthy of its name, the stones paving Golden Road shone from the searing rays above where it entered the royal capital.

Aransis was grand. Far more luxurious than my home, and I had always thought that was rather fine. But while Eldaborg had been nice and comfortable, dark but cozy on a winter night by the fire, this was a city of light with much open space. All life seemed to radiate from the palace, towering above us, although it was a way off. White and gold folded into each other, crescent arches and spiraling stairs going up, up, reaching for the gods.

It was, no doubt, an immense city, vast beyond anything these feet had stepped inside before. Despite this, the spacious streets were devoid of people. Plants hung from the walls of nearly every chalky house we passed, their flowers and unfamiliar orange and pink fruits the only life I recognized. Those, and the occasional stray cat staring at us from the shadows of the side alleys.

"It looks like a city for ghosts."

"It's dayburn. People keep to the shadows, or preferably inside, resting." Sirion appeared eager to do the same, a sheen of sweat on his forehead and waterskin diligently used.

"Midday?" I pulled the hood further around me. "Fits well. Your sun burns."

"Yes. You should avoid activities outside or at least have enough water. Most caravans find an oasis for this time of day, and work and trade stop. We should find somewhere too." Sirion did a turn, steering us down another broad road while sweeping his gaze over the buildings. "I think it was here somewhere..."

I quenched a tired sigh, settling for a sup from the waterskin. We were the only beings exposed to the sun, walking deeper and deeper through those empty, cobbled streets. Despite the clean, bright, and beautiful state of the roads and houses, I could not help glancing at all the black, blank windows, as if eyes from inside stripped me naked for their display. It was stupid, really because this was a city at sleep. I would welcome some shelter, at least I agreed with Sirion on this. And besides— "I'm hungry."

"Of course, you are."

Sirion the Rude. As if my stomach was really that noisy. He didn't even do me the honor of receiving my glare, turning his back on me as he steered us toward a wooden door with dragon carvings. He gave me the reins, though, walking inside and leaving me alone out there with two drowsy camels. Both Balt and Sirion's mount were content with the sudden rest, looking ready to lie down right in the middle of the road. I pulled at the reins. The camels stretched their necks, but their hooves remained planted solidly on the paved ground. "What am I supposed to do now?"

The door opened and a boy ran out, snatching the reins almost before he came up from his quick bow.

"Oh! Definitely not a ghost town!"

With lazy steps, Sirion appeared in the doorway. "Come in, Vildi."

"Bye, Balt, see you later." Feeling no worse than the tiredness of the ride, I was surely safe to walk inside. My stomach seemed to think so too, rumbling to the promising whiff of a warm lunch.

Oil lamps lit up the tavern, glowing with merry light against white walls. A man stood behind a counter, bowing as I entered. There was no one else in the room.

"Sit down, and I'll get us some food," Sirion said.

I found a table in the corner and a seat facing the door. If someone came in, I would see it. I kept the hood up, shielding my hair.

Sirion talked with the tavern owner. I heard their continuous string of sounds, lilting up and down like a song, in which the only word I knew was 'Sirion.' Lakari had a beautiful language, though incomprehensible. Now and then the man behind the counter would bow, Sirion nodding in response. Once he gestured in my direction, and I caught sight of his growing grin. Sirion looked different, somehow, in this setting. Relaxed, content with himself and his surroundings, a smile often rising to his lips.

Sirion joined me after a few minutes as the tavern owner disappeared.

"I bet you're bored with rations and stale food." With a dry twinkle in his eyes, Sirion reclined in the chair with an arm slung over its backrest. "I know I am."

"What did you order?"

"A Lakari specialty." He smirked, eyes crinkling in the corners.

My stomach did an unpleasant turn. "Do I want to know?"

"Depends. Do you eat—"

"No. It's fine." I put up my hand. "I'd rather have the surprise. It's food either way."

"Very well."

My gaze slid away from a travel worn, self-satisfied Sirion to rest upon more pleasant visions, like the painting on the wall. A city of cubic sandstone houses lay spread out in a flat landscape, with a scattering of green along a wide river. Behind them was a palace, immense in width what it lacked in height. The perspective of the painting allowed for a heightened view, revealing a blue spot in the middle of the grand building. An oasis?

I squinted, trying to get a proper look despite the dim room. "That's not Aransis, is it? The palace looks different."

Sirion turned to follow my gaze. "It's not. That's Irisis."

I waited, eventually lifting an eyebrow.

My stranger-savior leaned forward, chin resting in his hand. "The founding city of Lakari. Or, at least, how the artist envisioned it."

"Oh." Irisis, the dead city Kaira had told me about, back at the inn. How had she fared, with a guest missing? Where did Sir Sigve go, after I left him? Searching, of course, though surely, he kept traveling with the caravan. The desert was dangerous alone; Sir Sigve didn't go out there by—

"The water in the middle, that's the Desert Diamond. Heard of it?" Sirion swept his hand in an arch toward the painting.

"The Desert Diamond . . . I think I did, actually. Kaira told me about it, before—" I blinked, lowering my head until hair pooled on the polished surface in front of me. "I got lost. I was with a caravan headed for Aransis."

"So." Sirion leaned back in his chair. "We're here now. What do you plan to do?"

I looked down at the worn table. Despite the general luxury of the establishment, the surface before me was full of nicks and scratches in the otherwise shiny finish. It was either old or exposed to regular rough treatment, as was often the case at home. "I have to find S—Papa. Maybe I can send him a message? He's coming here with the caravan from Fiar, oh, and I have to give Balt back to the caravan." I clenched my fists to keep my fingers from fidgeting. The caravan certainly included two men, searching for the princess who had slipped away from *The Thirsty Traveler* and their reach. How was I going to deliver Balt, rejoin with Sir Sigve, and still avoid them? If I stayed hidden until Sir Sigve entered the city, let him find me—but would he even be safe alongside me in Aransis? Perhaps if we left immediately. "I think a letter would be best. Perhaps someone can send a messenger, tell them where to find Balt?"

A jar containing something creamy white was placed between us. Nodding to the servant as our food arrived, Sirion met my eyes, his pointy finger drumming against the table. "I know how to get ink and paper. But you should consider going to the authorities."

"And where would that be?" Something smelled absolutely irresistible. I couldn't look away from the plate placed in front of me. A steak lay like a precious pearl in the middle, a deep orange glaze spreading from its top to the sides like a veil. Fresh fruits adorned the meat, cut in thin, delicate slices.

"The palace," Sirion said, and I nearly choked.

Coughing, I drank some water to recover. "The palace? Would they really help a nobody like me?"

Sirion met my eyes, a slight smile forming on his lips.

My stomach lurched. "The food is here. We should eat."

"As you wish." My savior and escort busied himself with his steak, no longer looking up.

"So, what is this?" The meat was red beneath a sizzling, nutty crust. It was juicy like only fresh game could be, with the tenderness of youth. And the glaze was some form of sweet, rich sauce Torvald could never create.

Sirion glanced up. "Changed your mind?"

I looked down at the plate. It smelled so good. "I've mostly seen one kind of animal around, and Lakari has a history of starvation." According to Kaira, at least. "If you starve, you eat."

"True," Sirion said. He put his fork down. "Have you ever sta—"

"Yes."

It was my best meal in a long time. When I finished eating, scraping off every last trace of sauce from the plate, even honey cake would be beyond me to consume. My stomach thanked me. Full, finally. The tavern owner never lost his delighted front, a perfect version of politeness as he bowed and waved goodbye to his sudden guests, despite how we must have disturbed his rest during dayburn. I gave him a parting wave.

By the time we moved out, a few people had re-entered the streets. Some were setting up their wares for the afternoon sales. A few carts and wagons drove through the airy streets, some of them pulled by camels, some by donkeys. I almost missed the sight of horses. We were not the only persons walking, visiting the capital, a few of them stopping at the allure of a fine silk fabric or the whiff of savory food. Some, like us, were simply content with taking in the view.

"The people of Aransis love their dragons, don't they?" There was another one above the door we passed. And across the street was a door with two dragons coiling around each other, as if embracing. By the center of the open square in front of us, I glimpsed a marble statue.

"Definitely. Liva and Avil are loved by all." Sirion steered us past a beaming lady and her assortment of displayed jewelry. "You'll see more of them soon."

I glanced up. The palace was much closer now. My shoulders slumped. There was no avoiding it, was there? The situation was too dire to allow for privacy. Perhaps it would be tolerable. I hardly looked like a princess with my hair free of the usual braids and pins and a dress swept through dust. No suitor would be tempted by this. And Lakari was far, far from Rimdalir. They would not have heard of my more... *unfavorable* reputation. They could shelter me. I would reunite with Sir Sigve, safe within the towering palace walls. And surely, my attackers would be unable to find me, reach me. Right?

"Here." Sirion took my sleeve, guiding me down another wide and spacious road. Before us the palace reached for the sun, crowned by its golden rays.

Perhaps it was the quality of the area we ventured through, but I had never before seen a place with so many polite people. A merchant bowed and beamed at us even though we didn't stop to buy a single plush carpet.

A few citizens bowed in passing, and Sirion greeted them with smiles and a few words. He seemed to know everybody, and they all knew him. His easy attitude and the way people looked at him reminded me of Madalyn. She, too, had a personality that attracts others. So easy to love. Sure, she was demure compared to Sirion, her voice soft and words chosen with delicate precision, but the way they could both please others by just being themselves reminded me just how different I was.

Perhaps the reason wasn't Sirion at all. Despite the vast city, the community must be tight knit, giving away such a friendly atmosphere. It was almost enough to relax, but I kept the hood just in case. From inside it, I still saw the great, ornamented houses. For each new street we crossed, the buildings were a bit grander—from rough to polished stones or the colored glass embedded in the walls and set aglow by the sun. As Eldaborg carved the three wolves into oak, the high class in Aransis decorated their homes with dragons, suns and desert. Even with the hood shielding me they were impossible to miss, just like the white smiles of happy Lakarians, chatting in their lilting, singing language. I found joy spreading from my chest through my lips, settling in my eyes. To live like this . . .

I heard the clatter of hooves. Like a slow rumble on the horizon it began, growing until it filled the entire space with a thunderstorm trapped between the buildings. For the first time in Lakari, I saw horses. Two big, black, majestic and muscular beasts, pulling a wagon rushing through the street. Magnificent.

"It's not supposed to go that fast," Sirion said, brows furrowed.

"No? Why is—"

"Vildi, get o—"

A man pushed himself between us—patchy brown—the entire force of his running form shoving into me, my shoulder. I fell, the road and a few stray pebbles scraping against my skin while Sirion yelled something but the thunder was upon me. And I saw legs. Legs and hooves. Everywhere.

HOGNE'S CHOICE

Dim light teased my eyes to announce a new day on the horizon as the grainy bed beneath me demanded my immediate departure. From my itching skin I half expected to be covered in horseshoe marks, stamped into me. There were none.

I fell back in the sand, regretting it immediately. The grains really did get in everywhere. With hands rubbing vigorously at my eyes, I suppressed a sigh. The men were in Aransis. I hadn't even found Sir Sigve, all I had achieved was eating the equivalent of a horse, and then gotten pushed and run down by actual horses. There would be no new visit to the capital for me.

At the other side of our camp, Sirion stirred. He sat up, blinking with heavy lids.

All right, let's do this. "Did you sleep well?" I shook sand out of the blanket he had lent me.

He looked tired beyond drowsy, perhaps more so because of the contrast to his easygoing grin while wandering the streets of Aransis. "Not really," he said, stretching.

"I know, the sand isn't exactly a soft bed."

"It's not," Sirion agreed. A grimace pulled at his face. "Did you have breakfast yet?"

I shook my head. "Just woke." After eating fresh glazed meat and fruit, going back to scraps would be tough. My food didn't improve from my imagination when exposed to the light of day. In fact, a meal this drab and dreary possessed excellent camouflage against the sand. Maybe I should wish for the appearance of dry rations, then no one would be able to find me.

Sirion dished out his own food. Only a glance was needed to discover its far superior quality. "Want some of mine?"

"No thank you, I'm fine." It was a sad moment for my stomach.

With his cloak on, I couldn't see the dagger at his belt. I, on the other hand, was exposed, not only to the sun, but whoever we eventually might meet. Though in the end, neither blade nor cloak had helped a bit, had they?

Sirion glanced up from his delicious looking ham. "So, where do you want me to take you?"

Grinding a tough piece between my teeth, I had a hard time pulling my attention away from his diminishing meal, meeting his eyes with some reluctance.

"You're lost, right? I'll escort you back to civilization."

I swallowed. "Aren't you headed for Aransis?"

"Yes." Sirion's eyes followed the horizon, his hands clasped firmly together. "I'll take you there."

"But I'm not going to the capital. We'll have to split up." Fiar should be safe, at least for a short while.

"You're not used to the desert. You'd die." As if it was a foregone conclusion. True, my performance so far hadn't been stellar, but at least I had learned. And I would find Golden Road just fine by myself now. Probably.

I grit my teeth and pulled forth a smile. "I'll be fine. I'm headed for Fiar. I got separated from Papa, but if I just get to port, he'll find me."

"Aransis is shorter—"

"I'm not going to Aransis!"

Sirion leaned back, his long fingers sinking down in the sand. "All right. We're going to Fiar."

"You're coming with me?" I stood up, shaking off the crumbles of an unsatisfactory meal.

"You don't know where to go." Sirion got on his feet, eyes trailing me as he began gathering his belongings. "I have a place not far from here; we can stay there tonight. From there it's only a long day's ride to Fiar."

Sirion's tone of exasperation almost matched Sir Sigve. What would Hogne have done? I could imagine him telling me not to be foolish. I averted my eyes from Sirion's intense stare, before a flush could flare in my cheeks. A wasteland awaited beyond the dunes, empty except for scorpions, scavenging birds and wolves.

"Fine. I'll go with you." At least my companion was not a blond, slimy worm. And Sirion knew his way around the desert.

BALANCE

∾

At the end of an afternoon with mostly friendly conversation, my spirit dampened as surely as the sun sank to a brown horizon. We were still in the middle of nowhere, and the only thing I had seen for hours, besides Sirion's unnerving smirk, was sand. A stretch of it as big as any sea. Fortunately, I was patient by nature, one of my more redeeming qualities.

"You know, there is something bothering me . . ."

"Yes?" Sirion looked over, all open and ready to help.

"Yes, there was this thing . . ."

"Okay?" I could hear his composure cracking in the corners.

"I seem to remember you telling me something. Hm, what could it be?"

Sirion had not started out fresh either, but the signs of fatigue bore down on him now. He was pale despite his golden tan and short-tempered beyond the redemption of his superior food. "Just get to the point."

"Yes, I distinctly remember you saying your place was *near*."

"Relatively, yes. Nothing is near that remote dump you got yourself lost in."

I snorted. "You found me despite the remote dump."

"But I'm good at navigating the desert." Sirion stretched his muscles, releasing the reins for a moment to let the camel roam. "It really was in the middle of nowhere."

"Then how did you—"

"Except for its proximity to Aransis. We can still go there, you know?" Sirion turned, eyebrows arched. Color stood in his cheeks, a hint of red. So, even the Great Navigator, Desert Journeyman Sirion was affected by the heat.

"Sirion, when *will* we arrive at this place of yours?"

"By the end of the day." Sirion seemed entirely fine with the prospect, if his smile was to be trusted. I had to force down a tired sigh. If I never saw a desert after this, it would be too soon.

There was a slim silver lining for our situation: we had plenty of water and some food too. Sir Sigve would have liked my meals, something about how all this dried sustenance was good for my figure. I always thought he was slightly afraid of Mother, whom he had to answer to when we eventually returned to Eldaborg. She would be pleased with the shape of me, if nothing else.

Finally—when the first scatter of stars blinked in the sky—I saw a building in the distance, and we arrived shortly after. I gave my thanks, a hushed word of gratitude to the gods. I could conclude two things: if Sirion wanted to kill me, I would be dead already. And he had, in fact, escorted me *somewhere*, as promised. At least he hadn't lied, although he should have been hard pressed to benefit from leading me further into nothingness. Still, I would be a fool not to worry.

It was a lonely spot of sorts, placed there because of the pond-sized oasis beside it. The single building was modest and old, yet it was so heavily carved throughout the stone walls in its whole, small entirety, it must have belonged to someone rich. All the same, it looked abandoned and forlorn. "We seldom use it," Sirion rather redundantly told me. "There's not much need to travel here anymore."

"It's fine." With the rising moon and deep darkness came the desert chill, and anywhere to hold off the sand and keep me warm would do. Besides, Sirion had so far carried on exactly like promised, keeping a healthy distance between us while doing so.

We placed the camels in a stable built into the back of the house, giving them water and food. Sirion showed me how to take care of the animals, and though it didn't seem entirely natural to him, he was much better than me. "I traveled alone for a while. Had to learn it all," he said. Before I could ask anything, he continued: "Let's get us some dinner. Looking at those two munching makes me hungry." He didn't wait for me as he left. Well, talking was overrated. We would part ways soon—with some luck—anyway. The less I knew about him, the less he would feel entitled to know about me.

Whatever his faults, Sirion was right. Balt chewed his meal with half-closed eyes, looking like he *really* enjoyed it. My stomach rumbled, ignoring my excellent upbringing. I was lucky Maya could not hear me, or worse, Mother—though I could hardly help it. I patted my poor empty middle. There was no one around to impress, so a few growls hardly mattered.

Dinner was as simple as they came. I devoured the last of my rations. Sirion sat across from me, quite near considering the size of the wooden table, tearing off chunks of meat while he looked through me. A silence settled in the quiet way we both ate, the dark corners of a room which had been empty for a long time, and the questions hanging unasked between us. Across from me sat a man who had shown up from nowhere. His eyelids slipped, hiding blue depths. In the dimming light from the setting sun, dark shadows settled around him like a cloak, and he seemed to welcome the night. Such a contrast to the man who had greeted his peers, chipper and cheerful, who had led me through a city of light with confident strides. And he was set on helping me, with little to win other than my sarcasm and dubious gratitude. I almost asked why, opening my mouth a few times and saving myself only by stuffing dried fruit in it.

Sirion closed his eyes, his movements sluggish as if forced through mud. With a start, his head slipped off his hand. Despite his quick smile, pretending he wasn't falling asleep on the spot, he soon slumped again.

I reached out with a show of compassion and kindness. The man might be a little haughty, but he *had* saved me. "It's late. Let's call it a night."

"Yes, that's a good idea." He rose and signaled for me to follow, bringing me further into the house.

"Why *are* you so tired?" Wasn't he used to the desert?

"Didn't I tell you? I haven't slept much in a while." He sent me a heavy look, and a twinge of guilt twisted inside me, which was ridiculous because it was neither my fault nor responsibility. "We'll rest here tomorrow. I'll take you back in two days."

Alone inside this tiny building, where we would breathe each other's still air and one could not pass through the kitchen—by the brilliant idea of an oversized table—without brushing against the other? A whole day, with none of the distance traveling by camel would provide, in a place with nothing to do but study the other, asking questions. "No way!"

"Way." He sighed, eyes slipping for a moment before he glanced at me again. It appeared to cost him great effort. "Look, I'm exhausted. My camel's been driven much harder than I'd prefer, and he needs rest too. We shouldn't take the trip to Fiar in this state."

"But . . ." A whole day? I should get to Fiar before men in blotchy brown realized there was no Alvildi in Aransis.

"You don't like it? Well, tough luck. I'm staying here tomorrow. You have no choice, unless you'd like to try the desert alone again." Sirion crossed his arms.

"Fine." I balled a fistful of sleeves in my palms. If only I could do the same with his smug face.

He opened a door and waved me inside. The room was pleasant. Intricate carvings along the ceiling and once bright colors on the walls. A gentle light seeped through a lone window. More important, there was a bed with blankets. "This'll be your room. You can manage, right?" An insulting brow rose before me.

"Yes, of course." I was not a northern princess for nothing. It was just a room.

Sirion nodded, staggering out over the threshold. "Sleep well, Vildi."

The door slammed shut with a hollow thud. I was alone again, in this dark emptiness. Surrounded by comfort and relative safety, everything was as fine as the situation allowed. It was new. Foreign. An exploration of the bed revealed fluffy pillows draped in luxurious fabrics. Feather light veils draped so as to invite sleep. My hand throbbed, as if to make sure last night stayed fresh in my memory. A sting.

It was so, so cold. I crept under the blankets, wanting more than anything to sleep this entire misadventure off like a nasty headache, putting it firmly behind me. Cursed be the do-overs. What Do-Again could be worth dying for? Even worse if I were to die asleep, entering another infinite loop. Sirion had no idea what he had saved me from.

He was here, somewhere in this house. I was not alone, not completely.

My skin itched, a faint, phantom imprint of hooves. Even though I must have dozed off, I was still painfully aware and dreading the echo of dreams, writhing in thin blankets and for hours unable to relax.

9

A HOUSE IN THE DESERT

I crawled out of the nest my body had carved for me throughout the night, more fatigued than before I fell asleep. I probably looked the part too, being in the old building with a man I knew nothing about, on the run from two men who wanted who-knows-what with me, enduring haunting dreams of living and reliving horrific deaths. The sad truth was, I was entitled to my tired state.

The light of day allowed me to take in the details that had been hidden by candlelight the night before. I trudged into what must have been a small kitchen, with a stove and a fireplace, some utensils hanging on the wall, and several closets. All the handles were shaped with odd twists and knots, the metal dull due to lack of use. Upon closer look, I could make out a bent head upon a sleek and gnarled body, ending in a coiled tail. A dragon. The place would have looked grand for sure, if not for a cover of dust dimming it all down and stray sand sprinkling the floor. Not to mention the travel-worn inhabitants it now housed.

"Good morning!" Sirion greeted me with a wide, relaxed smile. Apparently, he had slept *very* well. He seemed fresh, rested, and ready for anything.

I couldn't help being a little jealous . . . and a little wary. "You scare me."

"Huh? Why?" He scrunched his eyebrows. Without the lines of exhaustion dominating his features as the morning sun played across his face, I could see he was only a few years older than me.

"You should know," I informed him, "I retain a healthy amount of skepticism. Discontent is much easier to trust. What is that good mood even about?" Being stuck alone with a stranger in the desert wasn't exactly my version of fun.

His face darkened a little, and he appeared more like the person I met yesterday. "Well, I slept for once." He sent me a piercing look and ticked it off on his finger. "I saved you," he ticked another finger off, "and I'm basically a hero." The third finger went down. With each finger, his mood improved again. He was like a cat purring in self-satisfaction by the end.

"A hero?" I nearly laughed. Not even Lord Gaute had ever called himself that, despite all his great and important deeds.

"Absolutely. Have some breakfast." Sirion slid a plate across the table, and I almost agreed with him. There were little dried fruits, yellow and pink and appealing, tempting me with innocent sweetness. A piece of bread sat beside them, and I held it between my fingertips up to my nose. It *smelled* fine, at least.

"Really? It's not poisoned, Vildi."

I smiled brightly. "Of course not."

He sighed, staring down at my plate. "Why would I save you just to kill you later? It makes no sense."

"You're still a *stranger*."

Sirion leaned over the table, cheek resting in his palm. "You say that like it's a capital offense. I can't help being a stranger until we get to know each other."

I didn't answer.

"Here." He reached over and broke off a piece, chewing with slow savor. "See?"

"Hey, that's *my* food." My poor mauled bread, now only three quarters its original size. I pulled the rest of my breakfast closer, ready to guard it if the need should arise. He had taken me by surprise, but I would not be played for a fool twice.

Sirion snorted. "You're unbelievable."

"No, I'm hungry." Even to myself I sounded sullen. "Food is serious for me," I said, forcing my voice into friendlier tones.

Sirion studied me for a few seconds before cracking a smile and brushing away my brusqueness like specks of dust. "You like tea?"

At home, Mother imported tea from the aristocrats across the ocean. It was a bitter brew, only drinkable with generous amounts of sugar, and then only through tremendous willpower. It was expensive on all accounts, and usually I got away with a no.

"Ah, haven't tasted it before?" He looked upon me with mock pity, appearing almost sincere. "This is the one thing I excel at making; be grateful you'll get the privilege of tasting it." As I scrunched up my nose, he laughed. "Well, it'll be decent, at least."

"I somehow doubt that."

"You'll like it." He started fiddling with two cups, some brown, crushed tea leaves, and a kettle containing boiling water. It took no more than a few minutes.

Sirion pressed the steaming brew into my hands. I blew small rings on its surface, obscuring the blank, dim reflection of my face. It reminded me of breaths of wind stirring the lake back home. Perhaps it would taste like it too, dark and murky forest water. As hot vapor stopped coming from the drink, I had to stop my stalling. Cursing my manners, I lifted the cup to my lips and let the tiniest sip enter my mouth. Maya and Mother would be so proud.

The tea was nothing as expected. I had another sip, bolder this time, and was rewarded. It was sweet, hot, and rich in flavor. Before I felt ready, the cup was empty, barely a drop left at the bottom, and Sirion looked pleased. Happy, even.

"Here." He reached over, pouring for us both to the brim, then reclined with his own cup cradled in his hands. "It's the best drink around. Well, at least among those lacking alcohol."

I hummed noncommittally. Still, I gulped it down. It beat lukewarm, stagnant water any day. Maybe that was why. And it had a hint of saccharine instead of being bitter. Better yet, it was sweet enough for Sir Sigve to disapprove. I could enjoy it without being eyed as he fought a fierce battle to not comment on my figure.

Sirion seemed content to lounge, arm slung over the back of his chair as he watched me, and I let my gaze wander, pretending he wasn't there.

∼

Balt and his companion greeted us good morning. They were already digging into their breakfast.

Sirion followed me into Balt's box. Somehow it could hold a full grown, albeit small camel and a man of unbound confidence, with enough space to spare for a merchant's daughter stuffed into the corner.

As Sirion leaned over, hands running along Balt's flank then down his legs, I stood there staring like a useless princess. A hand crept to the pocket of my dress, finding the cool metal of my Lakarian coin to flip over and over. "Balt is fine, isn't he?"

"Could be worse. Helps that he's young." Fingers snagged in shaggy mane, ran down Balt's ruffled coat and left a trace where dust and stray straw had been swept away. "He needs proper care, just like you and me. First, you need to brush him. Don't you have animals where you come from?"

"We have horses of cou—oh." Stupid. I had been to stables before even though a stableboy usually presented the horse fully equipped whenever I fancied a ride. But I had brushed my horse on occasion too. "Okay, I understand."

"Good." Sirion signaled for me to come closer. "There's a slight swelling in his left leg. Feel this?" He took my hand

and guided it, sliding my palm against rough fur along the leg to the ground.

"It's warm."

"Yes. Did you notice the soft bump? Right here. Like a bag of fluid, making way for your fingers."

"That's the swelling?"

Sirion nodded. "That's what it feels like."

"Poor Balt." I stroked his neck. Balt leaned in, feeling a little sorry for himself. He seemed to appreciate the comfort and care. "Is it entirely my fault?"

"Not at all." Sirion's face turned dark, lips thinning in a pinch. "These things develop over time. It's fairly common to work such animals too hard, all for the sake of a coin. Though I hardly have the right to criticize."

"Why not?" I went over to Sirion's camel and moved my hands down his legs. They were warm but not swollen.

"Doesn't matter much," he said, but then he relented. "Let's just say my trip here was less than pleasant."

I looked at the poor creature, The-Camel-Without-A-Name. "Then I'm sorry for you, my friend." No-Name leaned his head into my arms and blew a sad gust of air through his nose. He had every right to receive a little sympathy for having such a demanding owner.

Sirion lifted his gaze to some point high on the wall. "You do that."

Balt threw his head in indignation, stomping his foot impatiently.

"Balt, I haven't forgotten you. I would never." I returned to him, letting my fingers trace soothing patterns on his neck. I was like Madalyn when she consoled me as a baby, craving attention with my knees bruised and blue. Balt calmed down immediately. "What can we do to help him?"

Sirion glanced over at us, then his gaze dropped to those legs. "Not much, at least here. He needs time. We could rest for a few days, but it would make little difference. He needs proper, daily care."

Another thing I could do nothing about. If there was one thing Lakari excelled at teaching me, it was my own helplessness. Depressingly so. A person who could not stay alive by her own power had no hope of helping her companions, let alone her camel. I tugged on the sleeves trailing my arms, staring at the swelling.

"Hey, he's fine. He can take the trip back to Fiar. We'll take it nice and slow for him."

I nodded, not quite trusting my voice. Looking up, I saw Sirion's tilted lips, his eyes glinting diamond blue in this place where everything bore the color of sand. I drew a steadying breath. "So, we still leave tomorrow?"

"Yes."

"That's good," I said, resting my cheek against Balt's flank.

"You're in such a hurry to leave me." Sirion's gaze slid away. "That's not how it's supposed to be."

"I can't help it. Sorry." I skipped off, retrieved a brush, and settled to the task of grooming Balt's flaxen pelt.

"You don't *sound* sorry." Sirion watched for a moment, waiting. If I was silent, perhaps he would leave me alone. Instead, he came over, adjusting my grip and movements. "Long strokes," he murmured, suddenly right beside me and too close. Did this person know nothing of propriety?

"Thanks," I choked. "You can go."

"I'm dismissed?"

"Sure," I offered, intently brushing Balt and not looking anywhere else. I could not trust the color on my face. "I release you from my service. Happily."

"Good for you." Sirion found another brush and began his own work of grooming No-Name.

After Balt had finished his breakfast and his fur shone like ripened wheat swaying in the breeze, I led him outside. He would enjoy a walk, no one liked being closed up inside for long. Together we strolled in circles around the house.

I took care with my steps, avoiding the plants. There was only a scatter of them, but almost all had thorns or needles sticking out of their small, round bodies. Only a few of the bigger plants were of any use, and only for the shade they provided.

"What should I do, do you think?" I kicked a pile of sand, spraying it in all directions. "This is not what I had in mind when I left home." I waited for my companion to answer.

Balt shoved me with his muzzle, almost toppling me.

"I know, I know, I should not complain. I wished for adventure."

Balt gave me a new powerful nudge, his version of a friendly gesture.

"But I never imagined this." My fingers played with the rope when a gust threw sand in my eyes from a nearby dune. My hand snapped to my face, pulling on Balt—and he yanked right back. I fumbled as the rope tore through my fingers and sliced air like any decent whip, connecting with my leg. "Ouch." My gaze found Balt as he shook his head and sent me a disgruntled stare. "You're right, that was unnecessary." His legs seemed unharmed, thank the gods.

An angry red stripe ran down my shin. With my luck, it would scar, as most wounds did. Taking a second look, I saw how it curved like a snake or a wave. Well, at least there was that. It was just another mark in my collection, anyway. Smirking, I imagined Maya discovering the wound, throwing a fit. *What suitor will accept you now? You need to take care of yourself.* Victory for me. I felt a twinge in my chest and sighed.

Balt drew a little closer, deeming it rope-safe again, his shoulder almost touching mine.

I patted his neck, the fur soft beneath my fingers. "I have seen some spectacular places, though. Did you know there are cities made entirely of stone? And rivers so wide across you can't see the other side. Some people have their homes on boats, just moving toward wherever they find good fish and good company."

Our slow meander took us around a bend, continuing through a small crevice formed by the dunes. It was strange, how they felt and appeared so solid, and yet easily changed with the wind. Balt placed his cloven feet with care.

"It's just, I had only been in Eldaborg, you know? And I'd read all these amazing stories. I wanted to see it for myself, go on an adventure. *Experience* something." And, of course, getting away from clammy hands and a forced marriage. And a body pressing against mine in the darkness with nowhere—no! There was no worm here. A strangled laugh escaped my throat. "I suppose I achieved something. But it wasn't supposed to end up like this." Stuck in the middle of nowhere, running, nightmares, the pain . . .

Balt plodded on in attentive silence. Such a good listener.

"Who knows if I'll even see Eldaborg again or any part of Rimdalir, really. Sir Sigve is gone. But I had no choice, did I?" I examined our surroundings, but there was only sand nearby. "What are my options, do you think? Can I trust Sirion? Will he lead me out of here or will he take me somewhere else . . . but I don't have a choice there either. I can't find the road by myself, and I don't even know which direction Fiar is. I should have paid more attention to the stars or the sun, perhaps. But I just rushed out here, not thinking. Madalyn would have been able to navigate. Not me." I let my frustration out on an unfortunate pile on the ground, my foot cleaving through the bump to reveal a rock veiled by a layer of sand. And, unlike my descending toes, unwilling to move.

Balt blew air through his nose.

"Well, you can laugh," I said. "So, what *do* you think of Sirion?"

Balt nudged my shoulder, as if such a simple gesture could serve as an apology. Long lashes framed his sad, imploring eyes. I sighed. Reaching into my pocket, I pulled out a snack, and he devoured it faster than even I could manage.

"Of course, you think he's kind. He takes good care of *you*."

Balt munched happily.

"Well, perhaps me too. I have food. And he hasn't complained about how much I eat. And he doesn't ask so many questions anymore. Did you see him last night? When he got tired, and just stared out into nothing. He looked sad."

Throwing his head, Balt cried.

I shook my head. "I have no more food on me, sorry."

Balt rushed, taking big steps and making it harder to keep up. With me jogging after him, we rounded another dune and entered the oasis.

"Welcome back," Sirion said, smiling. He stood by the edge of the oasis, shirt rolled up over his arms as he dipped a bucket into the water.

Returning the gesture, I passed him quickly and followed Balt inside. "Now, what do you think?" I leaned in, my voice low. "About Sirion?"

Balt eyed me thoughtfully, shaking off some sand before he sunk to the floor. He went to sleep without giving a reply.

"What about you?" I asked No-Name. Loyal to his owner, he turned around to stare into the wall.

"I miss my family." Sight turning foggy, I blinked. "It wasn't supposed to be like this."

I dropped down next to Balt, sensing the warmth of another being, soft and comforting. His fur tickled my nose and the familiar scent of stable enveloped me.

"Maybe if I can get on a boat."

I need to go home.

∽

Sirion prepared dinner. It was not much, some greens and roots, a bit of meat, all of it warmed and mixed in a stew. But there was substance in the bits of ham and strength in the broth, an impressive meal for how little he had to work with.

My fork barely made a dent in the pile on the plate before me.

"Is it bad?"

My gaze snapped up at this breach of silence.

Sirion watched me with his hands clasped together, knuckles pale from strain.

I forced a chunk down, swallowing with lukewarm water. "It's fine." I swallowed hard to push down the ham lodging in my throat. If I ever managed to get myself out of Lakari and reached home, Mother would use the occasion to arrange a ball. A shudder traced down my back. But perhaps wasting away in a corner of the desert with my horrible visions was all that awaited me.

I glanced up from my meal. Sirion still stared, a furrow digging into his forehead.

"It's good. Really." To appease him, I took a big chunk, barely chewing before I swallowed. Coughing, I gripped the table's edge. Vegetables were stuck in my throat like the silent protests of a frozen body with a wandering worm's hands upon me, suffocating—

"Easy," Sirion said. "Here. Water."

Gulping it down, I could breathe anew. "Thanks," I rasped. "I'm fine." I stabbed a piece of meat with my fork. It slid right off, obstinate thing. Exhaling, I pierced it with absolute care, angling my fork so it could not escape because it was only a lump anyway and I was *hungry*, and to the glacial chasms of hell with it, why—

"Vildi?"

"I don't want to get married."

"What?"

"Why do I have to go through with it? I don't want to! Have someone else do it." Why did home have to equal marriage? Stupid, stupid suitors. "They have Brage too and okay he's only eight but I'm not the important one anyway, why do I have to marry?"

"I thought all girls your age, no—*any* age, cared about love and marriage and . . . that."

A drop of liquid fell on my food. Great. Now it would taste like salt too. Of all the stupid things I could focus on, Torvald seasoning his meals came to mind. The tears refused to stop. Why did I have to *cry* in front of Sirion?

"Vildi?" He was halfway out of his chair.

I swept my sleeve over my wet eyes, rubbing until they were dry, then looked up and met his eyes, troubled and dark blue, like seeing the brewing of a storm across a still faraway sky. I took a deep, dense, and hot breath. "I'm fine."

Sirion raked a hand through his raven-feather hair, resembling a bird barely scraping out of a fight. "I don't believe you."

I buried my face in my hands and pushed the tears away. I found Sirion's gaze as soon as I peeked out from between my fingers—waiting. His sharp brows creased, as if I was a mystery for him to understand. His lips were pressed together, tugging down.

I looked up again, sucking in sharp air. For a second, it felt like Hogne had looked back at me through those eyes. It was enough. "I want love. Of course, I do. Maybe. Eventually. After all the stories . . ." I pushed the plate away. "But not marriage!"

"Wait. Let me get this straight." Sirion pinched the bridge of his nose. "You want love. But you *don't* want to marry?"

"Love and marriage are completely unrelated." I wiped one last time, hoping my eyes were not flaring red.

He shook his head. "How so?"

Thank the gods my tears stopped. Solid ground was beneath my feet once more, and I slipped off a shoe to feel my toes sweep against the smooth stone floor. "Please. If you've read anything at all—that is if you *can* read—you should know. And if not, don't Lakarians tell stories? Most tales have at least a speck of love in them."

"In most of those stories, love ends in marriage," Sirion countered.

"Not necessarily. Like in those tragedies or adventure stories. Love is not bound or dependent on marriage." But why did I want love again?

A slow smile spread across his face. "That's true."

That fairy-tale lie. "You're right. Stories give me all I could want from romance."

"Rather than read about it, I'd like to live it." Contrary to his words, Sirion didn't seem ready to live anything.

I tilted my head, but his face was blank, the kind only possible by choice. "Have you experienced it before?"

"I have," he answered, voice flat. For some reason, I was not the upset one anymore.

"Maybe I'll stay away from love too," I finally said.

He snapped his head up. "What?"

"Well, my sister had love. It only made her sad."

He stared. "So you will not marry, and you will not love."

"Only sisterly love allowed," I decided, flashing a smirk. Sirion's expression didn't change, at least not the way I had intended. The table seemed a much better place to keep my gaze. "It's just . . . marrying someone I barely know, from a select few smug and snobby candidates, chosen by my mother . . . you can see why it doesn't tempt me? Love is different. Ideally, it should be something wonderful—like in the fairy tales. But I don't trust love."

"Then what can you trust?" Sirion asked.

I thought for a moment. "Only my own stubborn willfulness."

He gave me a fleeting glance and fell silent, eating as if the task needed all his concentration. Sirion didn't look up anymore—I could as well have not been in the room. Perhaps he was tired of me already. He *had* saved me. It was possible I appeared a little ungrateful.

I retrieved my dinner, determined to finish it this time. One bite, and then another. It piled up in my mouth until I had to force it down. I swallowed, drew a breath, felt my dry throat, and coughed behind a hand.

Sirion lifted his gaze.

"Thank you." There, I finally said it.

His thin lips tugged at the corners. "You're welcome."

"For dinner," I said, taking a big, demonstrative scoop. The stew still held some warmth, the vegetables were soft but resilient against my teeth, and I found the plate empty with a sting of regret.

"What?" Sirion blinked, before he let out a laugh. "Heh, I live to serve." He delivered a perfect, sweeping bow, snatching the plates as he came up.

I rolled my eyes. "I live to be served."

"Then we are well matched."

"In which case you match well with an impressive amount of people."

"Not at all." His demeanor was far too humble.

Despite the renewed silence, a strange elation lingered until shadows enveloped us. I ambled toward my room, closing the door on Sirion the Savior, studying me.

At the very least he deserved more than a lousy delivered 'thank you.' But that was all I had managed. There was nothing I could do but wait. And I had nothing to do here. I didn't have my horse, or my knitting projects, or the forest trails, no Madalyn and not a Sir Sigve I could tease. I even missed my lessons. I only had those few items I had picked up on the way before reaching Lakari.

Glancing at my sack, I sat for a moment longer before pulling it toward me. The single Lakarian coin was still in my pocket, heavy and shining as I held it up to the flickering flame of a candle. As I rummaged through my belongings, I found the beautiful golden thread I had bought at a tiny embroidery shop a couple months back. Cutting out a piece of dark blue cloth from a fabric I had saved, I began. I hadn't known what to do with them, anyway. Would he like it? My fingers froze around the needle. Maybe he would hate it. Well, I could still make it, if not for him, then at least Madalyn. The light from the moon and a small candle by my side was enough to let my hands and eyes work.

10

CHANGING WINDS

"Good morning, Vildi." Sirion pressed a cup of steaming tea into my waiting hands.

"Morning." I sat down opposite him, taking a careful sip. Already the fog seemed to dissipate from my mind. Together in the kitchen, blissful silence surrounded us, the sunshine of a fresh day filtering through the small windows. The possibilities given, the novelty of the experience, and the relative safety of this house—I closed my eyes, content to feel it upon the air, a simple pleasure of having survived another day, waking and finding a new one. I reached out blindly, and something dry and fruity appeared in my hand. "Thanks." I dug in with renewed vigor, appeasing my grumbling stomach. Tufts of bread materialized before me, perfectly balanced with a refill of hot, sweet tea.

"Ready to leave?" Sirion devoured the rest of his breakfast, his few belongings already packed and ready beside him.

I swallowed the remains of my food, nodding. After gathering my possessions and taking a final check of my room, I made sure to take plenty of water with me. I secured my sack to Balt's saddle, fastening the straps on his bridle, slung myself up, and was ready to go. The sky promised a warm day and although the lack of clouds was no surprise, the absence of even a gentle breeze was. We followed an old, sand riddled path. According to Sirion, it would eventually take us to Golden Road.

"Will we reach Fiar today?" I asked as we set out. Although I had to stay hidden, I would leave a letter for Sir Sigve—and Fiar should be safe. Goosebumps rose on my arms, sending a shiver through me. Surely the men were in Aransis, searching, not finding . . .

"Probably," Sirion said. "But not comfortably. It might be a better plan to arrive tomorrow."

"Camping in the sand?" I had the sudden urge to kick a stone again, if only one was available. "I don't look forward to that."

"Afraid so," Sirion answered. While his eyes were the color of the sky, a deep black defined the blue. They were much darker than the shades common to the people of Rimdalir. Sirion glanced at me, turning serious as he looked. "How are you, Vildi?"

What did he see? Did he notice my unease? "I'm fine," I said, putting on a smile.

Balt and No-Name trudged forward, a small swish heard whenever they shuffled sand with their hooves.

Sirion watched for a moment longer before relaxing his jaw. "Let's play a game."

"What kind of game?"

Sirion's lips quirked and a glint entered his eyes. "We'll . . . make guesses about each other. Ten tries, no lies. After all, we have been together for two days, and I still know next to nothing about you."

I narrowed my eyes. He didn't look away, gaze steady. Did he really just want to know me better? "And?"

"When I guess the most right and figure you out, I win."

As if it was so easy. A new kind of nerves played within me. "A contest? What is the prize?"

"What indeed . . . let's take that as it comes."

I was about to tell him no, make an excuse because . . . well, it was unlikely at this point, but what if he was with my attackers after all? Was he really taking me to Fiar? Perhaps I was already a prisoner, going along unknowingly . . . I shook my head. Sirion was my savior, and whatever else, at least he was kind, even pretending not to wait as I took too long to reply. But he might talk to the wrong people, spreading word of the foreign girl with blonde hair. Someone could have heard about the infamous second princess of Rimdalir. How should I refuse without sounding suspicious?

"You can start," Sirion offered.

It would be odd of me to decline. I would seem like I had something to hide, becoming even more of an interest to him. I bit my lip. Glanced at Sirion: waiting. Surely, I could endure a short, harmless interrogation? I said the first thing which came to my mind. "You like cake."

He laughed, a rich sound spilling between the dunes. "I suppose I do."

I looked away, face burning. Honey gold . . . how was I to blame for his skin and my deprivation of sweets? Fatal combination. And still he chuckled, waiting for my next attempt.

"You've worked as a caravan guide. That's why you know your way in the desert."

"Wrong," he said.

"Tea is your favorite drink," I tried. He insisted on having it with all meals.

"No, but close," he answered.

"Fine. You play an instrument." His hands were quite fine, delicate things.

"So personal," he teased. "No."

"You didn't really own the place we stayed at last night." His clothes were a bit worn, and though there was a quality in the leather and fabrics of his equipment, it was not new.

"Calling me a thief?" He raised an eyebrow. "Wrong."

"You are wealthy," I guessed. At least I thought he or his family must have been at some point, again judging by the house.

"I suppose I am." Sirion turned his gaze away from me.

"I'm done." Before he could protest, I continued. "I prefer to stop when the going is good. You have six tries, go."

Sirion shrugged, glancing over once before he concentrated on the path again. "You're a noble," he began.

"How do you figure?"

"That one was easy," he teased. "Your way of speaking, the clothes, skin, movements, posture," he listed, ticking each one off. His eyebrow rose. "Attitude," he finished.

I turned my nose to the sky. Let him read that!

Beside me I heard the telltale evidence of suppressed chuckles. It was my loss. Again.

With the smallest of peeks, I glimpsed the man riding beside me. Observed everything he had mentioned, how it applied to him. It was more a subtle trait for him than what I was used to, not flaunted but definitely there, once I knew to look. "Well, so are you," I said at last, words leaving me slowly.

"I won't deny it." He met my eyes with the steady, solid satisfaction of a tremendous ego.

I exhaled, looking ahead again. A *noble*. Well, of course he was. The gods had never given me a peasant boy for a rescue before, so why start now? Then again, wishing for a situation to be rescued in was to begin with the single most stupid idea of my life. If only the gods would stop granting the wishes of seven-year-old Vildi, ten years too late. My fingers found a loose thread on my dress and pulled. *I need to fix that later.* I hardly resembled a lady, but at least I wore a dress, despite the ease and comfort of traveling in pants. Although my disheveled state somehow appeared worse when compared to the standard of nobility. And Sirion knew. "Just continue, will you?"

"You hate nobles." From his voice it sounded like such a strange, unfathomable thing. "Even though you are one yourself."

"I don't *hate,* I just . . . really dislike them."

He arched a brow, casually making sure No-Name stayed close. "Why?"

I gazed down, thinking about it. "Well, formalities never sat well with me, and often parents are as bad as their sons, when it comes to marriage prospects. I can count on one hand—no, one *finger*, the number of nobles I like, excluding my family. And that one took me about ten years. Besides," I said, "have you ever read a fairy tale in which the hero is a noble? He's always a peasant, right?"

Sirion laughed. "I wouldn't say *always* . . . but we do have such stories."

"See?" I could not help the smugness spreading across my lips. I won that one, at least.

"You will soon count two fingers, though," Sirion said, smirking again. More irritating than him suddenly getting the last word was his confidence. I spotted no trace of doubt in him.

The worst of it was, I could not answer. I didn't *hate* Sirion. I didn't even dislike him. He was a bit infuriating, especially now, but he might be right. My hand came to rest upon the pocket of my dress. The soft square of its content hid just beneath the fabric. I sighed. "Next guess?"

"Your journey . . . I think you like to travel; you seem used to it. Although the desert must be new to you. I get the impression you are finished, though. Tired. You just want to go home."

My chest warmed at the thought. *Family. Madalyn. Safety.* "I'm going to, actually."

"Good for you." His voice reminded me of the desert. Dry and empty.

"Why, *thank* you." Sirion would have benefited from a lesson or two in conduct. Even I knew the polite art of pretending to be happy for someone else.

Sirion didn't dignify that with any response. His eyes were on me, searching for the answers to the person 'Vildi.' "You speak to your camel. And you mostly stayed yesterday because of Balt."

My gaze snapped from him to the sand. The dunes had such captivating, stunning shapes, and Sirion studied me until my skin crawled.

"I think you love animals. More perhaps, than people. Either that or you're incredibly lonely. Maybe both."

"That counts as two, I believe." I couldn't meet his eyes. His words hurt, even though he probably didn't mean them to.

"That's ... both ungenerous and magnanimous at the same time. I'm impressed by what you can manage. But fine. Am I right?"

"Yes, I guess so."

"On both accounts?"

I sighed, eventually nodding.

"All right!" Sirion's grin was insultingly bright. Didn't we *just*, as in seconds ago, establish my loneliness? It was rude, reacting like he did. Not that he seemed to care.

"By the gods' skaal! You have one left." With a parting glare, I turned away, my hair flowing around me.

He shrugged, the cloak rustling from his shoulders. "You're in great distress. You seem calm, but really there is more to your situation. And that by itself is quite impressive, given I found you in a recess of the desert, all alone, seconds from being poisoned. That's why you've displayed . . . well, a substantial amount of paranoia."

"It's true. The first part." It was entirely unfair—I had learned so little about him. This was not a game in which I could shine. I grit my teeth. "And I'm *not* paranoid." I ground my fears in genuine problems, thank you very much.

"Relax, I won't pry any further. And I've won, anyway." The way he stuck his nose in the air like any smug, satisfied noble, I could barely stand him. "I'm here if you want to talk about it, you know," he offered.

I shook my head. He had his chance to show just an ounce of empathy, and he blew it. Ahead of us, small grains of sand moved in waves over smooth stones.

"Vildi, I might be able to help."

I glanced over. Now he showed concern? With his earlier comments, why would he suddenly worry for me? I wanted to trust him. But wanting didn't make it so. "I—"

"Do you feel the wind?" He squinted at our surroundings, hand jerking up to force hair out of his eyes, though it blew away between his fingers.

"Yes?"

"It's picking up," Sirion said. He pointed to the top of a dune tipping over, sand rushing down its side. He peered at the ground where ripples moved over the surface. "Come!"

He nudged No-Name in the side, and the camel answered with an immediate run. Balt followed with no command, and suddenly I had my hands full keeping myself in the saddle. My hair stood out like a blonde curtain behind me, whipping with the wind.

No-Name raced across the sand, tearing up dust in his wake. Sirion, with his cloak billowing and flapping in the wind, seemed himself rock solid atop his camel. He looked back only once to make sure I was following. Well, I had no choice. I chanced a glance behind us and saw only brown on the horizon.

We had to swing around a dune blocking the path, and I discovered how climbing their hills in a plod was nothing like doing it at a full run. "Sirion!" My voice was barely a breeze against the gale. "What's happening?"

He shouted back, but the wind took his words.

Suddenly he tore off from the road, racing over dunes and down their sides, Balt still following close on No-Name's trail. I had to grasp Balt's mane to keep from falling, every step sending a jolt through the saddle and shaking me off balance. My knees and legs cramped from pinching and clamping close around his stomach, only urging him to go faster. I grit my teeth, chancing another glance at the approaching cloud. Past the blue, the sky was dark with dust.

We rode for what felt like a long time. Muscles down my legs screamed abuse while my stomach strived to keep me atop Balt's back. My fingers froze around the reins. The camels sprinted for us, running along the dunes, sometimes forcing their way over them, struggling through the deep sand. All the while the wind grew stronger, and the darkness closed in on us. Our animals heaved. Balt strained beneath me, each pull of his muscles more desperate, more painful than the last. His poor legs. We couldn't possibly keep this up.

Finally, Sirion pulled on his reins, breathing hard. No-Name fared better than Balt. Perhaps he had been raised for strenuous trips like this. Although we were no longer running at breakneck speed, Sirion kept us going at a fast trot along a valley of sorts. Getting more than a half-glance at the surrounding landscape, I noticed walls and stone peeking up from the sand. The jutting rooftops poking out from dunes, cubic houses half buried, empty black windows set in yellowing stone—we were in an old city. As we went further in and saw more of the buildings, I understood the structure and lay of roads and streets, open spaces for markets and bigger homes for the wealthy. Everything was embedded in layers of sand, thicker in areas which were more exposed, but nothing was spared a covering.

"We have to find shelter," Sirion said. "And it has to be big enough for all of us." He had to shout to make his voice carry over the wind. It was almost upon us, whipping at our surroundings, tearing into us.

"What about there," I yelled back, pointing at the gaping door of a large building, the first to escape a sandy burial. We should be able to get through, even with our camels.

Nodding, Sirion nudged No-Name again, crossing the distance while his clothes flailed as the wind ripped at him.

Sand peppered my hands, wanting to get through the thin protection of my lashes into my eyes, painful against my cheeks. Balt moved skittishly, showing clearer than words his dislike for the situation.

Sirion pulled No-Name through the doorway. I leaped off Balt, gripping the reins tight in my hand and dragging him along. Balt tore at the leather, white visible in his eyes—but he followed, thank the gods. As soon as I came through, Sirion blocked the opening with the heavy remains of a broken door. Inside, only a dim, gray light penetrated the darkness, coming through a window near the ceiling.

BALANCE

"I can't reach to seal it," Sirion said, looking up. There was a drizzling peppering sound against the door and the cry of wind coursing through empty streets. "Too late to find something else too. We must stay here."

My legs, as if weak twigs, struggled to keep me standing, ready to break with the burden. In the sudden stillness, pain slammed against my senses, an intense ache radiating throughout my entire body. I sank to the floor. "How long?" My voice was raspy, and I coughed on the last word.

"Difficult to say, but these things usually blow over after a while. Still, we'll probably be best off if we stay here tonight."

Balt closed in on me, blowing air and nuzzling against my hair. He needed a little reassurance and cuddling. I rubbed my palm gently over his front legs, finding them warm and throbbing. "The swelling is worse," I said, glad to have something to focus on. The improvised door creaked, painful moans like a dying animal. What if the sand piled up outside, what if we were buried inside a dune, stuck here—

"He should be better tomorrow." Sirion didn't sound so sure.

"I don't want to die," I whispered, throat choking up. "Not like this." Another loop, a coffin of sand and darkness and suffocation forever Do-Again and there was no air—

"You won't die. Vildi, I promise. Breathe. It's not that bad, we're safe as long as we stay here. You'll be fine. Take a breath with me, good, another . . ."

I exhaled, drew air in once, and then again as I felt warm arms around me.

"We're safe in here. Come, drink." Sirion sat down in front of me, pressing a waterskin into my hands. His eyes were dark, dark like the lake in summer.

Reaching out, I saw my hands trembling, giving me an unsteady grip on the smooth leather. The water helped alleviate my sore throat and the dryness in my mouth. I closed my eyes, breathing, sensing the liquid running through me like a soothing river.

Sirion let go, assured I could hold it by myself. Then he procured a bundle from his camel's saddle, unfurling it with a sharp shake and draped the blanket around my shoulders. Loosening the saddles from first No-Name and then Balt, he worked on caring for the camels, all the while mumbling soothing nothings in their ears.

He came over at last, another blanket hanging from his frame. He sat down next to me with our shoulders touching. "How do you feel?" he asked.

"Afraid," I said, voice cracking like skin boiling in the sun. "Cold." The wind was howling, and a small pyramid began to form by my foot, sand seeping through a gap in the ceiling above me. I could see another growing in the far corner of the room, and I swallowed, thick. The air was heavy, stagnant and dry as dust.

"The storm will pass," Sirion said. "Give me your hand."

I let my hand peek out from under the blanket, and he took it. "Your home, tell me about it." His voice was low, inviting.

"Home . . ." I closed my eyes, imagining Eldaborg, the scent of a smoldering fire and old wood. "It is nice, in its own way. In winter, the water clings to the trees like diamonds. Our breath turns to puffs of white curling through clear, fresh air. In some years, people freeze or starve, but with spring, life blooms everywhere. Fresh greens and small flowers. It's beautiful." The wind on my face, warm in summer like Mother caressing my cheek. Madalyn, smiling. Childhood. A time where I could laugh with Hogne, tricking him into carrying me on his back, or when we would sit in the grass talking while Madalyn and Eirik entwined hands, and we pretended not to notice. A time before suitors, when no one wished to marry me and everyone was Friend. When the content of dinner was my biggest problem, and life was *right*. "I miss it."

Sirion squeezed my hand, warm against my palm. "Why did you leave?"

"I . . ." A shiver ran down my back. "Well, the only thing I really truly hate is worms."

Sirion blinked.

I blinked back.

"Worms?"

"Worms," I confirmed. "Well, one. He was a suitor. A particularly bad one." Rude, intrusive, with his fingers locking me in place as he refused to let me go and whispered *my little star*, the breath of stale ale on my face—

"Did he do anything to you?"

My gaze snapped up. Sirion was in front of me. Sirion with his brows pulled down, darkening eyes, and fists clenching white around the waterskin. I shook my head.

Sirion exhaled.

The wind roared outside. Little daylight could penetrate the cracks to reach us. "Tell me something. Anything."

He cast his eyes down. Inhaled. "I lost those most dear to me some time ago. After that, the world was a dead place." He reached out—to embrace me?—but only offered water. "Meeting you, somehow it feels better. It's ironic. Lakari hasn't been too nice to you, has it? And meeting me hasn't really helped."

That's what he thought? "That's not true. Sirion, you saved me." I gave a resolute shake of my head.

He rewarded me with a slight smile. "It's okay. At the very least I found a purpose." He let his thumb trace a pattern in my palm, almost absentmindedly.

"A purpose?" Acute cold wrapped around me, squeezing my chest. I barely refrained from ripping my hand away.

Sirion looked up. "Oh yes. Keeping you alive is a struggle."

I huffed, forcing a laugh while my heart picked up speed. He didn't know how right he was.

"Why, isn't it true?" He raised a brow, all traces of levity gone, gaze unrelenting.

I scratched my itching arms.

At last, Sirion averted his eyes. "I have a sister."

I exhaled, chest letting go of a tight knot.

He continued, eyes trailing the floor in front of us. "She's a couple of years older than me. It was always us. Ilea got married two years ago, to the third prince of Tolona. I only met him twice, but still . . . I didn't get a good read on him." Sirion adjusted his position, a rustle of clothes filling the lull in his voice. "Tolona's been struggling with sickness. A few weeks ago, we heard there's been uprisings there, but we don't know how Ilea's doing."

If I was Madalyn, I could have hugged him, but there was nothing soothing about the presence of Vildi. I pushed dense air out of my chest. "Is Tolona very far away?"

"It's beyond the desert, in the mountains. Too far for comfort." With a swish of clothes, Sirion shuffled around in the dim darkness, unable to relax.

"Older sisters can be a trial, can't they? Although it's different, I know something about protecting sisters against marriage. What about you, Sirion? Are you well?"

"Thank you, Vildi." Sirion leaned back against the wall. "Well enough. Protecting you is a good distraction, I must admit."

I startled myself with the chuckles filling the room. "I can imagine."

Sirion joined my little laugh, yet the glimmer of a lighter mood faded fast. "I'll reach out to Ilea as soon as this all calms. She'll persevere in the meantime."

"I hope the gods watch over her," I said, unsure what else I could offer.

Sirion smiled wryly, handing over a piece of food. Because of the darkness, I didn't recognize it for salted, dried ham before I bit into it.

"Yours or mine?" he asked.

"Both," I concluded. And more quietly: "I hope they watch over us too."

Sirion leaned a little closer. "I'm sure they do."

II

CIRCLING THE SUN

The storm eventually passed. When we woke up the next morning, bodies stiff and sore from sleeping against a hard stone wall, the sun was already high in the sky and outside were piles of freshly heaped sand. At least the door opened easily, with nothing blocking our way out. Sirion explained to me how buildings were designed to circumvent the problem, sheltering windows and doors by leading the wind away from them.

The place we had stayed the night won little in terms of redeeming qualities come morning. I would swear on the gods' names there was sand on my tongue, whatever Sirion said, and the air was heavy. I had almost died again. Insisting on finding somewhere else to reside, I walked outside, Balt trudging after me.

Balt's legs were still warm from the hard ride yesterday, though No-Name fared somewhat better. We let them rest for the day. Sirion had regained some of that tired look, and I didn't need a mirror to know my appearance matched his. We were also running out of water, but Sirion knew somewhere close by to get more.

"We survived," I said, blinking up at the sunny, blue sky. After staying in the twilight darkness of the house for hours, the daylight was blinding. Sneezing twice in quick succession, I retreated to the merciful shadows of the building until my eyes could adjust.

Sirion walked out in the sun without those problems, stretching. "We did."

"It's a new day," I marveled. We had encountered a deadly phenomenon, and I had not died. No repetition. Just a simple turn of the stars and moon, along with a new sun.

"That's usually how it goes."

Deciding not to correct him as I hardly stood to gain from it, I stepped into the street again, feeling sneeze-safe. I could finally look at the city we had stormed past yesterday. The buildings were made of stones fitting tightly together, sandy yellow and coarse. Other than the wear of polishing grains on the wind, there was little actual damage to the constructions. Window shutters and doors were gone, but the buildings peaked proudly up from the sand.

"This must all be very old," I said, letting my hand slide across a rough surface. I could pry small granules out of the stone, if I wanted to. We passed a building with a gaping opening, half hidden inside a dune. A dead home, where people had once lived. Loved. Still, I couldn't imagine anything thriving in this place. I had nearly ended up like that too, half buried and forgotten, empty.

"They're from the foundation of Lakari," Sirion said, pulling me back from a dark turn of thoughts. "From when there was more than desert."

"Ah, the ruined city. Irisis, was it?" I had a sudden urge to laugh. "I heard about that. This is the type of adventure I wanted to have. Old civilizations, different cultures, wild, unbending nature . . ." My hand slid off the stone, slightly scraped and gritty. "Sirion, do you believe in magic?"

He blinked, looking more through me than anything. Although his eyes were fixed on me, he saw nothing. Blinking again, he seemed to regain awareness, or perhaps the world returned to his focus. "Magic? No. If something happens and we cannot explain it, we turn to our gods."

"We have gods too," I said. "But they don't cause magic. My sister has a bracelet of white stones. If removed, they always find their way back to her, to comfort her when she's in distress. The bracelet is only for Madalyn, though. I wanted one too, but I never found any. There is magic in those stones, but I don't think our gods caused it. Or . . . maybe they made the stones, long before my sister found them? I wouldn't know." I shuffled through a small dune, destroying it. In revenge, it collapsed around my feet, spilling sand in my shoes.

We walked down a channel running through the city. It was broad, curving along the edges to flatten out—and empty. It looked like, a long time ago, water had flown through it. We stepped over the edge on the other side, approaching a building which all other constructions seemed to radiate from. It was immense, standing tall and wide from the sand. The wind had not yet eroded all decorations carved into the stone, though the edges had lost some sharpness. Sirion took my hand and led me in front of it. "See? These are our gods."

There was a huge opening in the wall before us. Above it, so high I had to crane my neck to get a proper view, was a symbol. As with the coin, it appealed to me: the dragons the Lakarians seemed so fond of, circling a sun. "It's beautiful."

As if becoming one with the surroundings, still as a statue of stone, Sirion gazed at the crest above. "We see them sometimes, in the sky. Rashim, always. Liva and Avil, only rarely. But they are there. When the dragons shine around the sun for their people, they bring the divine rain. It is said a good year will follow." His smile held a nostalgic quality, and the grip on my hand seemed almost desperate. Watching him, an ache invaded my chest, an inexplicable sadness.

"Should we go inside?" I asked. "That's why we came here, right?"

Shaking himself out of his reverie, Sirion nodded. "I told you I used to travel a bit, remember? At some point I cleared a room in there, just in case. It's always smart to have some water and provisions stacked away at different spots in the desert."

"So you chose the biggest house around?" I flung my arms out, letting them circle me as I twirled around.

"Of course," he said, letting out a laugh. "Well, not really. But this used to be the royal palace; it was built with materials of higher quality. It's simply better preserved."

"Such practical reasoning." I tugged Balt along with me and went beneath the rounded gate. "I thought there would be something more fun to it."

"I think surviving sandstorms is plenty exciting."

"True." I repressed a shiver down my back. I held a steady, tight grip on Balt's reins as we walked inside. At least I was alive. I would prefer to stay that way.

We tied the camels up by the entrance, in a large side room designed for that very purpose. Sirion unloaded No-Name, who stretched in satisfaction. He placed the equipment on a shelf with no hesitation. An ingrained habit. We patted the animals, telling them we would be back, before entering through a door meant for men and not their mounts.

The inside was grand but old. It was also empty, our voices clinging hollow underneath high roofs. There was no proper furniture, though I spotted some stone tables and shelves in a few of the rooms we passed. Everything light enough to remove had been taken. Small piles of sand lay swept along walls and into corners, and our feet left a trail through the dust. At regular intervals I noticed the same symbol from before, two dragons forming a ring around the sun.

We passed a gaping entrance into a room. I peeked inside, stumbling against Sirion. A shrill scream echoed through the hall.

"It's okay, Vildi. There's nothing there, it's old and abandoned, I promise."

I swallowed down hard. Sirion's words scarcely helped against a room filled with dust and feces and dry bones, sand swept up at the entrance. A skull seemed to sneer at me with yellowing teeth. A den. "What kind of animal?" I asked, voice shaking.

"Desert hound." Sirion stepped closer, tugging on my hand until I followed. "Sorry, I had forgotten it was there."

Moving on, I didn't dare glance into the rooms we passed anymore. Eventually we branched off from the main hall through a corridor, entering a room decidedly different from the others. It bore the distinct signs of being lived in. Not much but enough. A slumped bag, a thin and worn straw mattress, and a table upon which a few dark green glass containers stood in a precise row. Two had something solid inside, and three contained dark liquids. I also recognized a waterskin and some utensils, a knife, candles, and equipment to kindle a fire. Sirion's room.

"I actually meant for us to stay here during the storm." Sirion found a couple of blankets, spreading them out on the floor as makeshift seats. "But sometimes you don't get that far."

"It's nice," I said, mostly because I didn't know what else to do. It *was* nice, but it also looked lonely.

"Don't tell anyone about it?" Sirion grimaced with a dry twinkle in his eyes. "It's so practical, having a place where no one can find you. I haven't shown anyone this place before. Well, I don't have much need for it now, but you never know."

"Will you not come here anymore?"

Sirion gave me an odd half-smile. "I might, of course, but I think my days roaming the desert are over."

A shiver overtook my shoulders, trailing down my back. "Mine too." I lifted my shoulders, letting them fall as I pushed the unease out of me. "I won't tell anyone." It was an easy promise. Who of consequence could I tell? I looked at our surroundings, thinking of our path here. Everything had been dead sand, not even a hint of a plant anywhere. "How were you able to stay here? There is no water."

"There is, actually. The Desert Diamond, a small oasis protected by the walls. In fact, they constructed this building around it, with the oasis in its center. But it's not sufficient to support a city, not even to fill this palace. Most people find the water bitter anyway, although I think it tastes sweet. The original water source is gone, and this one oasis is the only thing left. But," he said, "it's enough for me."

"I see." It sounded like a gem among rocks. "Can I see it?"

"I'll take you there later," Sirion promised. "But let's eat first."

I pushed a shriveled, pale fruit into my mouth, chewing vigorously through the tough fibers. Flexing my fingers, I stretched to snatch another piece from the plate. What did an oasis look like, tucked inside palace ruins? I ate through the giddiness springing to my chest.

Sirion hadn't even started eating, his hand too busy supporting his head as he yawned.

Swallowing, I seized a biscuit and although it was dry in my mouth, I forced it down. My feet tapped against the floor until I found Sirion staring, and then my toes curled inside worn shoes. In my chest, a flutter of excitement responded to a pull in my mind, as if I was about to find the sweetest honey cake.

Could Sirion not hurry up? His mouth should be put to good use eating, instead of sporting such a knowing smirk.

And his every gesture was of languid, lazy grace, as if to keep me waiting, separated from the water.

"Let's go," I said, swallowing the last bit of fruit as I rose. Maya would have frowned upon my manners.

"All right." Sirion followed me up and out of the room, still infuriatingly slow.

I took a few steps and stopped, looking down the hall and remembering all the side corridors we had passed. I had no idea where to go.

"Come." Sirion took my hand as he drifted past me, leading us further into the building. Our waterskins dangled in his other hand. I had completely forgotten about them, even though water was the real reason we were going.

My elation grew with each step, body light and happy, bubbly and bright all together, skipping along. As I was filled to the point of bursting, we walked through a final opening and stepped out into sunlight.

The Desert Diamond shone where water met shore, fracturing in ten shades of aquamarine until in the middle, a deep emerald hid its depths. The oasis was not big, just enough for a medium-sized house from Eldaborg to fit across its surface. Surrounding the water, grass and palm trees grew lush and fresh green, their leaves strong and bright. Large flowers in purple and white hung heavy from a plant twining around the palm trunks, bestowing a sweet fragrance upon the place. The old stone wall surrounded the oasis like a protective shield.

I walked to the edge of the small lake, stepping through the soft grass and sensing a breeze caressing my cheek. I glimpsed my own bliss, reflected off that beautiful, azure, glimmering water. I was home after a long journey, everything was right in the world, and I had finally found somewhere to belong, or rather, this had been my rightful place all along.

"And here it is, the Diamond of the Desert," Sirion said, pride in his voice. "I love this place. It has been special to me from the first time I laid eyes upon the water."

I nodded. No words would suffice.

"The water is sweet and like no other. You won't need to drink for hours—it will keep you strong." He drew close to the edge, filling both containers to the brim. "Of all the water sources around here, this is all which is left. But I've never seen it less than absolutely beautiful. It's easy to understand why the people built around it, long ago. Though few get to see it nowadays." He handed me one of the waterskins.

I took a careful sip, barely a mouthful. "Sweet," I commented.

"Right?" Sirion took a sip of his own, his gaze wandering from me to the lake.

There was a pull, a tug on my mind, out of reach as a butterfly would tease the edges of one's fingertips.

A shadow crossed the water. Glancing up at the sky, I saw only the glow of the sun and a clear, blue day. I squinted and it came back. Like a green shade within the water, circling the far lakeside. Perhaps a trick of the light. Palm trees leaned over the oasis, their branches almost touching the water. I had seen something similar at home, rustling leaves reflected off the lake's surface. Except here, there was no wind.

"Did you see that?" Another faint ripple flowed through the water.

Sirion looked from me to the oasis. "Oh, that. It's nothing to worry about. I see it sometimes, but there's never anything in the water."

"It was beautiful." As if a living, coiling emerald had been encased within crystal.

Sirion stretched, fingers reaching for the sky. "I agree."

I sat down, taking off my shoes. No more ripples came. With closed eyes, I felt the grass filtering through my fingers. The wind whispered in my ears. Warm water wrapped around my toes like a blanket, yet it was cool and soothing in my mouth. For the first time since arriving in Lakari I was safe, welcome, and cared for.

Sirion sat down beside me. "I know the feeling. I'm glad I could share this with you."

∼

As I turned my back on the Desert Diamond, my happiness drained as quickly as a leaky bucket lost water. Walking through hollow, abandoned halls of cold stone and stray sand was like waking up from a beautiful dream and realizing I was actually in a nightmare. I was on the run. Cut away from my guardian, these sandy ruin walls were the best protection I could hope for. With each step, a sense of loss reverberated through me.

"I know this feeling as well," Sirion said, looking at me. His hand swept toward a glass. "And I have medicine for it."

Turned out I could live very well on his kind of medicine.

"Can I ask you something?" Sirion asked rather redundantly, finishing his dinner with a drink from one of the green bottles on the table. It was a quite strong alcoholic brew, accentuating the effects of a day with sparse meals.

"Sure." My mood was somewhat improved again by the wine Sirion had offered me. It was good to relax with a drink in my hand. It was my third cup and really, all my strange experiences seemed like silly nightmares now. This hand clenched around the glass as if born to do so. All natural. I was definitely alive.

Smirking, Sirion handed me a waterskin. His eyes drove a stark resemblance to the Desert Diamond, right into me. "Drink," he commanded, sounding amused. "Or you'll regret it tomorrow."

The wine warmed me well. I had a fair tolerance for my age, and this was just enough to keep a bright mood, but not enough to make me sick. Shrugging, I accepted the water anyway, taking a small, polite sip before going back to the wonderful wine. "Did you know, Sirion, that your eyes look like the oasis?"

He threw his head back, laughing. "Drink more, Vildi."

"Wine or water?" I grinned, squinting at him.

"Whichever you prefer."

I took a good sup of each.

Sirion nodded, satisfied. "I've been thinking about what you said yesterday. You seem to accept me, despite knowing I'm of noble birth." Tilting his head, hair fell in front of his forehead. "Should I be proud of this accomplishment?"

"Well," I pondered. "Should you? It's not that I hate nobles." The wine worked wonders on my amiability.

"So you said."

"Yes. It's just a strong dislike." I put a finger in the air. "For example, they are easy to trust."

"Oh really," he asked, looking a little surprised. "How come?"

"Nobility," I set myself to explain, "can be trusted to be ambitious and self-serving. Eagerly vying for power, and yet yearning for indulgence."

Sirion's smirk grew for each word. "Not very flattering. But I can agree." He leaned forward, hands under his chin.

"Right?" I nodded. It was a perfect description of every suitor ever to step before me.

"What about royalty?"

"I don't know." My heartbeat stopped, then ran like the drums of a horse in gallop. Perhaps a sip of water to regain a clear head was a good idea, after all. "Maybe," I continued, choosing each word with greater care, "they would be less so. Because they already have everything. Except freedom. What do you think?"

"I think you are right, at least to some degree. Good observations."

"Thank you." I was oddly satisfied with that, feet happily bouncing Sirion's blanket on top of his makeshift bed.

"So . . . nobles are a greedy, lazy, power hungry breed. Where does that place me?" he asked.

"I don't know yet." A fistful of skirt wrinkled beyond redemption inside my clenched hand. "I don't know what you want from me." *But it is always something,* I thought. *And if not, that's just because you don't know who I am.*

"For the moment," Sirion said, "I only want to keep you safe. You happen to be in my care, after all."

"For the moment?"

His eyes, resisting the pull of dropping lids, rolled up as he sighed. "As soon as I take you out of the desert, you will go your own way and cease being my responsibility, won't you?"

"Definitely."

"But right now, I have a duty to protect you. It's an unthankful chore, sure, but—" laughing, he ducked away from the stray speck of sand I flicked his way. "At least it gives me purpose," he finished, looking suddenly solemn.

"Sirion?" Fumbling against my own numb clumsiness, I reached into a pocket and felt soft fabric against my fingers.

"Yes?"

"I have something for you. You know, as thanks for saving me—twice, for giving me food, teaching me to care for Balt and brewing tea . . . and we leave tomorrow, so I think you should have it today. It's stupid perhaps, and it's not enough and lousy as thanks, but . . ." Struggling with my words, I bit my lip.

Sirion's face changed, from wide eyes to bended lips and finally settling on a grin. "Really? For me?" He reached out, palm up. "Let me see."

The hand burned in my pocket. He would laugh. I could already see his smirk, and of course he would. He had no need for such an insignificant thing. Why did I do this again? So stupid.

Seeing me hesitate, Sirion raised an eyebrow. "Vildi? My gift?"

Tightly closing my eyes, I took my hand out.

"Oh." I felt him take it from me. "Vildi . . . thank you."

He sounded sincere. My eyes flew open to see Sirion in front of me, all traces of smugness or sarcasm gone.

"It's not much," I said. "Just something I made with materials I had on me."

"Thank you," he said again. His fingers traced the dragons, golden stitches on blue.

"I tried to make them look like the mark on the coins. I figured you liked the symbol, or at least dragons, since I saw it a lot around your house."

He nodded, eyes a little glazed. "They symbolize the foundation of Lakari. This, how the two come together, that's Hima."

It was the religion Kaira had told me about a few days ago. "The gift, right?"

Sirion's head snapped up. He opened his mouth as if he wanted to say something, but nothing came. Gazing down at the dragons, tracing the pattern, he nodded.

"I think it will hold well enough," I said, not quite knowing what to do. Perhaps he was a very religious person? Though by his reaction I hadn't offended him. Probably. "I sewed along the edges, so it won't unravel. I don't even know if you use or need a handkerchief. You can give it away, or throw it, I don't mind—"

"I like it. I'll use it." His lips curved into the beginning of a smile, careful and hesitant, blooming as a mild spring day. It was the sincerest expression I had seen on him yet. At that moment he looked younger, handsome, happy.

"The stitches are not even." Nails dug into my palms again. "Some of them are bigger than the others. Madalyn would have made it better. My sister."

"This is good," he protested. "I didn't think you could make such things."

"Well," I said, deciding not to point out how some of them were also skewed. "It's not by choice. Where I'm from, I would disgrace my name if I could not sew a proper dress for my coming of age. These skills are considered important, you see. Shows ability to provide and care for one's family, as any good woman should. According to Maya. And Mother, I guess."

"Look at that, you might become a splendid wife after all," Sirion said, shattering the mood.

"Never," I answered, surprised by my own laughter.

TRIUMPH AND FAILURE

I woke up with an *arm* around me. A crumpled shirt could not hide the snippet of golden skin or the smell of citrus and wine. My head thumped the truth of last night. For once, I was glad none of my family or acquaintances could see me. Maya might have cried. Mother would faint perhaps, or worse, run to my side with the wedding garbs. Being stranded in a desert with no witnesses did little to remedy the presence of his limb upon my waist or the steady, peaceful breaths mingling with mine. I lifted my gaze, looking straight into his face, made young by sleep's hold. My fingers twitched, fighting an urge to reach out.

This could not happen. Through a pounding in my head and the flush of heat from my beating heart, my body moved. My arms and legs pushed, shoving against groaning flesh until his arm flipped and his body rolled off the bedroll and onto the stone floor with a dull thud.

"Wha—why? By the agony of gnawing sand, a parched mouth and Rashim's searing heat, why did you have to push me?!" Glaring blue set upon me from within a frame of dark lashes.

Unable to hold his stare, I turned my head to the side. "I'm just reestablishing a sound distance of propriety," I said.

With a snort, Sirion shuffled to his feet. "Propriety. When did you ever care about that?"

"How would you know? I may care a great deal." At least my dress, although crumpled, was still in place. My composure, on the other hand, was in tatters. With burning cheeks and hands too restless to be still, I hardly knew what to do. All my years enduring lessons upon boring lessons, becoming a lady, and none had thought to prepare me for this. Beyond fleeting touch of hands and the occasional dance, a girl should be pure and demure. What better way to be sold off as a spouse? The customs of Rimdalir held a sickening absurdity in the light of reality.

Sirion provided breakfast despite the rough way he woke, thank the gods, though he had a peculiar look in his eyes the entire time. Perhaps he had trouble deciding between being offended or laughing at my flushing face.

The fault lay with the wine. I looked upon the green glass bottles in dismay. Three of them, all empty. A decent amount not even Father's men would drink without some effect, and it would definitely take more than a sip of water to rectify, no matter one's tolerance. Especially with a starved body or a tired mind, ready to forget life and death for a few hours.

At least we were still fully dressed. Besides, the touch of two arms while awake was less than one while asleep, so if dancing was acceptable, then this should be too. Furthermore, no person of importance would ever know about it. And there had been a storm. The wind was not of my doing, and we had no choice about our lodgings.

Matters resolved, I took the last bite from our shared plate and smiled at my companion. I could use some peace and tranquility. "So . . . let's go to the Desert Diamond."

Sirion looked from the empty plate to me, lifting an eyebrow. "Do you know how long you were staring at it yesterday?"

"Half an hour?" I guessed. "We have time for a small visit before we leave, don't we? I haven't been anywhere so . . ." *Beautiful, serene, or secluded,* I thought. Stun—why was he smirking at me?

"No, we don't have three hours to waste gawking, not if you want to reach Fiar before dayburn. I'd rather get along to Aransis too."

"You exaggerate, it wasn't *three* hours." I slumped back against the wall.

Sirion leaned against the other, crossing his arms. "No? Has anyone ever told you how you tend to space out?"

Only Maya, over and over again, and Sir Sigve recently while we watched a sunset against the sea, and perhaps Madalyn once or twice, and even Hogne. "All right. I do that. Sometimes." My hands opened, slack in my lap.

"If not for your stomach rumbling, you would have stayed there."

"I need food, it's who I am." I turned away, glad for the loose hair falling in front of me, hiding a flush of red. "But we can still take a short trip?"

"Did you know the Diamond of the Desert is a sacred place?"

"No." I cast my gaze to the dark corridor, blackness swallowing the meager candlelight with greedy tendrils. Who would have known such a wonderful place could exist beyond that gloom?

"It's a place for the gods." Sirion studied a spot on the wall, glancing my way once before he continued. "We actually have a ceremony here—though the last was held over seventy years ago."

Didn't Sarina say something about that? I wrung my memory, but found only fragments of a nightmare. "What kind of ceremony?"

Sirion demolished any attempt at order in his hair, his smile sharp as his scrutinizing eyes. "It's a ceremony of bonding."

I bit the inside of my cheek. "Why did we enter at all?"

"I thought you would like it." Sirion lifted his shoulders, letting them fall at once. He leaned back against the wall, letting muscles spill as he stretched his arms. "And you did. Well, of course you would. *I* like it. After the sandstorm and everything . . . you needed it. Being there feels good."

I drew a hand over my eyes. There was a lot of that 'everything,' more than he knew. I nodded, trying to ignore the satisfaction in his smirk. "Don't think I trust you yet."

"I know. *But* what choice do you have?" His expression, from the tilt of his lips to the gleam in his eyes, was radiant as sunshine. "In reality, you are completely at my mercy, yes?"

"That's why I don't trust you." I gave in with a smile. "Can I have it?"

He laughed. "My mercy?"

"Yes."

"Yes." He fell into a contemplative mood, watching me. "But you're right. I don't think you should trust anyone." A grim silence settled like a heavy blanket in the wake of his words.

We ate, flushing down dry food with sweet but lukewarm water. After packing our belongings, we reunited at last with our camels. Balt greeted me with an enthusiastic trumpet, munching something Sirion had given him. No-Name blinked with sleepy eyes, leisurely putting his hooves beneath him to stand for his owner.

Breakfast and the prospect of leaving a ghost city behind sat well with me. The chance of escaping the worst experience of my life also sparked some eagerness. "I'm going home, I can't believe it, I'll find my way back! Home!" I almost sang the words, flurrying about Balt, tightening straps and securing my few belongings. Sipping water from the Desert Diamond, I felt more like myself than in a long time. Ready to take on a challenge, mood steadily improving.

With slow movements, Sirion did the same. He looked as if yesterday's rest never happened. "That's good," he replied. A rueful, annoying smirk played across his lips. He should be happy for me.

"It definitely is!" I pushed myself up and threw my leg over Balt's back.

"Despite the worms?"

My mood instantly dampened. Well, home was home, regardless. "I think I'll be able to handle one greasy worm after this."

Sirion swung himself atop No-Name with effortless elegance. "You probably will."

Nodding, I brightened a bit. After this misadventure, a few lords and earls at home should be nothing. If I could find Sir Sigve, he would certainly do the honors of chasing out the vermin himself, sworn as he was to protect me.

Sirion signaled for his camel to move. "I know you'll be sad to leave me. Are you sure you'll not regret it?" His words flowed together like strings of a song. Poor No-Name. Must be tough, having to carry a man like him everywhere. Surely, the ego by itself imposed a crushing weight.

I gave Balt free reins, urging him to show this noble the dust of our backs.

No-Name trotted along with ease. Once again beside me, Sirion's lips went into a smile. Still, I traced no humor in his night-sky eyes. "What do you look most forward to?"

We passed the first cubic, half buried houses. Sun and dead sand, such a stark contrast to Eldaborg. Home. "Seeing my sister, perhaps." The road ahead didn't appear so grim anymore, even as black windows gaped at us on both sides.

"You're close then? That's nice. I have next to no contact with my brothers. Competition, I think. And my sisters are estranged. Like another species. Except Ilea, but . . ." he trailed off, watching the dry sand around him.

"My younger brother is like that," I said, hoping to ease the silence. "Must be the age difference."

"Maybe." Sirion's voice was light. When in a good mood, he looked very comfortable and relaxed. It was too easy to forget that he was still a stranger.

And yet, Sirion was my savior. But Fiar should be safe, against strangers, attackers. Against poison and daggers. At least for a while, as far as anywhere was safe for me. "Sirion, you're going to Aransis, are you not?"

"Yes."

"Good."

The silence afterward pressed down on us, strained and stretching. At least I knew, when the air no longer dried my skin and each breath became easier, that we drew near. Soon. I would find a boat, a ship to take me home.

I caught movement from the side, and then turned to see Sirion shaking his shoulders, as if attempting to shrug off something unpleasant. Catching my stare, he looked my way, revealing a crease between his elegant eyebrows. Each step led us closer to goodbye. My fingers clenched to channel a sudden constriction of my chest. What a strange moment of melancholy—Sirion was such a new acquaintance.

We turned around the bend of a dune, reaching a manmade path. "Guess this is goodbye," Sirion said. "This is Golden Road. Continue that way to reach Fiar." He pointed, turning No-Name in the other direction. "This way is Aransis. Are you sure?"

Between the gloom of leaving and glory of homecoming, my growing joy won out. I did a poor job of keeping the grin off my face, knowing I was about to return to something normal and safe. Forests, farmland, and my home perched on top of a cliff by the sea, where the chatter of seagulls joined the cacophony of crashing waves. And I would overcome a few pesky suitors for the pleasure of spending time with my family.

"I'm sure," I said. I tried to appear reassuring and calm, although the feeling was mostly foreign to my face. "Thank you for everything."

Sirion sighed. "I don't want you to leave."

"What?"

"Never mind." He exhaled as if getting rid of his soul, turning to stare at me. After a second, he averted his eyes. "You have to go, I know."

He looked forlorn, like a sad, wilting willow. It was such a contrast to his smug and satisfied self, especially because he was right. The sight bothered me, somehow, needling my heart as if I watched food gone to waste. And there was little I could do. I had so little comfort to give. Knowing only a need to lighten the mood, I opened my mouth. "Sirion?"

"Yes?" His gaze snapped to mine, with a glint ignited.

A memory of triumph and failure sparked an idea. "What did you want? Your prize for winning our game."

Sirion studied me, his serious face dissolving to an easy grin. "Don't need anything," he said. "Perhaps I'll ask for something next time we meet."

"Of course," I agreed. "Next time."

Sirion didn't quite look at me after that, and a stillness between us grew until it was a wedge. There were no more words as we departed, each in our own direction.

I was going home.

∽

Riding in silence along the road, I let windswept stone and cliffs guide me the rest of the way. Only me and Balt, one step after the other. Not a trace of life around us, and both Sirion and No-Name gone.

No nausea.

Balt led me to the stables. As we drew near, reaching the end—or start—of Golden Road, the few people in the streets stopped their work to stare at us. At me. The stable boy accepted the reins with a flaming face, gigantic eyes and a mouth suited to catch flies. He said nothing, though I think he tried.

Balt looked from me to the boy and back, blinking his beautiful lashes.

"I know. But I can't take you with me. I wish I could. But Balt, you wouldn't like the winter, you see. It's already hard on us who are used to it. You belong here in the sun."

Balt scoffed, air blowing in a huff through his nose. He tugged on the reins, almost pulling them out of the boy's hands.

"Goodbye, Balt. Thank you for taking care of me." I patted his neck, his soft fur, letting my hand slide down and fall to my side.

Balt turned his head to peer back as the stable boy led him away.

The wave I sent him was just as empty a gesture as the hole in my stomach. My eyes burning, I faced Fiar one last time.

Without Balt, I was truly on my own.

Home was only a long boat ride away, and I would soon see my family again. Five weeks with luck. Three if the winds were strong.

I meandered my way through the streets, passing the people of Lakari. A prickling sensation crawled up my back. Once or twice, I met the eyes of Lakarians as they lowered their hands mid-action to study the girl passing them. A middle-aged woman was quick to glance away. I shifted my attention, and a man's eyes snapped back to the wooden board in front of him.

It was not so strange, perhaps, considering the layers of dust on my clothes, small clouds spreading out when I shook the skirt. My hair hung loose and long, a non-existing style which would make me shunned in any society. That was the problem, of course. And to make matters worse, I was a young woman traveling by herself.

Really, though. These people were extraordinarily bad at minding their own business. But at least I didn't feel sick. The men were in Aransis and this was safe. Finally.

I pulled the remaining piece of blue fabric out of my bag, winding it around my head, hiding most of my blonde hair. Perhaps this style would be easier for people to accept, even if a few stray locks escaped confinement. At least it protected against the heat.

I was safe. The knife seemed to burn at my belt.

At last, I spotted the harbor and a familiar ship wobbling with the waves. The *Disandri* shone with golden letters across the rough, dark wood of the bow. I would get on board, out of sight, and stay there until the ship brought me away. I would leave a message for Sir Sigve, maybe even send a couple of letters, just to be sure he was told what had happened. All would be well. I could sit in the great hall again, share my stories with my people. My family.

I just needed to get on the ship, past the crew. I spotted a nice target and made my move. "Excuse me?"

A sailor napping to the last rays of sun woke up with a start, blinking owlishly at me.

"I came here on this ship, and was wondering . . ." there was something familiar about his empty, waiting eyes. "Never mind. This ship leaves in a fortnight, right?"

"No, miss. *Disandri* leaves in six days."

"Right." How incredibly stupid. The sailor seemed to agree. "Of course. I guess it has been . . . eight days since we arrived."

"Yes," he said, the edge in his voice was sharp as the crease between his eyes. Well, any decent member of society should be able to count on five—or ten—fingers without problems. Besides, I had cost him his lovely nap.

"Can I have a room?" I asked, making my voice gentle and amiable.

"Of course, miss." The sailor smiled with forced friendliness. "You want the same as before?"

I felt sweet relief, like a heavy burden lifting off my shoulders. Safe, at last. Out of this land in less than a week, and home within two months. Just in time for Madalyn's birthday. "That would be nice, but if not, I'll take any room you have." I gave him my best, pleasant expression. "I just want a spot on the return trip."

"You'll have it," the man promised. "I'll make sure you're on our list of passengers. Come back tomorrow, and we'll make the arrangements."

"I cannot stay here until we leave?"

"On the ship?" He laughed, apparently finding the idea ridiculous. "No miss, of course not. There are many fine inns in Fiar, I suggest you take one of 'em. Come back tomorrow to settle the payment and get written up."

"Well, thank you." I trudged away, his gaze burning down my neck. At least he helped straighten out my real-time perception.

Six days. How fast could the men get here from Aransis? I should have some time yet.

I returned to the busy Fiar roads, those of elegant western shops and equally eloquent residents. Sirion, even as a noble, had made no comments on my disheveled appearance, yet here I noticed more than one lingering look, hands lifted to hide their whispers. Most of them shunned me in their gracefully-pretending-to-be-discreet kind of way, giving me a wide breadth. Maya would have cried to see me fit in better between the lower class, the working and shabbier parts of town. My clothes were not in the best shape, after being pulled through more than their design ever intended. Strangely, being ignored felt better—like some twisted protection. Perhaps I *could* do this for six days. It was not so much, if no one knew me.

Thus, I ended up in a rather shady inn, with the only upside being the friendly looking woman who welcomed me and gave me a bowl of something resembling food. It smelled a bit like the gruel used to feed Tyra and the other horses at home. When the last spoon of sustenance entered my mouth, the door slammed behind me. I swallowed and turned to the sound. At the entrance was a man, big and bulky, draped in blotchy brown.

"Thank you for the meal." I forced a smile to the innkeeper, moving my gaze to the empty bowl on the table. The soup churned in my stomach. But there was a kitchen behind the counter, possibly even a back door . . . I rose with casual care, strolling across old, sandy stones.

"What fine golden hair." The man planted himself in front of me, sneering. "Princess Alvildi, I take it." He reached for me, grabbing my upper arm in a painful hold.

I should have known. I had a memory somewhere, telling me that escape was a feat simply not done. "Never heard of her; it's not me. Now if you'll excuse me . . ." I pulled at my arm.

The man smirked, eyes wide and dark and void of humor. "As if I don't know my target. This has been a mess of a mission, and I'm just ready to be done with it."

I glanced around me. No one rose to my defense, not even the woman who had kindly served me moments before. I half hoped Sir Sigve would jump forth from a table in the corner, a lecture on hand while demanding my release with his prized sword at the ready. No such thing happened.

What would Madalyn do? "Release me," I said, forcing any quiver out of my voice, summoning all the authority and strength I could pull forth. "I demand it."

"You do now," the stranger said. "'Fraid I can't do that."

He was close, eyes hard and breath sour from smoke and strong drinks. The few people present looked away except one, gawking with curious, wide eyes. A child—no help.

"Come along, now," the man said. He flicked his stained cloak, letting light glint off the weapon at his belt.

A dagger.

Struggling backward, I fumbled with my free hand for the one at my belt. My fingers shook around the handle as I raised it between us. If only Sir Sigve had trained me. If Father had allowed me to learn, like Madalyn had, if Hogne had taught me instead of protecting me . . .

"Women of the north learn to fight?" the man asked, sounding insultingly incredulous and amused. He gazed down at my small knife as if I was waving a toy.

"They do." I took one step back, hoping he paid more attention to my face than my feet. Rimdalir women *did* learn to fight, should they want to. He didn't need to know I was the exception.

"A'right." Glee glinted in his eyes and within a second he had unsheathed his own. Whatever moment had been there, whatever opportunity, I had wasted it. He lunged, his blade connecting with mine as I raised it in defense. A clash between his curved right-hand knife and my decorative one, and he twisted, slid past mine. A slight movement, a flick of his wrist, and I felt it thick and cold in my throat.

Red seeped from up there down my arm, sharp, going against the ebony handle and coating the blade, finally gathering in perfect spheres dripping to the ground. My body crumpled beneath me; my fingers were numb against the rough stone floor.

"Sorry 'bout the spill, ma'am."

DETERMINATION OF THE DESPERATE

My lungs heaved for sparse air as something heavy closed around me, holding me down. It was warm, circling my waist and pressing my body against his. Sirion. A new chance and *that* thing, cold inside my throat, was gone. A Do-Again, with a dream to guide my actions. Only a fraction of pain remained, itching like a weak resemblance of the real thing.

As my breath stilled, I heard more. And I understood. With so many nightmares, one could call me an expert, and the person beside me was struggling, gasping, in pain.

What would Madalyn do?

I turned, putting my arms around him as far as I could reach. I let him hold me too, because it might be improper, but it felt safe. Nothing else could matter.

Together, our hearts, both racing with the mare, calmed down. Our mingling breaths no longer quivered. Enveloped by a serene silence, I felt myself relax. Relief, not unlike how the air was easier to breathe after a violent thunderstorm. Deciding it was time to get up, I stirred, blinking. I peered right into dark blue eyes, clouded only by remains of sleep.

"I'm so sorry." His voice was hoarse, even vulnerable. Making no sense, although such nonsense was not uncommon for someone emerging from the clutches of sleep.

"Shh, it was a dream. Nothing real."

"Vildi." Sirion looked incredibly sad. His finger brushed with a light touch underneath my eye and came back with a drop shining on the tip. I didn't even know I had cried.

"I had a bad dream too," I said. "Happens a lot lately."

"I'm sorry."

"Not your fault." I laughed—it was a hollow tone. "And it's not real, anyway." At least it shouldn't have been.

"Only dreams," he followed, sounding just as empty as me.

"Will you tell me about your nightmare? Perhaps it helps to talk."

"I don't think it will." Sirion got up, eyes trailing away. "I'll prepare some breakfast."

Deciding not to press the matter, I shook out my blanket, folding it neatly. "And then we leave? I'll go back to port, find a ship, and then . . ." A small spark of energy emerged, like a flickering stubbornness refusing to die. "I'm going home!"

"Like that's any better," he mumbled, still looking anywhere but my vicinity.

"Well, I cease to be your burden, don't I?" I summoned a smile to counter his gloom. "Cheer up." For some strange reason, I couldn't bear to linger on dejection when Sirion was already so out of it. What an odd way he helped me.

Sirion kept to his silence, but at least he turned around. Upon meeting my eyes, his shoulders lost their tension. He came closer. "You want me to cheer up?"

I nodded, not entirely sure why it didn't feel like the right answer.

He took another step and stopped. His gaze . . . there was something in it, familiar though never before directed at me. For a moment, I could have sworn it was similar to how Jarle—my favorite noble—looked upon Madalyn. And then it was gone. "Never mind."

My hand slipped inside my pocket, finding the coin. The protrusion of dragons curling, twining into a heart, soothed my fingertips and the coolness of metal provided contrast to my burning cheeks.

I busied myself with preparing breakfast. At least on one point we agreed. I was still homeward bound. I *had* to find a way.

Despite this, Sirion was in a fairly good mood, even smiling through the mouthfuls of food. We packed our belongings, groomed our camels, and set off. As we came closer to our juncture, his spirit dampened.

"What will you do when you get there?" Sirion didn't look over, his words spoken in a low voice.

"I don't know yet." Sneak onboard a ship? At least I knew to avoid any inns. Where would I be safe and sheltered? With vague, dream-like memories of my most recent try, finding the correct choice seemed difficult at best. Death in Fiar. Death in Aransis. And this should be—had to be—my last attempt, my final Do-Again. Not one in a string of pain.

"You must find your father, right?"

His words drew a blank in my mind. My stunned silence lasted a bit too long, but he didn't seem to notice. Or at least he refrained from commenting.

"Yes," I finally said. That *was* my story. Vildi Sigvesdatter, merchant's daughter. Though he already knew I was a noble, so perhaps my front had crumbled days ago.

"And then you'll go home?" Sirion asked, watching the path ahead and adjusting No-Name's course.

I let my hair fall forward. "Yes."

"Maybe I'll visit," he mused.

I snorted. "Right."

"I'm not welcome? After all, you don't *hate,* just strongly dislike nobles and suitors. Yes. You would not welcome me," he decided.

Turning toward him, I didn't know if I should protest or agree, certainly not extend an invitation. Sirion was a stranger. I didn't know what words would win out until I saw his face. That smirk.

"Who knows," I said. "It's a mystery. You can find out or not." I stayed serious for about the span of three of Balt's steps, before I dissolved in laughter and Sirion with me. It was not the kind of carefree laugh I could share with Madalyn, or the sarcastic humor I could imagine having with Hogne. Hollow, as if trying to hide empty words and an impossible future. Laughing, because crying would be so much harder. Rimdalir and Lakari, they were different worlds, or could as well be. And I might never make it home.

At least it served as a distraction, though brief. The amusement bled out, leaving me frozen and a little sick, struggling to swallow through a sour taste in my mouth.

This time I knew I was walking into a death trap. And yet I intended to go. The short relief, the breather of the last days had ended, and Fiar was the only destination left for me. If I could get on a ship, I would find a way back to my family. Pretend to listen to Maya's lessons. Politely return Lady Liv's overbearing leer. Hug my brother. Let Mother caress my hair, as she used to when I was still a child, and lift the mead horn in a skaal or five with Father. See my sister smile.

Only a man and death stood between me and that future. I had to try.

"Here is the juncture," Sirion said. The windswept stones of Golden Road lay before us. To stay with him would be so easy.

"Yes. Well, thanks for everything and goodbye." My words tumbled out too fast. I didn't dare look at him, to see his eyes and perhaps falter, break down because I *knew* what waited but not how to avoid it. Sirion was nice. If I asked, he may come with me. But I could never inflict such a burden upon him.

What choice had I left?

"Vildi, don't go. You can come with me." It sounded so easy.

I turned, seeing Sirion and No-Name and the path leading to Aransis. There was no mocking smirk or badly concealed mirth. Just him, watching me with unblinking eyes.

"I can't come with you, Sirion. I have no reason to go there, and nowhere to stay. I'm going home." My hands fell down in front of me. Balt, ever the gentle soul, didn't even twitch.

"You could marry me." Sirion didn't ask. It was more a statement of plans, an offering of possibilities. Like: would you eat fish or meat for dinner, do you want the white or red dress? Do you want to marry or go home? Even worse was his earnest expression, the solemn way he spoke the words.

I waited for him to laugh, make a joke of it.

"We get along well enough," Sirion just said. "I like you."

Oh. He was serious. My heart beat hot and strong in my ears. The hand he had offered me clenched around No-Name's reins. Sirion's lips twitched, alluding to a smile that didn't take and although he stared straight at me, I could have sworn the red hue of his skin was more than a trick of sunlight. And there was a glint to his eyes, calling to something inside me, as if the promise held a glimpse of the gods' gilded halls. Sirion offered his life to a forlorn and lost stranger, asking to share everything with me. And I could give him nothing.

I lowered my gaze, twisting my fingers into knots. It wouldn't solve anything, would not get me home. Worse, it would put him in danger. And it was *marriage*. Drawing a trembling breath, I let it out with a solid push, leaving my body heavy and cold. "I don't really know you, Sirion. You've just met me. How can you seriously want to marry me?" As if a vague 'like' was anything to build on. Besides... perhaps Sirion was lucky enough to not have realized, but I could never forget the fairy-tale lie. I signaled for Balt to move on, turned away from that man and swallowed against the thickness in my throat.

"Vildi!" Sirion called, his voice commanding, demanding I stop. It felt like I had no will of my own, as if he froze me to the spot with only my name. I lifted my gaze to meet his. "Don't do anything foolish." With that, he turned from me and left me staring at his retreating back.

"Let's go, Balt," I mumbled. "We don't need him."

Balt shook his head, his shaggy mane flaring wildly around him, and I was left wondering if he'd agreed or refused my statement. Perhaps a bit of both.

Sneaking into the edges of Fiar, I quietly led Balt to his stable. We stayed in the shadows, letting no one notice us. Balt seemed to know his way, and by the last stretch it was more like him guiding me, saying: *this is my home.*

This time would be different.

My parents would be pleased to have me home, and after the effects of these last days, I'd probably escape any strict diets. What awaited after the happiness of getting their daughter back whole and safe, was endless lessons in behavior and conduct. I could live with that, for a while at least. *Marriage.* Well, that was a problem for later. *Sirion.* Had to forget him.

Mother, Father... Madalyn. I must have worried them, leaving like I did. It was why they sent Sir Sigve after me.

Perhaps I should be grateful. They had allowed me this adventure, giving me freedom. I was not the important one, thank you very much, and thank the gods. But looking at this dry place with people clinging to life despite the desert ever intruding on them, knowing what lurked behind any corner or turn—no. It was enough now.

I pulled out the blue fabric from my sack and swept it around my head, hiding most of my hair. Even though it was clumsily done, this make-shift shawl was better than nothing. Had to be. As we met with curious, blinking eyes and ears waving with the lazy movements of someone dozing in the sun, I let go of Balt's reins.

"Goodbye, Balt." I stretched, hugging him tightly. His pelt tickled my cheek, my nose. He was warm, so soft, leaning against me and his muzzle nuzzling my back.

Balt didn't comment on the wet spots I left on his neck or my arm sweeping over his eyes. He let me leave.

It was time to go back.

∾

I didn't dwell or waste any time. Spoke to nobody, kept to the shadows while sneaking from one alley to the next. My eyes trailed the ground as a good nobody, while each step landed on a new shade. Despite being a small but dense city seething with life and activity, I hoped a lone girl could be invisible like one sheep among many. Even one with lighter wool.

It took me ages—halfway through town I dragged my feet along, and by the end my head hurt. Dayburn had set in. And Sirion was still in the desert, exposed to the sun. *You could marry me.* My chest lurched, sharp and heavy thumps. Poor Sirion. Even if he meant it, surely, he understood it was impossible.

I reached the pier. The sailor sitting by the splendor of the *Disandri*, presumably to guard the ship, snored in the sun. My mind throbbed with a nightmare, a memory of rejection. Perhaps I could sneak past him. But we were not alone on this harbor and even if he didn't wake, a lone girl going onboard would seem extremely suspicious. Yet I knew six days was too much. I didn't even have one.

The next ship harbored dark men with blinding white grins. They seemed friendly enough, but the ship was headed further south. Completely wrong direction. It was a pity, for they looked like splendid company too, three of them even singing as they clinked their mugs together, with brew frothing over the edges. It reminded me of Father, of feasts. I was a little thirsty, but had no time to linger. I had to find a ship.

Of course, everything had been easier with Sir Sigve as a companion. As a young woman traveling alone, people eyed me with upturned noses and furrowed brows. The next three ships refused me. Phrases like "this is not a place for a little girl" or "I could not guarantee your safety, miss" followed me, and while the voices were full of pity, their gazes were condescending. They trailed down my worn appearance, lingering on my stomach. "We have no room for someone like you," one sailor even said. As if I was *that* kind of fugitive.

After walking the pier up and down, I had no choice but to trail back to the street. People were dangerous. Inns were dangerous. Sir Sigve was gone and only one other person had helped me in this cursed land, but he was gone because I made this choice.

Still... wasn't there a friendly girl in the market? Someone... or was it just the fragrance and savor of cake? She had been warm and caring, like Madalyn. Maybe she could help a poor, lost merchant's daughter.

I would have to find her. Walking through the market square in plain sight was beyond foolish perhaps, but I had no other brilliant idea swooping down to save me. I snuck through the streets, looked at no one and didn't linger, finally stepping out into the lion's den. The eyes of the stone dragons burned my neck as I hastened through the open space.

She sat at her stall, just as I remembered. The girl hummed a tune while rearranging her cakes, happily doing business with a man indulging his wife with a treat. As they disappeared, I stepped up.

"Welcome! What would you like—" The girl abruptly stopped, squealed, then let a small pastry slip through her fingers. With a quiet *thump* it met the ground, forever soiled. What a waste. "Princess Alvildi," she whispered.

"What?" My voice rang sharp between us. I closed my eyes, drawing upon stifling air until it seared at my lungs, and expelled it with care. Years of lessons in composure was the only force keeping me from falling apart. "You must be mistaken, but... thank you. Do I really look like a princess?" I twirled a stray lock of hair around my fingers, doing my best to look as if the day was bright and happy.

"Oh, I see. Please excuse me, Your Grace, of course you don't want to draw attention. It's admirable, for you to visit us like this." She was giggling, that girl, not believing me in the slightest. "Ah, I'm so honored! To think the princess would come before me, and it was only yesterday I learned about you."

"How?"

Sarina blinked. "How?"

"How did you know about me?" I clenched my eyes, unable to shut out the buzz of the market or Sarina's shuffling feet. I met her eyes. "No one's supposed to know who I am."

"Oh. Of course. Well, I heard it from Dalia who heard from her mother who was told by—well, I don't know. But everyone speaks of the northern princess with skin white as silk, hair touched by Rashim and eyes lush as Haya's floodplains."

"I see." My fingers went slack.

Sarina's brows furrowed and the smile drained off her wide mouth. "I hope I did not upset you."

I shook my head, unable to trust my voice.

"Please, would you take a cake, whichever you want."

My gaze zeroed in on a glazed, golden one, as if there could be no other. And surely, I deserved a bit of care and comfort.

She caught my longing eyes with the practiced ease of someone knowing her customers as well as their coin. "Here you go."

She placed the small cake between my fingers, and the tight knot in my stomach loosened a little. "Thank you, Sarina."

Her eyes widened to previously unknown dimensions. "Princess . . . you know my name!"

Whoops. It had just slipped off my tongue. "Ah, I . . . must have heard it somewhere."

The girl squealed. "I'm so honored the princess has heard and even remembers my name. Me! This must be the happiest day of my life!"

People turned toward the sound, ogling with dark orbs. If cake had been my medicine, it could not remedy the sea storming inside me now.

"Thanks. I hope you have greater pleasures in life than this, though."

Sarina ignored me with ease, lost in her star-struck happiness.

"Your payment." I dug through the deep pockets of my dress, scuffing against the knife rather than coins. Nothing. Then my sack, rummaging around, pushing items out of the way—when did I get it all?—until I found my sunken and small purse. If I met Sir Sigve again, I would be sure to carry more of our funds.

The market girl shook her head. "Oh no, I couldn't possibly—you're here, that is enough by far!"

I pressed some coins into her hand anyway. There were faces everywhere, people staring, peeling through the layers until they saw me, Alvildi, with no secrets and nowhere to hide. "Sarina. You know who I am. Please, I have come to *you*, seeking help. Will you help me?" It was fingers crossed for the perfect balance between reverence and pity.

Sarina almost fell off her stool. "I . . . I can help you? *You?* Your Grace, really?"

Her surprise lifted my lips with light. "Yes."

"How? Do you need cakes? I don't deliver . . . but for you, of course, I'll make an exception, naturally."

"Nothing like that." I took a deep breath. "I need a place to stay."

Her expression cleared like clouds dispersing in the sky. "Ah, of course. Well, there are several fine inns in this town, nothing to your standard of course, but if you would . . ."

"No. That's not quite right," I said.

Now she looked seriously confused.

"I need to be somewhere safe, with someone I can trust. I want to stay with *you*."

A myriad of feelings flitted across her face. She was easy to read, Sarina. Something along the lines of *not good enough* and *a dream come true*.

"Of—of course! You can take the bed. My place is small but clean, and this is such an honor, oh, what should I do?"

"Can I sit here with you in the meantime? I don't want to inconvenience you, and I definitely don't want any attention."

Sarina slid off her stool and gestured for me to come to her side of the table. She had such warmth in her.

I kept my gaze down, sat in the shadow of a building and behind a tableful of cakes. Hoping, putting my faith in this camouflage.

Sarina began expediting customers, picking out pastries and describing them, making sales. People went from her happy, coin purse a little lighter and waistband soon to be tighter. I had been one of them, once. What I would give to have that easy life again.

The weight of the cake was still in my hands. I deserved that pastry comfort.

The dough gave way to my teeth with ease, touching my tongue. Nothing. The rest of the pastry slipped between my fingers—I was beyond even the help of cake. Sirion might have had something witty to add to my situation. Sir Sigve would have been pleased, seeing it as restraints protecting my figure. If only I was with Madalyn again, she would have consoled me. Held me, braiding my hair by the warmth of the fireplace—she might even have made some inedible sweet buns in an attempt to replace the one I lost. Before the cake could swell in my mouth, I swallowed. *Home.* Yes, that was my destination, and nothing had really changed.

From behind the cake-stand I had an entirely different view of the market. Chaos aiding in secluding me. All around were colors. An energy to the air, a high spirit in the people. Children ran about, playing or going on errands. Sellers shouted the excellence of their wares to passersby with an enthusiasm not at all tainted by their repetitive line of work. Visitors let themselves be drawn into a flirting game of hackles, accepting flattery with more grace than parting with coins could usually inspire. From one moment to the next, it stopped.

Butterflies coursed through my body, with my limbs strong and ready to *fight, flight*—*run*. Forced myself to sit still, like a deer hiding in tall grass.

Someone, a young boy, pointed in my direction. The masses parted ways to let through three figures in black. Each from a different direction they came, making a formation, a triangle with me at the center. They strode forward, purpose their banner and determination their sword.

My death.

BALANCE

I rose with care, trying not to draw attention. With buckling knees, I had to lean on the table to keep upright. Inside of me, that sudden energy froze.

The men were already close and erasing the distance, the holes, there was nowhere to go.

No place would be safe.

As I had proven over and again, I could not fight them. There was nowhere to run. *Escaping*, that had been a silly, naïve dream.

From all parts of the market square, people turned to stare. Comprehension, unease, pity, *excitement*—there would be no help from the children, men, women, elderly, no one. No Sir Sigve, or Sirion, or Madalyn. Mother and Father . . .

I only had my knife. A quick slice. I drew a steadying breath.

What does it mean to die?

14

WHAT WAS LACKING

"I'm a dead man."

Phantom blood seeping down my hand, *red*, the cries, so much noise followed me when colors faded. It all disappeared when I opened my eyes and stared right into brilliant blue. His arm was slung around my waist. For the first time, waking up to something old was like a small victory. A new chance. A Do-Again of my own choice.

When he awoke, Sirion was in a foul mood. It was my fault, thrashing about with my nightmares and disturbing him. At least I didn't push him across the rough stone floor. If anything, he should be grateful. For me, the thought was scary—having lost the immediate response to waking up with this man beside me—and I did not want to get *used* to this. What would that say about me?

Sirion was still rubbing sleep from his eyes. He had yet to say anything.

My hands clenched around my blanket. "Good morning," I said.

After a shaky exhale, he pinched the bridge of his nose. Shook his head. Grunting, Sirion got to his feet and strode out of the room.

I sat in a sudden space of cold stone and silence. Was it that bad? After a while he returned, hair dripping and waterskins filled. Sirion placed the items on the table, then raked together a few of his belongings. The blankets were folded in messy rolls, not the tight, perfect cylinders I had seen him create before. He then set to prepare breakfast with a steady, grim determination, his eyes everywhere but on me.

"Did you sleep well?"

His eyes flashed my way before returning to his hands. His long fingers curled around a small knife handle, knuckles whitening to the task as he set the blade against meat and started shaving off slices to go with the dried mangos. Tea was next. With deeply rooted routines, he soon had a kettle ready, brew steaming hot inside. When he placed a second cup on the table, the sight of tea filling to the brim had never before inspired such relief in me.

I sighed, feeling boneless as I sat down to face Sirion. "I had a nightmare," I said at last.

After a fleeting glance, he nodded and continued the all-consuming task of looking down into the depth of his teacup, keeping religiously still.

With no idea what I had supposedly done to offend him and my attempts at conversation thwarted, we sat in an awkward hush. Perhaps I hit him while asleep? Kicked him repeatedly? Madalyn had never complained, but my sleeping habits might have developed some violent streaks, considering recent events.

"Did you sleep badly because of me?" I tried again.

Sirion buried his head in open hands. "I have a headache."

How stupid I had been, stating the obvious. Were those red marks on his cheeks? "I'm sorry." A piece of bread crumbled between my fingers. My split and torn nails, worn down from rough treatment on the road, which I might or might not have used on his face as I trashed and clawed against phantom foes.

"You don't need to apologize to me, Vildi." He looked so tired, as if lacking any shut-eye at all. His lines were deep, digging into the space around his eyes.

I closed my own. "I don't know what to do."

"About what?" Sirion lifted his gaze at last.

"My situation." What did I even want from this conversation?

"Sorry, don't mind my mood. It is not your fault." Sirion's eyes carried an apology, a soft exhale tilting his lips to tender warmth.

"Okay." I inhaled, discovering air which again was fresh and easy to breathe. Giving him a rueful grin, I shrugged. "I still don't know what to do. Seems like everything I try is wrong."

He blinked. Poor Sirion, being subject to my senseless rambling. Evading the crux of things, circling the problem, though unable to tell anyway. I knew he could not help me. But it felt good to talk about it, even like this.

"Sirion?"

"Yes?"

"Can we stay here a few days?" Five would suffice.

Sirion seemed to scowl at the meal sitting between us. "We have no food. Unless you want to live on one slice of fruit each day? We're eating the last of our rations right now."

"Oh." My teeth slowed down until the chewing stopped. With some trouble, I swallowed the precious mouthful. Only five days, and still too much.

"Besides, didn't you want to go home?" Sirion popped a slice of apricot in his mouth.

Eldaborg. Madalyn was waiting, perhaps a bit mad I had left her behind. Missing me. I should go back to her, relieve her of a princess-sized part of the pressure and attention. At least I could do some good. Brighten my days by offending the more unpleasant suitors, enough to make them leave. I would chase out a worm. And I could sit with my family again, eating under Mother's watchful eye, laughing with Father. Together we would empty barrels of mead. Could ride into the forest with my little brother, feel the wind on my face as I let my horse run at full speed. Would Tyra be available, or did they already put a foal on her? I squared my shoulders to the task at hand, returning to Rimdalir. "Yes, you're right. And I will. Never mind, I'll manage."

I snuck a glance at the man in front of me. Sirion had helped me, with no gain for himself, and he deserved better than the burden I might—would, with certainty—become if I stayed with him. Aransis was no safer than Fiar. Even if he offered again . . .

I was a danger to him. To everyone.

Sirion nodded and turned halfway away from me. His shoulders slumped around him, a dullness to his movements as he picked at his remaining meal.

We ate in silence after that, our last scraps of food. Our few belongings disappeared quickly into our bags. I fastened the knife at my belt, my palm lingering on the ebony handle for a moment. My pitiful protection. My hand clenched around it, the blade just on the edges of my fingertips and clean as if it had never been used. Do-Again a slice away. Glimpsing Sirion's frown, I closed my eyes. "I'm ready."

Sirion saddled our camels. We rode to the sound of slipping sand and the occasional gust of wind. But it always ended up that way, did it not? Perhaps there was not much to say. The decision was final, mutual.

We were about to split up, drawing near the same old juncture. Somehow, this time, the entire ordeal seemed lacking and dull. Another washed out repetition. But I still owed this man so much, more than he would ever know, and there was very little I could give. Well, maybe one thing, if he wanted it. "Sirion?"

"Yes?"

"You haven't claimed your prize." Even after one whole and two additional half—but for him forgotten—days of opportunities. Even though the whole 'ten tries, no lies' had been his idea.

"Huh?"

"For winning," I said. Decidedly so, with his six of six correct against my meager two.

Still, his eyes were blank.

"The game." I nudged Balt to take that extra step, daring myself to draw close.

Sirion stared at me.

My fingers itched, running restless against each other.

"It's fine. Don't need it."

"Oh."

He watched me, words appearing to burn on his tongue. "I'm not sure I should let you go by yourself," he said at last.

"I'm fine." There would be no deaths because of me. Besides, this was the last try. "I *will* make it. We will not meet again."

"I can come with you."

He could. I wouldn't be alone anymore. And perhaps he could protect me, just like Sir Sigve. Sir Sigve with his blood filtering through sand. Sir Sigve with his body broken on a tavern floor and daggers buried to the hilt inside him. I swallowed. Sirion. Sirion with a knife piercing his chest and the joke fading from his blue eyes, as if a cloud prevented the sun from shining on a lake. Sirion with his smile gone, froth coming out his mouth and— "I'm going alone."

"I hope you'll find your way." He didn't meet my eyes.

"Thank you. Really, for saving me. For everything." All our days together, those he remembered and those only alive in my memory. Pausing, I tried to ignore the push of tears and something heavy in my throat. "I wish you a happy life, Sirion."

He whirled around to look at me, and if I had ever seen determination in someone's eyes, that was it. "Vildi," he said, my name sounding odd from the tense set of his jaw. Sirion came closer, his arms sneaking around my back, running along my waist with a trail of flames, coming to rest at my hips. I was rooted, waiting. "Good luck." Abruptly, he let me go. The next moment, only dust and disturbed sand remained.

∼

Some hope returned as I again neared the outskirts of town. I knew so much. Surely, if I just tread with care, I would choose right and find my way home. This time for sure. It *had* to work.

"Hey, Balt?"

He flipped his ear back to listen.

"This time will be different. You'll see."

Balt snorted, tugging his head down as we descended a dune.

"I suppose that's right. You will not see it directly, but there will be no more Do-Agains. You'll finally be with your camel friends, and I'll be on my way to Rimdalir." My mind was heavy like my tired limbs. A hard knot held residence in my stomach, as black inside as my knuckles were white.

Balt trudged forward, climbing bravely atop heaps of sand. On the other side of a dune were the stables and Rahid with his caravan. Any further, and they would be able to spot us. We stopped, and I hopped off. Balt blinked with gentle, bewildered eyes.

"It's better to part here."

Balt tossed his head.

"Please." I felt like crying, as if this goodbye was one too many. "Balt." I leaned into his sturdy neck, let my arms circle around him. He relaxed into the embrace. My voice wouldn't come out right. Again, I tried. "I'll miss you."

He made his throaty sound, nudging my arm with the affection of a dear friend.

I let Balt loose. He would find his way without problems, and this time I could not afford to be seen.

He drifted about for a while, attempting to follow me even as I shooed him off. Confused, he tried again, and again I had to chase him away. Finally, Balt turned, plodding back to his home.

Alone.

My own steps took me circling around to enter Fiar a little way off the main road and the stables. The dunes were not particularly high here, close to the coast, but they were deep enough. Each step I sank down in sand, the track collapsing atop my foot faster than I yanked upward. Heaving myself up again seemed like an impossibly heavy task, though I managed somehow.

Finally, I was free of the dune and the ground was once more solid, rock hard against my thin shoes. With light steps, I almost flew across the distance. Even better, I faced the back walls of Fiar's small houses and snuck into the city from a deserted angle, unseen.

I didn't feel sick.

I went to the docks. A sailor glanced my way and a queasy twist lunged in my stomach. He had refused my request as I walked from ship to ship, enduring judging eyes.

Another sailor basked in the sunshine, the ship bobbing on gentle waves in the background. I sauntered up to the *Disandri,* right past the guard, lifting my head, trying to summon every speck of dignity, drawing upon the hundreds of lessons I had once fought to ignore. Madalyn would have been able to do it with ease and natural grace. For me, after months of pretending to be a simple merchant's daughter, putting on that air of royalty was hard. It had never been easy, but I tried. I walked up the ramp, done asking for permission.

"You're a little early, miss," the guard said, looking up from beneath his hat. Just my luck—why did he wake up at that particular moment? "Miss? Miss! Do you hear me? You cannot go there."

I didn't stop. "I'm just going to my cabin," I said, as if it was the most natural thing in the world. It fooled no one.

"You have to wait. No passengers are allowed to board the ship now. Please come back in a few days." His apologetic smile hardly helped.

I kept walking. "I am Princess Alvildi of Rimdalir, and my room is on this ship."

"Miss!" He grabbed my arm. "I don't care who you are. You will have to come with me." His grip tightened, no longer trying to be friendly. He dragged me down—it was either follow him or fall.

The sun glared at me, digging into my skin and sinking tendrils down my midsection. With my limbs numb and heavy, I noticed him releasing me and saw his mouth moving, telling me something. I shook my head. His pitying eyes followed me as I plodded away along the docks. From the other ships, more than a few sailors stared back.

I tried, I really did, but I couldn't summon up the courage, the strength to ask again. I was so, so tired. Turning, I wandered off the harbor, back into Fiar proper. My feet shuffled between stray cacti and my fingertips followed worn, old walls. My stomach was hollow, letting out the occasional grumble.

The streets were far from empty. People eyed me as if I was sick and kept their distance. It was stupid, of course, but I trudged forward in the middle of the avenue, kicking up dirt and pebbles on the way. Sneaking was pointless anyway, no?

Sarina sold her little cakes from her little market stall. What effort would it demand of me going over there, convincing her to take me in? A useless endeavor.

I hardly felt a thing. Only the wear and strain on my mind.

The sun was past its zenith, soon it would sink into the sea. Dragging myself around, I ended up at a new inn. The walls were light and the residents merry. Would it even matter? At least I got some supper, suited to calming both nerves and hunger.

It was almost time.

Cold sprung down my arms, nausea nestling in my belly. It was not the type of sickness from going hungry, solved by a good meal. The porridge in front of me sat forlorn, picked and prodded. Putting half a spoonful to my lips, I made another attempt but met the taste of ash, a lump growing in my mouth. My throat closed up. A shadow blocked the view out through the doorway. Forth from it, three men emerged.

Reliable like clockwork.

As on instinct, my hand flew to my belt. Even if it took a hundred attempts. Even if my mind frayed a little with each new death. My heart would be like steel. My fingers sensed nothing, nothing at all but clothes falling and folding in rivulets, empty beneath.

My knife was gone.

Arm sinking to my side, I released a long breath. What had I wanted to accomplish, anyway? To defend myself? Even Sir Sigve had failed to defeat them. Going back? But Sirion didn't want me around, given a choice. He had not offered again. That was only right with a burden like me. Marriage? Even his old proposal was empty—he had known I would refuse. The thought of repeating the day was as sickening as the sight of the men in front of me. It solved nothing.

The men advanced, their eyes zeroed in on me, and all around me people were moving away, leaving me open and all by myself on the floor as those predatory shadows neared. Alone.

My arms hung limp from my shoulders, my hands empty.

I had no strength, nothing left in my body. And so, it happened.

15

A DESOLATE NOTHING

I had been so stupid. Of course, I should have stayed with Sirion.

They surrounded me like an escort, but there was no mistaking my position as prisoner. They left little to no gap between them for my feet to shuffle across the ground, kicking up dirt as we moved through Fiar. Whenever I slowed down, a hand appeared to put pressure on my back, nudging me forward.

They loomed over me as a reminder I was tiny compared to these dark shadows. A crest sometimes peaked out from behind their deep green cloaks, golden against the black of their clothes. I hadn't gotten a proper look yet, but it was similar to those I had seen in the desert ruins: a ring, like the sun, and half a dragon circling it.

We entered the outskirts of this city of endings. I could not see Balt anywhere, but Rahid appeared as if summoned, four camels in tow.

"Your compensation." The leader of my captors dropped a heavy purse into waiting hands. He had a stern face, eyes tired and cold beneath coarse, short hair which held more gray than black. Apart from *'let us escort you, Your Grace,'* mocking my lack of choice in my own future, he had yet to say much of anything.

"Ah, my pleasure, absolutely a pleasure." Rahid produced a smug, groveling grin. His gaze didn't stray my way at all. No help from him—he was a person of business.

I didn't recognize any of the camels. "Rahid, did Balt return?"

Rahid blinked.

"The camel I rented," I explained.

His eyes flickered in my direction for a split second. "Ah, Great Princess," —not a title *I* recognized— "no worry, no. You esteemed self don't concern yourself with my camels." He bowed, beaming at a point somewhere to my left before he hurried away. Why would I ask if I didn't care? A push to my ribs reminded me of greater problems.

"Your Grace." Leader—which name he never dignified to indulge—gestured for me to come over, his youngling subordinate stressing the motion with another nudge. The sun sat low in the sky. They didn't mean to go further today?

They hoisted me up on a camel, mounting themselves moments after, heading straight for the desert. Why would they take me out there? They had always seemed content with doing me off at once. Maybe it was easier for them in a secluded place, with no one watching, saving them the trouble of explanations. Perhaps killing was the next best option to kidnapping. The words *'you are safe now'* held a meaning behind the jest I had taken them for. A victim with a sense of security made for a pleasant captive.

Golden Road was empty for as far as I could see. They kept a slow tempo. We rode in a loose formation with Leader first, then me, and the underlings taking up the rear.

"Where are you taking me?"

"We're escorting you to Aransis," one of the men said, his words lacking the trail of song so characteristic for the people of Lakari.

The youngest of the captors grinned as if we were the best of friends. He reached inside his coat to produce a piece of paper, waving it around with more heart than Father with his ale. "We have the royal decree if you want to see."

I crouched over a bout of nausea, goosebumps spreading as a wave up my arms. A Do-Again I couldn't remember? "What would be the use in that?" I already knew from the center of my bones to Sir Sigve's blood draining through sand—it was fake.

My new camel looked quick. Could I outrun them? I let my animal skid a little to the left, still in the path—a bit more, right on the edge—

"Oi, princess, straighten out!"

I dug my heels in the flanks of my poor animal and grasped loose strands of mane for my life, my future. We were running—shouts behind us—my mount was fast. Ahead of me was a protruding rock, too steep, I had to go around but to my left was the underlings in hot pursuit, to my right: Leader. It was over, a short stretch in.

"Please, Princess, don't make this difficult. We need you to come with us," Youngling said. With his smooth face, slightly skewed teeth and an attitude toward authorities, he appeared little to no older than me. He sighed, holding my camel still. "We're here to escort you."

"I don't want to be escorted anywhere," I answered, a stubborn streak flaring through my despair.

"We have our orders," the third man said, eyes flat and void behind tufts of dark brown hair. Streaks of silver glinted from his beard whenever he talked, though he was mostly silent. He had yet to show any emotion on his face. At least he didn't pretend with me, like Leader and Youngling did. I could trust him to be exactly what he appeared.

"This is for your own good," Leader lied, despite looking me straight in the eye. With brusque and forceful movements, he worked a knot, a rope tying the reins of my camel to his own saddle. The creature seemed to have no problems with the arrangements. That mount was no Balt, sadly. I felt no camaraderie with this camel. "What a waste of time," the man muttered, securing the final knot. His hands were of the tough, leathery type bearing faint scars in jagged bands, evidence of his experience.

The sky had taken on an indigo hue. Only a streak of orange lined the horizon.

They hoisted me up, slightly rougher than before. The young one gave me an apologetic look. "Don't try that again, Princess. The desert is dangerous. You must stay with us."

My eyes burned. I hardly knew how to respond. "I would rather have the desert." None of them heard me. Leader had already walked back to his camel.

BALANCE

We kept moving. They followed a little closer this time, even with my reins tied. Suffocating. I had nowhere to go, no place to rest my eyes where I wouldn't see *them*, and so I turned my gaze down. Hard, solid dirt, stones rounded by wind, smooth and numerous, all paving the ground. For each bend in the road, the terrain became rockier.

With the lead rope tying my camel to the leader's mount, I couldn't even attempt to outrun my captors. But perhaps I didn't have to. I didn't actually need to escape, I just had to be willing to die. To repeat. A simple Do-Again.

The sun touched the horizon and would soon be gone.

They had not strapped me to the saddle. The rocks were not jagged, but it should only matter that they were hard and sticking up irregularly along the road. It was a fair distance to the ground.

If I timed it right, aimed true from so high up, if I hit my head . . .

I flung myself off the mount.

Being airborne for that last second before the end, the moment stretched on, but I still knew it would be over in the blink of an eye, and I would wake up with Sirion beside me.

After the thud, I sensed only silence.

Abruptly, pain erupted within me. From my side, the arm taking the brunt of this fall and the air knocked out of me, though my head, ironically, I somehow managed to protect. Stupid instincts.

"Ah, Princess! Why did you do that? Who would even *do* something like this? So reckless." Youngling was off his animal in an instant, the others close at his feet.

"Are you hurt, Your Grace?" Leader looked down with a scowl as if I had personally offended him. He also appeared somewhat worried—wouldn't do to damage the goods, huh?

"Ah, ugh . . . no, not enough." With bruises blooming across my body and sharp pain, my head felt light. If I even twitched, I might throw up.

Youngling helped me to stand, moving slower than a snail, all the while keeping one arm around my waist. "Careful, steady. She's a little crazy, isn't she?" He nudged the third man while keeping a hand on my leg, hoisting me atop the camel.

The quiet one gave a grunt—neither assent nor disagreement. He barely seemed to acknowledge anything, the silent type.

Their leader gave them both a sharp glare. "You will *not* utter such words again. Better if you don't talk at all."

"Yes, Komir, sir," the young one replied.

Komir glanced at the sky, a deep, bone-tired sigh escaping him. "I would have liked more progress . . . but this will have to do. We'll make camp here."

"Understood," Silent said, the single word curt and clipped. The rude youngling nodded along, glowering at the ground.

They led me out of the road to a natural shelter formed of old rocks. They propped me against the stone wall, and through my haze of red pain I saw them buzzing in and out of focus. A fire sprang up in the middle of camp. Silent came by, pushing something into my hands. Dry, hard meat with no taste, and I had to tear off every scrap with my teeth.

BALANCE

I felt the ache recede with rest, enough to be more aware of my surroundings. The road was out of sight. If anyone traveled by, they might completely miss this inconspicuous campsite.

Komir sat by the fire, tearing off chunks of meat with a dark expression on his face. A little way off, Silent rolled out blankets in four piles. Presumably, one was for me.

Youngling sharpened his knives. First one, methodically and with sure movements as was his craftsmanship. Such loving, gentle care, executed for better killing later. After a while he began with a new knife, his tools following the curved blade with tender adoration. When he noticed my stare, he smiled, letting his thumb draw across the edge: the motion performed with absentminded familiarity. One drop of blood dripped to the ground.

Something cold spread from within me, overtaking my arms, hands, feet, numbing me until I had nothing more to give. Just sitting there with these men as my only company, looking, watching, with those sharp knives and unsettling grins.

In my childhood, Maya had whispered stories to the flickering fire as wax ran in thick droplets from our bedside candles. Her face had been scary and her voice fierce, saying: *don't let the mountain trolls take you.* I used to love her fairy tales.

I could not discern who they were, their intent, or their destination. Desert trolls? I was just like those fairy-tale princesses, but for me, no brave lad or prince was on their way to rescue me—not even Sirion—because we had cut our bonds, and I could not return. Sir Sigve, my protector, was not with me.

No way back. Regret or not, there were no second chances.

And if I remained a captive . . . these men clad in dark, surely, they had something in mind for me.

I felt the cold wash over me again, and I huddled with my arms wrapped around me against the desert freeze.

"Horasis, you get the first watch!" Komir's sharp voice threw my thoughts aside. "I expect proper behavior," he followed up, darkening a fraction more.

"Ah, yes, indeed!" The youngling—Horasis—bowed his head, all serious until Komir wandered off with a nod. Horasis turned to me, a jovial front melting into his features. His eyes sent a shiver down my back. The knives at his belt glinted in flickering red, orange flames—reflected in an instant and gone the next. "I will keep you safe, Your Grace."

I shut my eyes.

"You should rest, Princess Alvildi. Get some sleep." Komir's words were almost nice, his voice surely meant to be pleasant. He was cautious, I knew, when he helped me over to the bedrolls, hands careful not to hurt me. A repulsive touch on my skin.

But they did not tie me up.

It was a stroke of luck, likely given to me because I had managed to beat up my body just fine by myself. They expected no new resistance from the prisoner when even one captor was overwhelmingly stronger. They all slept, except that one unlucky guard. With less experience than his comrades, young and not gifted with any noticeable wit, if I should have any chance, this was the time.

Perhaps it would work.

I could not sleep even if I wanted to, thanks to the men on both sides of me who did not have that problem. Neither had Horasis. Although he sat propped up by the hard stone wall, his eyes slipped.

How could I possibly evade them in the desert? I was already hurt. And survive, without water, food . . . even if I took my mount, they would either wake up from the noise, catch up, or I would die alone between the dunes . . . but not before my chances of going back to a morning of freedom and safety disappeared forever. Sirion would not save me twice.

I didn't look forward to repeating. Not for what it cost me. More than the pain or the horrible, horrible familiarity, one wasn't supposed to live each day more than once. Still, I could not stay. What waited for me on the other end of this confinement was probably worse than death. And in that case . . . if I were to die, it would have to happen fast, or not at all. I could wake up with Sirion right there to hold me.

I had one chance: that red, curved blade.

Horasis' eyes closed one last time, soft snores joining the choir. I slid out of my blankets. He didn't move. I took a step forward and he stirred, mumbling something unintelligible as he came to rest again. I advanced once more.

A hand shot out and his fingers locked tightly around my arm. "Oi! What are you doing?" Horasis' large eyes went from mine to the arm he clenched, my fingers stretching uselessly toward the handle. Freedom was right there before me and still out of reach. "A knife is nothing for a little princess to handle," he snarled. His eyes were wide and frightened.

Someone stirred among the sleeping. "Horasis, what is this about?" Horasis shrank under the weight of his leader's heavy stare, impressive even in the clutches of sleep.

"She snuck up on me, sir. Tried to steal my knife."

"Isn't that your fault for letting it happen? Who was it that had *guard duty?*" Komir delivered a glare through his heavy, slipping lids.

Horasis folded further in on himself. "Me . . . sir. So sorry, sir."

"And you . . ." Komir turned his stern eyes on me. "Could you please not do that again?"

"Of course," I said, sneering. "I love being held captive, by all means, go on."

"You're not a captive." He yawned, rubbing a hand over his eyes. "We're escorting you."

"I see. *Escorting* me."

"Will you not cooperate?" Horasis asked, glancing at his tired leader.

I produced a flat stare. Even though they had forgotten, I remembered dark men and sharp knives a bit too well to be duped.

"Fine. I have to tie you up." Komir crawled out of his blankets, letting out a long breath like one would rid oneself of great evils. "Please forgive me, Your Grace. I'm sure you understand."

"I don't want to," I said, a stubbornness born within me.

Komir didn't dignify that with an answer.

He led me back to the blankets, and a rope found its way around my wrists. Komir had a grim expression throughout the entire ordeal, though I probably looked worse. At last, he was finished with me and stomped back to his bedroll.

As an afterthought, he turned one last time. "Horasis. If you sleep on watch again, you will be the one tied up. You should be aware that you are very close to losing your position."

With that happy thought, Komir went to sleep.

The fire was smoldering low, sparkling occasionally, simmering with slowly dying embers. Horasis sat straight and stiff, eyes wide and mouth ajar. He would not slumber again tonight. The sound of saw against unwilling wood already came from both the men flanking me, promising a long night.

It was too much—just this morning Sirion had been by my side. With the distant stars over me, the rope, and dark strangers my new reality, both Sirion and Balt felt eons away. Madalyn and home were a faded dream. Both paths I had missed, and now they were slipping through my fingers like the sands of time.

My eyes drooped.

I forced them to open, staring at the fire, peering at the stars, though there were no familiar patterns.

Without permission, my eyes closed again.

When I woke up, I sensed the aching protests of my bruised body and the harsh sun stabbing my eyes. After a night without dreams, I found myself still a captive. The three dark men hoisted me up on the camel and brought me further into a desolate nothing. This was my new reality.

Hope was gone.

SUNLIGHT ON SAND

Between their black silhouettes and sharp blades to the way they avoided other people like the plague, I had no room to escape. All we did was travel, kicking up clouds of dust as we went. There was no luster in the ruins we passed, and even the occasional glimmering oasis failed to soothe me.

They seemed to think a scrawny meal twice a day was plenty, and my stomach sputtered and grumbled until it could no longer rumble, settling for hollow, sullen silence. If this went on for long, I would soon shrink to something much thinner than my portraits attempted to present.

As my captors kindly reminded me, my appearance was far from pleasing.

BALANCE

I had barely rubbed sleep out of my eyes when Komir came looming, a frown firmly placed upon his face. "With all due respect, Your Grace, don't you have anything else to wear?" As if the small, sagging bag with my belongings had any room for an evening dress.

"I don't recognize this respect you speak of," I answered. If only acid could spill from a sour voice. "What does it matter how I look?" I would admit, though, clean clothes would have been nice, under other circumstances. "Am I to be sold?"

"Of *course* not." The man looked as if the very thought affronted him. Lying apparently came to him as easily as breathing. He gazed down his nose at me, lingering nowhere, looking generally displeased with the world. "It will just have to do, for now."

I shot him a nasty glare, wasted as he turned around to pack up camp, denying me even that small comfort. I slumped back down, closing my eyes for some short, stolen minutes. Sleep was only available for a few hours every night. Food shortage and sleep deprivation followed by extensive travel under the harsh sun throughout the day had worn me down.

"Wake her up, will you, Toleor?"

Feet shuffled closer. "Get ready," Silent said, intruding on my rest. His few words only added to the quiet in him, delivered with a low voice, his Alltongue gruff and punctuated. I tried to ignore his hand shaking me. "Don't go back to sleep. We're leaving soon." I heard him stretch with a groan as he stood up to gather his few belongings. Silent

Toleor was stoic and serious, dedicated and determined. Under other circumstances, I think I would have liked him. In some twisted way he reminded me of Hogne.

Perhaps it was dehydration or fatigue at work, but seeing him quietly lecture and chiding an outspoken Horasis, I felt a sting of nostalgia. The quiet, hardworking one, striving to achieve, working alongside the somewhat rude, talented friend to whom the results came easily. I missed the good summer days in the grass, bantering with Eirik as he struggled not to ogle Madalyn. Hugging Hogne. My sister's honest smile.

Kicking off my blanket, I stretched as far as my restraints allowed. With how the rocks dug into my back, only my tired state had let me fall asleep. Awake as I now was, staying on the ground seemed less tempting by the minute. With half-closed and blinking eyes, I sat up and chewed on the piece of meat Horasis handed me. Another day was about to begin, my fifth in this state.

I was still sore from my first day in captivity, and my skin bore marks of being scraped against coarse grains. Even worse were the cuts from my futile and less than lucky landing against rocks. My hands were always bound. Although my captors changed the ropes often to shake out sand, my wrists were red and raw. My hair tangled fast when left unattended. And who would have brushed it, anyway? I would rather cut it off. As it was, they made no attempts at grooming me—though they took excellent care of the camels. Prisoners were perhaps lower on the pecking order.

Safe to say, I no longer resembled a princess.

To be fair—they tried to take off the restraints again the second day, accompanied by scrutinizing eyes and a hearty display of fake royal decree. I behaved for hours without incident. In the late evening, as Komir and Silent Toleor had gone to sleep, I sneaked off toward the camels. But Horasis was way more alert this time, catching me even before I left the campfire's circle of light. The bindings never came off after that.

From being a dead place, cacti popped up more often on each side of the road, announcing a change in the landscape. The sun was only halfway up in the sky when I spotted buildings on the horizon. They grew as we got closer, their shapes a little too familiar: the white walls, small constructions getting bigger further in, leading up toward a towering palace at the very heart of the city. Aransis.

Last time with Sirion, we had strolled through the wide, light streets of Aransis' better areas. After the first few, bright roads, we took a turn and the familiarity ended. Although the city was constructed to let eyes always wander back to the palace, the streets we entered were narrow and dark. My captors didn't exactly sneak, but perhaps that would have looked even more suspicious. Instead, they indulged in dark alleys with dusty paths and the occasional signs of poverty. A few people played an instrument, their cases open to any coins a passerby could spare. The music held unfamiliar rhythms and tunes, in harmony with songs which words I didn't understand.

But as we moved deeper in, beggars replaced musicians. It was the kind I had seen in all cities of any significant size, as if extravagant riches always ran hand in hand with the greatest poverty. It was still a strange and sad sight for me. In Rimdalir, some were rich, and some were poor. But none were left without a roof over their head. Hands were never idle if they could do some good, honest work. Then again, Rimdalir was a small country, and even Eldaborg was a farmland town at its heart. Or perhaps it was the climate. A beggar without a home and a hearth would simply die come winter.

Aransis was different. It was a real city. Real beggars. I breathed a little easier, the twinge in my chest receding as we again entered brighter roads.

A woman crossed our path, carrying a basket full of sheets. She wore simple brown clothes, her hair covered by a green shawl. She looked like a mother, the strict but kind type. "Please." Despite an effort to yell, my voice came out raspy and raw from thirst and lack of use. "Help me?"

Komir hushed me to silence, glowering at my offense. "Don't mind her," he said, still watching me. "There is nothing to see here."

The woman stopped. Her gaze swept over us. After a hurried bow, she hastened off with the basket bumping against her legs.

No aid would be forthcoming from her. Not surprising, of course. What would a random woman be able to do, anyway? It was a fool's attempt, desperate hope. But maybe, just maybe, she would speak of a girl with blonde hair, would tell the right people—whoever they were—perhaps the authorities would get wind of a foreign girl being held captive in their city. By some streak of luck, Sir Sigve might hear the rumors.

"Don't talk to the people," Komir commanded.

"Why not?" I snapped. "You are no company."

Waiting for a rebuke, I shut my eyes. Once again, my mouth worked faster than my head. Well, my situation was about as bad as it could get already. And they wanted me alive, sadly, or I would have escaped this predicament on the very first day.

Komir said nothing against me. He did not lift his hand at me. He exhaled, motioning for us to continue down the road. "You are not presentable, Your Grace. You should not be seen looking like . . . that." His explanation did little for me. I already knew they strove to avoid attention.

"Would look too suspicious, huh?" I asked, wishing sarcasm would somehow become poisonous.

Horasis glanced at me. "Well, you would. And you need a bath, Princess."

Toleor shook his head, eyes narrowed in a glare. "You should not speak to the princess like that." He almost sounded angry with how he cut each word in its tail. Defending the captive? What a strange thing to do.

Shushing us, Komir led his little group with sure strides deep within the city walls. Each new road added to a network of similar paths, like a labyrinth of sandstone walls. He knew where to go.

For every street we crossed, the houses changed, getting bigger, cleaner, whiter. The people donned far too fine clothes to haul their laundry across streets or push carts overflowing with wares. Instead, they strode leisurely past the alleyways, some couples with linked hands, sometimes men enamored in what looked like deep and important discussions. Even when I called for them, they barely spared a glance at the travel worn group in the shadows of their homes.

Finally, we stopped in a side street outside an establishment of sorts. Dresses, shawls, and other garments for ladies of a certain class were on display. Komir hurried me inside.

A woman with deep red clothes in several loose-fitting layers greeted us with a seller's smile.

Komir answered, gesturing to my less than pristine attire and my possibly filthy face. The woman nodded, and her lips ever curved to please. They spoke Lakarian, that singing, incomprehensible language.

She closed in on me and began tugging on my clothes, prodding them with the tip of her finger. I didn't need to understand her spoken word to know she found them foul.

"Hello," I said.

No response.

"Don't you know Alltongue? I'm a captive, can't you see that? Will you save me?"

The woman frowned, looking at Komir. He shook his head. "Her grace has an interesting sense of humor," he said. Komir stood with a straight, stiff back, the kind meticulously drilled into the body from a young age, put to use in formal settings. Or, as Sir Sigve sometimes demonstrated, when one's sense of security was under attack.

"So far, I must consider Lakari less civil for each hour I spend here." Nails dug into my palms.

Komir shifted his weight.

"Kidnapping, captivity—even lack of the common language among such . . . fine society."

"I understand Her Grace well," the woman said, her Alltongue sharp and perfect but for a slight lilt.

"Oh." Of course, she was with them. Possibly the link between the men and their customers. They would sell me to someone wealthy, most likely a noble, rich man with a taste for young princess. The thought sent a shiver down my back.

Komir sat down, making himself comfortable. Clearly this could take a while.

The woman shushed me into a dark room behind the counter. As my eyes adjusted to the dim light, I saw two girls readying a bath, water frothing with soap.

"Please strip, Your Grace." The woman made a gesture to the general vicinity of the room, too vague to actually tell me anything. "My daughters will help you."

I eyed the bath. It looked wonderful, a promise of cleanliness. I could also make myself difficult, refuse to even lift the hem of my dress. What a meager help that would be. The only way out of the shop, from what I had observed, was going back again, passing Komir. Only in my imagination was I able to escape on my own—how many failed attempts had I experienced now? Even with Sir Sigve, it might not have been enough.

"She is awfully dirty," one of the girls noted, waiting on me with dimples and white teeth on display. She was the oldest by a couple of years at least, with the plump and simple beauty I had seen in a few of the wealthy people we had passed earlier. In Rimdalir she could have been a wife already.

"Dirtier than the floor at week's end," the other chimed in. She was still a solid foot within childhood, her amiable smile accentuating round cheeks.

"She is," I agreed. I didn't need a mirror to know they were right. I had not expected them to *say* it, though.

The water looked warm, filling the room with steam. The oldest girl poured something resembling oil in the tub, and the fragrance of jasmine enveloped us. She moved with leisure and grace, deceptively relaxed, as if I was one in a hundred filthy captives she had washed.

Eyes turned toward me. Eyebrows rose. I undid the buttons, one excruciating after another, pulling the dress over my head. At least I would get clean.

The girls scrubbed at my sore skin, their swabs flaying off grime from the road as well as crusts from my wounds.

"I wish my skin was so ghostly pale," the first girl said, poking me with an experimental air, amusing herself as I turned white from her touch, then red again as soon as she let go.

"Mother would never be able to send us out during dayburn," the other agreed.

"You can wear a cloak," I suggested, remembering the sun's heat like a finger getting too close to a fire. But any conversation was welcome if it could take the thoughts off my situation.

"I would not want to stay inside all the time," the first girl decided, ignoring me. "I don't need her skin."

"Neither would I," the younger said.

"Why don't you speak Lakarian, if you insist on insulting me?" I crossed my arms in front of my chest.

"Is my Alltongue bad?" the younger girl asked her sister.

The older girl shook her head. "It would be terribly rude to not speak so the customer understands. Mother is pleased with us."

The younger one beamed, returning to her swab, working with renewed vigor. My cuts burned.

Giggling among themselves as they worked, they turned my arms over and around, even going as far as scrubbing my nails.

"Don't you think her eyes look like the withering death?" the youngest girl said, leaning forward with a wide-eyed stare. I blinked, unable to hold her gaze.

"That only looks green because of the bottle," the other answered. "But I once saw a bottle of withering death in her shade exactly."

I didn't know what the 'withering death' was and had no desire to find out. Feeling my stomach churn, I swallowed and closed my eyes, blinking to keep tears away.

My hair refused to untangle, even though they poured oil in it and attempted to coax the brush through the knots again and again.

"Her hair is terribly fine," the oldest girl said. "So pale, like sunlight on sand."

"Reminds me of Liva and Avil." The other combed her fingers through my locks, yanking to a stop against a tangled mess.

"The dragons?" I asked.

"A pity it is in such poor condition," the first said, throwing me a reproachful look. As if that was *my* fault. And none of them bothered to give me an answer.

By the end of their handling of my body, I was in more pain than before, although I had to give them one thing—at least I was clean. Even my hair had come around, untangling and drying up fast to float about as I moved. From the light of slowly burning oil lamps, it seemed to shimmer and glow.

My old attire, created through painstaking hours with a sharp and unforgiving needle, was thrown away like filth. They laughed at my protests, frolicking about as they forced me into new and 'much better' clothes. The fabrics were soft, silky, emitting a sweet fragrance, and above all: they were clean. And they were easy to move in. On the downside, they clung to my frame, revealing more than my old ball gowns, with only sheer, see-through texture shielding me from the eyes of men. Had the attire attracted even a hundred suitors, Mother would not dress me in such garbs.

My shoulders were *bare*, and certain... assets accentuated, with how deep the neckline cut down—both back and front. The skirt was long and flowing and *would* have been decent, if not for the *splits* at the side, and barely some flimsy, transparent fabric beneath. The only thing familiar with this get-up was the belt at my waist.

It was a gown fitting its purpose—to sell me.

The lady from before, the owner of the establishment, came in, examining me with her cold eyes. "Good, she's finished," she said. With hands at my back pressing me forward, I walked with tentative steps out to the front room. I tried forcing the blush off my face, to little success.

"We could do nothing to remove her cuts and bruises," the shop owner said with disdain, eyes scrutinizing everything from bare arms to bound waistline. "But we put on some salve, and it should heal."

Komir looked pleased for once. He was not alone. Horasis the Rude almost devoured me with his eyes until Toleor gave him a sharp hit to the back of the head. I could imagine Hogne standing there in Toleor's stead, turning away for my sake, grinning and giving me a wink when no one was watching. Silent Toleor, of course, did none of those things.

"For your silence, ma'am," Komir rumbled, and a purse of merry coins found a home in the hands of a delighted, nodding seamstress.

"Of course. You know you have my discretion, Komir." The woman bowed down, generously showing off her cleavage. When she came up, I glimpsed gold between her fingers. She would keep her word.

When we left the shop, my old clothes lay in an abandoned bundle on the floor, along with my dignity.

THE NORTHERN STAR

My captors did not hide anymore. They marched down the main road, surrounding me like barriers to the world beyond. Between their dark forms, the tall buildings, and the people watching us, I became a small, insignificant thing. Alone. Even my camel was foreign, despite our days together. He was no Balt.

Few people occupied the streets, but a crowd would not have helped. The people who saw us moved aside to let us pass, bows and reverence following in our wake. Young girls, old men, motherly women coming to buy groceries—it did not matter. There would be no aid from them.

It got worse.

We were headed to the heart of the city, with elegantly dressed people strolling around as if the world held no problems. A place filled with nobles. The sun crowned the palace, illuminating white stone. Immense walls with long shadows. Big, ornamented gates opened upon our arrival, the sun with its circling dragons shining proudly above us as we passed beneath, a sound like thunder vibrating through the air as gate doors slammed shut behind us.

Each of my small steps sent a pling through the halls as the soles of my new shoes connected with hard stone. The corridors ran deep. They might as well have taken me into a mountain, despite how spacious and bright the place was. For each new path, door, corner and turn, I got more lost. I would never find the way out by myself, and it could just as easily have been a troll waiting for me in the innermost chambers.

How did the stories go, all those folklores about princesses and the Hulder race? What fate awaited the stolen and spellbound girls?

Do-Again offered no escape. What choices were left? Even if I used weeks finding an exit, surely in such a vast palace one could hide and live off snatched food until a way out appeared? But this was such a grand place, of white marble and gold, and I had yet to see a dark corner. Passing a window, I looked outside. With a dizzy, spinning head, I decided to keep some distance to the view for a while. Climbing was out of the question.

The *Disandri* had left while I was in captivity. Turned back home, probably without Sir Sigve and definitely without me. Was I to be a captive in the Lakarian court? What did Lakari want from Rimdalir, a small kingdom so far away? We were not rich by these standards, and my parents could offer nothing such a grand place didn't already have in abundance.

"We are close, Princess. Please behave." Komir talked with a rumbling voice carrying far through the corridors, a frown digging deeper into his features each time he peered at me. Even his underlings appeared concerned, Horasis, fidgeting restlessly, Toleor, always silent, pursing his lips. As if noticing my lingering gazes at the doors and windows, Horasis produced a shawl from a satchel and draped it around my arms and back. It looked pretty enough and hid parts of my bare shoulders and the less than pristine state of my skin. No amount of scrubbing had removed the purple yellowing bruises or the myriads of tiny cuts. The thin cloth hung loose, but it allowed them to inconspicuously hold on to the ends and again, in a sense, tie me up. They could pull and yank at me on a whim. Silent Toleor kept a tight grip on both the shawl and the scowl adorning his face.

We came to a corridor grander than the last, entering a room whose sole purpose seemed to be the doors across the marbled floor. A room for waiting. Inside, restless and pensive, I finally found a familiar face. I wanted to run to him, embrace him, even let him ruffle my hair as if I was ten years old again, and above all: let him escort me home. "Sir Sigve!"

Upon hearing my voice, he turned. "Lady Vildi!" With tension dissolving from his features, my companion looked ten years younger. He rushed to my side. "Thank the gods."

"You're here! I was afraid you'd—but you're fine. You're well and here and—and everything will be fine." I sniffled, feeling my tears threatening to breach the surface.

Sir Sigve's lips twitched as I fumbled through my words. "I am glad to see you safe, my lady." Then, as the novelty of relief lifted, his face stiffened. "Though you would have been all along, had you stayed with me." His voice was curt and clipped. I had lied and abandoned him in the middle of nowhere . . . I even forgot to leave a note. Yes, he was surely enraged, and had every reason to be.

I glanced around us, taking a step closer. "Do you know anything, Sir Sigve? Please, since you're here, you must know what this is all about. I . . . I'm scared." Toleor still held the shawl. Komir stood like a solid, frozen trunk. Horasis turned his gaze away from me. My captors were so skilled in pretending everything was fine.

"If you had stayed with me, Lady Vildi, you would have had nothing to fear," Sir Sigve said, his composure cracking word by word. The benefits of his relief faded a bit too fast for my liking. "Ah, yes, and thank you for asking, my lady. 'Are you well, Sigve, how have you been since I *left you in the desert.*'" Sir Sigve's eyes flattened to slits. "After you *abandoned* me without a word, I went to Aransis. I had hoped to find you here, but of course you were nowhere to be found, and no message either. I contacted the authorities, as you can see, and it turned out we were expected. They had already sent out an escort to fetch you, which I suppose would be these gentlemen." He gestured to my captors. "Well, that is how I ended up here."

"These gentlemen, as you call them, explained nothing to me." I clenched my fists, my polished nails biting flesh. Komir stared ahead with a stiff glare, not reacting to my words. Lying. As if I hadn't died over and over by their hands.

"You never listen," Sir Sigve said, not softening up at all. His scowl would put Maya's to shame. "If you hadn't *left* like you did . . ."

"We told you many times, Your Grace, that we were escorting you," Horasis chimed in.

"You could not expect me to believe you after everything." I gave the man one of my prized glares, though he hardly even blinked. "I'm sorry for leaving you," I tried, turning back to Sir Sigve. "I had reason to—"

"You can thank the gods you are still alive." Color rose in Sir Sigve's face, his fingers whitening around the hilt of his sword as each word whipped at me. "Going into the desert alone as you did."

"I know! Okay? I know that. I had a good reason." My voice sounded thin. Despite my best effort to push them down, tears filled my eyes. I cast my gaze away, finding the black streaks in the marble floor a relief.

Sir Sigve sighed, relenting. "At least you are safe now."

I glanced at my captors. Safe, he said. Their knives were half hidden by their cloaks, peeking out just enough to never let me forget their existence. Silent Toleor clenched the shawl that was holding me in place. I swallowed. "Sir Sigve, please. Let us go home?"

"My lady . . ."

"We can pick strawberries by the roadside, ride in the forest and eat Torvald's sweet buns. Let's celebrate Madalyn's birthday together."

"I'm afraid not." Pinching the bridge of his nose as if attempting to stave off a headache, Sir Sigve closed his eyes.

In the silence that his voice left behind, the rustling of clothes and the intake and exhale of breaths became sharp, jarring noise in my ears. Even the spacious chamber seemed to push in on me with three captors surrounding me and Sir Sigve standing still and unmoving, unrelenting.

My first tear fell. I squashed down the rest of them with a deep breath. "Why am I here? Do you know?"

"Yes, my lady . . ." His eyes shifted, as if something fascinating caught his attention beyond my shoulder. A piece of paper stuck out from one of his pockets. "You have an audience with the royal family. It is marriage, Princess."

Someone in heaven was having great fun from within their gilded hall. *Don't laugh at me,* I thought, looking up. Not one god deigned to reply, of course. Only Hogne cared for me.

Coughing, Sir Sigve claimed my attention anew. "There was another letter, apparently. Meant to reach us as we came to Lakari, but we left Fiar too soon to receive it."

"How did they know where we would . . ." I trailed off. The reason held my gaze without a shred of shame or remorse. "Lovely." I hadn't known he reported home, but I should have expected it.

"I didn't know, Lady Vildi. I also thought we could return to Eldaborg."

I failed to meet Sir Sigve's eyes. Snatching the offensive piece of paper from his outstretched hand, my fingers fumbled to unfold it. The message was written in an elegant hand, letters long and curling at the ends. Mother.

Rimdalir offers, upon the Crown Prince of Lakari, their alliance by the hand of its Northern Star, Her Grace, Princess Alvildi Gudmundsdatter . . .

I crunched the piece of paper within my fist. The only difference between being made a plaything as a prisoner and getting married off was this: in the latter case, there would be no rescue. They would rather throw a huge feast through Eldaborg, or the whole of Rimdalir even. Seven nights, seven days and all that. And it was irreversible.

"Sir Sigve..." A nervous laugh escaped me. "Surely, I don't *have* to go through with this?"

My former companion—my family, really—cast his eyes away, out through the window to an orange sky and freedom out of reach. "I am truly sorry, Lady Vildi. There is nothing I can do."

"Why?" My throat constricted.

"It has already been agreed upon by your parents and his." Sir Sigve bowed his head, as if he could excuse Mother and Father for selling me out. Or perhaps he lamented being the reason they discovered this opportunity to ruin my life.

"But... but if I... why would Lakari want me?" My mind raced, fumbling after some solid argument, finding only questions. "What can I do for these people? And the *crown prince?* Please tell me this is a joke—I'm not fit to be queen! I'm not Madalyn."

No one answered.

Wait. "I can make them break the agreement. These things are never truly settled before they meet the candidate, anyway."

"That's usually true." Sir Sigve dragged his words as one pulling teeth. Fingers combed through his beard as his gaze once again trailed past my shoulder. "By the letter, it seems that was the intention in your visiting this court. But after I arrived here, they have made it clear they now insist on the match."

"Still, if I only show them how—"

"My lady!" Was that fear flashing through his eyes? "You will *not* behave as you did back home. These people will not accept your insults as brazenly as your father did." A crease appeared between his brows. "I doubt it would work, anyway. As I said, they seem set on this marriage, despite the situation already being quite unfortunate. Something about their traditions. They seem to consider the bond already made."

An urge to tear at my clothes, run, smash something, *anything,* bubbled inside me. It was impossible, though. Bad behavior was my greatest weapon too. For it to be ineffective was almost unbelievable. If I was absolutely nasty, even these people would not want me. "An audience, you said? I could—"

Sir Sigve shook his head. "Don't even think about it! It will not work."

"But . . . this is me. And marriage. How can Mother and Father consider this a good idea? I won't go through with it!" This was *my* life on the line.

The shawl tightened around my arms, released the next second. A warning. My life was already in their hands.

Sir Sigve's gaze hardened. "Now, Lady Vildi, I'll be with you throughout it all. I will stay by your side, most likely after the wedding too." His voice strained against his own statement. He braved onwards anyway, always loyal. "You will neither be alone nor abandoned in this land."

"I have . . . no way to escape?" A bird passed the window, letting a breeze carry her far away.

"No, my lady."

The bird was a speck in the sky. "What if I say 'no' at the ceremony?"

"I doubt you would get the chance. *Or* like the consequences if you do."

The bird was gone. "I will be married to a stranger." The pressure threatened to again break out from behind my eyes.

Sir Sigve watched me with something akin to sympathy. "I'm afraid so." His gaze trailed away, landing on my wrists. "Why is my lady *bound?*"

Komir coughed, straightening his back even further. "Of course, only for her own safety. We could not risk her getting hurt, and the roads can be dangerous. It would not be necessary if she didn't try to escape."

"For us as well. I don't want to be stabbed while I sleep," Horasis said. "I don't understand what His Grace wants with her anyway, suicidal and craz—" A hand over his mouth abruptly cut him off. Maybe also Toleor's elbow in his ribs. I secretly hoped it had been painful. It felt like justice, just a little.

Toleor slowly released his grip on me as a man in fine robes with an upturned nose strutted up to us. "It is time. Please follow me."

He led us through the door, the type which cracks in the middle and opens to the side, complete with bowing footmen and fanfare. We arrived in a throne room decorated with golden dragons and a well of flowers on white walls, its ceiling a long way up and vast windows letting sun and wind in.

"Her Grace, Princess Alvildi of Rimdalir and her escort, Sir Sigve Sturlason." The announcer had a clear and strong voice, giving me no room to sneak off into a corner. Well, the men surrounding me had a share in the blame. Again, all eyes were on me. Including the beady pair of the person in regal attire up front, seated on an enormous, wide throne of white marble and golden framing, puffy orange silk pillows stacked around and beneath his royal shriveled limbs. A shiver ran down my back. Was I to be married away to that old *thing*?

Komir strode up to the man, bowing before the throne. "I could not deliver Her Grace unscathed to you, King Illion. I am prepared to repent."

"Did you try?" My shrill voice received only silence in the vast space around me.

The king stared down at us from his podium, looking thin and haughty on a seat large enough for two to share comfortably, with precious metals clinking as he moved. "We *forgive* you, Komir. You did *well* in getting her here *at all*, as we understand." He talked as if every other word held special importance, making it all sound rather odd. "Leave us. *Everyone*," he emphasized, wizened pale-blue eyes sweeping over his court of elegant and improperly dressed folk.

People shuffled out of the room, expensive red and green fabrics swishing with their steps. Before they left, they all dipped into deep bows. The audience chamber looked even bigger after its inhabitants, my escorts included, disappeared.

"I'll be right outside, Lady Vildi." Sir Sigve put a heavy hand on my shoulder, letting it warm me for a second before he turned to leave. "Take courage."

The doors closed with a sharp and final *bang*, leaving me alone on the floor in front of Lakari's stern and odd king.

Well, almost.

As I let my gaze wander away from the commanding sight up front, I found the person sitting to the side of the throne. Despite the shadows almost touching him and the unfamiliar, loose and rich clothes he wore, I knew him. The way he lounged in his chair. The smirk lingering across his lips.

"Sirion," I breathed, taking two steps toward him. My heart skipped a beat, and I felt this tiny shiver of . . . relief? It nestled within me, latched onto something in my chest. Sirion was my savior. I could run to him, and he would protect me. Even if he didn't care for me, he would help. It was *Sirion* sitting there before me. It was him, and yet my feet froze to the floor.

"Vildi," he acknowledged. His hair stuck up at odd angles. "Welcome. Seems like I don't have to go to Rimdalir for you after all." With his place up there, an unreachable distance away from me, Sirion seemed to have settled into his role just comfortably. Lounging, his legs stretched agreeably, arms idly resting with a glass of wine in one hand, grapes within easy reach of the other.

I stood in front of him, on display in these foreign clothes, far from home. Sirion was my intended. And his grin grew for each second that he held my gaze. As if the world was bright and beautiful, he beamed down at me.

I had thrown myself off a camel to reach him. I had been a captive because of him. It was for his sake Lakari forced this marriage. Sirion. But of course: he was a noble.

"It *shocks* us," the king boomed, his voice lilting up and down with every word. "That a princess, worse, *our* next queen, would not *present* herself to us when she arrived in *our* kingdom." He shook his head, earnestly grieving my deplorable actions. "And you even *ran*. It is a *disgrace*, and we *would* annul this betrothal, if not for certain *circumstances*."

"Well, I was shocked too," I snapped, renewed anger fueling me past the initial speechless surprise. "I didn't even know anything. Why would I ever want to present myself?"

The king regarded me as something akin to an insect underneath his boot. His wrinkled face contorted in a grimace. "If *you* had let my men escort you, as was *proper*, this would have been avoided. Please *show us* at least a *speck* of dignity."

An absolutely immense headache threatened to announce itself. "Escort? There was nothing proper about it, a—"

"Propriety *demands*—"

"Your soldiers killed me! Did you know?" My voice fell dead to the floor, silence ringing stronger than any shouts in their wake.

"Vildi," Sirion said, words slow and careful. Any trace of his usual smile had disappeared. "Those were not our men."

I blinked.

Sirion's expression didn't change.

"What?"

"We don't know who was after you, but this was an attack on the crown, through you." Sirion's hand came up to upset already agitated hair. "We're trying to find out who they are, but we have so little to go on. You should be safe within the palace walls, though. And you'll have guards just in case."

"With *unrest* stirring within Tolona, our nation needs to show *strength*. There should *always* be two *together* on the throne of Lakari," the king supplied. "And I am *alone.*" He looked quite concerned, even sad. I almost felt sorry for the old king. But these were Lakari matters dooming me to marriage. "My son *needs* a wife."

"You benefit from this alliance, I'm sure. And such a marriage will be nothing more than a trade between two countries." I admit, I sounded more than a little bitter. To them, any girl would do, anyone could fill that vacant spot on the throne. I was nothing more than a convenient solution, unwittingly knocking on their door in their hour of need. Still, my voice hardly carried through this enormous stone room.

With his lilting, singing Alltongue, the King cut off my rant. "A throne of one is *wrong*, weakness is being *alone*." His hands spread as if presenting some great, verbose treasure, gold glinting off his fingers.

He was playing a game I knew well. This king wanted security for his kingdom, for his son. Surely, he would respond to reason? "You must see, I am neither suited nor inclined to sit on your throne. Rimdalir is far away and cannot offer Lakari more than an alliance in name. You must find your queen somewhere else."

Siron's foot tapped against the floor. His gaze darted over to the king before snapping right back to me.

With his high throne and crown, that old, wrinkly man slit his eyes as if I was a pesky fly buzzing rudely in his grand presence. "You will honor the *promise* made and marry my son. This is your *duty* as a woman, as a princess to your homeland, and to your *parents*."

Mother's voice rang in my mind like an echo of Lakari's old king. *Your duty, Alvildi, as a princess of Rimdalir . . .*

everything I had left to escape. "I will have you know, I did not come here as a princess, but an adventurer."

Sirion shifted his weight in the chair, eyes widening at each word.

"Even if I was aware of these . . . arrangements, why would I give myself away to a stranger?"

On his throne, the prince flinched.

That old king appeared unfazed by my speech, though perhaps he reached peak disapproval a long time ago. Like typical noble arrogance, more used to people groveling at their feet than someone standing up against them. They stood between me and home. As if cloaked by silence, Sirion stared me down.

"I came here to explore, not for *marriage*." I nearly spit out the word. It was not supposed to happen like this, and a new flame of anger flared past my exhaustion. "Sirion, you know I don't want to marry."

Finally, those blue eyes slid away.

My heart beat the drums of life, of power and helplessness, strength and weakness in my ears.

Sirion lifted his head, revealing eyes as dark as a deep sea, where a victim could easily drown. "Why would I want someone so dead set on not having me?" Studying his hands, he lifted the glass between long fingers to take a sip of wine. "You're not the only one forced in this situation. Did you really think your parents would let you leave for this journey without some motive? I have a father too, as you can see." Sirion gestured flippantly in the direction of the king. "This entire thing—that's between them."

"Why didn't you tell me—" The question stilled in my throat. After all, I had not told him either. Still, was it possible for him to have been unaware? Coincidences like that simply did not happen, right? Besides, *he* wasn't surprised.

"Your family apparently saw this as an opportunity. Something to benefit both kingdoms. And getting a leash on their disobedient daughter, it was a win-win situation." The words of the king had cut, but this was worse. Sirion plucked a grape, crushing it with his teeth with a well-known, careless elegance. "Their Northern Star."

Numb, I felt a coldness from my fingers creeping up my arms, reaching inside me to weigh me down. I swallowed against the nausea, fighting for control. Tried to push past the memories of unwanted, wandering hands, an intimate and oily voice whispering *'my little star,'* the sneer as he peered down and up again. He was not here, of course. Only the title had followed me. Letting my nails bite into skin, the sting brought me back. "I did not choose that name." Old and familiar fury flooded in, filling me with ice.

"I can imagine," Sirion said, grimacing. "A frozen beauty, I heard, unreachable like your namesake. Cold and uncaring."

"Let me go home." Somehow, with a tight grip around the skirt, I kept the shaking out of my voice. The shawl around my shoulders hung loose, tips trailing the ground. Quality shackles of red thread, even if no visible hands clenched around the ends anymore.

"For better or worse, you will end up by my side." Gazing down as he did, Sirion's eyes were cast in the flickering shade from his hair in the candlelight. "It was decided as you stepped on Lakari ground. None of us can change that, even if we, as you put it, 'let you go.'"

"Then why in glacial hell did you help me?"

The king wrung his lips in disgust. Well, I would be the most unpleasant queen they ever had.

Sirion smirked, lacking even the decency to be at least a little unsettled. "Well... a test of destiny, perhaps. Or maybe the superior strength of my character. I couldn't very well let a damsel in distress die." He raised his head, observing me from his high place. "As a gentleman, it was my duty to escort you. You can leave if you want. But the match is decided. The easiest and safest way would be for you to stay."

"We have sent words to your *parents*," the old fossil droned from his throne, shuffling about. Perhaps the fluffy pillows made for uncomfortable seating, if one occupied them long enough. "With a month and a half to the *wedding*, they should have sufficient time to send a *representative*, should they want to."

That was it. Even Father would not help me this time. It hurt. Blinking did not stop the water from rising, and there would be no comfort. Every effort to conceal my unsteady voice fell short. "If that is all, please excuse me." I turned, walking alone under the enormous roof toward my new imprisonment.

"Vildi," Sirion called, forcing me to halt and look at him. "I don't agree, you know, on your title. With your eyes I would rather say you resemble a spring day."

Despite myself, I laughed. Didn't he know a spring day in Eldaborg could be awfully rainy and cold?

THE CROWN PRINCE OF LAKARI

"Call me if you need anything," Sir Sigve said. "I'll be just down the hall."

"Thank you." My voice was void of its usual vigor.

"Princess Alvildi." He never called me that. "I believe you'll do fine."

Piece by piece I shrunk in on myself, trying to keep my tears at bay. "I hope so," I said, my words falling thin through the hallway.

My former companion nodded, fingers repeatedly clenching and releasing the hilt of his sword. "I'm sorry I can't take you home, my lady. If I could, I would."

"I know." My gaze slid away from Sir Sigve's gray, serious eyes.

Sir Sigve stood with firmly planted feet, his hand smoothing slightly tousled beard. "You're strong, Little Princess." It was a kind lie, a small comfort. Still, a lie.

I managed to slightly curl my lips. "This situation . . . it's worse than hearing the gods feast in the sky."

"Worse than the day after drinking a barrel of mead, I imagine," Sir Sigve said, his baby crow's feet crinkling in a smile.

"Worse than having to listen to Lord Gaute's self-glorification. Worse than the worm." I laughed. It was better than crying, anyway.

Sir Sigve lingered, looking like something burned in his mind. Finally, he asked. "You knew the prince already?"

I nodded. My fingers played along the splits in my dress, yanking and possibly fraying some expensive fabrics. "Met him in the desert. He saved me. But he didn't tell me anything. Why didn't he tell me?" The tip of my shoe found the floor, rediscovering why kicking stone was a bad idea. I clenched my teeth. "Stupid Sirion. He couldn't have stumbled upon me by chance."

"By the gods' skaal," Sir Sigve said, hand clamped around the hilt of his sword. "It seems unlikely."

"He even asked me to marry him. Was he laughing the entire time?" I shut my eyes tight. From pain, from the fading light. Nails dug into my palms.

"Lady Vildi." Sir Sigve embraced me, his arms a bit stiff and odd through the gesture.

"I just . . . I don't know anymore."

"I understand. I'm here, my lady."

With relief from finally having someone on my side, a fresh burst of tears-to-be came over me. I nodded, not trusting my voice.

Sir Sigve released me with the same slow care he would have given a baby Brage. "The Lakarians are strange," he mused. "They seem unnecessarily complex. They don't always tell you what they think up front. But they are good people, from what I've seen."

I grabbed his arm, sensing my fingers pinching him and yet unable to let go. Sir Sigve didn't even flinch. "I can't be their queen! I'm not suited."

"I wish I could do something, but I can't. You decide how this turns out, what kind of queen you'll become. How your marriage will be. If you can give it a chance."

"Well," I laughed, the sound coming from a void inside me, "I have little choice."

"The gods watch over you, Lady Vildi. And now I need to sleep. Remember, I'm just down the hall."

"Goodnight, Sir Sigve. Thank you for being here." *For supporting me, even though you always wanted to go home.*

He nodded, trudging across the marble floor, disappearing through a door. Sir Sigve would be close, just like he told me. He would stay for me. Because of me, he would let go of the life he built for himself at home. His position as Father's right-hand man, gone. His role as mentor to the fighters of Eldaborg, dissolved. His love for Maya—a love he may still be denying—sacrificed. If I had listened before, taken his advice, a person so much older and wiser than me . . . but I had stubbornly insisted on having an adventure, and he shared the punishment for my folly.

With a deep breath, I closed the door. My new room was about thrice as big as my old one, light and airy where I was used to gnarled wood and furniture made to make the most of the cramped-up space. When the sun properly left the sky, I would likely be able to see the stars. Shimmering curtains framed immense windows, white walls were crowned with a salon, an immense bed, closets, and any other practical luxury I might want. It suited a princess, like how a five-year-old girl imagines such a room should be. And I had it alone. Unlike home, it had none of the cozy, small nooks and marks which years of living gave a room. Perhaps there never could be, when the walls and floor were cold stone instead of dark wood. It had no sister.

Somewhere in the palace, Sirion had his quarters.

Collapsing on the bed, I let my tears go. For stupidity. For Sigve. I shed a few for my life. For home, and my family. Everything emptied into a soft, green pillow as the sun's radiance disappeared and evening crept into the room. When I was finally hollow, my lids slipped. I was ready to sleep, preferably for weeks.

Vibrant, sharp bangs startled me out of nothingness. "Vildi?"

I closed my eyes a little tighter.

"Vildi, please?" Someone was at the door, making a ruckus as if he wanted to tear the barrier down. I buried myself deeper into the pillow, though in the subsequent silence I heard the person sigh. "I'm coming in."

"No, don't co—" Creaking to announce its offense, the door opened. I dug myself out of the soft fluff to glare at the intruder. "Don't think I'll forgiv—Sirion!"

Sirion closed the door. He drew a hand over his drooping, drawn eyes, expelling breath like the plague. "Just so you should know. This wasn't easy for me either."

"Why, was it worse than being held captive and taken against your will just to be told you're being married off to someone you barely know, and have no say in it?" I rose, crossing my arms in front of me. "Tell me, Sirion, was it worse?"

Sirion, on his way across the room, halted in his steps. When he moved again, it was like seeing a person trying to plow through a field of fresh snow. Finally, he slumped down in one of the chairs by the window. "No, it was not."

"Thought so. You can go now."

Closing his eyes, Sirion drew a deep breath. "Please Vildi, we need to talk."

"Apparently we don't. You must have known who I was, all those days in the desert. You said nothing then, why should you now?"

"Yes." How easily he admitted it, meeting my eyes without hesitation. "How was I supposed to tell you, Vildi? You didn't trust me. You didn't want to come with me. And you definitely didn't want to get married. When would have been the right time to say: 'and by the way, Vildi, you are my fiancée'? You wanted to go home. I didn't want to ruin that. Besides, I had trouble enough making you accept help even though your life depended on it, and I *could not* risk ruining that."

"Well, what about in the house, when I told you I didn't want to get married? Or what about when I talked about home, and you knew I would never return?"

For each of my words, Sirion sank in on himself. He sat looking stone-faced, eyes frozen as ice. "Of course. Yes, I could have told you. Maybe I should have." He looked down. "It wasn't supposed to be like this."

"Definitely not," I agreed, sitting opposite him, the green pillow held in a tight grip.

"I can't change it." He leaned back all the way, staring up at the ceiling. "Not this." As if he even wanted to.

"You can choose someone else."

"I had a wife before." He didn't stir from his slumped position, watching a design of roses and golden swirls carved into white marble overhead. The room was only lit by a few candles, and the sun had disappeared. "I didn't choose Ashia either. We were . . . nineteen and twenty, and still too young. But she was kind and graceful, warm and helpful, more concerned with others than herself. We were happy."

I swallowed, watching my knuckles paling against each other. Ashia. I should have said something yet found no words. I who had refused his proposal when he offered, I who had shied away from his help, had openly mocked the notion of marriage before his father, I had no right to feel jealous now. And I could not take his hand, however much his fingers trembled.

"She died—" Sirion drew a breath, exhaling shakily. "Together with our daughter, two-and-a-half years ago. And I—I'm not good with death."

"I'm sorry." My weak voice could as well have tried to stave off a blizzard's chill. Sirion was so far gone, he didn't even seem to hear me. His fine hands lay between us and my fingers twitched.

"If she had survived, you would have been free. Except—of course it was meant to be this way. I *can't* change it."

And so, I was to fill her place. Ashia, the loved one. "She sounds like Madalyn," I said, somehow not choking on the words.

"Sorry." Sirion sat up, meeting my eyes. "I'm sorry it's like this. Lakari problems, Lakari traditions and gods. But you're a part of it now. You can go home, and it would change nothing."

If I went home . . . Mother had arranged this match and Lakari had accepted, even though it was me. And how would Father refuse something like this? Sirion was right.

"Again, I feel too young," he said, tufts of hair hanging sad in front of his eyes.

I arched an eyebrow.

"Twenty-three."

My other eyebrow joined the first. "You're not too young, Sirion, you're an old man." Well, it was better than forty still.

He cracked a smile, though it dissipated fast. "And you're even younger than I was the first time."

I struggled against the word. "Seventeen."

"Too young." Sirion's gaze slid away, escaping out the window.

"I still don't understand." He didn't seem to want this after all. "This situation . . ."

Sirion looked like he too needed a pillow to bury himself in. "A few weeks ago, a letter arrived at the palace. A portrait was delivered soon after. It was decided we should give you an audience, let us meet and see if there was any water in the desert, if you understand my meaning."

I nodded.

Sirion sighed, fingers creeping up to scrape nails through his hair. With his continual pulling of the strands, it was amazing he had any left. "But you didn't come. Without the formalities . . . I was just Sirion, and you were Vildi. You needed saving, and you didn't trust me—"

"I still don't," I told him.

He grimaced. "I understand that. I'm sorry. Really, more than you know, for everything. This is forced upon you, and I can't change it." Lowering his gaze, he looked like the tired, worn person from the desert. One with little hope, and even less to live for. Having to marry because of the throne and a threat from the neighboring country and being stuck with . . . me. A person so unsuited to be queen. Worse, getting a queen who opposed the idea. Of all the girls in the world, he lost his love and got me instead. The obstinate, childish, infamous, spoiled, and rude second princess of Rimdalir. He glanced at me. "It's not supposed to be like this." His eyes fled to the stars. "This is my little sister Liria's dream, and nothing could be better. For me, experiencing this—but it's all wrong. For you, this is awful."

A fresh burst of tears almost escaped. "I want to go home."

"I know."

"I don't want this." I muffled my words into the fluffy silk.

"I know," he said again, voice breaking like waves against the shore.

"I'm so angry."

Somehow that made him laugh. "That's good."

"It is?" I chanced a glance up from my pillow. Sirion gave me a somewhat guarded look.

"Yes," he confirmed. "You have every right to be angry. I was selfish for not telling you who I was, and this would never have happened to you if not for me. Be mad at me. But don't be so sad."

Just Sirion. Just Vildi. He was right. It was selfish, a convenient lie. Going around, pretending to be something else. A nobody. Like, for example, a merchant's daughter. There was no answer I could give him.

"I care, Vildi. I did before I even met you." Sirion reached out a hand, but I couldn't take it. It lingered in the air between us in a painful, prolonged silence. Finally, he drew the hand back, turning away. He stood up, about to leave through the door. "Being the only one who feels something is hard."

With another glance up at him, I felt myself shatter all over again. For me. For him. But there might be something I could do, one small thing I could give. "The entire time I was captive," I began. Drew a deep breath, steadied myself. "I wanted to go back to you the entire time. I even tried a few times. Failed, of course." I laughed, but it still sounded a little hollow.

Sirion stilled. Slowly, as if he walked through water, he came back and sat down again with a blank face. His eyes, wide and vulnerable, fell on my hands. With a sudden, shuddering breath, Sirion snatched my arms to turn them this way and that, where my bruises were scattered like dry pine needles after a good shake of a gods' midwinter tree.

He let go as if burned, his gaze stiff and staring at a point across the room.

"I'm fine. I'm not hurt; it looks worse than it is." Those were apparently the right words because he relaxed, turning back to watch me. I attempted a smile. "You were my savior, the only good thing in my life—except Balt—after I came here. And then I'm told I'm about to be married to a stranger, but suddenly it's *you,* the one I—but it was all wrong."

Sirion stared, eyes like voids. "You care." His voice was flat. Abruptly he collapsed backward, the haunted look swept aside as if it had never been there. "That's a relief."

Affronted, I scooted away and clutched my pillow tighter. "Not really. I can't trust you."

"You will, eventually." He sounded so sure, laughed a little even. "And you *care.*" I felt his joy upon me, tangible in the air as if no problems were left in the world. "Of course, you love me, it would be strange if you didn't."

Drums beat red in my ears. I threw the pillow at his face. "I don't love you. Don't be delusional."

Sirion threw the pillow back into my arms. "You will."

I decided to ignore that. His arrogance was boundless, and he was a prince. Sirion smirked, and a smug satisfaction settled in his blue eyes. I would dearly have preferred a peasant boy. Like Hogne. It was supposed to be a fairy tale. My own lad, coming to my rescue ... well, that was one childhood dream smashed to smithereens. And Sirion was the man I was now forcefully engaged to.

"I know nothing about you," I said.

"That, I can fix." His twisted lips and the teasing glint in his eyes sent a thrill through me. "I am Sirion, and I happen to be the Crown Prince of Lakari. I'm also the man you lived with for a few days, who enjoys making tea for grumpy people in the mornings. What do you want to know?"

"Easy as that?"

He nodded.

"I don't even know where to begin," I said, burying my face in the green plush. "I thought I had thousands of questions, but I can't remember them."

"Then I fear you are doomed to ignorance," he shrugged.

I scowled, almost throwing the pillow again.

"No?" He laughed. "Well, I was born here. I have an older sister, Ilea, as you know. I also have two younger brothers and three very silly younger sisters who are quite curious about you. I don't talk much with them, but we have always been on good terms. My older sister Ilea taught me to ride, and she used to share morning tea with me. When Mother died, Ilea was there for me. And again with . . . well. She married, left Lakari, and we haven't spoken since. It's been almost two years now." Sirion blinked, glancing my way with a slight bend of his lips. "I like being outside. Traveled a lot growing up. Seeing the kingdom and meeting people was an important part of my education." He paused, gazing down at his hands. "After Ashia, I was alone for a while."

"And now?"

Lifting his head, Sirion set his eyes on me and smiled. "Now I'm getting married. And I'll do my best. I have a purpose, and I have someone I care about."

With his words, it sounded all too easy.

"You want to go outside? We have a garden." He sat up, stretching, still way too satisfied.

"Sirion . . . look outside."

He did. The sun was almost gone, shadows reaching deep into my room. "It's not *that* late."

After everything and all the anger draining out, I felt the urge to collapse backward on the bed. Sleep. Wake up. Maybe somehow this had been another nightmare and I would be home, sharing the dream with Madalyn, and we could laugh at the thought of a person more conceited than Lord Gaute. The Prince of Lakari with his love and his sorrow and—I closed my eyes. When I opened them a second later, Sirion still lingered.

I bent forward, pressing fingers to my forehead. "For me it is. I've been traveling for days, and not even by choice. My life just took a drastic turn for the worse" —he winced— "and I'm tired. Just . . . let me sleep."

I hid a yawn behind my hand. My limbs were like lead. Something, flitting outside the reach of my mind, lurked in the hollowness of me.

"Of course, you're tired. You should rest," Sirion relented, his hands at ease for once. "All right. I'll see you tomorrow."

I waved him away, shambling to the bed. "Yes, yes. Sure." I clawed my way beneath a blanket and felt him tug it around me. After a breath or two, the door closed behind him, and I was alone. Curling in on myself, I could not banish the lurching, heavy lump swelling in my stomach, my chest, throat—

FALLING GROUND

During my first two weeks in the palace, I did an outstanding job of avoiding Sirion. Leaving my room early each morning, exploring corridors and chambers until I was thoroughly lost and had to wait for a servant to cross my path and lead me back. It was hardly my fault. Each hall looked like the former and ran smoothly into the next, a labyrinth unlike anything I had seen before. If I *happened* to miss him at a few junctures, that was only natural for such a place. An entire day might disappear, though I inevitably saw him at dinner. Despite these events being of a formal character, I had yet to spoil one—for neither king nor prince seemed inclined to reconsider the absurdity of me as a bride. And because evening meals were held with his family of siblings and a displaced king, made complete by servants lining the walls on beck and call, there was not much conversation around the table. Even if I sat beside him, at most we could exchange some hushed words occasionally, if so inclined.

And if I ever saw Sirion during the day, his look of growing frustration got tucked away as I smiled at him and exchanged polite pleasantries. I did not work against my role as a fiancée. I just . . . happened to be everywhere he was not, most of the time. Sir Sigve noticed, of course. When he asked me about it, dissatisfaction written across his features, I did a poor job with my explanation. Perhaps the cause was marriage itself. Or being so aware of my inferiority to Sirion's first wife, the perfect, loved one. It could be the deep-rooted, constant reminder that I was unsuited for the position, and not knowing how to fix it. Fix me. Mayhap the sorrow of having to let a childhood dream go. Whatever the reason, looking into Sirion's eyes was too difficult for me.

A sunshine side appeared as my servants gave me new clothes—local style, but clearly intended for me, made to mimic the dresses from my home. The likeness started and ended with the belt around my waist. They were sheer, light fabrics, loose and comfortable if not a little too revealing. Still, much better than what I had seen other women wear on occasions. Most importantly, the clothes were clean and so was I. The baths they provided me were absolutely luxurious.

I was mostly alone. Sometimes I walked with Sir Sigve, although ever since he discovered training grounds the first week, I didn't see much of him. It was good for him to have something to do. Just as swords were a specialty of Eldaborg and the best archers came from Silverberg, apparently the fighting school of Lakari had refined the art of knife throwing, though I already knew that from first-hand experience. And even if I had possessed the curiosity to learn, my clumsiness banned me from touching any sharp-edged objects. Sir Sigve dutifully saw to that.

I needed some healthy, good relationships, and Horasis hardly counted. Even though I met Silent Toleor in the halls sometimes, I had trouble exchanging more than a few halting words. I had yet to see him smile, although he gave an awkward nod whenever he saw me. Now that I knew he wouldn't kill me, I found it sort of adorable in a very Hognesque way.

"Cheer up, Princess," Horasis said in the spirit of helpful guardian-ism.

"I can't help it, can I?" I glanced behind me, but the hall was still empty on my trail. "I'm not made for this, any of it."

"I know nothing about that." Horasis shrugged. "Born to a family of soldiers, ended up exactly where I'm supposed to be. Aren't you a princess?"

"No one ever killed each other in Rimdalir. We were farmers." I shuffled my feet, grieving the lack of convenient stones to kick. "Three weeks of watching shadows."

"I'm here to do that for you. You're safe in the palace, Princess." Horasis opened a door, sending me through. Outside was a burst of fresh air against my face. The palace courtyard was in a pristine state of order one would never find in Eldaborg. Instead of packed dirt and hay littering the ground, each cobbled stone was placed tight against the next, left bare to refract rays of sun. The wall surrounding the area was three men high, and yet its shadow only covered a small strip of the ground. Planted trees were pruned to resemble sculptures, ensuring endless maintenance.

On a side path, Toleor wandered between those trees, moving his gaze from one place to another, scrutinizing anything from the palace walls to the gate.

"Toleor," Horasis said, waving a hand. "Lost something?"

"No." Toleor, in his silent, contemplative way, sat down on a bench. "Needed fresh air."

"Did something happen?" I sat down on the bench across from his, folding my skirt so it wouldn't snag or rip when I stood again. These Lakarian dresses were delicate things.

"Your Grace." Toleor greeted me with a short jerk of his head. "It's my family. Got a letter this morning. Sickness."

"I'm sorry." Poor Toleor. His words loaded upon my heart and my breakfast felt like a pile of rocks. "I hope they get well soon."

He stared at the ground.

"Can't you do anything?" Horasis scratched at his neck. "Send them medicine or return home for a while?"

Silent Toleor glanced up, brows tightly drawn over his brown eyes. "I do what I can."

I hardly knew what to say, and the silence stood as a wall between us until the shadows reached the path and I had to go. Once again, Madalyn would have managed so much better than me. I plodded away, swamped with silks and jewelry while a man worried for the safety of his loved ones. And yet I had dinner to attend.

∾

Almost four full weeks of dread and boredom.

At least there were no more attacks, no new Do-Agains. I had nothing to do but wander. Once or twice, I thought I detected the flicker of a dark cloak, or the glint of steel as light touched the shadows. I asked Horasis about it once, and he said in plain and clear words I was paranoid. I left it at that, after days and days of nothing happening. Having to admit he might be right was, in a way, a relief. If my fear was ungrounded, I had nothing to be afraid of anymore. I could live with these sights, knowing they were tricks of the mind.

I soaked in a morning bath as my new lady's maids stood at stumped attention. They no longer tried to do the washing for me, at last believing me when I said I could do it myself. My skin would not be subject to their harsh scrubbing anymore. Now they just lingered in their corner, murmuring in a language I didn't understand.

I reveled in the warm, scented water, relieving my shoulders and neck of stress. Submerged, I blew out air, bubbles popping above me. Coming up with the skin on the tip of my fingers scrunched like old fruit, I was finished. The girls worked effectively to dry and dress me.

I had talked with a few girls my age, but getting through to them was difficult, perhaps because of the general attitude of the people. They stared and they mumbled, doing a poor job of hiding their attention as they held delicate hands up before their mouths. I didn't need to hear their words. I knew they found me queer and possibly crude. The rule that 'a lady should speak with the soft care of a whispering wind,' as Mother had bestowed upon me years ago, seemed to stand strong in any society. But beyond that, there was an incredulity in their eyes, a veiled, strange disbelief. I was not *that* much different from what was expected of a princess from the north.

On my way back from the bath to my room, I passed two of the palace's noble guests, a man and his wife. They stilled as they saw me, making their curtsy look like mockery, penetrating gazes and their hushed whispers following me down the hall.

After endlessly branching paths, I closed the doors on these halls, my new shadow and my small army of ladies-in-waiting, letting out a relieved breath. Falling onto the bed, I almost fell asleep to the warm day. When the sun stood at its peak, there was little else a body could manage.

My alone time was cut short. The door opened, shutting close the next moment with a sharp *bang*. "Please, leave me, I want—"

"My lady, what a deplorable state I find you in." She came into my room like a hurricane, scowling from the first glimpse as if I was five again, having raided the kitchen and soiled my clothes with cake.

I whirled around, throwing myself off the bed. "Maya!" I barreled into her and buried myself, my tears, in the soft fabric draped across her shoulder.

Maya only hesitated for a moment, though soon her stern bearings melted away and she embraced me like a mother. "Shh, little princess, everything is fine now. I'm here to stay; I'll take care of you always. You are *not* alone anymore."

Hearing her endearment, feeling her warm arms around me, I could have been a child again, just receiving her comfort and care.

"But really, Lady Vildi, I am so relieved I brought your summer dresses. We can't have you walking around so ... so ... *undressed.*" Maya eyed my attire like Father would glower at a failed batch of ale. "I have seen more skin after I arrived here than my entire life combined, I'm sure."

"Yes, it feels like that, doesn't it?"

As if summoned, two boxes of luggage were delivered to my room. The poor servants, breathing hard even as they bowed in the doorway, had been forced to drag my possessions all the way up those winding stairs. "Ah, there it is. Your belongings, my lady."

My carved animals of birch and pine soon decorated the chamber, and my jewel box sat on a small, delicate table beneath the mirror. My wardrobe had expanded.

"I have some other dresses, don't I?" I plucked at the sleeve, almost coarse to the touch after wearing the silks and sheer fabrics of Lakari.

"Of course." Maya strapped the last buckles and ribbons on my dress, and the heavy linen fabric fell beyond my wrists and past the ankles to the floor. The belt was looser around my waist than I remembered, yet every breath I drew was dense as if the air thickened and churned in my constrained chest.

"Do I have to wear this?" I shifted my weight and felt the dress drag along.

"You're decent again, finally!" Maya nodded, satisfaction pouring out of her firmly crossed arms, her crisp nod. "You look beautiful, befit a princess of Rimdalir."

In the mirror, I met the eyes of a Vildi wearing that dress. The fabric had a midnight blue, soft quality, with heavy silver linings and a brooch. With some help, I had spent countless hours sewing the delicate stitches. It had been my most expensive attire, and the last time I wore it was the night I left home. Under my hands, my stomach jolted like a nervous horse. And the imprint of worm hands wandering, burning, sickening— "Thank you, Maya. But I finally understand why the people of Lakari wear light and indecent clothes."

"And? No reason for you to stoop to their level."

"Yes, it is. Sorry, but this dress is coming off *right now*." Goosebumps spread across my skin and still my neck was clammy and gross.

"I will not accept this." Maya placed her hands on her hips, leaning forward with *that* expression. It had prompted five-year-old me into submission on several occasions.

"Right. Now." My body was so warm, my face flushing as if I was running a fever. I fanned myself with my hand to no apparent effect. I tugged at the collar. "Don't worry, Maya. You'll be comfortable in the local style soon enough. Didn't you say you're staying? I know Sir Sigve is. Perhaps these light clothes are just what you need."

Red flushed her cheeks and Maya, twelve years my senior, looked pointedly away.

"It's fine," I consoled her. "I'm sure we'll be able to wear these on occasions in winter." If there even existed periods of less warmth in these parts. I somehow doubted it.

"I cannot accep—my lady, don't undress yourself!"

Ignoring her, I continued the meticulous process of loosening all the straps on my dress, just as Maya swapped at my hands. As I didn't stop, she threw herself into the work of fastening every strap and brooch I had unclasped.

The sun reached its peak, and at the end of our heated battle, both Maya and I were comfortable in perfectly indecent clothes.

∽

"Why is he following us?" Maya looked over her shoulder, a frown firmly settled on her face. We were walking down a corridor leading to the gardens, where we had been summoned for lunch. It was even beyond me to decline a direct invitation.

"Don't mind my shadow," I said. "It's better to ignore it."

"You hurt my feelings, Princess," the shadow answered, a very unhurt grin on his face. "Horasis Lagir, my lady. Assigned to guard our future queen." He bowed with a flourish, making Maya blink.

"I'm no lady, I'm a maid. And why would my lady need guards?" Maya didn't take her eyes off poor Horasis, instead stepping closer to me and positioning herself between us. This was her first time away from Rimdalir, and she seemed a bit mistrusting to her new surroundings. I could relate; they differed greatly from Eldaborg.

"Just a precaution." Horasis touched the knives strapped to his belt. At first it had been an intimidating motion, but during these last weeks I had seen him do it many times.

Maya narrowed her eyes, glaring at my guard. She didn't seem inclined to share his comfort in the gesture.

"I'm not trying to escape anymore," I said. Maya should be spared the details of gruff men and their bloodied knives. Skipping ahead, I twirled around to give my shadow a mock glare. "And I still have a little trouble trusting you, to be honest."

"As long as you don't make my life difficult by jumping out a window, I don't mind," Horasis declared magnanimously. Maybe he had trouble trusting me too.

"Don't worry, I won't." My feet shuffled across the white marble, trying to avoid the black streaks and swirls embedded into it. "Where's Toleor? Couldn't he guard me too?"

"He could. He's had some night shifts with me, but mostly he's got other responsibilities. But I'm here to protect you." Horasis' beaming smile made him look almost as young as me, although with a happiness I could hardly match. "You're safe with me."

"Are all Lakarian men so confident?"

Horasis shrugged. "Probably not. I've earned my confidence."

"I prefer Toleor, silent and thoughtful. Like Hogne."

I glimpsed Maya from the corner of my eyes, studying me.

"I'm fine, just miss him is all."

"Of course, you do." Maya stepped closer, giving my hand a squeeze in the shelter of our skirts. Horasis studied us with furrowed brows, but he said no more.

Another turn took me squinting against sunlight.

The garden was vast, and I had yet to explore it all. I knew the palace walls surrounded it, but with palm trees and hedges crisscrossing through the gently sloping area, I could only see a bit to each side by the entrance before foliage obscured further view. The grass was lush, a road running through the lawn toward the center of the area. Several smaller paths crossed ours, disappearing behind fragrant jasmine bushes while flowers adorned small beds along them.

"How are you able to keep such a garden with the desert just outside the city?" Even with this general area being more than desert, I had only seen spiky, solitary plants spread across the landscape as we neared the capital.

"Haya River," Horasis said. "It runs through Aransis."

"Meaning you built the city along it?" I hadn't noticed a river anywhere. I squinted against the sun, glimpsing light reflecting in water from narrow channels running through the lawn.

"Yes," Horasis said, seeming a bit surprised. His expectations of me must have been poor indeed for such a small deduction to impress him.

A low table filled with local delicacies immediately captured my attention, until I realized it lacked cake. Sirion was waiting for us, meeting our presence with pleasantly tilted lips and eyes reflecting the sky. His little sister Liria sat with him, her face brightening as we drifted closer. She was younger than me by a couple of years. Liria seldom stopped staring given the chance, proven night after night at dinner. Just as during the evenings, I tried to ignore both siblings and the guards behind them.

"Welcome," Sirion said. "I'm glad you decided to join me for tea, Vildi." He stood up, giving a perfect, crisp bow.

I put forth my best pleasing smile, reserved for such special occasions. "Of course. I didn't have a choice." My eyes were content lingering somewhere past his shoulder. An interesting assembly of fruit hung in clusters from the palm's thick crowns.

"I hope your journey was pleasant and that you're settling in well, Maya," my intended said, ignoring my blunt remark with an elegant shift of attention.

"Quite well, Your Grace." Maya lowered her gaze, her curtsy deep.

"Good." Despite his cheerful front, Sirion's hand seemed restless. It kept creeping upward whenever he glanced my way, falling back in his lap each time he noticed. "I heard your family is coming soon too?" he braved on, looking at me again.

"Yes, so I heard." I folded the skirt daintily around me. "Mother would never want to miss my . . . wedding." I had to push the word out through my mouth, force my leaden tongue to form the sounds.

"They are very welcome." Sirion shifted, stretching his legs. Long fingers drummed against his thigh.

"Thank you." I averted my gaze to a group of trees, where birds chirped sharp and clear. Madalyn would not come. She had her birthday in three weeks and with it a ball, her duty as heir to Rimdalir. Without doubt, Mother would never permit her to skip such golden occasions to hold house for a suitable assembly of suitors, royal wedding or not.

Liria gestured for us to sit on the other side of the table. "Please, eat with us." Her voice was low and light, almost like music when she talked. With the potential to be a wonderful singer, it was a shame she preferred staring.

Broad leaves hung from trees above, providing a pleasant shade. A breeze blew life to my hair, finding a few strands to tease out of Maya's strict braids. Before my stomach could announce its growing needs, I filled a plate with a little of everything. The fruits were delicious, and even Maya took her share. The salted meat tasted a bit odd and was left mostly untouched.

"Vildi, there is something we should talk about," Sirion said, a pensive look about him. Even his uneasy smile was gone, lips pressed tight together.

His sister stared at him with her sparkling eyes. A sigh escaped Liria as she looked from Sirion to me.

Sirion spun a cup of tea between his hands. Hot vapor left the drink, surely burning his fingers, and he put down the cup, exhaling. "Would you walk with me after we finish eating?"

All eyes turned on me. Liria with excitement, Maya with her expectations, and Sirion waiting for my answer. My head bobbed in a nod.

"Excellent." Sirion broke into a grin, reclining against a pile of pillows.

"Can I come too?" Liria asked, looking as if she didn't want to miss out on the great happenings of the year. In Rimdalir, those might be the autumn hunts or the spring feast. I had no idea what Lakarians considered fun, but relationship issues seemed to be it.

Sirion let out a laugh. "No, of course not. This is between me and my fiancée."

His choice of words tasted sour on my tongue. I put down the remaining piece of meat, my appetite gone. "Will you show me the river?" At least I could get some exploring out of it.

"It's a bit far, but I'll take you." He made a grand, sweeping gesture with his hand. From our seats at an elevated plateau, we had an excellent view of our surroundings. The Lakarians must be very proud of their royal garden, with its flood of exotic, purple flowers and green, green lawn. "This is where we'll get married in two weeks." Sirion had been in a bright mood from the moment we arrived, but upon closer observation the lines in his face were obvious, eyes dim behind slipping lids.

"But you'll also have the Ceremony of Bonding," Liria said, still studying me as if I was a rare specimen of sorts. "You'll get to see the Desert Diamond." Excited fingers tucked hair away from her face. She turned to her brother with a little-sister smile I knew all too well, though her version might have more impact on the recipient. "Sirion, I want to come too." Liria popped a red grape into her mouth.

"No." Sirion drew a hand over his eyes. "You're not supposed to talk about it, you know. We cannot trust that Vildi is safe beyond these walls. We still don't know who is trying to hurt her."

"Oh." Liria hung her head like a sad sunflower.

I was a bit tired myself, despite sleeping well at night. Actually, it was more of a lightness, my surroundings wobbling in gentle waves, as if I had been spinning and abruptly came to a stop. The sun found me through a filter of leaves, hot and draining. I reached for my cup, sensed a glint of reflected light and a sound like steel hitting steel. Horasis gaped, fingers outstretched and shock in his eyes. A confusion of limbs and legs scrambled to get earth beneath their feet, and orders were shouted over my head. The ground fell toward me.

Vaguely I heard Sirion's voice. "Vildi! Komir, fetch som—"

∼

I woke up to a throbbing headache and evening darkness. My hand was warm, another hand holding it tight and tender. Sirion sat by my bed, half asleep with hair like a wilderness, though stirring as soon as I moved. A blanket slipped down around my waist. "What happened?" I asked, voice rasping through my sore throat.

Sirion blinked, peering at me with bleary eyes and looking as if he needed the bed more. "I'm sorry, Vildi." Stretching, he shook himself properly awake, reclaiming my hand. "I shouldn't have taken you outside so close to dayburn. You're not used to the temperatures yet. You fainted."

"Heatstroke?"

He confirmed with a nod, his gaze trained on our hands.

"Where is Maya?"

He seemed to hesitate. "Sleeping. She was affected as well," he said at last. "She'll be fine, same as you."

Had I really been that warm? But... "We sat in the shadows, and we drank tea. What were the sounds I heard?" And... Horasis, looking as if he had just thrown a knife, turning to stare at me with a strange mix of relief and fear in his eyes.

Sirion was silent.

"Tell me," I insisted, clutching the sheets. "What happened?"

Sighing, Sirion leaned back in his chair. "I didn't want you to worry; I thought you collapsed before you could notice. It was the meat, a mild poison—anything more, and it would not have passed the test of the tasters. They most likely intended to strike when our minds were muddled and our bodies weak, and with few guards to defend us."

Clenching my cold, white hands around the blanket, I felt a familiar, heavy nausea return. "But we didn't die." No nightmares. Just my room, evening sky decorating the window, flickering candlelight illuminating the somewhat crude wooden carvings from home, standing in stark contrast to the grand Lakarian style of furniture and ornamented walls. No repeat.

"No." Sirion pried my fingers off the sheets to intertwine with his. "I recognized the symptoms, and we got an antidote quickly. Besides, none of us ate much of the meat."

"It tasted strange."

He nodded. "But the truly dangerous thing was the knife thrown at you. Thankfully, Horasis intercepted with his own."

"He did?" It lined up well with my memories. Still, being able to hit a knife in flight? "Is that even possible?"

"That's why he's assigned as your guard," Sirion confirmed. "Incredible aim and good instincts."

"Makes sense," I decided. "It's not his conversational skills, after all." The joke fell flat between us. "I must thank him."

"It was too close, this time." A grove dug into the space between Sirion's eyes, forcing upon him the weight of every one of his twenty-three years. If I stretched out a hand, I could trail the line of his tense jaw. "Vildi . . . I'm sorry you were put in danger. We didn't get the men behind the attack, and we must assume there's someone within the walls. Still, you are safe with me."

"Safe," I mumbled, some of my bitterness seeping into the word. If nothing else, Sirion held my gaze with steady eyes, believing everything he said.

THE ONLY LOVE ALLOWED

I had barely finished breakfast when someone knocked. The person on the other side let the door swing open before I had time to react—which made the initial politeness rather redundant. Sirion stood in the doorway. "You have a visitor." The brilliant smile, his complete lack of a frown caused one to settle on my face instead.

"Please," I said, my voice dry. "You usually skip the formalities, anyway. Come in." These had been a few nice, calm days, spent reminiscing with Maya, completely fiancé-free. I should have expected them not to last. "Have you found anything?"

For a moment, a cloud seemed to pass across his sunny demeanor. "No, nothing. The search is slow, with so little to go on. But I'm not here for that." Glancing behind himself, he brightened, opening wide the gateway to my private sanctuary. Sirion looked like a little kid just dying to spill his secret. "Your visitor is not me . . . so, I'll leave you to it." And out the door he disappeared.

In his stead, a slim and petite figure slipped inside, rushing to embrace me. "Vildi, little sister, have they treated you well?"

"Madalyn!" She was warm, she was family, and I fell into her, letting her hold me.

"It's all fine now, Vildi," she said, with a velvet voice and fingers stroking soothing circles on my back. I might have spilled a tear or two into her silver-blonde hair. I had many of them to shed and share, it seemed.

"Why are . . . *how* are you here?" I choked on my voice, fisted my hands into her dress and made some irredeemable wrinkles, but I did not care. Neither did Madalyn. My sister only held me tighter. She should have been at home, fending off suitors to prepare for her twenty-first birthday.

"You know, the . . ." Madalyn stopped, conflicting feelings revealing themselves in her few words—and in what she didn't say.

"The wedding," I finished, strangely calm about it.

"Yes." The word was a whisper between us. She bit her lip, a troubled look on her delicate features. "All this time, I was worried. Receiving Sir Sigve's letters never really helped."

"Are you angry?" I held my breath, clinging to her a little stronger.

"For leaving?" Madalyn looked away for a moment, a frown burrowing between her eyes. "I wish you had told me." My sister sighed, hands going limp in her lap. "But I'm not angry."

"Wouldn't you have tried to stop me?"

She glanced down at her bracelet, fingers clutching a few of the white stones. They were dim, almost gray despite the well-lit room. "I doubt if I could. I understand it well, the need to get away. But you left without a word, and . . ." her voice went out, and she drew a quick breath. "Finding you gone . . . you scared me, Vildi."

"It all happened so fast. I couldn't stay . . . I'm sorry." I glanced up, seeing the gentle, lovely face of my sister peering down at me.

Frost entered her eyes. "Was it Vinjar?"

I cast my gaze to the floor. Finally, I nodded, sure I would cry anew if I looked up.

Madalyn's hand came to grip her stones, nails scraping the white so hard, I thought I saw sparks. "If he *ever* shows himself before me again . . ." She glanced down, and the fierceness lifted from her eyes, leaving only love. "My poor, little sister. It's fine now." She held forgiveness, understanding, care, warmth: embracing me. She deserved the world.

"It's not that bad. Nothing really happened, but . . . well, that nothing was still too much. I had to get away from the suitors, the balls, the expectations, the stares, that name. And him." Soon the tears would spill again. My mind grasped for something else to talk about. The worm was not worth wasting my precious time with Madalyn. "I had a gift for you . . . but it disappeared." I looked around my room, the few items which had found their way here, through me or

Maya. There was not much. "It was supposed to be a necklace, but I bought a knife instead. It's gone, though. I have something else." Madalyn smiled from my mumbling as I fetched my travel bag, pulling out blue fabric and half a spool of golden thread. Thank the gods the fine material had survived the turbulent travels.

"Thank you," Madalyn said, hand sliding over silk. "This is beautiful." She unfolded the cloth, revealing a handkerchief-sized square missing.

"I had to use some of it," I explained. "But I think you should be able to use the rest, make something nice."

"I'll try. I'll treasure it."

"Though you don't need it to be pretty. I know one person at home who would like you even in rags."

Madalyn blinked. She was not supposed to bear such a bewildered expression. Where was her blush? I had even given my blessing before I left, and still here we stood. So, he had made no progress, my one and only favorite noble.

"Never mind." The sun was about to peek around the corner and spill in through the window. Soon we would be able to see every speck of dust in the air.

"We are very different, you and I. You've never been bound by the shackles of duty, always stayed free and true to yourself." Madalyn separated three thick locks from my hair, her nimble fingers working on a braid. "But perhaps you were never as free as I thought."

I met the bluebell eyes of my sister. In that moment, we shared something. This intangible mutual feeling. We were both princesses of Rimdalir.

I leaned against her, tucking myself in her embrace. "I think I fooled myself. This freedom I claimed was an illusion. But I don't think you'll be forced into marriage. You'll be queen, the best we ever had."

Madalyn's pleasant expression turned stiff. I could have bitten my tongue in that same instant. "It is expected," she said, her tone flat. She was right, as always. It was required of her, keeping the blood flowing through generations of throne sitters.

A thread dangled from my dress, and my fingers plucked and pulled on it. "I still think you'll get to choose."

Madalyn froze, as if chilled by winter. After a moment, she gazed out the window. "I kind of wish we could both leave, see all the wonders of the world together. I'm glad you saw some of it before you came here. Is the prince an agreeable person?"

My heart beat his name in my mind. *Sirion*. "He can be rude. And arrogant." Sometimes a storm, the next second showing kindness—unpredictable. He was hard to explain. "Rather than nice . . ."

My sister's eyebrow twitched, the corner of her lip tugging a fraction down.

"He is kind. It might even be tolerable, eventually." Sensing my cheeks growing warm, I let some hair fall to the front.

Madalyn spread her lips in a radiant smile. The stones shone as if a spring sun had set upon them. "Good."

"Well, it's not like I have a choice, anyway."

"You've always escaped engagement before, though. I can't imagine you didn't try." She gave me a teasing, knowing look.

"Oh, I did," I confirmed. "To the best of my ability." I kicked the table, resulting in instant regret as my toe punished me, throbbing pain to the tip of my nail. Stupid silk shoes. Stupid stone. The marble glimmered up at me with no forthcoming apology. "They refused to relent, and they are absolutely adamant."

A rare flicker of shock passed through Madalyn's eyes.

My lips tugged down, barely hiding clenched teeth. "Yes. It *is* strange. He hasn't told me anything."

"And did you try to talk it out?"

"Of course not. I've been avoiding him," I said, sitting up straight.

My sister's hands stilled in my hair. "That's not good, Vildi. You are getting married in a few days, you need to talk."

"I can't face him."

Madalyn took my hand, leaning forward to find my fleeing gaze. "Why? Don't you think he cares? I've only seen him fleetingly, but with how he looked at you I doubt he—"

"No," I interrupted. "Yes. I don't know."

"And you never will if you don't face him," she said, so very right.

"He loved his first wife. I'm a girl he happened upon in the desert, whom he has to marry for some obscure reason." Perhaps it was a question of propriety? I bit my lip. Desperation?

"Vildi, promise me you'll try."

"I think he needs an heir." A grimace pulled at my face. Would he still want me if he could see me now?

Madalyn's eyes softened. "As any heir to a throne does."

"Too true." I almost kicked the table again. "But I don't understand how anyone could be *that* desperate."

My sister reached for my hand. "I know you weren't trained for this. I think even being the queen of Rimdalir would be easier than ruling a vast kingdom like Lakari. The truth of a ruler is, if the people starve or die of sickness, it's on you for not providing food and medicine. You will have a duty and need to take responsibility." Madalyn looked pained, hurting for me. "Vildi, please talk to—"

I was saved by the door being flung open. "Oh, my sweet baby girl! I am so happy for you." Mother floated in, her dress trailing her as a flowing river. She went straight to me, planting a feather-light kiss on my cheek. Her finger already spun around a stray lock of my hair, tucking it in place.

My gaze snapped up. "Mother." I took the hand she presented, and her warmth seeped through.

"Mother," Madalyn echoed with a small curtsy.

From behind Mother's frame, clutching her skirts tightly, Brage poked his head out.

"And of course, Brage. Come here, you." I bent down and opened my arms. My little brother rushed at me, giggling into my hair as we embraced in a tight bear-like hug rivaling Father's. Mother hummed, and I had to let go. When I rose, my back was ramrod straight.

She was dazzling, our mother, radiating joy in her graceful way. "My little girl is finally getting married. And a prince! Trust me, the relief was great when we received their reply of consent on the marriage, although many of your suitors lost heart upon hearing the news." She closed her eyes as if savoring the moment.

"It seems I am. As for my suitors, I daresay they will learn to live with disappointment."

"Indeed, they shall. And sweet Madalyn is unmarried still." Mother stroked my sister's cheek, her eyes soft. "Although your time is coming, my sweetest. You are already twenty-one soon. We can't keep postponing it forever." As she turned back to me, the tight lines of her lips dissolved. "Lord Jarle sends his regards, Alvildi."

"Oh, that's nice." I turned to Madalyn with a smirk. "You'll have to bring him my sincere gratitude once you get home."

Madalyn blinked, the stones at her wrist flashing too fast for me to catch the change before they turned the usual, pleasant white. "Of course, I will tell him for you, Vildi."

Mother set her ice blue eyes upon me. "Lord Gaute wanted me to deliver his sincere congratulations, my sweet. He's a fine man." Her gaze trailed away, fixing on my sister.

Madalyn closed her hand around her stones again, hair falling in front of her eyes. I took her free hand, giving it a squeeze. "Take care when you go back, sister."

"Don't worry, I will." Madalyn turned to me, her face stiff from forcing pleasantries, an expression cultivated to fool everyone. It had never fooled me.

A small hand tugged at a fluttering piece of my dress, and I looked down into vast, gray eyes. "*I* will! Vildi."

"Yes, you must take care too, Brage. You're a man in our family. Son of Gudmund. Will you protect Madalyn from the big, bad people?" I lowered down to his ear and whispered, for him only: "They're all worms." I widened my eyes to emphasize.

He nodded solemnly, as serious as only an eight-year-old boy can be.

Mother didn't seem to follow our conversation. Well, nobody ever acted with less than absolute respect under her gaze; she could not possibly understand. "Oh, enough of that. Prince Sirion was quite polite and perfectly presentable at our reception, don't you think, Madalyn my sweetest?"

"Yes, Mother, he was well mannered."

Mother nodded sagely. "Well, of course. He is a *prince*." With how she uttered the word, I was happy Father was not present to listen. Mother looked practically in love herself.

"Well mannered, huh?" I struggled not to laugh.

"You are very lucky, my sweet. He does not even care for the discrepancy with your portrait."

"Oh, yes, Mother. That must indeed be his most redeeming quality."

"If only he was deaf." Mother frowned, her eyes hardening. "Then he would be *perfect*. You can under no circumstances use such a tone on him, Alvildi."

My laughter bubbled out. "Trust me, *that* is not a concern. At all."

Mother was not one to let go of a well-crafted expression of disdain. But after a bated breath, she sighed. "I see you tended to your figure. Considering how hard this is for you, I am proud."

I shook my head. "No need. It was completely involuntary." Somehow my angelic smile didn't sit as well with Mother as Madalyn's would have. "The people of Lakari have a great love for dried food, you see."

Both Mother and Madalyn stared, their perplexed eyes blinking once, twice. I beamed back. "I am so happy to see you again. My family."

No need to mention the cakes my fiancè provided me, a desert dessert after every drawn-out dinner. His most redeeming quality indeed.

21

LIFELONG DUTY

I always imagined, even reluctantly, sewing my wedding dress. Much like most of the fabric pushed my way nowadays, this gown was of shimmering silk. Green to match my eyes, or so they said, while the dragons represented Hima. Their tails entwined in the back; their bodies followed the rim of the skirt and rose to meet in the front, foreheads touching. The embroidery was delicate, tiny stitches made with a thin golden thread. It was, in every aspect, excellent craftsmanship. I had no say in its creation.

A stranger stared back at me from the reflection on the wall. "How did I ever end up with this?" With fidgeting, restless limbs, I saw the person in the mirror flinch.

"Ah, yes." Maya sighed, unable to hide her joy as she fussed with my face. "This is such a miracle!"

From the corner, I heard Sir Sigve suppress a laugh. How inappropriate. This was not a good time to find one's sense of humor.

In a few hours, I would be married.

"I didn't agree to this." I swallowed against nausea rising through my throat. "How did I end up like this?"

Somewhere along the way I had taken several wrong turns. Even with the ability to do it over, which actions and decisions in the millions of many would I need to change? I glanced out the window. Perhaps Horasis was right, and I was a little crazy. Then again, what did he know, youngling as he was? He had a few years on me, true, but I would never hide food in my pockets like he did. And it was not only because my new dresses lacked pockets altogether, or because Madalyn never would, or because I was to become queen and the way down was long, long—

"Are you unwell, my lady?" Sir Sigve took a step closer, hand going to his sword—as if he could protect me from my own wedding.

I averted my eyes from the window. There was no point in returning to a morning where nothing would change. Shaking my head, I let Maya fasten my hair, until it curled up in an intricate design in front and the sides, falling sleek and loose down my back. She worked around the strange jewelry twinned into my hair, a golden chain framing my face with a green gem resting on my forehead. A similar, unfamiliar weight of tiny emeralds hung from my ears.

At least it's Sirion.

"Thank you," I said, pushing my lips to show only cheer to my waiting companions. "I'm fine. Nerves, that's all."

I would spend my life apologizing to my past self. *Married.* I should have tried harder at some time or another these last weeks. But really, Sirion was to blame. Smirking, sad, but brilliant in moments of sincere happiness. Pretending to care. Perhaps, in his own way, caring. But lying nonetheless, never telling everything. Kindness?

He had not chosen me. It was a matter of practicality, benefits, and needs. 'A throne of one is wrong' and so forth. The worst, most despicable type of marriage. Still, this was our situation.

"You only need to get through the ceremony," Sir Sigve said. What a poor attempt to console me. "There'll be cake afterward."

"True." This was nothing more than a string of events I had to live through. A wedding. A feast. The Desert Diamond and a second ceremony, someday soon. The rest of my life. I drew a breath—and let it go, together with that flowing ribbon I had crinkled inside my fist. "Let's go."

I'm sorry, my naïve fifteen-year-old self—this is happening.

Guards led our party from my room through the long, bright halls to the outside.

A plateau made of the palace itself opened up for the garden, water running through channels and feeding plants thriving in shadows or basking in sunlight. I would soon see him.

As I stepped into the light, a murmur blew through the crowd. People on both sides bowed as we passed them, the procession with me in front drifting along a path to the heart of the garden. A shuffling of sorts happened to my left, with the court trying to catch a glimpse as a princess of

Rimdalir—the unimportant, insolent one—stepped forward to become their queen-to-be.

Sirion, waiting in the shade of a palm tree, reached out a hand for me as my procession approached. His loose attire matched mine in green and gold, though his was made to accentuate his muscular build. Sirion's smile was unable to hide the uncertainty in his eyes. Hesitating for a moment, I felt Maya deliver a discreet nudge to my back, then I relented. I took his hand. Sirion's shoulders sank a fraction, fingers closing around mine.

"So. The ceremony will be outside, like you said." My palm burned.

"Yes, it will."

We strolled together, steps adjusting to each other. If not for all the people staring us down, I might have imagined it a simple afternoon walk.

"How fortunate to be blessed with such wonderful weather."

Snorting, Sirion rolled his eyes. "Lucky."

"So, *why* are we outside?" I asked. Perhaps sanity was still within my grasp. Weddings happened all the time. They were trivial matters. Like the weather. "It's too hot, isn't it?"

"Because of the sun. Our union must happen under the eyes of our gods."

"What about mine?" I fixed my eyes on the broad leaf of a palm tree as we trailed underneath it. "Never mind. They're surely throwing a feast bigger than Father will when Mother comes home. Even Hogne would reproach me for disobeying."

"Are you thinking of escaping?" Sirion appeared uncomfortable, shuffling and fidgeting even as he led me deeper into the garden.

"Do you know a way?"

Sirion shook his head. "I'm sorry this marriage will take place despite your wishes."

"But not sorry enough to stop it from happening."

He nodded, tightening his hold around my fingers.

The people on my side bowed as we passed, the unlucky ones sweating in the sun. None of them met my eyes.

Sirion exhaled, his fine clothes shifting with his movements in the light. "This wedding, this string of formalities, is what we do for the world. What comes after is for only us."

My cheeks flushed. What after could there be, other than a crown that did not fit, and a cold throne? Sirion had said so himself, he'd left his heart in the past.

As if someone else commanded my body, I felt strangely empty. But this was happening, and it was happening to me. The path ahead became ever shorter, each slow step carrying me closer to transcending a boundary from which there would be no going back. Those vows might be only formalities, but Sirion knew as well as I how irrevocable they would be.

"Vildi, I'll try. I promise you," Sirion said, voice low and yet intense. His eyes bore into me, as if to imprint his very thoughts upon me, burrow into my heart and soul to nestle there, melt his being into mine. I felt him there, as well as his hand was real against my skin. Sealing his presence in my life, Sirion tangled his fingers further in mine. We neared the end of the road. "Even if I had a choice, I would have chosen you."

Studying the sand underneath my feet, I stepped carefully so as not to get grains in my delicate silk shoes—I could do without that discomfort. The silence pressed down on us like the heat from the sun, but I had no words to offer him.

As we passed Toleor, I met his solemn gaze, the only spectator not swept up by jubilation. Perhaps his heart bled for me. He knew I didn't want this, and he would wish me the best, just like Hogne. Or it was simply old habits. My chest stung, not letting me forget how I missed my peasant boy.

Trailing up a few stone steps, we knelt down in front of an altar. A priest stood before us, an older man with white and golden robes. His face showed no emotion, but his stare made my skin prickle, his tightly pressed lips signaling either displeasure or a belief in solemn self-importance. Maybe both. Sirion's family stood fanned out to the side with the stern king to the immediate right, and my family stood on mine.

Father graced us with his absence. Eldaborg was never left unattended and with both Mother and Madalyn, even Sir Sigve gone, he had to stay behind. In matters of duty, he was reliable, my father. I would have liked to take one more skaal with him.

Mother dabbed discreetly at her eyes, celebrating this merry occasion. My sister looked upon us with a beautiful smile—only she knew what hid behind it. Her bracelet sparkled like diamonds one moment, growing dull the next. Brage squinted against the sun; threw his head around to stare at the altar; calm only long enough to gape at the attires of white, red and blue before he spotted the butterflies swarming a cluster of purple flowers. His gaze was something I recognized. With his first time traveling outside Eldaborg, the world was his adventure. Brage had caught on to the festive atmosphere, and his cheerful grin spun forth a flicker of warmth in me.

Beside me was my own, lifelong duty. To serve and be served. The garden was filled with people curtsying before me. All of Lakari, and Sirion. I expelled air, for once finding the next breath easy. *I would have chosen you.* "I'll try," I finally whispered, too low for anyone but Sirion to hear. I sensed a light pressure in my palm.

"As the tale has been entrusted from father to son for as long as men have walked among the dunes, so will I also tell this story." With an even, powerful voice belying his age, the priest began as if reciting a dear childhood memory.

"At the start of days there was only Rashim, the sun, watching from above the empty, unending desert. But even gods grow lonely when the days number the eternal. He cast out two flickering flames, letting them grow and take the shape of the dragons: Liva and Avil. Circling the sun, the dragons found in each other strength and love. A spark sprang forth between them, and thus their union lit the desert with life. After breathing life into the world, the dragons waited, watching.

"But their beautiful world of life was not perfect. Marred with war, sickness, and famine, their people were soon dying. In heavy sorrow and motherly love, the dragon Liva reached out to the dragon Avil, and together they bestowed a gift to man and woman. With the protection of love, they brought peace to the people, shaping the foundation of Lakari.

"Still Liva and Avil watch their people. On warm days we can see the dragons glowing, circling the sun. Today we celebrate the gift of Himayatan as we unite the next king and queen of Lakari."

I glanced up. The sun glared back. I saw nothing in it but heat. In Rimdalir, warmth was life and winter was an enemy. Here the life-giving sun might mean death, and yet the people worshipped it.

My hands were stiff and cold, even with how hot and stuffed it was inside this circle. Sirion held a mask of solemnity, although behind was something else. Or perhaps it was my imagination, the satisfaction curling around his "yes."

The priest shifted his gaze to me. An entire nation set their heavy stares on me, their queen-to-be. My stomach flopped. Queasy, with the hanging plants and altar swimming in my vision, I swallowed. My fingers twitched. Someone squeezed my hand, warm and steady. Sirion. Standing so close to me, I heard his heart beating, even and strong, and I drew a breath. "Yes."

I gave away my freedom to him.

I glimpsed Mother's tears—the happiest day of her life. A daughter married with a foot solidly on the safe side of twenty; the Rebel Princess of Rimdalir was finally tied down, and I no longer threatened to disgrace them all.

The rest of the ceremony was an austere, stiff thing, morphing into a huge celebration. Laughter and brew flowed with the same freedom as a mountain stream in spring and even our reverent King succumbed to the merry atmosphere.

"Come, Vildi. I think you'll like this next part." Sirion held firm on my hand as a crowd of strangers and family alike flocked us, cheering us on in a rush through the garden. Down a corridor, crossing a hall and past the main gate, we came out on the other side of the palace to the sight of a huge beast, towering above a sea of camels.

My hands flew to my mouth, barely containing a squeal. "An elephant? I've only ever read of those." My steps quickened, and in spite of the dress, I dashed forward.

Sirion caught my hand. "Easy, Vildi. You'll only trip on your dress or fall down the stairs."

I cast my eyes down. "It's one, wide step, Sirion. I'll be fine." I trod with care, lifting the hem of my gown above ground to give my shoes freedom.

We proceeded through the only path in a forest of potential phlegm spitters, emerging on the other side safe and dry. Perhaps camels were more well-mannered than I gave them credit for. At last, we faced the elephant, close enough to see every furrow in its clean, gray skin and feel the air move as it flapped its ears.

"Did they scrub you too, poor you? And just for this. They did me too, see?" I tilted my head, showing off my own speckless cheek.

"Poor you." Sirion chuckled, giving my pristine state the barest of glance. "Here. Let her choose if she wants physical contact. Elephants are gentle, but they want respect."

With Sirion to pace me, I slowed, reining in my eagerness to a soft, outstretched hand for the creature to greet. "That's just like my sister. Nice to meet you, Elegant Elephant."

The tip of her trunk, graceful as the best of dancers, uncurled to tickle my palm. Long lashes swept down across gray cheeks, framing huge eyes like nothing I had ever before seen. The elephant blew air through the trunk, a fanfare welcoming us to join her.

"Elephants are intelligent and loyal," Sirion said. He gave the trunk a pat.

Elegant shook her ears, creating a cool breeze rustling through our clothes.

"Are you ready?" Sirion turned to me, his eyes alight with glittering cheer.

A contraption of thick, black leather went around the creature's stomach, crowned on top by a platform with a couch of sorts. Plush green pillows promised comfort while an overhang of golden cloth was set to provide much needed shade. "Are you sure it's safe?" It appeared like a ramshackle construction to me, despite the fine materials used in its build. A pretty exterior didn't ensure quality, a fact I could never forget.

The animal groaned, lowering herself to the ground.

Sirion tugged at my hand, flashing a grin. "It's safe. You did well with your camel; this will be easy. And you're not doing it alone. I happen to be an experienced elephant rider, I'll let you know."

"I'm sure you are." I gripped the handle and pushed myself up, finding it quite easy to thread on the readied footholds to reach the pillows, even managing to spare my dress any harm.

Sirion was quick to follow, leaping up and landing without a moment's hesitation, as if he'd done this every single day of his life.

Slowly, Elegant put her front legs underneath her, extending them. We swayed backward against the back of our couch. With her back legs she pushed, and we had to hold onto the railing in front of us to not fall forward. Each of her steps hit the stone as thunder, vibrating through our seat.

People danced in the streets, music floating from one musician to the next. Our procession moved along a great road through the city, showing off the newlyweds with every sway of the elephant. Our guards flanked us, some on camels and others on their feet. I spotted both Horasis and Toleor among them.

Sirion's little sisters, Liria especially, viewed the proceedings with dreamy eyes, admiration, awe, and acute fascination. With the last glance I had of them, they dove deep down into the throes of a giggling mess.

As we passed, every person turned toward us, craning their necks, children being hoisted on shoulders to get a view, a glance, a glimmer of a snippet of a dress. The people of Lakari. Something fluffy and wild burst in my stomach anew. I would be queen, in a few months—far too soon. A *ruler*. But not alone. Well, thank the gods there was some sense left in this world.

"I know they're supposed to, but . . . they're all staring."

"Because you're beautiful, Vildi." Sirion didn't even blink, examining the crowd on his side as he waved and smiled.

I threw him a quick glance only to meet with blue, finding the swarm of citizens to be safer after all.

Sirion was not done. "You see, you bear the gods in you. The dragons in your hair and life in your eyes."

"So does half of Rimdalir." I let out a laugh, though it was short lived. Below us, Toleor and Horasis were gone in the crowd, this mass of humans and camels moving as a churning sea.

"No. You're a treasure, Vildi, to Lakari."

To Lakari. How great. I was a hunting trophy after all. People studied me as I passed them, shining, brown eyes all gazing up.

My right hand, placed inside his, was so warm. On my left hand, the fingers clenched cold around my emerald-golden dress. A glance, and my gaze was arrested in his. "On the subject of eyes . . . Sirion, yours remind me of looking into the rifts of a glacier."

He laughed. "That's ice, isn't it? Frozen water? That might be my best compliment yet."

"Poor you. Here's a better one for you. They remind me of the oasis. The Desert Diamond."

Sirion leaned back against the pillows, his mouth releasing a small sigh. "I look forward to going back. All of this is formalities. The Desert Diamond . . . that's when our real bond will form."

"So you say. I rather think the cake tonight will do the honors."

Sirion shook his head, amusement running on his lips. "Knowing you, that might be true."

I leaned closer, examining the stark black rims encasing ice-blue within. How strange.

"Vildi?"

One seldom saw such a shade of blue even in Rimdalir.

"You're staring."

Sirion was close. A faint red dusted his cheekbones as he leaned toward me. His lips. A myriad of wings fluttered and flailed inside me, flaring a wave of heat from toes to fingertips. "Oh . . . I thought—why do you have blue eyes?"

Sirion collapsed backward into the pillows, laughing behind the hand covering his face. "Good question," he managed.

Leaning toward my own side of the seat, I sniffed. "Well, all Lakarians have brown eyes. Just look."

"Yes." Chuckles still escaped Sirion. "Except my family. We're all born like this, the entire royal line. We think it's our connection with the gods. Our children will be the same."

Children. My fists found silk to ruin within their grip. The sun stood high now, but from zenith it was only one path—straight down. Apart from being a nice commodity of trade, every princess' duty in history had been to produce heirs, and I would be a fool to think I could be different.

But my husband was Sirion. If there was one kindness in this, that was it. I snuck a peek at the man by my side. His gaze had slid away to meet the love of the masses below, but I knew if he turned, those eyes could sweep through me with the power of a sea in a storm. And if his words were true, someday, a baby would blink up at me with those same, ocean blue orbs. Button nose, a small, pursed mouth, perhaps with skin in a hue between fair and gold. Apart from Brage, I had little experience with the tiny creatures. Brage had been rusty-blond from birth. My child . . . Sirion's child, would it have raven tufts on its head like his father?

A feast had been prepared for us as we came back, and our wedding dinner was delicious. After a few drinks I laughed with ease, a genuine happiness, and even though I knew it was fleeting, I was too far gone to care. Better yet was the bounty of cakes and pastries served afterward. Didn't I once say this was a country of cake? The king stared and Sirion laughed, but why should I care? In a few sparkling moments there was only honey, and dough, and me.

There were quite a few speeches, and poets singing their praise to the lovely couple, the lands, and Himayatan. Strong drinks set everyone ablaze in celebration. All around was this *happiness*, so tangible in the air I could taste it.

Sirion held my hand throughout the entire evening, warm and soothing. His gaze seldom left me for long, though he played his official role splendidly, giving away 'thank you's and other formal pleasantries with ease. I almost believed him. If he was disappointed, he hid it very, very well.

The feast, though nothing like the rowdy, hearty events at home, blurred in voices and plastered pleasantries, the swish of fine fabrics flashing in the corner of my sight as sweet wine and even sweeter pastries found their way within reach. Steadily but quite sudden the sand had run out on the day. A hand kept a solid grip around mine as we weaved through corridors and upstairs. Marble spun in my vision, coming to a stop as my toes wriggled against a plush carpet. Silks fell from my frame as servant girls fastened fluttering ribbons and adjusted my hair to fall like a waterfall down my back. I extended my arms in front of me and the white chiffon of my shift followed. The sound of a door swinging open had me turn and there stood Sirion, his sculpted shoulders, sharp cheekbones, and deep, stormy eyes. And we were alone in my room.

With stumbling steps, I went to him. "Sirion?"

"Yes, Vildi?" I swayed like the breeze. He steadied me like an expert sailor on churning water.

"What's the withering death?"

"What?" His face wouldn't stay focused for me. I wanted to see his smile in front of me. Why didn't he keep the fog away from my eyes?

"The with'ring greens. Like my eyes." My tongue curled with happiness around the sound of the 's.' Like Sirion.

Something took a good grip on my arm. A quiet laughter reached my ear, but my hand couldn't get a hold of it. "It's what people drink to forget the consequential headache which follows a night of celebration." Sirion's voice floated in the great space of lit candles and moonlight.

"Oh."

My body leaned against his. Sirion's heartbeat was in my ear, a scent of citrus and smoke tingling my senses.

"Sirion?"

"Yes?"

I reached up, filtering my fingers in his raven hair. "Not a peasant boy. You're not my fairy-tale lad, but—for a noble, you might be tol'rable."

"You don't say."

He led me to the bed, catching me before I could stumble. Putting me on the sheets and tucking the blankets around me, he stroked my hair like one would pet a helpless kitten. "Sleep well, Vildi."

He left.

22

TEA AND TREPIDATION

I woke up alone. This was normal, of course, and I had done so for months, ever since leaving Madalyn alone in our old bedroom. Alone was good. Normal was good. I blinked, and sunlight touched my finger. There was a ring on that finger, setting off an abrupt squeeze in my heart. He had left.

In my rambling, shambling, alcohol doused state, Sirion had simply led me to the bed and fled out the door. I had done what I did best, the very thing I had sworn myself to do in a throne-room months ago and again when I set foot at Lakarian court. I had ruined everything.

Whatever I had imagined from my first night as a married woman, being left alone was not among my expectations, and it was my fault.

BALANCE

I flung a dress above my head, tugging it in place as I scurried out the door. I hit Horasis with my leg and almost fell atop of him, catching myself with a hair's breadth to go. Horasis mumbled, turning toward the wall to snore lightly against it. Yesterday must have been long for him too.

I sped down the corridor, breaching daybreak rays seeping through the windows.

"Madalyn, Maya, please let me in."

The door creaked. "Vildi?" My sister blinked at me. Blue, like his, but lighter, bearing love as only Madalyn could.

"He left." I said, sniffling, my nose dense.

Maya's head emerged over Madalyn's shoulder. She rubbed sleep from her eyes, her dark blonde hair free from the usual shackles and flowing down her back. "Oh, Little Lady."

"Maya, he left."

"Come in, come here, I'm sure it's not so bad." Maya pulled at my hand, tugging me inside their sleeping quarters.

"Vildi, what happened?" I sensed Madalyn's arm around me, guiding me to a couch.

"Sirion." I clenched my free hand, wrinkling a fistful of silk. What had I said to him, the night before? That he was tolerable? Well, what a great compliment that was. No wonder he left. Who would want a drunk, obstinate, and rude girl by their side? Oh, by the gods, he must have felt so disappointed, having lost the graceful, beautiful Ashia and being stuck with Vildi. "How little he must think of me now."

"I'm sorry?" Madalyn's mouth forgot to close.

"Last night." I flung my arms out. "I promised to try, but he left me alone, and now I'm too late. He didn't even stay to talk. He's given up. Of course, he has, they all do in the end, and he's been patient for weeks already. Sirion gave up on me."

"I'm sure it's not that bad, Lady Vildi." Maya stroked my back, up and down and soothing.

"It is. And I can't even go back and Do-Again, because this is a new day already and any way, I did this for weeks. Last night was only one drop in a cup filled to the brim."

"Vildi, you only have now. We must all live with our choices. But you can decide for today, and tomorrow, and every day still ahead of you." Madalyn spun a lock of my hair, placing it behind my ear. I felt it loosen and flop inelegantly down moments after. Stubborn hair.

Maya stroked my cheek as if I was five and had scrubbed my knees. "If you talk with him, I'm sure he'll explain. It will be fine, little princess, so don't cry."

"Cry?" I blinked. "I . . . oh. I am."

Maya laughed. Madalyn patted under my eye with the hem of her dress. They both looked as if I presented them the midwinter feast, the first spring flower and the autumn fire all at once.

"I have to talk with him."

They both nodded. Maya dabbed at the corner of her eyes.

"Hogne would be proud, little sister."

I cast my gaze down to my lap, allowing myself to sink into the comfort of his name. "I know he is." If only Hogne was here as well.

"I'm proud of you too." Madalyn embraced me, the white stones at her wrist glowing stronger than I had ever seen them.

"Thank you," I breathed. Bouncing off the couch, I sprinted out the room and down the hall. I knew what to do. My tears tempted a slight smile, growing with each step until it hurt my cheeks. My hair flared behind me, as if carried by the wind. With chest heaving against the words, I pressed forth, the staff gaped at me before finally heeding my request.

∽

Less than an hour after waking up, I found myself outside a door. Not any door either. This particular door hid my husband on the other side. With a deep breath, steadying a peace offering on the tray in my arms, I knocked. Nothing happened. My knuckles rapped against the wood with increasing force until at last I heard shuffling inside. As if reluctant to move at all, the door creaked on its hinges.

"Vildi?" Sirion blinked at me, eyes bleary, hair tousled fresh from bed. "I thought you'd sleep much longer."

The strangled sound escaping me was not the natural laugh I had imagined. "I'm a princess of Rimdalir. Alcohol is not new to me. I only have a small headache, slight nausea, and the urge to bury myself beneath dark blankets and not come up again . . ."

"I see." Sirion's lip curled for my benefit, the same type of indulging smile I had received from the grownups as a child.

"Well, that's who I was, at least. But I'm not anymore, am I?" The thought was strange. I tucked it away somewhere deep down in my stomach, underneath a lump from which it would never again emerge, could do no harm. "Here." I held the tray out.

"Tea?" He took my offering, peering at the can, and leaned down to take a whiff. "Did you make it?"

I chewed on the inside of my cheek. "Yes." But perhaps I should have let the servants do it after all? They had looked horrified as I swished around, taking my liberties in their kitchen—and what if I did it wrong. The tea could be really bitter or taste nothing at all, or perhaps I used too much sugar and he'd feel terrible after a single sip. My lips felt numb forming the words, "For you." My foot scraped against the floor. Even after all the times I had seen him do it, every cup he had made for me, why hadn't I paid more attention?

His expression was frozen in that bland, polite grimace. He was probably too well-mannered, too kind, to not drink, even with such an unimpressive gift. And I might be too late, anyway. In the desert we had at least been able to talk, although we barely knew each other. Now we were as tightly bound as the gods would allow and still each word hung heavy in the air, building upon a wall I had nursed these past weeks without noticing. Not thinking.

I dove back into the depths. Nothing left to lose, was there? "Sirion, I'm sorry. Lakari should have a better queen-to-be than me. And you deserve more than—more than me."

His face was stone. No, a tilt of his head, lips bending up—was he laughing?

I felt my cheeks burn. Could I sound any more pretentious? I let my gaze fall away from his summer-night eyes. Inhaled hot, still air. I was too far in now, and if he found me ridiculous or childish, so be it. "This is it. I want to make the most of this, even though I'm starting late. I realize that I am. And I created this distance. I had trouble accepting—well, everything."

"Stop. It's fine." Sirion glanced past me, up and down the corridor, then took my hand. His touch burned. "Let's talk more inside. A hall is not the right place for this, I think."

Sirion's chambers were big and spacious. We entered a room for waiting, pleasant but sparse as any seldom used room would be. It led to a living room with a couch, a salon table, and elegant yet comfortable chairs. A scent of sandalwood curled around my senses, originating from a glowing rod of incense in the corner. Paintings decorated the walls, showing lush forests and vast mountains, bustling cities and foreign cultures. Small, curious objects stood on proud display atop a shelf, like seeing through a window upon a world outside Lakari. A bookshelf of glittering midnight stone held row upon row of leather-bound books, scrolls, and tomes. Underneath a stack of papers, a map of thick parchment jutted out, exposing faint lines and shapes where light touched its surface.

Sirion put my possibly mortifying gift of tea on the table, gesturing for me to sit. He lounged in a chaise across from me, with nothing to betray his thoughts about this invasion from a person he had well and truly left behind last night. But yesterday, under the burning sun of his gods, Sirion had said he would try. *I would have chosen you.*

My feet slipped out of thin shoes to feel the plush, red carpet covering his floor. The fibers tickled my skin, welcoming my toes within their embrace with a silky texture rivaling my new gown. I glanced down, seeing my feet caress the visage of a dragon.

As the burning sensation in my cheeks receded so did the grip on my voice. "Sirion, how are we supposed to live together, do this thing? *Marriage?*" The word sounded woolen, as if my tongue was too thick to bend properly around it.

"We'll be fine, Vildi." Sirion poured tea into the two cups. He encircled one in his palms. "Warm." He lifted it up to his nose. "Smells good."

As if we were back in his small desert home, sitting in the kitchen with only an oversized table separating us, I reached for the cup he had placed before me. It was hot against my cold fingers. "You gave me your mercy, before. Do I still have it?"

"I'll do my best to take care of you," he answered instead, gaze fully trained on the drink.

"Is it the same?"

Sirion met my eyes. "It's the best I can do. I can promise . . . you will be safe. And I hope you'll be happy. Eventually".

I wanted to protest. After so many attacks, promising safety seemed like a tall order. Still, he had absolute confidence, jaw set in hard, determined lines, eyes unyielding, looking like he desperately wanted me to understand.

"I believe you," I said. I drew a breath, releasing it was easier than expected. "I'll trust you." Not that I had much of a choice, but I kept those words locked inside me because finally, I pulled forth something in him: a tentative but warm smile.

Noticing his empty cup, I gave it a generous refill. Sirion reached out, plucking the kettle from me to fill mine.

"Sirion, do you remember our game?"

Sirion put his chin in hand. "You mean the guessing game?"

"Yes. It was supposed to be ten tries, but I broke it off because I was scared. You know, I was on the run and didn't want to be identified . . ."

"I remember. But Vildi—"

"And you won, but I thought if you wanted to, we could do those last few tries now. I think we each had four left?"

"We could of course, but . . ." Sirion cast his gaze down, brows drawn tight against a furrow between his eyes. A chuckle escaped his lips, as if he had trouble choosing between laughter or dismay.

"I know you already won." I turned toward the window. From Sirion's room, the sun was still hidden behind a wall. Instead, I viewed the vast, spotless sky. One rarely saw this in Rimdalir: the lack of even one puff of a cloud, except to announce the clear blue of midwinter chill. In Lakari, the sky offered little else.

"Vildi, that's not it. If anything, you won by default."

I blinked. Twisting toward him, I was met with Sirion's wry amusement.

"But you got everything . . . you guessed right every time. Every. Single. Time. Sirion, you cheated!"

Sirion's deep laugh couldn't hide the red rising to his cheeks. "I did."

I fell back on the couch. "And I thought I was so bad at it."

"I'm sorry. In normal circumstances, I don't think I would have done better than you. Hearing these things from you—talking about them—it was different from simple prior knowledge. It was fun. Real."

"You tricked me. I was going to ask if you wanted a prize too."

Sirion shrugged. "I don't deserve one."

"You don't."

"But I would like for us to complete the game, if you still want to."

I eyed him. "No cheating?"

"None."

"Well then. Four tries, no lies. Start."

He leaned back, examining me. Eventually, he spoke. "You had a happy childhood. You love your family, and they love you."

"Almost everything was good about my childhood, thinking back."

Sirion grew serious as he studied me. "You mentioned magic once. Mysteries, the unfathomable, fairy tales: they all fascinate you."

"They definitely do." A shiver traced down my back. "A bit too much, it seems. I received more than my share." A wish the gods could have refrained from granting, in my humble opinion.

"It will get better, Vildi."

Poor, naïve Sirion. I was only a knife-throw away from new Do-Agains. Only a slice in my sleep from entering infinite death. Because . . . if they killed me, it would happen, would it not? Was there a possibility I could die without waking up? What force ruled the repeated days? A chill spread up from my fingertips, and I huddled in my own arms.

With folded hands supporting his chin, Sirion scrutinized my curled-up form. "Your aversion to marriage . . . it must be more than the candidates." He inhaled as if bracing for impact. "Your parents."

Dry chuckles left me. "Good guess. It's not my parents. They are odd together, but they love each other."

"I'm glad. Mine shared respect, fondness perhaps, but not love."

"I'm sorry."

Sirion's shoulders slumped. "It's common. We will be an exception, and I'm happy about that."

My eyebrow arched in response to his words. "You seem so sure."

"Because I am." Sirion lifted his cup of tea, as if giving a skaal before he took a graceful sip. "You're in love with me."

Blood rushed to my face, drums beating hard as my gaze leapt down to my lap. "You have one left."

He nodded, knuckles pale from his tight grip on the cup. "There was at least one suitor you had a good relationship with, the one you mentioned yesterday. Hogne? Your single, favorite noble." Sirion scowled, as a man forced to swallow a particularly distasteful stew or one of Madalyn's failed sweet buns.

"Hogne? He wasn't a suitor, he's more . . . an older brother? He's still looking out for me, protecting me . . ." I traced a white swirl in the otherwise dark onyx table, feeling a small sting in my heart. "Not a suitor. Though I loved him. And as for my favorite noble, I came to like Jarle because he never showed interest in me. He's staying true to his feelings and to Madalyn, and I respect that. But my real suitors . . . no. I must admit, I disliked or despised them all."

Sirion put his cup down, filling both mine and his one last time. "I see. So I had it wrong."

"You get no point for that guess."

"I'm fine with that. I got answers."

I cracked a smile. "Ready?"

Sirion gave me a nod.

It was my turn to lean forward, observing every small movement of the man before me without shame or retribution. He met my eyes for a full minute before he blinked, blue sliding away to focus elsewhere. His loose, simple woolen shirt moved along without sound. His hair stood at odd angles, though this was my fault, surprising him before he had a chance to meet me in his own time. If not for his quality clothes and the pristine state of his skin, Sirion would have made for a fine peasant. "At some point in your life, you didn't want to be king."

Sirion's eyes widened. "Correct. How did you know?"

I exhaled. "Because you've run away from responsibility at least once. And I know a few things about that. You had a hideout in the ruins, Sirion."

"After . . . after Ashia."

A stone loaded itself upon my chest. I swallowed. "Yes."

"Vildi?"

"Yes?"

"That counts as two, I believe."

I let out a surprised laugh. "How generous. How utterly un-magnanimous."

"I'm a fast learner," Sirion said, grinning with all his white teeth. A future king and his duties, indeed.

Opening my hands in my lap, I tilted my head, meeting his gaze from under my lashes. "Well, I must allow it, mustn't I?"

Sirion just shrugged. Honestly, why couldn't my teeth have been that nice?

"Well, I'll make my last two count. First: despite your arrogance, you are kind and caring. You might even be quite selfless."

"Thank you? I think?" Sirion blinked.

"It's a good thing." A flicker of laughter and light swept through me, gone as I drew a breath. I fisted a part of my dress, keeping level with his gaze, though just barely. A myriad of butterflies sprung forth inside of me. "Yesterday evening, you left out of consideration for me."

Sirion lost his own smile. His fine hands still held the cup of tea I had brought, although by now it was empty. "Yes. For you. But for me as well. I want us to start something together, something to last. I want to do this right."

"Is there even a right way?"

A tiny tug teased his lips. "Perhaps not. But there are better and worse." Sirion raked through his raven-feather hair, making it look as if a strong wind had blown through the room. "Tell me, Vildi, what your suitor did to you. The worm."

My hands balled into small, helpless little fists. I glimpsed Sirion behind the hair that hung in front of my eyes, awaiting a reply. I bit the inside of my cheek.

A hand reached out to embrace one of my clenched hands, another breached the light curtain to stroke my cheek, tucking some of the hair away as it retreated. "Please, Vildi."

"There is not much to say." My voice was a whisper, mist dispersing upon leaving me, unable to sustain shape in the outside world.

"Will you try?"

I nodded. "Vinjar . . . I think Mother always envisioned him for me. He was a duke from her homeland, you see, and through our marriage the ties between Rimdalir and Getjyr would stand strong. He knew this, of course. When he arrived at my fifteenth birthday, I was his possession. I was to be his obedient, graceful little *star*." I wiped my eyes. "That didn't sit well with me. And he wanted this, but if Madalyn was close, he couldn't take his eyes off her. And I understand because everyone loves Madalyn, and she deserves their love. She is born to beauty and grace, of course he would notice her. But he did this, and still he wanted me. A spare, perhaps? Although most suitors were the same. It was *how* he did it. Those ogling eyes, going up and down and lingering, his oily voice, his condescending way of thinking we were nothing but decoration . . . and I turned seventeen. The great hall was thick with a tint of ale, and one would have to lean in to be heard. *He* was at my ball, of course. He . . . caught me as I drew fresh air outside. He was close. Didn't let go, with those hands, his drunken breath and his voice, *my little star,* and I couldn't move—unable to break free. He slithered against my body and his fingers groped against my dress, seeking skin and he pressed against me as my back pressed against the wall. No one was there to see, to hear, to help. Then—at last—my hands moved, shoved, and I broke free."

I glanced up. Again, there was a storm in Sirion's eyes.

"And that was that. The worm let go of me at last. I just . . . I had enough. So I left. Sir Sigve caught up with me the very next day, as I was haggling for passage on a ship. Apparently, Father had allowed me to go, if he stayed with me. And now you know everything about Vinjar the Worm."

"I want to kill him."

"You'll never get the opportunity. Madalyn will get to him first." I managed a smile.

"Your sister? I wouldn't have guessed." Sirion grinned. "I like her better now."

"Madalyn is great." I felt the tension leaving me and with it, laughter returning.

Sirion shifted, letting go of my hand. He turned to the window, eyes flitting my way once before fixing his gaze on the empty sky. "I'm glad you came here."

I glanced at my cup. There was still a little left, swirling at the bottom, too cold now to tempt me. Tea was better if Sirion prepared it. I put the cup down on the table, able to give my husband a nod.

He reclaimed my hand, almost engulfing it within his. "We don't know each other like we should, and our circumstances are not the best. Still, I feel alive again. I'm no longer alone, Vildi."

I barely refrained from drying off my hands on the sheer, creamy fabrics of the skirt, ruining the dress forever. If I disappeared or died, would he bear it well? I had heard the stories. A little had slipped in our conversations as well. I knew he struggled the last time. Sirion's voice was low, intense as if speaking directly to my heart. As if wanting to escape reason, my heart yearned to listen.

"I'm connected to you through a bond neither of us can break." The rings glinted in emerald and gold, as if to confirm his words. "Vildi, you are stronger than you think. And beautiful. You make me laugh, and, well, there's something good in my life again." With a sardonic twist of his lips, Sirion shrugged. "I can no longer ask you to marry me. Instead . . ." He sank to the floor by my feet, holding my gaze arrested in his as fingers entwined with mine. Deep hurt and deeper hope was in the slight tremble of his hands; his mouth, caught in a fight between uncertainty and joy. Sirion drew breath like a man drowning, breaching the surface after a long time. "Alvildi, will you share your life with me?"

It was like a thorn being yanked out, leaving me raw but relieved. Like his extended hand pulled me up from icy water, as I did the same for him. I laughed, throwing myself forward, embracing Sirion with all that was me. "I think I can do that."

Sirion put his arms around me, warm and alive, and so was I. There was also the benefit of his shoulder hiding my flush. His single word, "good," vibrated from his chest through me.

REUNION OF FRIENDS

Time ceased to exist as sandalwood and citrus embraced my senses. His pulse, throbbing in his neck against my lips, beating the rhythm of his heart through my body, spurring fire through my veins until only Sirion, close, close, registered in my mind.

Abruptly, I could again feel the lack of sunshine through the window. Sirion released me to the presence of his wide couch, a breeze rustling past us from the open window and a sudden gap where before only light clothes had separated him from me.

Unable to hide flushing cheeks, I settled with my hands bundled before me. "It seems I won our game, Sirion."

"You did. No cheating either."

"Do I get a prize?"

Sirion tilted his head, hair falling in front of his eyes. His eyes slid down, snapping up the same second and he grinned, his expression matching the thrill in my chest. "What do you want?"

My gaze took to wandering, past his lips and down—to the safety of my slightly tanned hands, with white lines faint in my palms. A blonde curtain followed. I had forgotten to set up my hair before I stormed to his door. With some luck, any tangle ignored in my haste was hidden by the sheer amount of hair, despite our proximity.

"I actually do have something for you." Disappearing for a moment, he came back with a bundle.

"Thank you." I reached for it, but only reluctantly did he let go. It was heavy for its small size, hiding a hard object within. As I unfolded the cloth, something shone in reflected light from the lamps: a blade with an ebony handle gleaming beneath my fingers. I lifted my gaze to meet Sirion's serious eyes. "That's my knife."

"It is," he admitted.

"You stole it."

"Yes." He didn't even sound the least bit remorseful. "And I give it back only for your defense. I don't want you to be without something to protect yourself with when we leave for the Desert Diamond. But please, Vildi, don't do anything foolish. Don't use it to hurt yourself."

"Why would I—" Well, if Komir and Horasis had reported on my behavior, maybe such an admonition was not entirely unfounded. And Sir Sigve had surely outed my skills with sharp objects. The first princess of Rimdalir in the memory of men to be banned from fighting, and in general handling anything more lethal than a sewing needle. There was nothing to do but yield to my fate. I clenched Madalyn's supposed gift between my fingers, the blade sharp and fine as the day I bought it. Unused. Madalyn would forgive me for keeping the knife a few more days. Sirion had no clue how clumsy I was or he would never have given it back. "Very well. Defense only."

"Good. I would have liked to delay the trip to be honest, but it's tradition for people like us. Can't be avoided. It's like . . . a confirmation or solidification of our bond."

"Why? Isn't that what a wedding is all about?"

Sirion pulled his brows together. "I'm not sure how to explain it. I guess it's a question of sanity as much as anything, equilibrium of the mind. I'm not entirely sure what to expect, to be honest."

"But you . . ." I dropped my eyes to the floor, finding my Lakarian coin in an invisible pocket of the dress. It had been with me ever since it came into my possession, as if calling me to its home. My fingers started playing with the piece, flipping it from pinky to thumb. "You didn't do this with Ashia?"

"No." Sirion gazed out the window. "No one alive has witnessed the Ceremony of Bonding. But this is . . . personal? It's between us and the gods. Anyway," he continued, shaking himself out of his musings, "as we still don't know our attackers, we must be careful. There was another attempt yesterday. Did you notice?"

My heart stilled. "I didn't," I said, body weighed down like a fear hanging over you so long it grows numb.

"I'm glad." Sirion looked more bitter than anything, the lack of information possibly gnawing at him. "I didn't want you to worry about that as well; you had enough already."

"What happened?"

"Our guards spotted people moving close during our ride through the city. There was also a skirmish at the ceremony itself. Several people must be involved, and I don't think they're from Lakari."

"There's at least two." As far as my nightmare memories could tell. "Maybe three?" Because there had been two working together to create the accident of me being run down by a horse-driven carriage. In addition, one man had waited in Fiar.

"Yes." Sirion clenched his hands. "And at least one has access to the palace. They are still so elusive."

The stone lodged in my stomach grew to the size of a boulder, taking up all the space in me. "Only exposing themselves if they were sure of success."

"Yes. I think so too."

I glared down at my small hands. Even with a knife, I was helpless. A lady through and through, although even Mother would not have liked this if she knew.

Sirion put his arms around me, sharing his warmth. Only then did I notice myself shaking against his frame. "Until we get them, we must be careful. Therefore, only a handful of people know about our departure tomorrow, and they will come along to protect us. You can bring Sir Sigve, if you want. I think you should."

"All right." Having my companion with me again would help. "I'll be prepared." Maybe Sirion would feel safer, at least, if I had this blade on me. I clenched the knife handle until my knuckles turned white.

"Here," Sirion said, adjusting my grip. "Like this." His breath touched my face, so, so close. His hands covered mine.

Did he know how many scars had been inflicted from my clumsy hands? What if I lost the knife and it cut him or severed the tips of his fingers? My own fingers twitched. The knife slipped in my slick grip.

With a quick dive, Sirion pinched the blade between his index finger and thumb. He gave it back handle-first, a crease nestling between his eyes. His hand brushed across mine as he let go.

Well, at least we both had our toes intact, despite my blundering hands. "Thank you," I said, face stiff.

Sirion leaned back on the couch, giving a sharp nod even as he avoided my eyes.

My thoughts, my words, they were stuck somewhere in my chest or my throat, squeezing. We were silent for a second, a minute, the moment dragging on and still his eyes were rigid, staring as if there was nothing more mesmerizing than the wall.

"I'm sorry." I blinked. There was a push between my eyes as a headache greeted me, pressing out tears with its arrival. "I didn't mean . . . you shouldn't come close to me while I'm holding something sharp. What if it slips and the pointy end cuts you?" I put the knife back in its protective leather case, every movement performed with precision and care.

Sirion turned to look at me again, eyebrows arched.

I met his eyes. "I don't mind holding hands."

Without hesitation he snatched my outstretched limb, his face relaxing as if nothing had plagued him. "Of course, you don't."

"Did you just manipulate me?"

"Maybe? I might have had a stronger reaction than was called for." Sirion shrugged, his smirk not dimming even a smudgeon.

"What am I to do now?"

"You could reclaim your hand," Sirion said. But his grip felt nice and warm for my cold fingers. "You could hug me again."

I blew at a piece of hair. It fell right back. "You always present me with such easy choices."

"I'm here to serve." He spread his arms to the side, slumped yet elegant as he reclined on his part of the couch. A moment later, I snuck my arms around his neck, my heart loud against his chest, his beats just as loud against mine.

"You know what?" My voice, muffled from his shirt, still carried to him. "I actually look forward to seeing the oasis again. The Desert Diamond. Being there felt nice."

"Of course, it did," Sirion said. "I like it, why shouldn't you?"

"So everyone must think as you do." I pushed myself away, leaving him sitting there blinking up at me. I pulled the reins on my smile just as it simmered under the surface.

He grinned. "Why not?"

I opened my mouth, then closed it without finding proper words.

"I changed my mind." Sirion leaned back, his gaze still trained on me. "I don't want competition."

BALANCE

"As if that even matters anymore." I blew on a lock of hair. The door across the room tempted me anew. I should take a bath, soak down in hot water until my skin turned red and scrunched-up like sun-dried fruit.

"I have one more thing for you," Sirion said, perhaps trying to pacify me. "This time, it truly is a gift. Just let me get into some proper clothes, and then I'll take you there."

"Well . . ." I glanced down at the knife, once again strapped to my belt. "All right."

Sirion moved at a snail's pace as he readied himself, and I sat on his coach, locking my fingers together as I waited. What could it be? What shape would it have? Was it edible? Another gift of jewelry to mark me as his own, brand me with his insignia as men seemed fond of doing? I would make an exception for Sirion. Take it with gratitude, even if it turned out to be something gaudy. I still recalled the feeling of cool metal around my wrist as Lord Gaute tried to brand me with his family crest on my fifteenth birthday. Sirion was no Gaute, thank the gods.

Soon we were walking hand in hand through long halls and lit corridors. Eventually we let the doors shut with a heavy thud behind us as we reached the palace courtyard. With the brilliant blue and open, immense sky, my smile bloomed. The breeze stroked my cheek, brushing through my hair. I closed my eyes and knew the cold was far away. Maybe this day could be happy—perhaps they all could.

And Sirion would remain beside me. The knot made by our hands sent warmth between us. "This is so strange."

"What is?" Sirion sensed my halting movements and tugged lightly.

"Being married."

He frowned, turning elsewhere while forgetting I had to follow, our hands still linked. I stumbled a step or two before catching up.

"I spent so much time running from this, ever since I was fifteen. All of Madalyn's suitors who had failed to win her suddenly shifted to me, giving me the same words and empty promises." A grimace pulled at my face. "I wanted nothing to do with it."

"And now?" Sirion's steps were long, almost too fast. I tugged on his hand, and he slowed down.

"It's not so bad," I relented, peeking up at him. Sirion's mood had improved. The day seemed bright, as if storm clouds had parted to let the sun shine.

"Not so bad, huh?" He saw right through me, didn't he?

"Well, and you love me," I sang, skipping some steps ahead and glancing back with a teasing grin.

Sirion stilled, joy abruptly gone. "I never said I did."

My cheeks burned at his words, and I ducked my head, happy for my tousled, unbraided hair as it fell in front of my face. I searched my mind for a sharp remark, but they all vanished without a trace. Where was my sarcasm when I needed it? If our marriage was a game, only Sirion knew the rules. But what had I expected, really? I should never forget the fairy-tale lie.

He chuckled, snatching my hand. "I do, though. I'm in love with you."

I released a breath, a laugh, feeling my shoulders slump as relief swept through me.

"We need to go in here." Sirion led me along through a small door. It had nothing of the oversized opulence otherwise observed throughout the palace, and it was intended for servants rather than us. A sweet fragrance reached us from within.

"What is it?" Could it possibly be . . . cake?

Sirion shook his head, keeping a good grip on his secretive smirk. "It's a surprise."

Turning a corner and passing another door, he guided me through a thousand similar looking corridors, which I could never hope to navigate myself. "Is this the quickest way?" I wondered, and Sirion's gaze fled past my shoulder.

"No, but I get to show you some of the old place. It never hurts to know where the paths lead, even if you don't use them often." He suddenly twirled me around, making my skirt flare until I came to a stop against him, meeting his gleaming eyes. "And I get to show the world my beautiful wife."

Sirion was . . . proud? Of me? Not Madalyn, not a perfect princess. Me. "You want to show me off?" The notion was so typical for a suitor. I could only laugh. Our hands swung between us as we moved through the light halls, passing the sun's rays as they hit white marble in a glimmer of diamonds, beautiful as ice flakes grown upon snow.

I'm sure we passed several kitchens, smells wafting from them as we went by. I wondered if there was cake? Sunlight hit us as we stepped through a modest size door that lead to the stables.

Sirion flexed his fingers, as if hit by nerves. Still, he faced me with radiance. "My future queen must have her own mount, don't you think?"

They had horses, elegant with long and slender limbs, much different from the sturdy breed back home. More exotic yet were the elephants, Elegant among them. The friendly creatures had an exclusive, enormous garden. A few animals were nearby the gate. The reason became apparent as Sirion reached into a hidden pocket and produced some treats. He put a biscuit into my palm, and a young trunk curled around it with the grace of a dancer.

Sirion snatched my hand afterward, tugging me along. No elephant for me, though I wasn't sure I would have had much use for one, anyway.

Like any respectable palace, they had a decent establishment for camels. A long row of these creatures examined us beneath their drooping lids, probably concluding we were out of spitting range.

Sirion steered us with sure, quick strides. Of all the camels sticking their shaggy heads out, watching us pass with lazy, sleepy eyes, one made a sound as we drew near. He gazed back with dark brown, beautiful, serene eyes, shaking his shining mane.

"Hello No-Name, good to see you," I cooed, letting go of Sirion in favor of his mount.

"No-Name?" Sirion's eyebrow crept up as a smirk came to his lips.

"Yes," I chirped, still busy nuzzling and scratching the perfect spot, the root of his mane. No-Name ignored Sirion, leaning toward me.

The neighboring camel stuck his head out. I froze. "Balt?"

Balt blinked at me. Then he called out, fervently bobbing his head as if to urge me over, pushing tears to my eyes.

"He's yours."

I sucked in a breath. "Truly?"

Sirion's teeth glinted white. "Bought him from the caravan business in Fiar just a few days ago."

Within two heartbeats, I held Balt tight. "I missed you so much!"

Behind me, I heard Sirion mumble. "That's a warmer greeting than *I* received."

I met his gaze, watching laughter dancing in the blue. Sirion had saved Balt. "Thank you." My voice allowed no more than a whisper. "Sirion, thank you so much." I stroked Balt's silky hairs, resting my forehead against his. "You will have a good life here, Balt. I'll take care of you."

Balt blew some warmth out of his nose.

"Would you like a ride now?" Sirion asked, moving toward his own mount.

"Yes."

"When we have dealt with the attacks, we should take a trip just for us. I'm having our house—the small one we stayed in—restored and renewed."

"The one with all the dragon handles? Your family home?"

Sirion's grin grew, as did the light in his eyes. "Yes. It'll be our own place, to be alone on occasions if you want."

I stretched out my hand, letting his fingers intertwine in mine. "I'd like that."

24

DESERT DIAMOND

Our party, including a priestess, Komir, Horasis, Toleor, Sir Sigve and, of course, Sirion and myself, departed for the Desert Diamond before the sun rose the next morning. No one bid us farewell, and we left the castle through a tunnel leading our party directly into the desert.

Priestess Risa was a gentle woman in her forties, with a long braid of black and silver running down her loose, light attire. She was seldom caught without a smile, but neither did she laugh. She kept us company in the evenings, helping with the meals and telling stories from Lakari's history and religion. She spoke of the royal line, how every known occurrence of Hima was followed by war, drought, or other disasters. *Hima never comes alone.* I received a solid education in everything which might go wrong in this desert kingdom, and the royal family, blessed with solving these problems. How great that my 'yes' was not only to Sirion, but this plethora of challenges as well. The worst of it was, Risa told of these events in the same manner Sir Sigve would comment on the weather, always with her low voice and solemn expression. She seemed in a constant state of serene bliss, and at times, uttered the names of her gods.

With such a company, I almost preferred our guards. Horasis joked around, trying to coax Toleor into joining him. Toleor, in his stoic ways, refrained with admirable perseverance, though one could observe his annoyance through the twitching tick of his left eye. How long then would I need to tease him, to make him crack a smile? Hogne was never this stingy with his mirth.

Komir surprised me, sometimes rewarding us with a rich and deep laugh, reminding me with a twinge of Father. The first time it happened, Sir Sigve looked my way with a rueful twitch of his mouth.

Sirion rode beside me the whole way, talking of small things like how to read the wind running across the sand, near invisible landmarks of the kind very useful for a trained eye, or how to trust your camel to find solid footholds even in rocky, steep paths. Hearing about such normal matters set me at ease. I would absolutely not think about knives and poison and being pushed in front of running horses. With Sirion and I traveling in the middle of the group, our escort flanked us, making a first line of defense should anything happen.

We rode hard and long, the days stretching forever before abruptly ending with the cold, starry night sky. I half expected armed men to pounce on us at every turn and dune top. For each bend in the path, I waited, alert and afraid, but nothing happened. The third evening, Toleor lit a fire for the luxury of properly prepared food and hot tea. "No signs of life," he told me. "We can afford one warm dinner."

As Komir stirred and Toleor chopped vegetables, with stew boiling over the flames, no wind was needed for the rich aroma of red meat to reach me. My stomach announced its appreciation. "I can't wait," I said, hoping my grin distracted from an oncoming blush.

"You never can, Princess." Horasis forced his existence into our conversation and the circle of food admiration.

"You're no better." I gave him a mock glare. "How many times has your stomach rumbled in my presence?" Not to mention the dried mango he always carried around, now also for my benefit. It was not the sort of thing one could hide from me.

Horasis gave a toothy smile, bowing with a flourish of arms.

"None of you have to wait," Toleor said. "It's almost done."

"Dinner?" Sirion abandoned the camels to join us. Sir Sigve came trudging in his trail.

"Yes." Excitement bubbled within me. My last meal was a solid half day ago.

"Your Grace." Toleor filled the first bowl, giving it to Sirion.

Sirion passed it on to me. "Sounds like your hunger is more urgent."

"Why, thank you." I held my head high, keeping a steel grip on my dignity—and my dinner—as I chose a spot beside Balt, on the far side of camp. Sirion sauntered behind me, a new bowl in hand.

One after another, our party left the center of camp to join us. Apparently, no one would eat within the warm glow of our bonfire, despite the beautiful sparks crackling and beckoning us in the cool evening air.

I shifted, the grains burrowing past my clothes and into my shoes. Whenever I moved, there would be sand. "Do you really want to sit here?"

"This is not my preferred place, my lady, but I follow you, as you know all too well." Sir Sigve gave the ground a hard glare.

"Where else would we be?" Horasis asked, flopping down on my other side.

"We thank Rashim for this meal. The third time Hima manifested," Risa began, seating herself with a grace and pose shaming my own, "long years of starvation swept upon the land. Liva and Avil—"

"This is good," I said, blowing on a spoonful and cutting another lecture short. As if I ever needed a reminder of going hungry. "Thank you for making this, Toleor."

Toleor nodded.

"I don't think I've had this dish before." Sirion seemed to contemplate the food being ground between his teeth, his eyes glazed as he gazed upon air. "I thought I'd tried most everything."

"Recipe from home." Toleor peered down at his own bowl.

Horasis grinned, the half-processed food in his mouth only concealed by the darkening night. "We're lucky to have

Toleor with us. I love food, but you don't want to taste a meal I've made."

I let out a laugh. "I'll believe that."

"Hey!"

"May I offer my sincere gratitude and best wishes to your family, Toleor." This warm meal was exactly what I had needed. The fresh vegetables, spices, and steak shared their summer flavors and brought out the savory taste in the stew.

Nodding again, Silent Toleor kept his gaze down. For once agreeing with my appreciation for food, he clutched the bowl with the passion befitting the truly precious. He took his compliments just as Hogne, with red in his cheek belying his serious mien.

∿

We entered the ruins on the fourth day, passing each building with slow, painful steps. Horasis and Toleor scouted ahead, checking for anything amiss. A gust of wind blew grains across the street in front of us. I saw no tracks. The sand piled up along house walls, windswept and perfect like on an undisturbed, sandy beach. We placed the camels on the inside of the palace walls, our steps thumping with hollow thuds in the empty halls. It was just as Sirion and I had left it all those weeks ago. Sand and dust gathering on the floor, rooms stripped of belongings.

I kept my gaze straight as Madalyn's arrows, unbending like Mother's back. Sir Sigve was with me, following close behind. In a few hours we would share two horn's worth of ale with a cheer rivaling Father's. Surely, we would laugh and joke about the tense atmosphere I now conjured for us all.

The next room we passed was the desert hound den, but I would not look inside. Then came a chamber like a gaping hole in the darkness, but nothing happened as Toleor passed it. Soon done. I would skaal for Hogne. Perhaps Sirion would join me, raising his glass as we celebrated another ceremony coming to an end.

My dress was of the nice, impractical sort. Flowing in soft waves of white, it trailed the floor with a chain of emerald and gold hugging my hips. Anything more than a careful walk, and I would surely stumble and fall. The ebony knife bumped against my leg, its leather case warm against my thigh. But what could a dagger in my hands do against trained fighters? Its weight was a meager comfort.

If my steps were long and quick as the entrance of another black room appeared beside me, nobody commented. Did my heart hammer in their ears, as it did in mine? Our party consisted of so many skilled fighters—they could take out a man or two without a problem, and none of us would come to harm.

Another room behind us. Was that a rustling from the next opening? Nails bit into my palms. Priestess Risa's long, dark hair swayed with each step she took in front of me. The thumps of our steps, our breaths as we exhaled were the only sounds running through the hall.

"You are safe, Your Grace." Toleor's gruff, low voice was suddenly beside me.

The torchlights didn't quite reach, and my smile was lost to the shadows. Still, my shoulders let go of their tension, and my breaths came easier. If I closed my eyes, I could imagine Hogne walking right there along with me, step by step.

Fingers touched the hand on my other side, trailing down my palm and closing around my fingers. Sirion. His warmth seeped into my cold limbs. "We're nearly there."

A hum began in my chest as we drew close to the center, a longing growing stronger and presenting the need for lush grass to tickle my bare feet, see the glittering water surrounded by life. Sirion glanced down at me, smirking. Perhaps he felt it too.

As we came to the exit, the priestess asked our guards to wait inside by the entrance. The Diamond of the Desert was a holy place, the ceremony sacred. Horasis looked about as pleased as Sir Sigve by the strict order to stay put, leaving us "foolishly defenseless," as he called it. Our gentle priestess didn't relent in the least, arching a brow to reveal a stubborn streak behind her amiable front. "It's perfectly safe within the Diamond of the Desert," she said, turning away from him to inspect us. "It's a place for Liva, Avil, and Hima. Take off your shoes."

With bare feet, Sirion and I walked hand in hand through the doorway, following priestess Risa. The sunlight was gentle on my face as we emerged from the shade into open space. My stress, fear, the prickly sensation in my neck, the urge to look back and search for someone watching me from the shadows, all those worries lifted. As my bare soles touched the sunlit ground, a sense of belonging swelled inside me, as if light spread from the depths of a murky pond, chasing darkness. It was the strangest feeling, though familiar, similar to what I had experienced the last time. Serene. We tread through the grass, enveloped by a sweet fragrance of flowers. The air was mild yet warm, embracing us in safety like a mother. Sirion gave me a relaxed smile, and

I felt myself reciprocate, laughter bubbling to the surface from a happiness deep within me.

The priestess trod with precision and care to the edge of the oasis, breaching its surface with a wide, golden bowl, and just as carefully rose with water brimming inside it. Small droplets rained like diamonds from its edges. "Come closer."

We stepped toward her, our toes tickled by cool droplets. I was exactly where I should be.

Risa placed the bowl between our fingers, our hands still linked. The fine details of the ornaments rose beneath my fingertips. Within the water, something caught the light with shimmering green. Scales. Shapes circling, glistening beneath the surface, soothing. Everything was right in the world. As if we had done it together a thousand times, we lifted the bowl, placing the rim to our lips to sip from opposite ends.

The water was sweet and fresh, cool and rich. I had tasted nothing better. It filled me, a sensation running through my body from my very core to the tips of my fingers and toes. Strength, awareness, the world crystallizing in perfect clarity, as if the water had rinsed my eyes of a fog I never even knew existed. I sensed so much. The lush grass singing with happiness in the sunshine. The vibrant purple, jubilant flowers, dripping nectar into the lake. The oasis like liquid aquamarine and the blue, blue sky. Above us, the sun. At the center of all stood Sirion. Himself, inside and out, my feelings mirrored in his eyes.

Lowering the bowl, we remained perfectly still in this new world of ours, looking at each other while Risa took the bowl from our hands. She walked out of the Desert Diamond in silence.

"Is it done?" My whispering voice entwined with the wind.

Sirion's fingertips touched mine, sparking warmth between us. A wisp of breath, his voice was rough as he spoke: "Yes."

I stepped forward, my toes brushing his.

Sirion's arms circled my waist, drawing me closer. My body melted into his, with flush and softness and wonder as if the gods had made us to fit. My nose, buried in the crook of his neck, caught a scent of citrus.

"How do you feel, Vildi?"

"Good." Light, as if my feet might take flight on gilded wings, as if my heart could soar and a heaven of honey cake and mead was forever with me.

I felt his chuckle rumbling through my chest. Sirion withdrew his warmth, his hands cupping my face as he met my gaze. And his eyes. They were brilliant blue, like sapphires in sunlight, clear and happy without reserve. And without hesitation, with our hearts beating in tune, connected through light and love, our lips met. Tender and thunder alike, it was Sirion and it was us, together in dance.

Abruptly, it ended. Sirion broke away, breathless as his heart and mine sang of connection with each drumming thud. His hand slid down my cheek, tracing a burning path from my shoulder along my arms to entwine with my fingers.

My steps tread an easy and soft path back, the strength lingering within me. As we emerged from the outside, Sir Sigve's eyebrow crept up as he watched me. It was understandable, seeing as I had been tired and anxious only a small eternity ago. Even as we walked through the corridors and the clarity of my sight faded, the elation stayed.

I caught Horasis and Toleor glancing at us—me—through the darkness but found I didn't mind. Clearly, the ceremony had given us more than water to quench our thirst. I arched an eyebrow in question.

Sirion caught my inquiry. He swung our arms with a lazy nonchalance, the knot of our hands swaying back and forth. "Our bond."

Priestess Risa turned with a serene happiness splayed on her lips as if she, too, had tasted the water. "The Diamond of the Desert grants clarity, drawn from the light in the hearts of men. It's a sacred ceremony, as old as Lakari. In fact, it is said that Liva and Avil themselves shared of the Desert Diamond's water, upon the precipice of their love." She spiraled into a new string of godly appreciation.

Sirion glanced my way, rolling his eyes.

Happy for the shadows hiding my lingering, bright smile, I looked down at our linked hands.

Balt and the other camels waited patiently for us by the palace entrance. After the dim darkness of the unlit corridors, the light of day was blinding white. We squinted and blinked against the strong, glaring sun.

We had not taken ten steps before I heard a dull thud and saw Risa collapse by my feet, a knife protruding out of her chest.

A SLIVER OF PAIN

"On defense! Surround and protect," Komir bellowed. His weapons were already out, glinting as he lowered himself in a crouch. New knives flashed through the air. Both Horasis and Komir whirled around, knocking blades off course while I struggled with even tracing their paths.

Six men emerged, running at full speed, flanking us from left and right. My stomach plummeted and lurched as I noticed their dark, patchy cloaks. I recognized at least two of these men, their mad grins as they yelled, as if seen through the fog of a dream. Blotchy brown. And a third man, greeting me in the palace corridors, his face now contorted in a fighting glee.

My knees weakened, threatening to buckle under my weight. I knew these men, I knew them like the edge of a blade against my throat, slicing, plunging into my stomach. My body knew these men and tore a scream out of my throat.

"Vildi!" Sirion clutched my hand, steadying me against his chest, but I heard his heartbeat like quick drums. "I will not let them hurt you, not again."

Our guards held their stance, Horasis and Sir Sigve engaging on our left, Toleor and Komir on our right. Risa was so pale. The woman lay frighteningly still, blood pooling around the wound, staining her clothes. She made no sound.

"Leave her, Vildi." Sirion pulled and tore at my arm. "We need to move." He dragged me along, Balt and No-Name following with fear spilling in their eyes, the other camels protesting on the reins.

Komir fought two men at once, taking one out with a sweep, exposing himself to an attack at the same time. He hit the other attacker, collapsing himself in the next breath with a hand to his sliced chest and red trickling through his fingers.

"We need to help." I tugged on my arm, but got nowhere.

Sirion backed us up another step, his eyes huge and raw. "We cannot help them now. I cannot risk it."

"But—"

"No! We must get you somewhere safe. Come!"

A knife hissed past us, hitting a camel. It screamed in pain, pulling on the reins until they slipped out of Sirion's grasp, the poor animal scrambling in a frenzy through the sand. Cursing, Sirion lost the others as they followed the first creature in senseless panic, white visible in their wide eyes.

Sand rushed up my ankles with every slow step as my muscles strained to comply. "They're dying because of me. Risa, Komir . . ."

"Stay away, run!" Horasis' voice cut off as he parried a slice toward his stomach, letting the momentum of the movement spin and carry him away.

"Sirion, please."

We struggled up a dune as Sirion held on to me, his jaw tense and teeth clenched tight. Away from the fight.

My old companion chafed at his movements, cuts crossing in thin, red lines against the white of his attire. A man fell as Sir Sigve spun his blade in an arch, the other crouching low and advancing. One step, another, and the distance between us grew. I could only glimpse them like fractures of a broken mirror, stolen visions as Sirion pulled me along.

"I will help them, Vildi."

Back-to-back, Sir Sigve and Horasis engaged the last two men. For each beat of my heart drumming red in my ears, for each breath which could be the last and for every knife flying through the air, our companions were one step further out of reach.

With one hand clutching mine, Sirion drew his knife. His knuckles paled as he crushed the handle within his fist, and his eyes were wide and veiled with torment. All because of me. Because I was a burden, the useless wife he had to protect. Because my only true skill was to die.

One attacker still advanced on us, halted only in his path by Toleor. For everything good in the world, we had to win fast. Priestess Risa didn't move, and Komir paled with each wasted moment.

"Please, Vildi." Sirion's voice rang through the dark fog of my mind. "I promise I will help them but for now we need to leave."

The dress caught between my legs, chafing against my steps as I struggled to keep up. I heard the fabric rip and tear in the seams. I stumbled against my husband, looking up as a whistle pierced the air and Sirion's cheek split with blood. With a grimace, he fought against the sand encasing our feet, hindering our escape even as the red seeped down his face.

Toleor pushed in front of us, knocking Sirion out of the way as he deflected a knife. Sirion staggered, falling, his head slamming through sand and revealing solid stone beneath. For a sickening moment, his eyes glazed. My husband blinked, shaking his head. He struggled to his feet, reaching for me. His hand was cold against my skin, pulling me along yet again as his breath ran ragged like mine. Sirion could die.

Sirion and I, we were alone. Isolated, too far away to be of aid even as Toleor fought to protect us. Still, it would be fine. Had to be. Toleor and the last man seemed evenly matched as the fight drew them closer, knives hacking air. I would not lose Toleor—my poor peasant boy, my second Hogne. A sweep, Toleor ducked, spinning and slashing; the attacker dodged, drawing near but my Silent Toleor kept him engaged. Every move was met with the perfect counter, each sweep avoided with the ease of a dance. Even as the fight pulled them closer, my guardian fought with fierce concentration in his dark eyes. Hogne was looking out for me. Toleor would protect me.

I would not lose Sirion to this fight.

With a scar twisting his upper lip in a grin, the attacker spun his knives, blades shining with a wicked edge. Ready to slice. Toleor tilted his head, his dagger sharp between them. A last defense. They watched each other, shadowing each other's movements for a long, awful moment, before the attacker smirked, and Toleor turned his back on him. Together, weapons raised, they rounded on us.

This was a misunderstanding. I blinked. Hogne would never—although this was Toleor. My heart twisted pain and fire through my chest yet Toleor held his blade, tip turned toward me, gaze serious and cold.

Sirion narrowed his eyes, pushing me behind him. "You betray us?" He stepped backward, forcing me to follow.

"No." Toleor spun his knife with lazy familiarity, settling it in his grip. "I was never of Lakari to begin with."

"Not of—Toleor. Who gave you this order?"

A second dagger appeared in Toleor's free hand. His gruff voice gave a short bark of laughter. "Don't you know?"

The other man took one step closer. Glancing from us to his knife, he flicked it at Sirion with an almost experimental air. Sirion knocked the weapon off course with his own. I could only imagine the amount of practice and experience needed to achieve such precision and control. The attacker just shrugged. As on cue, both he and Silent sprinted toward us.

Sir Sigve was too far off, fighting and struggling against blades cleaving the air.

Pushed on the defense, Horasis backed up step by step. Komir lay unmoving in the sand with his hands and clothes bloody red.

Risa was dead.

Sir Sigve's sword connected; a man collapsed. But there was just too little time, and the distance might as well be infinite.

Between them and us were Silent and the last man. We were alone. Helpless. How could Sirion fight, how could he win against two trained killers, weighed down with me? He would lose, protecting a useless, young girl. The others, if they were even able, would get here too late.

Sirion would die.

I swallowed, pushing back a wave of dizziness. My husband stood in front of me, crouching, ready to defend me: a princess of Rimdalir. Everything lay before me with perfect clarity. Like with his cheek, he would bleed from a thousand small cuts, and the blood would gush out to smear against his golden skin. His eyes would dim until the storm dwindled and fizzled out. Sirion's blood would paint the sand a crimson sea.

Only a few meters left, the men stormed us with fierce grins. It was the first time I saw Toleor smile.

I was helpless, but there was one thing I could do. Rewind. Just another Do-Again.

I found the hilt of my blade, steadying myself. Surely, it would work. Please, just one more time. *Gods, give me strength. Hogne, lend me courage.* I pushed in front of Sirion.

Silent halted with wide eyed surprise and the stranger paused, barely a stretch of sand left. He seemed to consider this new situation for something like a split second. Judging, deciding I was harmless—running straight toward me.

I locked eyes with him. My fingers froze as ice around the ebony handle, nausea churning like a hurricane. What if it didn't work? But my heart clenched with pain from years ago and a wild fear pulsed through my mind, spurring me on—to let Sirion survive. I felt every inch of my body, every nerve standing on edge as I threw myself in my attacker's path. His knife or mine—a quick slice. It was only pain.

With a wicked, scarred sneer, the attacker lifted his blade to descend upon me—and he collapsed, Sir Sigve's sword impaling him from behind. Dagger in hand, Toleor reached for me, only to crumble by my feet. The sun reflected in three knives: one piercing the back of his knee, a second between his shoulder blades and the last in his chest. Toleor hacked blood, turning once more his face toward the sky. To me, standing before him. "You cannot . . . run." Then, only his empty stare remained.

Neither had touched me.

Further away, Horasis stood with planted feet and outstretched fingers, his face marred with the deed. And it hit me: he had killed his friend.

Beside me, Sirion let his arm drop. "Please, *never* do that again, Vildi." He embraced me, clutching my body to him with locked hands. Shaking. The knife slipped through my fingers, settling unused and untainted in the sand.

Perhaps it was the sun. The heat. The lack of a slice, when a moment before I had prepared for death. All at once tension left my body, and the world tilted, turning black.

26

PERFECT PROTECTION

I had to face three men when I woke up, and none of them were too pleased with me. Well, despite what he said, Sir Sigve was proud. I could see it in his eyes and the small smile hidden behind his tight lips. Horasis chewed on me for putting myself in danger, *'making his job difficult.'* They had been afraid for me. There was little I could say to that. Worst was Sirion. He was pale, refusing to let go of my hand as he stared into nothing. The sight clenched a clammy fist around my heart, turning my explanations to a fumbling mess. For what could I say to defend my actions? To him, I had put myself in danger. Without a Do-Again, my life had been a heartbeat from forfeit.

I chanced a glance at the other side of our camp, where Komir rested with a slash down his chest and his throwing arm limp in an improvised sling. The bleeding had stopped, and he was in no real danger. But Priestess Risa was dead. They had wrapped her in a blanket and begun the work of making a pyre. A body buried in the sand would dry up, forever preserved. Worse yet, scavengers might get to her. Horasis told me we would hold a ceremony before leaving.

Behind the ruins of a house, the smoke already sieved up from a stack of seven bodies. Soon the sparks would fly. I drew my legs tight against my chest. "Do you think it's over?"

As Sirion didn't answer and with Komir sleeping, Horasis shook his head. "Don't think so." He grimaced, glancing away. Ember glows reflected in his watery eyes. "Don't recognize those other men, but Toleor had family in Tolona."

Despite the sun shining down on us, shivers from inside of me rode through my body. "Why?"

Horasis shrugged, feet shuffling about in the sand. "Don't know why they attacked. Tolona depends on Lakari, they've always been good neighbors." He held out a blanket. "Here, Princess. You look cold."

I pulled it around me, burying myself to the ears.

After a curt bow, Horasis trudged back to the work at hand. With Sir Sigve's help, he lit the pyre, and his words drifted across camp. "Embraced by fire, Liva and Avil's love reach you, may the sun forever shine on you. May you rest with Rashim."

Peeking at the bright flames, I swallowed against the unladylike urge to hurl the contents of my stomach upon the ground. Fumes spread out to obscure the horizon, a stench burning in my nose and settling like a suffocating blanket over Irisis' ruins. With small, measured breaths through my mouth, I turned away from the sight of camp and flames to instead face my husband.

Sirion sat with his head buried in his arms, as if sick to his stomach. To him, perhaps it seemed like I flung myself at any blade happening to cross my path, as if at any moment, he could be widowed anew. But he would have to look at me eventually, and we should talk. Besides, this was bigger than me. With sweaty palms and a load in my heart, I drew a breath. "What now? Sirion, this is bad, isn't it?" I glanced at his stiff and silent form. "What about your sister?"

A hand jerked up to tug at his hair. "I know." Sirion drew long fingers over his eyes. "I need to contact her. Ilea is strong, but whatever is happening in Tolona now, it isn't good."

"What should we do?"

"We?" Sirion turned to stare at me, his thoughts hidden by shadow. He shook his head, eyes drifting off. "Well, I don't know yet. Traveling there could be dangerous."

"Toleor mentioned sickness in his family." My free fingers traced a path in the sand, creating rings looping into each other.

Sirion clutched my hand, forehead resting on his knees. "There was a plague in Tolona recently. We heard about the uprising soon after. The kingdom is poor with limited resources, which is why Lakari provides aid. In fact, Ilea's marriage into their royal family was supposed to strengthen that alliance."

"Arranged marriage." With a sweep, all my rings were destroyed. The pointy finger started anew.

Sirion glanced at me. "Yes. In Tolona's favor."

"I want to help. I know I can help." I tried a smile, though the pungent taint of flesh and burned hair allowed for no more than a skewed grimace. My finger dug down, tracing the same circle over and over again.

The grip around my hand tensed. "Like you did today?" Sirion's face contorted in pain. "I'm supposed to protect *you*."

"I'll be careful." The words 'I will not do it again' got stuck inside me. I didn't regret it. My blade shimmered with innocence and beauty in the sun. "If it helps, you can have it back." I held the knife out to Sirion, who seemed to only grasp it by force of habit, his eyes drained as he stared at my offering. "Better?"

He didn't respond. The knife slipped from his palm to roll down his lap, landing in the sand.

"I'll do my best. I promise you that." The ring in the sand was deep, so many rounds needed to create its steep walls. Over and over again. I could make my time a game, balancing on a knife's edge between life and death. Finding that one choice to change it all, so Risa could fold her hands and speak the names of her gods, so Komir once again could fight and laugh, and Sirion . . . he would be free of the turbulence coursing through his eyes, heavy in his heart. "Sirion . . ." I bit my lip. Would he believe me?

Like a man facing his nightmares, Sirion's gaze lifted to me, betrayed by fingers drumming against his thighs.

My voice got stuck in my throat. My heart hammered with the ferocity of a runaway horse, struggling to escape, but Sirion looked at me as if in a heartbeat, he would lose me. With fingers cramped around my skirt, I drew a breath. "I would not have died. I can't. My day just . . . starts over."

Like a torrent of water, my words spilled into his silence. "I was never truly in danger. Please believe me. But I could take the pain, it was the only thing I *could* do. The day would repeat, and I would have known about the attack." I looked at the knife lying between us. "If I just do a Do-Again . . . everything will be fine. No one needs to die—"

"Don't," he snapped, following my gaze. There was some spark in his eyes, the downward pull of his lips as a hand swept the blade out of my reach. "I know you'd go until your mind breaks. Don't. It's too late, anyway. Vildi, we cannot help them anymore."

"You don't understand, Sirion—"

"You cannot help them, Vildi. Neither can I. If I was faster, stronger . . . braver. But I'm not." Sirion buried his face in trembling hands, his knuckles whitening as he pressed them against deep-seated eyes. Through the collapsed form of my husband, I heard him release a quivering breath. "It is too late to start over."

My thoughts came to a halt, his words ringing in their stead like a bell chiming a truth out of my grasp. "I—"

"From the moment you fell unconscious." Sirion met my eyes with his frigid, blue gaze, hands still in front of him. "I know, Vildi. It's Hima."

"Hima . . ." I dragged the word from my lips and it fell to the ground between us. A gift from the gods, a simple name that Kaira, Risa, even Sirion had talked about. And everything that happened to me from the moment I set foot in Lakari, from familiar streets to the attacks in my dreams, being trapped in my body with the sting of a scorpion until Sirion found me—they came together like so many fine stitches on a single thread. Every ill-considered attempt to change events. "My Do-Agains . . . you *knew?*"

"Of course." Sirion folded his hands, brows furrowing together. "I thought you did too. That you understood. The special wedding ceremony, and today . . . though with the attacks, the palace has been, well—I wanted to—*should* have talked to you about it regardless, but I didn't get the chance these last weeks; I was going to that day in the garden but—"

"We were attacked. And I've been avoiding you." The world once more seemed to tilt. "You *knew*." I looked down at the knife resting with Sirion. The knife I had once used to take my life. "That's why you took it. How?"

"How did I know?" Sirion's eyes were lit, intent with determination. "You can ask me."

My words were slow to form. "Sirion, why didn't I die the first day I entered Lakari?"

He nodded. "In a way, it's the ultimate protection. Starting over again if things don't work out, when everything seems hopeless. Remembering, and choosing differently. Hima."

"That's why you 'had no choice.'" I swallowed, looking down at my wringing fingers.

Sirion watched me with level eyes, not denying.

All of it—the bond, the sensation inside me, came from this thing. *Magic*. How utterly stupid. Why else would I have these feelings? It was nothing more than a ruse, a spell to serve a purpose. It was why Sirion was drawn to me, why Lakari had insisted on him marrying me. For this, one lesson should have sufficed: the fairy-tale lie. Could he hear my heart hammering? Even as the corners of my lips yearned to sink, I forced them to lift.

Sirion's return gesture was small but seemed sincere. "The gods have given us Hima. You belong with me, and I belong with you. It's a bond neither of us can break."

A bond of magic.

I fell back in the sand. "You're right. I should have realized."

His smile disappeared, and his eyes slid away from me. "Hima is a wonderful thing. It's born from Liva and Avil's love, and I'm lucky to experience it, I know. But I hate it. Death for life. Bending the mind to the point of breaking, welcoming pain for a second chance. Love for the price of suffering."

I glanced at him. *Love.* He believed that? Sirion clenched the poor knife, glaring as if it had hurt me on purpose—and I recognized that gaze. It was the same expression from the first time I saw him, when he yanked my arm away from the scorpion. My savior of the desert. My traitorous heart clenched at the sight and despite the truth hammering in my mind, emotions made my voice mellow. "Sirion, how did you find me?"

His face was carefully blank. "I share your dreams every time you reset. Your . . . 'Do-Again's?"

"The nightmares?" All my nights wringing myself in the blankets and his own restless sleep . . .

Sirion grimaced, raking a ring clad hand through his poor mauled hair. "The days which disappear come back to us in those dreams. Did you notice they got clearer each time? That's your mind getting used to the gift."

"Oh, by the gods' skaal, save me," I mumbled, hiding my burning face in my arms. He had seen the entirety of my stupidity. Me refusing to be a proper lady, stuffing myself with cake, me not caring if I appeared rude, me hearing his story . . .

"They're only fragments. No need to look *that* embarrassed. Although now I wonder about everything I *didn't* dream."

"Don't." His annoying smirk didn't falter one bit. The sand should swallow me this instant, and I wouldn't mind. I peeked at him and saw his grin. "Really, it's nothing."

"Perhaps I'll dream it." He waggled his eyebrow. It should have been completely ridiculous, and it was inappropriate because we had such an important conversation, but somehow with him it looked good. So unfair.

"Please. Can't you just . . . not have those dreams?" The sky was clear and blue, blue, blue.

"Sure. If you promise not to die anytime soon."

"That's not fair." Where was a well-timed sandstorm when needed?

"As if your demand was any more reasonable," Sirion's voice told me.

"It was a logical thing to ask." Could I ask him not to look at me for the next ten years?

He snorted. "Sure."

"I can't trust your dreams now, can I?"

"Well, I can't trust you with your life, you know. You have an extraordinary talent for finding idiotic ways to die."

"As if I can control that." I gave up, crawling up on my knees, looking at him. His blue, blue, blue eyes. Magic thumped emotions through my chest. I blew a stray lock of hair out of my face, although it fell back at once. "Do you dream of me every night? Or just when, you know, the time . . . reset . . . thing."

"Every time you . . . reset. Yes." He grabbed a fist of sand, letting the grains fall down through his fingers. His stare was a bit too intense. "But all dreams are not like that."

I felt my face burn ten shades of flames. "I did *not* need to know that!" I reached for my sack and buried myself in it, wishing for a pillow. "By the gods, why did I even ask?"

"Curiosity," he supplied helpfully.

"Great."

He poked my cheek. "Vildi?"

I glanced at him. He looked content, like the anxiety was almost gone. Good. Better than agony and apathy, anyhow. Sirion should not look so pained. "Sirion, if I had gotten home, what would you have done?"

"I don't know. Maybe I would have visited Rimdalir, become one of your hated suitors."

I snorted, surprising myself. "I can't imagine it."

"Why?" Sirion reclined back against a stone wall, stretching his legs.

"I don't know how you behave while drunk. We drink a lot, you see, at our balls." Though there would be no more balls for me. No suitors, of course. But neither family. "In Rimdalir, you're only as strong as how much you can drink as we skaal for our gods."

"That's a strange custom."

"Is it? Our gods drink, fight, and love with passion. Why shouldn't we?"

"With passion?" Sirion watched me, a smirk seeping into his features. "I think I like that."

"Don't read too much into it," I said, mostly out of habit. Too tired to fight against my beguiled heart, I settled beside my husband, leaning against his shoulder.

Balt trotted over, nuzzling his nose in my hair. My friend.

With the sun behind him, No-Name resembled a proud steed on the ridge of the nearest dune, casting his thoughtful eyes across the ruins.

Truthfully, I was relieved to just have Sirion beside me, both of us safe and holding onto each other. I could figure out the rest later.

Sirion clenched my hand, his elation fading away. "Vildi, Hima never comes alone."

SIRION

Being the Crown Prince had its perks, but dealing with official—and political—matters was not one of them. Certainly not this one.

"Your orders, Your Grace?" Komir gazed stiffly out the window, hands clasped behind his back. I could almost see his hair graying by the minute from the strain of the last few months, and this certainly didn't help.

Then again, my hair might suffer too, if this continued. As soon as I became a married man, thus eligible for the throne again, my father had handed over a flock of his advisors and generals with a certain glee in his eyes. Now, certain matters were for me to solve.

I stared at the half-written letter in my hand, a blotch of ink blooming at the end of an unfinished sentence. *The assassins have proven to be of Tolonan origin. Please, Ilea, be carefu—*

I heaved a sigh, dropping my pen. A few droplets of ink sprayed the letter further, though it hardly mattered anymore.

"There is really no trace of the messenger?"

"None."

"And the one before?"

"None." Komir's words put a flaming torch to the funeral pyre of my hope. The messengers had crossed the border to Tolona but failed to return. All of them.

"We have to keep trying." My sister was deep in that viper's nest of a place.

"Do you want me to send another messenger, Your Grace?"

The unspoken words hung between us, heavier than the ones he had said aloud: Do you want to send another person to his almost certain demise?

"Yes. No." I tore through my hair, unable to contain my frustration. My fear. "We could send an official delegate." But what man, noble or otherwise, would risk such a mission, even if promised their weight in gold? An idiot, perhaps, or a reckless one—and both would be more likely to escalate the situation than abate it.

There really was only one solution. "I should go myself." They couldn't exactly kill me, even if they tried.

Komir gave me an unimpressed look, likely wishing he could tell me I was both foolish and reckless. For once, my title was useful for something—though knowing old Komir, he would find a way past the restrictions of decorum to get his message across. "With all due respect, Your Grace, I find it very unlikely that your father will consent to sending his heir over the border into enemy territory. Especially when said heir has been targeted recently."

"Why do you always have to be right?" I wanted to slam my head into the desk—very un-princely. Besides, it wasn't me they had targeted. No. They had chosen who they believed to be the easier victim: the unsuspecting princess who had been tricked into marrying me. And they had succeeded, multiple times.

A shudder ran down my spine from the memory of the nightmares, her deaths, and the onslaught of visions of a single scorpion. My desperate search in the desert, trying to find a lost, reckless girl.

And I had found her. My bride, Alvildi. Another reckless soul, who would allow me to ascend the throne.

"What can Tolona gain from keeping me off the throne?" I mumbled. "And how?"

Komir stared out the window, his expression stone.

Maybe some kind of extortion. After all, they had my sister Ilea, a beloved princess of Lakari. And we had fed them the means ourselves, marrying her away for an alliance that, safe to say, had fallen through.

How did this tie up to Vildi? How had they known? The few people we could have asked were dead. And we had to tread carefully with those remaining, lest we get a rebellion at our door.

From ruffian assassins to elite soldiers, how far did this reach? Tolonans had pursued military careers in Lakari for the better part of three centuries—as a secure way of sending money back to their families. And we had welcomed them with open arms.

"How large a portion of our troops are compromised?" I asked, half dreading and half hoping for an answer.

"We cannot say at the moment," Komir said, "as we cannot differentiate between those directly involved, those indirectly involved, and those in the unknown. Certainly, the amount of people hailing from Tolona is great, but then you need to consider the second and third generation residents, and if we should count those with shared parentage with Lakari. If you include those . . ."

I repressed an urge to slam my head on the desk. "Then we have no idea how big a problem this is."

"We will continue our inspections, Your Grace."

"Please do."

My fingers splayed across the vellum of my letter, the wedding ring gleaming in the sun: Avil, one half of the symbol of Hima, always with me. And Liva was always with Vildi, protecting her with the gift of love. And yet . . .

"Pardon, Prince Sirion, but may I suggest summoning the Crown Princess, so that she may share in this meeting?" Meaning: I was stupid for trying to do this by myself, when Lakarian tradition and rule clearly stated that the throne should be shared by two.

"Thank you, Komir. Vildi still needs time to settle into the new chambers and adjust without her family." The letter crumbled under my straining fingertips. Why would I ever involve my bride in something as dangerous as this? The attacks on her life should never have happened to begin with, and it was my duty to protect her from ever experiencing them again. No more assassinations. No more deaths.

Yet more and more, this carried the rotten stench of war.

BONUS CONTENT

A widowed crown prince. An unwanted bride.
Old magic to twist their fates.
Subscribe at inghildokland.com to read about
Sirion's first meeting with his fated bride!

An Author's Wish

Thank you for reading
Balance!

Your honest review will help future readers decide
if they want to take a chance on a
new-to-them author.

If you enjoyed this book and think other readers
might too, please consider leaving a quick review.

All authors appreciate this so much. Thank you!

— *Inghild*

Also by Inghild Økland

Balance Series
Madalyn
Balance
The Fairy-Tale Lie
Ishimin
(more to come)
Balance Novella
The Jewel of the Amber Court
Balance Short Stories (newsletter-exclusive)
The Unwanted Bride
My Peasant Boy
A Prince and his Bride
The Maid and the Swordsman

Dark Spelled Romantasies
Spelled & Forgotten
(more to come)
Dark Spelled Romantasies Novella
Loved & Ensnared

ABOUT THE AUTHOR

Fantasy has kept a special place in my heart ever since I was only 7 years old, snuggling up to my sister and father as he read *Lord of the Rings*.

Now a soil scientist by day, writer by night, I enjoy my days living off tea, dreaming up stories, and consuming a healthy dose of heart-pounding romantic fantasy.

ACKNOWLEDGMENTS

Four years ago, Balance appeared to me in a vivid dream. When I woke up, I ran to my computer, Vildi's sassy voice coming to me in a rapid stream, as if saying, "keep up, will you?"

Balance is my debut novel, and it demanded a lot of work. From a first draft of 40K, rife with plot holes and a shallowness I'm embarrassed to admit to, it grew and unfolded, reaching new depths with every edit. And it was all thanks to my beta readers and editors.

Disa, thank you for everything you give me. You read, you support, you listen, and give advice with endless patience. Thank you for being my dear sister.

Michael, I'll never forget your reaction after reading Balance, urging me to keep writing. You have no idea how much that meant.

Pål, thank you for your guidance, for brainstorming with me, easing my panic, and finding solutions to all those faults in the story. Thank you for all our evenings of wine, anime, and book writing talks. Thank you for being my close friend.

Ingeborg, dear Sunshine of mine, words can't really do you justice, and not in this limited space. Thank you for reading, encouraging me, supporting me, validating me at every turn. For being you, for being there for me, thank you.

Attila, my dear office neighbor, thank you for your support, and for the motivational boost you gave me. Whenever I felt down, I had your kind words to think back on, knowing someone liked even this faulty 40K story of mine. Balance has doubled since then, and I can't wait to hear what you'll think now.

Thank you, Line, for challenging me, pushing my book out of that awful, shallow state and to that first glimmer of something better.

Amber, thank you for your insight, which fixed some of the remaining big weaknesses, making the story likeable. Thank you for sticking with me after too, for all our conversations and for sharing your stories. I Love everything you write.

Julianne, thank you for your feedback, your support, for your friendship, and for sharing your lovely books with me. I look forward to our continued growth together as romance fantasy authors.

Ulana, thank you for every call, all your advice, encouragement, and endless enthusiasm. Your books are an inspiration, and I'm grateful that you're sharing this process with me. Balance is not only better because of you, but you make this journey fun and exciting.

To my other beta readers, Anette, Nora, Lisa, Navyblue07, and iloveoatmeal019, thank you so much. You all contributed to this story, and I can point out parts in the story that improved, adjusted or changed because you helped me. Lisa, thank you for creating the dragons that decorate the book. They are stunning, and I love them so much. I put them wherever I'm able, as you might have noticed.

Rachel, thank you for being my content editor, for all your suggestions and all the adjustments, for all your insight which made the locations more lifelike and the characters more realistic. Thank you for pushing Balance to become so much better, and for your support every step of the way.

Lauren, thank you for your copy/line edit, which fixed the stumbling blocks in the story and made it run so much smoother than before. And thanks to your advice, I included a kiss in a certain scene, which made the book more wholesome, I think.

Rebecca, thank you for your proofreading, for making sure the readers can have a pleasant reading experience without errors to distract them. Also, thank you for the copy edits you also gave me, removing those last awkward spots in the story.

With my three editors, Balance reached a quality I would have no hope of grasping by myself. You pushed me to work harder, not settling with half done, and I learned so much. Thank you.

Merilliza, it is an honor to have your art wrapped around my first book. I loved the illustration from the moment I saw it, and Vildi came to life with your stunning art. This cover is more than I ever imagined, and everything I dreamt it would be. Thank you so much.

To my family and friends, thank you for sticking with me during this time. You all had to endure my raving, rambling, one-track mind. You've all given me patience and support, encouraging me to seize this opportunity. I'm grateful to you, and I love you all.

Lastly, I want to thank Self-Publishing School for teaching me about the self-published author's thorny path. Thank you for pushing me to work hard, rather than waiting to catch lightning in a bottle. Thank you, my fellow students, for being an awesome community, and Nola and Sherri especially, for beta reading Balance and giving me so much support in the time after.

Thank you, Barbara, for coaching me, for all your help and guidance. I'm taking my first step today to building my author career, and I thank you and SPS for that.

Made in the USA
Middletown, DE
11 October 2024